"Do we want to make a life of music?
I can say that I, personally, don't
know. You'd have to ask the others
what they think."

"Here's a question," Mr. Morgan says,
sitting down across from me. "Are
you guys interested in finding out?"

Ransom

Start to Finish

Book Design: Mike Fontenot

Cover Design: Mike Fontenot

Cover Art: Dara Newville and Mike Fontenot

Special thanks to Miss Dara Newville for all her efforts in getting the artwork on the back cover finished. You are an incredible artist, and you totally rock, kid! ☺

Special thanks to Mrs. Kimberly Geswein for giving me permission to use a number of her fonts (*especially* the insanely cool smilie faces) in the telling all of this, and the Audio Distortion stories. All of her work can be found at http://www.kimberlygeswein.com. Go check it out!

Printing History: Original – May 2015

PRINTED IN THE UNITED STATES OF AMERICA

ISBN-13: 978-0-9861824-0-2

ISBN-10: 0-9861824-0-0

10 9 8 7 6 5 4 3 2 1

"In ten hours, there's gonna be twenty thousand people in here…"
Misty Maitland – Lead Vocals

"You are just sooo freakin' weird, Misty Maitland, I swear…"
Martin Masterson – Keyboards

"It's like I have no idea who I am anymore… who any of us are."
Ariel Williams – Rhythm Guitar

"You are as amazing, as you are totally freakin' insane, Misty Maitland."
Rhyan Crossman – Drums

"I can't believe we get to do this twice a week, for the next three months!"
Vanessa Preston – Bass Guitar

"no freakin' way…"
Joshua Miller – Lead Guitar

Prologue

Riley Mitchell

My name is Riley Mitchell.

Or, if you prefer, Riley Morgan.

And yes... my father is *Audio Distortion's* drummer.

A few years ago, I wrote a series of stories about my father's band, and the amazing journey the five of them embarked on – and are still traveling.

Those of you, who may have read those stories, might remember that, at the end of the last book, I suggested I might write the stories of the other bands that directly influenced my life as I was growing up.

It's taken a while, but you are holding the results.

I struggled for a while with how to tell this story – start at the beginning, or simply pick up where *Audio Distortion's* story ended. It was my sister-in-law, Carla, who helped me make that decision.

Everyone has heard the one about the four people, on four corners of an intersection, who all see the exact same accident, and yet, give four completely different accounts, of what happened. In this case, a lot of *Ransom's* story is contained in the six *Audio Distortion* stories I previously wrote, but the thing is – according to Carla – the parts about *Ransom*, were told by the members of *Audio Distortion*.

That's not really *Ransom's* story, now is it?

So, knowing I had to tell the entire story – start to finish – I kissed my husband, and my kids, and set off to find *Ransom*...

I figured, where better to start, than with the bubbly lead singer?

Kansas, here I come.

Really?

Misty Maitland

When Riley shows up at our house, on a sunny spring afternoon, I'm surprised to say the least. She comes in, I close the door, and she follows me to the kitchen.

When she tells me what she wants...

"I want to write *Ransom's* story – start to finish."

...I stand staring at her, speechless, for a good thirty seconds.

"Misty?"

"Huh? Ohhh... sorry. You're serious, aren't you?" I ask.

"Well... yeah," she replies, and as an afterthought adds, "Is that still hot?" and points at the coffee maker.

"Uh-huh, I just made it," I reply, pulling a cup off a hook and handing it to her.

"And why the whole 'shocked' thing anyhow?" she asks, filling her cup.

"Well..."

"It's what I do, remember?" she replies, to my 'less than an answer'.

"But… well… *why us?*" I ask, pulling out a chair and sitting down at the kitchen table.

"You guys were a very intricate part of my parent's lives – and mine – for a really long time. So… why not *Ransom?*" she replies, taking a seat next to me. "I believe it's a story that needs telling…"

I sip my coffee, and, still a bit stunned, again stare at her for moment.

"Thing is… *it has to be told by the six of you.*"

The moment she says it, I get a rush of goose bumps, as I wonder what the others are going to say.

"Besides… it's been three years since you guys let it go, and went about living your lives, so I'll bet your fans will be all over this, the moment it is released."

Although I'm staring at her, my mind has already slipped into memories of a somewhat forgotten past. When I turn and glance into the living room, I see the giant image of the six of us, standing on a stage, the *Begin Again* album cover filling the huge monitor behind us, and it all instantly floods right back into me…

Being Discovered

Ariel Williams

I'm walking down the hall, and am just short of the teacher's lounge, headed for a math class, when I see her – and my heart stops. She's following Mrs. Perkins into the lounge.

"No freakin' way!" I mumble out loud, much to the surprise of more than one of my fellow students.

When I reach the door, I slow enough that I can see through the small window, and sure enough, there she is, pouring coffee into a cup. I can't help it – I stop dead in my tracks. 'What' I ask myself, 'would the lead guitarist of one of the biggest pop bands ever, be doing in the teacher's lounge of a high school, in the middle-of-nowhere Kansas?'

Suddenly, someone grabs my arm, and starts pulling me down the hall.

"Come on, Ariel! You are not going to believe this!" Vanessa screams, almost pulling me off my feet.

Before I can respond, we've turned the corner at the end of the hall, and are two-thirds of the way to the music room.

"Nessa! I have a math class now…" I say, trying to break her grip on my arm.

"Too bad. *This* will make being late totally freakin' worth it!"

We slide to a stop directly outside the music room, and the moment I look inside, my entire world simply stops.

Sitting on Mrs. Perkins' desk, is none other than Willie Morgan – drummer for *Audio Distortion*. He's laughing and joking with some freshman, and seems like anything but a superstar.

"No way…" I mumble.

"Why would *he* be in Kansas – of all places?" Vanessa asks.

The moment she says it, I hear heels on the floor behind us, and when I turn around, find Mrs. Perkins and Emily Táo walking toward us.

"Same reason *she* would be, I suppose…" I reply to Vanessa, pointing past her, down the hall.

The moment Mrs. Perkins sees us, she waves and calls to us.

"Ariel! Vanessa!"

"Yes ma'am," we say at the same time.

The two of them stop in front of us, and the disbelieving looks on our faces, give us away.

"Well… it's apparent you already know who she," she points at Ms. Táo, "is, so I'll just tell you what's up. They are giving a talk for the music students during fourth period this afternoon, here in the music room. Most of the teachers know about it, so if you need to get out of a class, they will let you. I'm keeping a list, so don't even think about…"

"Yeah, right," I mumble. "I'd pretty much miss graduation for this…"

Ms. Táo laughs, and Mrs. Perkins says, "I know there's a class you are supposed to be in, so…"

"Yes ma'am" we say, again simultaneously, and then turn and head off in different directions.

For the next two and a half hours, my heart is racing…

Opportunities

Joshua Miller

I thought Martin was full of crap – to be honest with you. But when I walk into the music room and find Ariel, Vanessa, and Rhyan all sitting in the front row, I begin to wonder.

"Martin says that the lead guitarist and drummer of…" is as far as I get, before Ariel points at the door. When I turn and look, in walks Willie Morgan and Emily Táo, followed closely by Mrs. Perkins.

"So…" Mr. Morgan says, grinning like he's nuts, "any musicians in here?"

They spend the next hour telling us about themselves, their music, and finally, their studio. They explain that Discovery Studios is in search of the next *Audio Distortion*, but as yet, haven't found them. Finally, when the hour is up, they tell the twenty-two of us in the room that, if anyone is interested, they'll hang around after school, and jam with us.

Yeah… right… *'interested'*…

An hour and a half later, the four of us are standing around, goofing off with some freshman, waiting for Martin to show up – hard to be a 'band' without all your members. Anyhow, because we're all totally into music, we always jump at the chance to help other kids who share our passion. Rhyan is diligently trying to show Noah parts of a *Next Page* song, and Ariel is talking frets with a different girl.

The second the door opens, all eighteen heads in the room turn to look.

"Okay guys and girls, shall we make some music?" Ms. Táo yells.

Watching the two of them interacting with all of us for close to two hours is totally amazing. It's not kids and pop stars – it's just a bunch of musicians. Eventually, they ask if any of us actually play together. Seconds after Mr. Morgan asks the question, a huffing and puffing Martin comes busting into the room, which makes everyone laugh. I turn to look at Vanessa and see that she is whispering to Noah. When I start to say something, she puts her finger to her lips telling me to be quiet.

Once everyone quits laughing, Martin sits down, and Ms. Táo takes over.

"So... not a single 'band' in the room, huh?"

Noah slowly raises his hand, and Chip – sitting on the other side of him – looks like he's gonna faint when he does.

"We sorta are. But we're still just learning..."

"Got a song you can play?" Mr. Morgan asks.

"Well..." Noah starts to say, and is interrupted by James, their bass player.

"We do," James says, "but it will suck. We just aren't that good yet."

"'Suck' is what we did for almost three months when we started playing together," Ms. Táo says, following it with a laugh. "You feel like entertaining us?"

Chip, Noah, James and Conner set up with the school equipment, and tear through a metal song (that's what they are into) and although it's just loud noise to most of us, Ms. Táo seems interested.

"Well guys, I didn't hear any bad notes, and it did seem to flow, but you aren't playing *together*."

"Yeah," Mr. Morgan adds, "you and you," he points at Noah and James, "are at least a couple of beats ahead of the them," he finishes by pointing at Conner and Chip.

"Sync up and you guys will have something," Ms. Táo says, smiling.

"Practice, practice…"

"*PRACTICE!*" everyone in the room yells at the same time.

"Exactly. So, I need a restroom," Ms. Táo says, holding up her hands.

"There's one in the teacher's lounge," Vanessa says.

"Closer?"

"End of the hall on the left," Carolyn, a freshman, offers.

"Cool. Back in a bit," Ms. Táo says, and disappears out the door.

"I need a soda machine," Mr. Morgan says.

"Teacher's lounge is the closest one," Martin says.

"Cool… and maybe I can find your teacher as well. Back in a flash…"

The moment they are both gone, the five of us get into a circle…

Hesitance

Jean Perkins

The moment they walk in, I get excited.

"Well?"

"Kinda weird, actually," Emily offers. "None of them said anything."

"Yeah," Willie adds, feeding coins into the soda machine, "they didn't even admit to playing together."

"What?"

"It happens, Jean. Lots of kids don't handle the spotlight very well..." Emily says.

When I laugh, so does Willie.

"Heard about Emma, have you?" he asks.

"Anyone who loves music knows your story, guys. Every kid, in every one of my classes, can recite it almost word for word."

"So..." Emily says, taking Willie's Pepsi, and guzzling it.

"I'm really sorry guys. I wouldn't have told Janet about them unless I thought they were interested. Looks like I've wasted your time..."

"Oh… I don't know about that," Emily says, grinning.

"Huh?"

"She's been watching out the window…" Willie offers, getting another soda from the machine.

"So far, about half the kids have filtered out and headed home. The five of them are still in there…"

"What we need from you, Jean, is a means to sneak up on them…"

Even as the shock of what is happening sweeps over me, I find myself wondering if all the members of *Audio Distortion* are as in tune to each other as these two are…

BOO!

Joshua Miller

We were playing a cover of *Teenage Dream* by Katy Perry – Ariel was doing the vocals – when Ms. Táo and Mr. Morgan snuck up on us. We even had someone hanging out in the hall to tell us when they came back – which sorta backfired. Although they seemed to like what they heard – much to our total astonishment – we could all see something was bugging them. They told us they wanted to talk to us, but that it would have to wait until the next day...

Today.

When I get a note from the office during third period, telling me to report to Mrs. Perkins office, I almost weird out...

"You sent for me Mrs. Perkins?" I ask, as I knock on her open door. Immediately, I hear a voice behind me, and at the same time, someone shoves me through the door.

"No... we did," Mr. Morgan says, as Ms. Táo laughs.

"What was with the whole 'being secret' thing yesterday anyhow?" she asks, closing the door behind her.

"Well... I... uh..."

"Oh stop it, Joshua!" Mrs. Perkins blurts out, glaring at me. "They are just a couple of musicians who really want to help you guys..."

I'm honestly not sure why, but the moment Mrs. Perkins jumps on me, my whole attitude changes. In that single instant, I no longer see 'superstars', but instead, only a really cool drummer and guitarist...

"Okay... why us?"

"Are you freakin' kidding me?" Mr. Morgan blurts out.

"The moment we walked in on you guys, we saw ourselves, Josh. I heard Stanley and me playing off each other like we've been doing since the very first time we played together. Until yesterday, I'd never seen a lead and keyboardist as in tune as Stan and I..."

Yeah... I'm very close to freaking out. Seriously. Even Mrs. Perkins sees it.

"I'm not sure what to say... honest to God..."

"Tell us that you and your bandmates are *serious* about music... that all five of you are as passionate about it, as me and my bandmates are..." Ms. Táo says.

As I sit looking from Ms. Táo, to Mr. Morgan, to Mrs. Perkins, I get the strangest rush, and for some reason, I just know...

"We are. We all totally love music. Do we want to make a life of it? I can say that I, personally, don't know. You'd have to ask the others what they think."

"Here's a question," Mr. Morgan says, sitting down across from me. "Are you guys interested in finding out?"

As fast as my heart is beating, I really have no idea what I'm about to get myself into...

The Missing Link

Joshua Miller

It's been a week since music turned our lives inside out. The amusing part came when *Mrs. Faintree* explained to us that she hadn't been *Ms. Táo*, in well over a year. Poor Vanessa – the one who called her Ms. Táo – turned six shades of red, she was so embarrassed. She told us we were free to use their first names – they were cool with it – and the five of us all mumbled 'yeah, right' at the same time, which made Mrs. Perkins crack up.

We've each talked to them one-on-one, and a couple of times they talked to one or two of us together. On Wednesday, they got us together in the music room again, and talked us into playing – for *everyone*. Just to be smart alecks, we played one of their songs, and it didn't turn out half bad.

But, Martin and I can still see that there is something about us – something that isn't working for them.

"So…" Mrs. Faintree says, sitting down with a cup of coffee, "Willie and I spent last night talking…"

"...about us..." Vanessa mumbles, the tone of her voice telling all of us what she's thinking.

"Yep," she quickly replies.

"And we've decided to work with you guys, assuming you are interested."

We all turn and immediately look at Mr. Morgan.

"seriously?" Ariel pretty much mumbles.

"Yes, 'seriously'. But... there's one big parameter..."

"None of us can sing..." Rhyan blurts out, sounding a bit dejected.

When the two of them turn, look at each other, and smile, I think all five of us relax.

"Yeah... you need a singer," Mr. Morgan says.

"How do you feel about getting a new band member?" Mrs. Faintree asks, as if testing us.

"It will be weird, but I think we can live with it. Do you know of someone?"

"Nope... and I wouldn't presume to pick one for you. I just need to know you guys are open to the idea," she replies.

"If we're going to try this," Martin says, "we'd like to succeed. We're all pretty sure you guys know how to make that happen, so whatever you guys say, we're up for."

"It won't work if we're just telling you what to do, guys. It has to be a team effort. You have to *participate*..." Mrs. Faintree says, finishing her coffee, and putting the cup down.

"You guys have to *want* this," Mr. Morgan offers.

Finally, my dad – who along with all the other parents, has been in the room the entire time – speaks up.

"These guys," my dad says, pointing at Mr. Morgan and Mrs. Faintree, "are chancing a lot on the five of you. I will say

I don't get it, but they seem pretty passionate about what they see in you. *Do not* waste their time and effort."

"The five of you have been at this since you started high school," Mrs. Preston says, "and I've heard all of you discuss 'what if' ever since. This... *right now*... is 'what if'. Like Adam just said, *do not* waste their time and effort."

"I gave up my garage two summers ago," Mr. Crossman offers, "so you guys would have a place to rehearse and play. You guys went after it like kids possessed. You will have to give that same effort here..."

"Times ten," Mrs. Faintree adds, smiling.

Suddenly, Mrs. Perkins stands up, and looks at each of us. After a second, she steps around her desk, and leans against the front of it.

"When the five of you first started this, I made a comment..." she starts to say, and almost automatically, the five of us respond...

"If you're going to do it, don't half-ass it!"

The funny part is, all our parents break up laughing.

"Well," Mrs. Faintree says, "our charter is leaving from Dodge City in about four hours, so we need to head that way."

When she stands up, Mr. Morgan laughs, and stays seated.

"You go get the stuff from the Inn, and I'll talk to these guys," he points at our parents, instead of the five of us, "for a bit, if that's cool?"

"Gotta drive past here anyhow. See you in about thirty minutes."

"I'll walk you out," Mrs. Perkins says, and stands to follow her. "And you five," she points at us, "need to get lost..."

We laugh and as we are going out the door behind Mrs. Perkins and Mrs. Faintree, Rhyan says, "We'll be in the music room when you want us!"

A Voice

Misty Maitland

"I have to get home, Misty. Are you gonna hang around?"

"Yeah – I gotta figure this out. If I need help, at least Mr. Parks will be around," I reply.

"Okay… see ya!"

As Ronnie turns and walks off, I put my ear buds back in and hit play. Katy Perry picks up right where she left off…

I have to figure this math out, before the test on Monday. Fortunately, my teacher is at school today, even though it's Saturday. So, I turn the page, and keep going.

When Katy Perry is finished belting out *Hot-n-Cold*, I know that my favorite song is next on the play list. The moment Colbie Caillat starts singing *I Do*… so do I. I like the song so much, I really don't care who hears me singing it.

As I'm turning another page in my Calculus book, I see movement next to the music building. A short lady, with some really interesting hair comes out, closely followed by Mrs. Perkins, the music teacher. I return my attention to my book, and the moment the song's chorus starts, the goofy

high school kid in me burst out, and I start singing so loudly,
I can hear myself over the music in my ears…

You make we wanna say
I do, I do, I do, do do do do do do doo
Yeah, I do, I do, I do, do do do do do do doo
Because every time before it's been like
Maybe yes and maybe no
I can live without it, I can let it go
Ooh, what did I get myself into
You make we wanna say I do, I do, I do, I do, I do

I'm already into the next stanza, when I see a pair of
sneakers stop on the grass in front of me, inches from my
math book. The very second I lift my head, my heart almost
stops – and as totally bizarre as it is, I never stop singing…

Everyone at school knows they are here. Everyone
pretty much knows why, too. Even though they don't have a
real name yet, Josh's band is probably the best one in a
hundred mile circle around Ransom. High schools as far
away as Garden City and Dodge City have called and asked
them to play dances and parties. And I'm pretty sure every
girl in the freshman class of Western Plains High, has a
crush on Josh.

Without saying a single word, Ms. Emily Táo – lead
guitarist of the massively famous *Audio Distortion* – kneels
down in front of me, smiles, pulls the bud from my right ear,
sticks it in her own, and does nothing more than listen.

And yes, for some totally insane and unexplained
reason, I keep singing…

So can we say
I do, I do, I do, do do do do do do doo
Oh baby, I do, I do, I do, do do do do do do doo
Cause every time before it's been like
Maybe yes and maybe no
I won't live without it, I won't let it go

 Riley Morgan

What more can I get myself into
You make we wanna say

Once the song ends, still not having said a single word, she laughs, winks at me, puts the bud back in my ear, stands up, and goes right back into the building the way she came out, again, with Mrs. Perkins right behind her.

And yes, it's the strangest thing that has ever happened to me in the fifteen years I've been on earth.

Coalescence

Martin Masterson

When, on Monday afternoon, Misty Maitland comes into the music room, right behind Mrs. Perkins, and the two people who were *supposed* to have left on Saturday, all of us sorta freak out.

Because I'm the only one who actually knows her (she's absurdly smart, and is the only freshman in our Advanced Calculus class) I decide to speak to her.

"Hey, Misty!"

"Hey, Martin..." she mumbles, sounding way nervous.

"Tell me what songs you guys know – songs you have played for audiences," Mrs. Faintree immediately says.

"Huh?" Rhyan blurts out.

"We want you guys to play something all the way through, so we can show you something..." Mr. Morgan adds.

"Well..." Vanessa says, looking at me, and I just shrug.

"We know a couple of your songs, start to finish," Josh says, walking over and turning on his amp.

Ransom: Start to Finish

The very second Mrs. Faintree *and* Mrs. Perkins look at Misty, and she blushes, I know something is up. Without waiting for the others, I start the intro to *Being Noticed*, and Rhyan joins me instantly. Seconds later, Vanessa and Josh jump in, and I again glance at Misty who, for some reason, looks totally petrified. I watch her cross the room and stop in front of the windows.

"no freakin' way..." I mumble, barely loud enough to be heard, and wondering...

Vanessa and Rhyan look at me, and when Ariel – who isn't playing – looks at me too, I shake my head telling her *not* to sing... even though she's the one who usually would. I'm pretty sure I know what's about to happen... even if I still can't believe it.

The moment we hit the bridge from the intro into the song, standing with her back to all of us, looking out the window, Misty Maitland *opens her mouth...*

> *On a quiet night*
> *I was cleaning tables*
> *Watching the band*
> *Knowing they're able*

The five of us actually lose it. Rhyan messes up, and then Josh does too. Ariel is so stunned, she drops into a chair right behind her, her guitar still hanging from her shoulders, and stares at Misty. I quickly flap my hand, to get everyone's attention, and mouth the words *'keep playing!'* hoping Misty doesn't notice our stunned response to her totally amazing voice.

> *Wondering when*
> *The their time will come*
> *Wondering when*
> *Someone will notice*

The moment she starts the chorus, just as if they've been doing it all along, Vanessa and Ariel add the backup vocals.

We're here!
Night after night
We're here!
Under the lights
Hoping we'll get noticed...

The moment she hears them, Misty turns to face us, and we all see the tears trickling down her cheeks. *This...* is the single moment, when the six of us understand – without saying anything.

We are a band...

And of all the songs we could have played, we pick the one that best defines our lives at this very moment in time.

By the time we're done, there are about thirty people – students, teachers, and some staff members – filling half the room and lining the hall too. The round of applause that follows pretty much freaks us all out.

When I glance across the room and see Mrs. Faintree high-fiving Mr. Morgan, I know that our lives are about to get totally crazy...

"You have all the basics – you just need
to find **each other**..."

~ Emily Faintree 

The Learning Curve

Misty Maitland

The next six months of our lives are insane. I discover that at fifteen, I have no concept of what it takes to become a recording artist.

While we are trying to finish the school year – which for Rhyan and Martin, is their last – the five of them practice. A lot. At one point, Ariel's fingers even begin to bleed.

That's when I finally understand just how badly the five of them want this…

I get to work with a 'vocal coach'. Apparently, she works for Discovery Studios. I think I work harder during the last two weeks of school, than I did the entire rest of the year.

Vocal Registers. Modal Voice. Falsetto. Pitch. Range. Resonance. Tone.

I'm pretty sure I spend more time *studying*, than I do actually singing. But, like I said before, once I understand how committed the others are, no way am I slacking up.

Once Rhyan and Martin get through the whole graduation thing, the trips to Discovery Studios begin. And once they get us into their world, Mr. Morgan and Mrs.

Faintree wear us out – mercilessly. The cool thing is that they agree to work with three songs Ariel, Martin, and Vanessa have been working on for the last year or so. Day and night for two straight weeks, the five of them completely immerse themselves in the music.

Wednesday, of our third week, I meet Emma Greene – the lead singer for *Audio Distortion*. And yeah, I'm a bit star-struck. Heck, I *am* fifteen, remember?

Her very first question to the band is how we would feel about performing a ballad as our first released song. When Rhyan points at me and mentions *Destined To Be*, I'm certain I turn ten shades of red. Although it seems I can sing pretty much anything, slow, touching songs are what I love, so I'm immediately excited.

This is when we discover that Ms. Greene is here to write a song for us – something original. Something that will get the world's attention. Because she wants the song to be 'personal', Ms. Greene spends a week talking to us, asking questions, and generally learning about the six kids from Kansas.

Then, without warning, she simply disappears for a couple of days. When she turns up again, she pulls *me* aside, smiles, and hands me a stack of pages, full of lyrics. Then, she sits me down, and over the next week, makes me participate in creating our band's very first original song. I learn more from her in four weeks, than at any other time in my life. Watching her 'create' is... well, I don't know how to explain it.

When Ms. Greene feels the song is finished, she hands me the first copy, and once I read it, I cry. And once the other band members see the title – *hostage* – we all know where the story came from.

The whole process is an amazing education – especially for a fifteen year old from Kansas...

 Riley Morgan

It takes my bandmates, with the help of Mrs. Faintree, Mr. Morgan, and Mr. Campbell, another three weeks to get the music right. Then… we are ready to try it.

The first time I actually sing the song, *everyone* pretty much freaks. Although we're pretty sure the members of *Audio Distortion* have a handle on things, none of us has even the slightest idea how completely out of hand this is going to get.

A few days later, Ms. Greene leaves, and we too, go home. For the next four months, it's practice, practice, practice. We go back and forth between Ransom and Discovery Studios, at least five times. At home we spend all our free time in the music room at school, or in Rhyan's garage.

Eventually, it's time to *record*, and I'm *petrified*. I find myself wishing Ms. Greene was still around, to… well… I dunno. She's a vocalist too… and… well…

Anyhow, once they find out that we are making our first attempt at recording, some of our parents come with us. I think they're more excited than we are. Even though they keep butting into things, Mrs. Faintree is amazing, dealing with them.

Having practiced endlessly for three days, Mrs. Faintree insists I rest my voice while the others iron out some issues with the music. Now, sitting alone (which I kinda need) in the kitchen of Discovery Studios, I'm about to make a real contribution to our band, and it happens by total accident.

I'm paging through Ariel's sketch pad (she's actually an amazing artist) looking at all the names the five of them are considering…

Flip Side (has Vanessa name next it)

Silo 6 (gotta be Rhyan… silly farm boy that he is)

Bits and Pieces (in Ariel's handwriting)

As If! (not sure who came up with this one)

Short Fuse (Vanessa again, no doubt)
Mission Critical (Josh... for sure)

Although we've all gotten close over the last six months, I still feel like I'm an outsider of sorts – the five of them have been at this since junior high school – so I decide not to offer any suggestions as to a band name, although Vanessa did ask once. As I turn the page, to see if the list continues, something slips out of the back cover, and lands in my lap. I pick it up, sit staring at it for few seconds, then suddenly, I just 'get it'.

With a silly smirk covering my face, I'm still staring at the postcard in my hand, when I hear a voice behind me.

"Find anything you like?" Ariel asks, taking a seat next to me.

"I wasn't trying to be nosey... I swear..." I blurt out, sounding a bit defensive.

"You're part of the band too, you know," Josh offers, taking a seat on the opposite side of the table from me.

I watch as the rest of them come in, and Rhyan goes right to the refrigerator.

"I guess... I was just thinking..." I reply, as a case of nerves sweeps over me.

"So share," comes from Martin, as he stops next to me and puts a hand on my shoulder.

"Well..." I offer, glancing up at Martin.

"Spill it!" Rhyan says, as he starts guzzling from a carton of orange juice he found in the fridge.

"It just seems to me, that with all the passion you guys are putting into this, your name..."

Ariel interrupts me, with a slug in the arm.

"*OUR* name...!"

Before I can stop it, a huge smile spreads across my face.

                                        Riley Morgan

"Okay... *our* name, should be more than just something catchy or cliché. It should give people a reason to listen to *our* music. It should be simple, and tell the world everything there is to know about *us*..."

"For example?" Martin asks, now totally serious.

I glance around, and finding questioning looks on all their faces, I make a decision. I take the postcard – which is still in my hand – and lay it address side up, in the middle of the table, and watch as all their eyes go directly to it. They stare at it for a few seconds, then one at a time, turn and look at me.

"What..." I ask, as I reach out and put my finger on the postcard, "...can tell the world anything more about the six of us..." I pause and slide my finger over the big postmark – *Ransom, KS 67572* – at the top, "...than *this?*"

"Oh..." comes from Ariel, her eyes locked to my finger.

"My..." comes out of Vanessa's mouth just as quickly.

"God..." Josh finishes in a mumbled tone, as he picks up the post card and stares at it.

"And not a single one of us, even considered it..." Martin says, staring at me in stunned disbelief.

"I *knew* there was a reason HE let us find you, Misty Maitland..." comes from Rhyan, as he puts down the carton in his hand, and give me a big sloppy kiss, right on the lips.

I, of course, turn six shades of red, as the others start laughing. Seconds later I'm surrounded by arms, as the five of them do their 'group hug' thing. And yeah, I start crying.

And so, *Ransom* is born...

"So..." Rhyan offers, picking up his drum sticks from the counter, "what do you say *Ransom* goes and records their very first song?!"

This is the most relaxed we've been in the last year – but it doesn't last long.

Six hours, and eight attempts later, Josh and Rhyan are as close to having a meltdown, as two guys can get – I swear.

"Relax guys – you've never done any of this before," Mrs. Faintree offers.

Mr. Morgan laughs – again. He seems to find all of it insanely amusing for some reason, and yet is totally dedicated to the entire process.

"I need coffee," he says, standing up and disappearing from sight as he closes the curtains on the booth window.

"You guys work on it a bit between you. You have all the basics – you just need to find *each other*..."

"Like we did that first time... in the music room..." Ariel mumbles.

"Uh-huh," Mrs. Faintree adds, "exactly. We'll be back in a bit."

With that, she turns and just before she disappears out the door, adds, "And for crying out loud, quit 'trying', and just let it come to you..."

The second she's out of sight, Vanessa asks, "Any ideas?"

"I keep blowing it..." Rhyan says, shaking his head.

"Talk to us," comes from Josh.

"I dunno, it's something in the way Misty is singing the last line of the first verse – the short double tap on 'let go of my heart'..."

Remembering what Josh said at the kitchen table, and totally understanding what Rhyan means, I finally decide to speak up, even as scared as I am...

"It just seems like there has to be some kind of break there..." I almost mumble.

"Hey," Ariel offers, appearing excited at the idea I'm trying to help, "Sing the last two lines, with no music... I have an idea."

"With the double up?" I ask, my heart now racing.

"Uh-huh..." she replies, winking at me.

I smile, turn on the mic, and when Rhyan gives me a beat with his sticks, I do what Ariel asks...

*"from so deep in my soul, the pain is so great...
why won't you please... let go... let go of my heart..."*

Ariel picks up the sheet music, and as Vanessa and Josh look over her shoulder, she scribbles something on the page. In seconds, Josh and Vanessa are grinning like fools – apparently understanding what she's written – and Ariel steps over to me.

"We're going to shorten these chords," she points at the page, "and you need to lose this break, and this refrain, double this whole phrase up, and sing it as a single line," she again points at the page, which I take and look at.

Although I still can't actually read music, the five of them have been working overtime trying to help me with it – and I have a pretty good understanding of the process.

"Okay... so double it up really quick?"

"Exactly!" Ariel replies, putting a hand on my shoulder, "and we will echo you on the repeat."

"Rhyan?" I say, nodding at him and immediately getting a few clicks of his sticks. Once I have the rhythm, I sing the same two lines, with Ariel and Vanessa joining me...

*"from so deep in my soul, the pain is so great...
why won't you please..."* I sing alone.

"won't you please" Ariel and Vanessa sing with me.

"let go of my heart..." I finish.

The very second it happens, we all know it. Everyone gets back into position, and after a five count from Rhyan, we play the song – *our song* – start to finish.

Damn near *perfectly*...

It's the most amazing three and a half minutes of our lives, and we all feel it. The very second it's over, *every one of us* takes a deep breath, a few sips of water, and lets it sink in. That's when Vanessa notices my tears...

"Misty?"

"I'm fine... shaking like a leaf, but okay. Remember, I'm still learning... and I'll probably weird out at times, okay?"

The five of them crack up, and both Vanessa and Ariel step over and hug me.

After a few more seconds, Josh adjusts his guitar and commandingly says, "Again guys."

We play it three more times over the next half hour. On our last pass, our parents come wandering in, and stand silently watching. My mom is standing next to Rhyan's dad, who has his hand on Mrs. Williams' shoulder, and she's in tears.

Ransom – the newest pop band around, is about to take the world by storm, thanks solely to two amazing musicians, who have an incredible amount of faith in us.

And... we will soon discover that Mr. Morgan can't be trusted...

Playback

Joshua Miller

Misty and I are hugging our moms, and without warning, the studio is filled with *hostage – and* it's so close to perfect, no one but us would know it isn't.

Well... us and Mr. Morgan, who is pulling the shades of the booth, back up.

"I hate to ruin this Kodak Moment guys, but you're still on my clock," he yells, over the end of the song. "Parents, I need my studio secure, please."

After our parents quietly disappear into the hall, Mrs. Faintree closes the door and goes into the booth.

"Just like the last pass, guys – no screwing around. Josh, give me a C Major so I can check the levels and the echo."

I do as ordered, and the moment he nods at us, we make some music. And again, it's so close to perfect, it's *amazing.* The intense emotion generated by Misty's voice, as she pours every ounce of herself into the song, pretty much freaks everyone out.

We give Mr. Morgan two more passes, and then lay down three other songs, we've been working on. It's amazing, and after four continuous hours, we finally take a break.

We're gathered in the kitchen, making sandwiches, when out of nowhere, Misty walks over, hugs me, then turns and looks at the others.

"Thank you – all of you – for giving me this amazing chance. You could have chosen any singer you wanted, but you gave me a chance. My heart will always belong to the five of you…"

Then she steps over to Martin, goes up on her tiptoes, and gently kisses his cheek. He, of course, blushes like crazy.

"And thank you for understanding… from the very moment I walked into the music room."

Ariel and Vanessa put down what they are holding, and wrap their arms around her.

"We," Vanessa says, pointing at all of us, "are *Ransom*, because of you. Never forget that."

"Yeah, and now," Rhyan says laughing, "eat something before you blow away." He hands her a plate of food as everyone laughs.

We spend the next two hours, laughing and joking and learning about each other. We share things we would otherwise never have shared with anyone.

Ransom is ready to be famous…

At least we think we are…

"You're stuck on **song** – think **record!**"

~ Willie Morgan 

Trust

Ariel Williams

"I want to give it away, guys. Free download from our site."

All of us are staring her, not sure if she's messing with us or not. When none of us says anything, Mr. Campbell – who turned up this morning – speaks up.

"I'm sure you guys all remember our band…"

"duh?" Vanessa mumbles, making everyone laugh.

"Well, guys, she…" he points directly at Mrs. Faintree who is sitting on her desk, "singlehandedly made *Audio Distortion* happen."

"Without Emily's insane ideas, none of this," Mr. Morgan waves his hands to indicate the entire studio, "would exist. The six of you wouldn't be doing what you are doing…."

"Guys…" Mrs. Faintree adds, sliding off her desk and crossing the room, "I think I can make this happen just the way you want it to…"

"She knows what she's doing guys…" Mr. Morgan quickly adds.

"All you gotta do is trust her..." Mr. Campbell adds.

"With the help of people smarter than us, we got our chance. Now, it's your turn. Do it my way, and in six months, everyone on the planet will know who *Ransom* is..."

"Can we ask our parents?" Josh quickly asks.

"Sure..." Mrs. Faintree replies, as Mr. Morgan opens the door and our parents – who have apparently been listening – appear.

It's my dad who speaks first.

"I have absolutely no doubt that they want you guys to succeed. Look at what they've invested so far, kids..."

Then Mrs. Crossman.

"I would suggest the six of you listen to them, unless of course, over the last eleven months you've acquired more knowledge of the music business than they have..."

"But..." I start to say.

"Ariel," Mr. Morgan says, shaking his head and again, laughing. "You're stuck on *song* – think *record!*"

The very second he says it, I'm pretty sure every single teenage light bulb in the room starts glowing.

Yep... *this* is what they do.

After a split second of contemplation, six voices say 'okay' simultaneously.

And so it begins...

Going Viral

Vanessa Preston

So... let's discuss insanity for a moment.

I'm three months short of seventeen, and I'm pretty sure I know everything.

Well... I used to think so.

Mr. Morgan had a friend of his completely redo our 'website' – if you can even call it that. We use it mostly for people getting downloads of stuff we played – at school dances and places like that. We had a blog too, which I'm pretty sure ten people total, ever read. Just before we left to go home again, he showed us the final product – and the five us stood there with ours mouths hanging open.

Oh... and the insane part? The button right in the middle of the main page that says *hostage* in my handwriting. The exact same button is on the Discovery Studios site, with a flashing icon that says *'the next number one song'*.

Yeah, right. That one cracked us up.

So, here's the absurdly bizarre part...

Mrs. Faintree was so completely right – about everything.

No sooner than we pile into Ryhan's mom's van for the ride home from the airport, *all* our phones go off at the same time. We all get the same message from Discovery Studios – *'check your website, then check ours'*.

Martin gets to ours first…

"No freaking way!" he blurts out, still tapping on his iPad like a crazy man.

"o… m… g…" Ariel and I say at the same time.

"It gets even weirder guys…" Rhyan offers, getting so pale, you would think he was dead. "Look at the DS site…"

What, you ask, can completely freak out six high school kids like this?

Between the two sites, and in just the twelve hours since it was posted, *hostage* has been downloaded 37,000 times. And, on the DS website, they've already created a couple of forums – with well over 3400 members between them! – and they all want to know the same thing…

'Who are these guys!' and 'Do they have a CD?'

Uh-huh… complete and total *insanity*.

NONE of us says another word, all the way home.

Our parents however, are laughing their heads off.

Road Trip!

Martin Masterson

We're sitting around a huge table, inside Lucky Guess Records – a fitting name for the record label representing us, considering how *Ransom* came to be.

The deadly serious guy at the head of the table, is Mr. Richard Galley – producer. More importantly, he's *Audio Distortion's* producer. We're hoping he becomes ours as well.

"Emily, if you weren't so good at what you do, I'd kick your butt..."

Mrs. Faintree and Mr. Morgan crack up.

"It worked, didn't it, Rick?" Mr. Morgan asks.

"Yeah, I'd say a quarter-million downloads in six months, constitutes 'worked'."

"And the 6,700 pre-orders on the CD confirm it," a blonde woman – whose name is apparently Terri – says, as she shuffles some paper.

It took us another four months after Mrs. Faintree brought us to Los Angeles, to actually finish our first CD – eleven songs that, in our youthful opinions, all totally rock.

The bizarre thing (I know I keep saying that, but they just keep happening it seems) that freaked us all out, is that shortly after it swept the web, *hostage* ended up on the radio... and, as totally insane as it was, snuck right up on what is the hottest group in the world at the moment...

Next Page

Their song *Just for Fun*, is number one at the moment, and for some reason, everyone thinks *hostage* is about to bump it.

All this, from five high school musicians, from the middle of nowhere Kansas, and one cute, freckle-faced, sixteen-year-old, with an unbelievable voice.

Go figure.

"So, parents..." Mr. Galley says, ending my daydream. "Are you going to let me send them on a short tour, and get them some exposure?"

"What?" we blurt out at the same time, making all the adults laugh.

"Short circuit, guys – colleges, and small venues. *Ransom*, along with a couple of other groups, plays three songs, at each location," Mrs. Faintree says.

Every one of us looks right at our parents.

"School?" Mr. Williams asks.

"We've planned for that," Mr. Galley says. "You three..." he points at Josh, Ariel and Vanessa, "have graduation the weekend before school is out, right?"

"Yes sir," they reply in unison.

"Well then, school is out the Thursday following graduation, and we've set it up so that the tour starts on the following Saturday. Everything will be in place, and all the kids need to do, is get there."

"I'm in charge of that," the blonde lady says. "I'm also the 'chaperone'," she adds, glancing at each of us.

"Voice of experience, guys," Mr. Morgan says, trying not to laugh, "Mrs. Maxwell takes absolutely no crap…"

"amen…" Mrs. Faintree mumbles, which makes everyone laugh again.

"And us?" Mrs. Maitland asks.

"I'm open to suggestions," Mr. Galley replies. "It's a Lucky Guess road show, but you guys are the final word."

We watch as our parents whisper amongst themselves, and then Mr. Crossman becomes the spokesman.

"At this point, we…" he points at the other parents, "are pretty much out of the picture…"

Misty quickly interrupts him…

"Our parents will never be out of the picture," she blurts out, "no matter how old we get. And… I still have two years before I won't require a babysitter…"

The six of us start laughing, and our parents get a little teary eyed.

"None of you needs a babysitter – we raised you, so we know. But…" he turns and looks at Mrs. Williams, "Maddy and I would love the chance to watch this… from close up… even if it's just once."

"How about this then," Mr. Galley offers, "you all come to the opening show at The Pit…"

"The Pit?" my mom asks.

"University of New Mexico," Mrs. Faintree says, "pretty good acoustics too."

"After that, if you want to stay, we'll put you up. Sound fair?"

All of the parents nod their agreement.

Then, Mr. Galley drops a bomb on us – one that none of us would have expected in a million years…

"And just so you know, *Ransom* is *closing* the show each night. Having heard your music, the other bands said they'd rather not play after you guys, if they can avoid it."

Although we don't really get it, Mr. Morgan and Mrs. Faintree certainly do. They leap from their seats, and yell at the same time, then high five each other.

And once again, the room is filled with laughter.

Life In The Fast Lane (sorta)

Martin Masterson

We survive our first 'tour'…

Sixteen shows in sixteen weeks.

The school agrees to let Misty start two weeks late, with the understanding she will catch up. The cool thing is, the teachers get together, and send her all the work she will miss, and each of us pitches in to make certain she gets it done. The girl is deadly serious about graduating, and walking with her class, just like the rest of us did.

Mrs. Maitland and Mrs. Crossman stay with us the whole time, and we involve them in pretty much everything.

Turns out, we are the youngest group on the tour. As a matter of fact, two of the groups have done similar tours before, but didn't develop a following. The members all say they're going back to school, to study and find their ways, and will come back to music later, if it works out that way.

As we're setting up for the final show at the University of Texas, Melvin – the bass player for *Back Alley* – walks up to Joshua, a huge grin covering his face, and hands him something. Seconds later, a stunned and disbelieving

Joshua, walks over and hands a single page to me. It's a printout of Billboard's latest posting, and there, at the top of the page, next to a *giant* **1**, is...well... us! *hostage* actually made it to number 1 on Billboard's Hot 100 – as bizarre as that is. All the girls, including Misty and Rhyan's moms, break into tears.

And, as if that alone isn't insane enough, just before the show, every single one of the members of the other bands, form a line, and tell us the show doesn't start until we *all* sign every copy of *hostage* they have.

Thirty-one copies (some of the roadies got into it as well), and 186 signatures later, *Shot In The Dark* takes the stage, and opens the show.

Seventy-five minutes later, it's our turn, and after fifteen other shows where Misty Maitland was just our bubbly lead singer, tonight, in the darkness of the Bass Concert Hall, she steps up and becomes our *frontman*.

Even as we are plugging up, and Rhyan is getting his drums lined up, Misty's voice fills the hall...

"Hey guys!" she yells into her mic. *"Wanna hear something pretty freakin' cool?"*

Somehow, an astute technician quickly puts a single spotlight on her, as she smiles and holds up the page I gave her moments before we came on stage.

"We just found out that hostage is number one on the Billboard Hot 100!"

The place goes nuts... and for the first time in our very short lives, we actually feel like 'pop stars'...

"So..." Misty continues, giggling like the sixteen year old she is, "Do we play it first, or last?"

Within seconds 3000 voices are chanting *hos-tage! hos-tage!* over and over. Misty turns and looks at us, and with the biggest grin I've ever seen on anyone, says, "Guess that answers that question, guys..."

In thirty seconds, we are ten bars deep into *hostage*, and by the time we're done, it's easily our best performance of the song, and by far, *the best show of the entire tour*. Even Mrs. Maxwell is totally blown away.

Two hours after it's over, we each get a call from Mr. Galley, congratulating us, and telling us we've become the talk of the music world – including our last performance, which has somehow already made the music news.

Insane... to the tenth power...

Lessons In Creation

Martin Masterson

Once Misty starts school again, our lives as pop stars go on hold. Fortunately, Ransom is small enough, that we don't have to endure the silliness of being 'celebrities'. To everyone back home, we're just us.

Two weeks after we get back, we get our first real taste of fame – in the form of checks, from Lucky Guess Records. Mr. Galley sent them together, by courier, to Mr. Crossman.

As we stand together in the Crossman's living room, carefully tearing open the envelopes, you can tell it's taking all of Mr. Crossman's willpower not to break up laughing.

The checks are identical – except for the names – and once we see them, six mouths suck in huge breaths at the exact same moment.

Needless to say, *none of us* has ever seen a check with five digits to the left of the decimal – let alone one with our name on it. Attached to each check is a handwritten note...

Congrats! You sold out your first tour!
It just gets crazier from here, honest.

Stare at this for a while, let it sink in, then cash it and spend it wisely.
Rick

Yeah... we all drop into chairs instantly, and just sit staring at each other for a couple of minutes. Rhyan's dad eventually gives in, cracks up, and disappears into the kitchen, leaving us dazed and confused.

The six of us do a lot of interviews over the months following the tour, but it's always done so that it doesn't interfere with Misty's classes. And, as weird as it will sound, that's a band rule – not a parent rule. Understanding that Misty wasn't willing to skip classes for interviews, all of the radio and TV stations were willing to settle for the five of us.

Even though we eventually grasp the concept of getting paid to make music, boredom quickly sets in, and everyone except Misty – who is diligently trying to finish high school – finds a part time job in town and we spend most of our free time trying to learn to write. We quickly realize we aren't lyricists, and decide to stick to music.

Finally, the first week of June, Misty Maitland becomes a graduate. And although all of us are front and center, what really trips everyone out, is how many people from the label turn up. Even Mrs. Faintree and Mr. Morgan come.

Now without any limitations, over the following summer, we throw ourselves entirely into music. We make multiple trips to Lucky Guess and more than a few to Discovery Studios, as we try to answer our first record with an even better second one.

It doesn't take us long to understand that doing so, is considerably harder than it sounds.

On *hostage* we had more knowledgeable help than any three bands could have asked for. This time we decide to try and do it ourselves.

Silly kids...

Anyhow, on a cool September afternoon, I'm headed for Rhyan's house after work – we're going to keep trying with the composition thing – when I see Misty. She's sitting by herself, at the lone picnic table, outside our famous Dairy Queen. Once I turn around, I can see she's diligently (and furiously) scribbling in a huge notebook on the table in front of her. As my truck rolls to a stop on the gravel behind her, she never even flinches.

"Hey Misty!"

When she doesn't respond, I finally see the chords from her ear buds as they slip inside the collar of her jacket on each side, and laugh. I put the truck in park, shut it off, and get out, still with no reaction from Misty.

When I'm within arm's reach of her, I start to put a hand on her shoulder, but when my eyes see what's in the notebook, I hesitate.

I've only read four or five lines before my heart takes off...

Misty suddenly stops writing, reaches out, grabs the steaming cup on the table, and takes a big drink. I take a step toward her, and I guess my shadow on the table, freaks her out.

The cup and pencil go flying, and poor Misty launches herself off the bench and into a standing position as she spins around to face me.

"DAMN IT, MARTIN!" she pretty much screams at me, while at the same time, pulling the buds from her ears.

I on the other hand, slowly take a seat where she'd been, and start reading.

Page after page, my heart races faster and faster. After close to a minute, Misty steps over and puts a hand on my shoulder.

"You owe me a hot chocolate, butthead..."

"Cool..." I reply, never taking my eyes off the notebook. I reach into my shirt pocket, pull out a $5.00 bill and hand it to her, still never looking at her. I hear her giggling, as she turns and heads for the order window.

As I continue to read, I realize that Misty's voice is only part of the reason God let our paths cross. I'm reading the other part...

Apparently, Misty Maitland has an amazing way with words. Seems she has chronicled the entire existence of *Ransom*, since the day it began, right here in this notebook.

A minute, and five or six pages later, Misty reappears, drops some change into my shirt pocket, takes a seat next to me, and puts a cup down in front of me.

When I stop reading and turn to face her, the look on my face pretty much freaks her out.

"That's why I didn't show you guys. I knew it would piss you off..." she mumbles, dropping her eyes, and pulling her hair back.

"You are just *sooo* freakin' weird, Misty Maitland, I swear..." I reply, following it with a laugh.

I reach out, gently lift her chin until our eyes meet again, and find a few tiny little tears in hers. Then, for some totally unexplained reason, I lean over and gently kiss her.

"Just like you did that very first day in the music room, you are about to once again, save *Ransom*, girl."

I turn, close her notebook, stand up and pull her to her feet as well.

"In the truck – and *do not* spill the hot chocolate, got it?"

She smiles, nods, picks up the cup of coffee she got me, and within seconds we are headed for Rhyan's. Even as I am trying to drive and dial my phone, she reaches out and takes it from me.

"Who are you trying to call?"

"Vanessa and Ariel. They need to meet us at Rhyan's."

"What about Josh?"

"He's going to be there," I reply, as I watch her type a text to the girls, and send it.

Just as I am turning into Rhyan's driveway, Misty again turns and looks at me.

"So… tell me the truth – how much trouble am I in?"

I put the truck in park, turn it off, and turn to face her.

"A lot," I reply, a huge, goofy grin covering my face. "But not for what you think…"

Unrealized Talent

Misty Maitland

I'm sitting quietly on Rhyan's couch, sipping my hot chocolate. Martin is sitting at his keyboard, scribbling on some sheet music. The rest of *Ransom* is sifting through my notebook, in some kind of weird stunned silence. We've been here for forty-five minutes, and since Martin handed them the notebook, not a single one of them has said a word.

Yeah... I'm pretty much petrified.

When I stand up to put my cup in the trash, I hear Vanessa call to me from across the room.

"Misty – come here."

I drop the cup in the trash, turn and cross the garage to where the four of them are standing around an old dining room table. When I'm within feet of them, Rhyan pulls out a chair, and indicates he wants me to sit down, which I do.

"We need you to combine these," Josh says, flipping back and forth between a couple of pages in the book, "and tell the same story, in five stanzas."

"Huh?" I blurt out, looking at each of them.

Ariel slides some blank sheet music pages in front of me, and hands me a pencil.

"Seems you have written our next title song, girl, it just needs a little rearranging..."

I shrug, grab a lined pad that's next to me, and pull the notebook over in front of me. Once I copy the pages they're interested in, I push everything away except the lined pad, and sit quietly staring at it for a few minutes. The rest of them turn, and without another word, cross the room stopping next to Martin, and start talking to him about what he's working on.

The pages they want me to work on, are about all the madness of getting famous. It's mostly about the emotional roller coaster a certain fifteen-year-old, was on, for most of the journey. It's about watching it all through my eyes...

Because the others are insanely passionate about music, they were all in it with both feet from the beginning. I, on the other hand, was pretty much just 'caught up' in it, and went along for the ride.

When I close my eyes, and lay my head on my arms on the table, none of them says a word. For about five minutes, I let my mind wander back to all the insanity our lives became...

When I lift my head, I pick up the pencil, and just start writing. For three hours, Misty Maitland throws herself entirely into creating her very first song...

When I'm finished, I realize that everyone is gone. Only Rhyan is there, and he's sound asleep on the couch. With a big smile, I put an old wool blanket over him, lay the final version of the lyrics on the table next to him, and slip out the side door of the garage.

It's not quite 11:00 pm, and I think about calling my mom. Because I only live three blocks from Rhyan, I know that I'll be home before she could even answer the phone, so instead, I bounce along in an amazing mood, wondering how much more insane, I've just made our lives…

Excited (again)

Ariel Williams

The next morning, Vanessa and I pretty much bust into Misty's bedroom around 8:00 am... which of course freaks her out.

While her mom stands in the doorway watching (and trying her very best not to break out in laughter), we roll Misty out of bed, and help her pack her backpack with stuff she will need. And no, we don't even give her a chance to wake up.

"Guys!" she blurts out, as we are stuffing things into the backpack, "what's going on?"

"My mom is taking us to the airport," I reply, giggling and shoving her past her mom and into the bathroom across the hall. "Mr. Galley is waiting for us in LA."

"We're going to LA?" we hear through the closed door, as the shower starts to run.

"Yes we are..." Vanessa mumbles, as we both smile at Mrs. Maitland.

"I haven't seen you guys this excited in as long as I can remember," Mrs. Maitland offers.

"Misty has given us a direction, Mrs. M – without even realizing it."

"Yeah," I add, "and I personally think it's going to be amazing!"

"'*It*'?"

"Yes, ma'am – our next CD.

"You have enough songs for another CD? *Already?*" she blurts out, while at the same time, we hear the shower shut off.

"Not quite," Vanessa offers, "but with the help of people way smarter than we are, I'll bet that in sixty days, we will."

The moment Misty appears in the bathroom doorway, we rush her into her room and have her dressed (sorta) and headed for my mom's van.

"Call me when you get there so I won't worry!" Mrs. Maitland calls out as the three of us go down the front steps.

"Yes ma'am!" three voices reply in unison.

An hour later, after a totally quiet ride, Misty finally breaks the silence.

"I wasn't purposely keeping it from you guys..."

"We know," Josh says, stifling a laugh and squeezing one of her hands.

"I was just... well... worried, I guess."

"About?" Rhyan asks.

"That you'd be pissed off I was keeping notes on stuff that's kinda private..."

Martin, who is sitting up front with my mom, turns in his seat, grins like a fool, and then hands Misty her notebook.

"We don't care where the inspiration comes from girl, just promise us you will never stop writing..."

Riley Morgan

And yet another bond is formed between the members of *Ransom* – in a minivan, speeding along through the wheat fields of Kansas.

"Well, the fame part isn't that big a
deal, really. It's keeping up with all the
expectations that seems to be kicking
our butts."

~ Joshua Miller 

Mentors

Misty Maitland

The first thing we encounter at LGR, is the rumor mill. After hearing the same thing in three different conversations around the building, we go straight to Mrs. Maxwell's office...

"Sorry for just butting in Mrs. Maxwell, but..." is as far as Vanessa gets.

"Yes, guys, it's true," she says, laughing.

At the same time, we hear a female voice – that even after all this time, I recognize instantly – behind us say, "Excuse me guys, I need to talk to Terri." Then none other than Ms. Emma Greene – who we later discover is actually *Mrs. Campbell* – slips between us and goes to Mrs. Maxwell's desk.

"no freakin' way..." Ariel mumbles, while at the same time, Vanessa goes totally pale.

The moment she hears Ariel, she spins around, and realizes who we are.

"OMG! *Ransom!*" she blurts out, then walks back over to us, and starts hugging people.

"Hey girl," she says when she gets to me, my eyes now full of tears.

"Hey, Emma. My heart is *so* happy you found your way... and that it led you back home..." I reply, much to the complete astonishment of my friends.

When we hug each other, the intense emotion is apparent to everyone in the room. Once we break our embrace, Emma turns and looks at the others.

"So... how is the whole fame thing treating you then?"

"Well," Josh quickly offers, "the fame part isn't that big a deal, really. It's keeping up with all the expectations that seems to be kicking our butts."

Everyone quickly agrees with him, which makes Mrs. Maxwell laugh.

"Been there, done that!" Emma replies. "You aren't giving up are you?"

"No... not at all," I offer, a big grin on my face. "They found my notebook..."

"So... you're here to record?"

"Well... to try anyhow," Rhyan says, fighting a laugh.

"So are we!" Emma says, pausing and looking at each of us. "Keep in mind guys," she adds, looking deadly serious, "your second record will be the hardest one you will have to write. Don't give up – no matter what. Just believe you can do it..."

We say "Yes ma'am," almost in unison.

Emma turns, looks at Mrs. Maxwell, and says, "We set up in Studio Two, and are ready when our engineer is..."

"Cool. Let me see what these guys want, and I'll be down directly. Twenty minutes?"

"See ya!" Emma replies. When she turns toward the door, she pauses and again looks at the six of us.

"You guys need *anything*, all you have to do is ask, understood?"

"Yes ma'am..." we all mumble at the same time, pretty much stunned, as she turns and slips back out the door.

"So guys..." Mrs. Maxwell says, making all of us turn and look at her.

"Can we watch, Mrs. M?" Vanessa blurts out.

"Huh?" she replies.

"Audio Distortion... can we watch them record?"

She cracks up laughing, stands up, and says, "Why the heck not? Come on..."

Five minutes later, we – along with most of the staff – are standing in the box, waiting. The moment I see Ms. Meredith with an acoustic bass, Mrs. Faintree with an acoustic twelve-string, and nothing but a snare, one tom-tom, and a single cymbal in front of Mr. Morgan, I get the most intense rush of goose bumps I ever have. The first few lines Emma sings, and the tempo of the song, actually make my heart race. Truth is, I'm pretty sure everyone present gets a little teary-eyed.

The total silence that follows their performance... well... there's really no way to describe it. No cheering, no clapping. Just two dozen totally stunned *fans*...

Begin Again is undoubtedly going to be massive...

Harder Than We Thought

Joshua Miller

After two months of nothing but working, we have seven songs that everyone seems to like – including Mr. Galley. Parker Lindstrom – a really good song writer – helps us a good bit. The thing we all find a bit mystifying is that she never once tries to change any of the songs.

A note here, a word there, finding a bridge or a new break, or just adjusting tempo. When she finds out that Misty wrote all our lyrics, the two of them get pretty close.

And... even as we work, Misty keeps writing. At random points in the day, we find her in a corner somewhere, scribbling away. On a couple of occasions, Vanessa and Ariel wake up in the middle of the night to her tapping a pencil in rhythm as she is writing.

So... our problem. Yeah, we have one.

The one song we so desperately want to work – won't. The song we discovered in Rhyan's garage simply won't come together the way we want it to.

After ninety days of stressing ourselves, Mr. Galley tells us to let it go – to go back to our lives, and take a break from music.

We're sitting together in Studio Two, when out of nowhere, Mrs. Faintree turns up in the box, and does nothing more than stare at us for a couple of minutes. Then, she disappears again, and we sit staring at each other, curious.

Having already packed our equipment, we leave the studio, only to find Mrs. Faintree standing outside with a rather odd smirk on her face, and Mr. Galley standing next to her.

"Big white passenger van, right outside the door. All your stuff is in it," she says, and then tosses Martin a set of keys. "You're driving. I'll be there in a second…"

When all we do is stand there, totally confused, Mr. Galley laughs.

"Really?" he says, shaking his head.

All our 'light bulbs' go on at the same time, and we turn and go out the door next to us. Even as we pile into the van, we each know that whatever is about to happen, it will be yet another defining point in *Ransom's* history…

Who Are We?

Martin Masterson

I drive for about three hours, and then Rhyan drives for close to four. Mrs. Faintree drives the rest of the way.

At around 11:30 pm we pull into Discovery Studios.

"You know where the beds are guys – go get some sleep. Meet me in the kitchen around 8:00, I'll make some breakfast and we'll talk."

Five voices mumble *yes ma'am* at the same time, and we do as instructed.

The interesting part comes when Misty – already half asleep – crawls into the same bed I'm in, and is sound asleep within minutes.

"So..." I say into the darkness, "am I the only one who is confused?"

"Yeah, right..." I hear Vanessa say.

After a few seconds of silence, it's Ariel who says, what all of us are feeling.

"It's like I have no idea who I am anymore... who any of us are."

"Who *Ransom* is..." Josh adds.

After another brief silence, I say, "Well guys, this is where *Ransom* began. Hopefully, with a little luck, we can answer those questions..."

We lay quietly for a good five minutes, and then, out of nowhere, the person I *thought* was asleep, jabs me in the side, and makes a comment of her own.

"And maybe, we can figure out that damn song..."

All of us laugh... and I gently kiss Misty on the head.

Fifteen minutes later, all of us are off in dreamland.

"…if you are going to figure this out,
you will have to let go of the pop stars,
and the number one recording artist
you've become, and go back to being
the six kids we discovered in a
classroom in Kansas…"

~ Willie Morgan 

Answering The Questions

Martin Masterson

Here's where *Ransom* actually moves past being a band, and becomes family.

Around 7:15 the next morning, cute little Misty Maitland wakes up to find she is sleeping on my chest. In a moment of temporary terror, she lifts her head, and blurts out, *"oh my god..."* which of course, incites mass laughter from everyone else in the room.

After we're all showered and changed, we head for the kitchen – and the moment Rhyan smells the bacon, it all becomes comical. Not having actually eaten a 'real' meal since we left Ransom, the moment we see what is waiting on us, we simply let go. Within seconds, we are once again, six goofy kids from Kansas, not stressed out pop stars...

"So..." Mrs. Faintree says, as we are all around the table, stuffing our faces. "I heard it all."

We all pause and glance at her.

"You two," she points at Ariel and Misty, "made me cry."

"Not an easy task, either," Mr. Morgan adds.

"I have no idea how you did it – whether you," she points at Ariel, "played to her voice, or if you," she turns and points at Misty, who is again blushing, "simply sang over her near perfect acoustic guitar. But I am here to tell you, *Trying To Hold On* is going to chart..."

Stunned silence. None of us can say a word. Then, after about thirty seconds, Mrs. Faintree puts an end to breakfast.

"I also know what your problem is..."

Six forks hit the table at the same time, and all we can do is stare at her.

"And no, I'm not going to tell you what it is. If this song is going to be all that the six of you want it to be, *you* have to figure it out – between you."

Yeah, all our hearts are racing.

"I brought you here because you have history here. Talk to each other, read the lyrics together. Consider the music both together and individually..."

"What I am going to tell you," Mr. Morgan says, looking at Mrs. Faintree, "under protest, is that if you are going to figure this out, you will have to let go of the pop stars, and the number one recording artists you've become, and go back to being the six kids we discovered in a classroom in Kansas..."

Then, together they stand up and head for the door. Just before they go out, Mrs. Faintree has one last comment...

"And from this point forward, I'm Emily and he's Willie. No exceptions. You're all adults now, but more importantly, we're all musicians..."

And then, we find ourselves alone... lost in thought.

"This isn't about Ransom... or about our label... or about expectations. This guys, is about the six of us, creating a totally kick-butt song — *our way.*"

~ Misty Maitland 

Why Me?

Misty Maitland

Willie and Emily are right. Being here is way different than being at Lucky Guess. Truth is, here there is zero pressure.

We hang out, talk, play a lot, and even get to watch a couple of other artist lay down tracks of their own. We're all blown away when both of them actually recognize us. This is also when the six of us realize that in addition to being an amazing drummer, Willie Morgan is probably the best engineer we've ever seen – perhaps even better than Mrs. Maxwell. At times, I would swear the guy hears things, no one else does...

It's been five days, and although we're still pretty much clueless, the pressure to figure out why, simply isn't there.

I'm sitting on one end of the deck, staring at the lake, and writing, on and off. I flip to the back of my notebook, and with a grin, pull out the lyrics to the song that has become our nemesis. As I am reading (for the millionth time) the first stanza, I hear a guitar. When I move the well-worn page, I see Joshua sitting Indian style on the grass, alone, ripping some kind of crazy lead riff. It makes me laugh, because we've all come to realize that this is his way of letting go of things. He just plays... and plays... and then plays some more. Always, by himself.

He isn't that far away so, even though he's not plugged up, I can make out most of the notes he's playing. In seconds, my mind is putting the lyrics together with the tempo and chords Josh is playing, and in the blink of an eye, it makes total sense.

"could it really be that simple?" I mumble, as I stare at the pages in my hand, still visualizing.

Then, just like it did with the band name, something in my head simply clicks, and totally by chance, *I figure out how to make the song work!*

I let the notebook fall to the deck, jump up with the lyrics in one hand and the music in the other, and race down the stairs, dropping to my knees in front of Josh.

"Do it again!" I pretty much yell at him.

"What?" he blurts out.

"Play the most brain mangling lead riff you ever have..."

Something in my eyes must give away the importance of what is happening, because the guy closes his eyes, and plays the most intense riff I have ever heard.

"Is it yours, Josh? Did you actually write that?" I blurt out, pulling a pen from his pocket and scribbling on the sheet music.

"Uh, yeah, years ago. I used to want to play speed metal," he replies, actually blushing.

I jump up, grab his hand, and pull him to his feet.

"Man... this is going to be beyond epic – come on..."

He follows me into the house through the kitchen, where we find Ariel and Vanessa talking to Emily.

"You guys," I blurt out, pointing at the girls, "are with us."

"Misty?" Emily starts to say.

"In a minute, Emily, in a minute. Where is Rhyan?"

"In the upper studio with Willie," she replies, now also understanding – perhaps more than my bandmates – that I'm totally locked onto something.

I turn that direction, and almost walk into Martin, who has a handful of sheet music.

"Come on awesome keyboardist, we are about to make this happen…"

They follow me up the stairs, none of them saying anything, and when we reach the studio, Emily takes a turn and goes into the booth. Willie and Rhyan are sitting in the booth, discussing something, when I point at Rhyan, say "Now, please," and point at the drum kit behind me. The moment he holds up his hand as if to say 'in a second', Ariel pretty much screams at him.

"Damn it! Get your butt out here, Rhyan!"

In a heartbeat, he's standing next to the drums, sticks in hand, and I quickly walk over to him.

"How many times have we played this stupid song?" I ask, waving the sheet music in his face.

"Crap, Misty, I quit counting," Rhyan quickly replies, somehow knowing exactly which song I'm talking about.

"Well then, play it one more time, except this time…"

I hold up one of the pages of sheet music and let him look at it – at the spot where I made just one small change.

He looks from the page, to me, and back at the page.

"You're our tempo, dude. They," I point at the others, who now have powered instruments, "are *all* going to be playing off you."

"*Seriously?*" he asks, again looking at the change I made. "What about you, Misty? Can *you* get there?" He reaches out, and taps the page, where I made the change.

"As serious as a heart attack, Rhyan. And don't you even worry about the vocals. You are about to hear a Misty, you have never heard before…" I reply, my face now covered by a seriously sinister grin.

"You are as amazing, as you are totally freakin' insane, Misty Maitland."

At this point, *everyone* is staring at us.

"And, just in case you need some motivation," I add, as he takes his stool, and stomps the bass pedal a couple of times, "I've decided what the title is going to be – *no discussion…*"

I hold up the back of the lyrics pages, where in huge block letters I wrote…

HIGH SPEED RUSH

The huge grin on his face tells me this is so totally going to work.

I spin around, my heart racing almost out of control, and not even realizing I've pretty much taken charge, look at the others who have been standing quietly, listening.

"The five of you have played together for so long, that following one another is second nature. I know, because I've seen you do it. Do that now… follow him," I pause and point at Rhyan. "It's the same song, with one little change…"

They all look at one another, then back at me.

"This isn't about *Ransom*… or about our label… or about expectations. This guys, is about the six of us, creating a totally kick-butt song – *our way*. Josh?"

"Yeah?"

"*Exactly* like you did it in the yard…"

With a totally evil grin, Josh reaches over, spins the volume knob on his amp as far as it will go, and then does exactly what I ask – totally shredding what is now the intro to *High Speed Rush*.

The very moment he hits the last chord, Rhyan is all over it, and within seconds, Ariel, Vanessa, and Martin are in perfect unison. At the first bridge, Misty Maitland becomes a rock singer.

No more smooth, calming, ballad voice.

No more bubbly, happy, pop song voice.

Just a very serious, very intense, rock voice, that creates notes I didn't even know I had in me.

And even as Josh plays screaming chord after screaming chord, Ariel has her fuzzed out guitar playing each note right behind him, with almost an echoing effect.

And yes, the moment I turn myself loose, my bandmate's mouths all drop open. I'm pretty sure Emily and Willie freak out too. Halfway through the song, where we had been struggling with fill, and transition, Joshua simply takes over. The very moment he heard Rhyan's drums, he understood my tempo change, and immediately turned his fingers, and his heart, loose.

To be perfectly honest with you, it's even more intense than the first time we played *hostage* all the way through…

The moment it's over, the five of them do nothing more than stand staring at me. With a huge grin, I hold up the same page I showed Rhyan before we started – the one with the title on it…

"No freakin' kidding…" Vanessa blurts out.

"Ditto…" Martin mumbles.

"And do you know *why* this is going to be the title?" I ask, tapping on the page.

The five of them stand staring at me, totally stunned and pretty much speechless. I on the other hand, am seconds away from full on laughter.

"Because… while there is no way I could have picked five better 'best friends'… this…" I again tap on the words *HIGH SPEED RUSH* on the page I'm holding, "is what my damn life has been like since the day I met you crazies!"

Even as the five of them break up in laughter, a deep male voice fills the studio.

"Excuse me… but who the hell are you guys, and how did you get into my studio?" Willie says, as Emily sits laughing next to him.

"From where I'm sitting, it seems creating *'your way'*, works just fine…" Emily says, as she shakes her head, high-fives Willie, and goes right on laughing.

At this point, there is only one thought circling my mind… just how intensely pissed off is Mr. Galley going to be, when he finds out that his latest 'pop' band's new title song is… well… you get the idea.

"nener-nener-nener"

~ Emily Faintree 

Equalization

Joshua Miller

The next afternoon, I walk into Emily's office, not realizing she's on the phone. When she sees me, she laughs, and points at a chair opposite her desk. Then, she lifts her finger to her lips, grins, and puts the call on speaker. The moment I hear Mr. Galley, I almost panic.

"Seriously? Misty pulled this off?"

"She most certainly did! She convinced them to do it *their way* – not everyone else's. And, when you hear the song, I have fifty bucks that says you get your underwear all kinds wadded up..." Emily replies.

"Crap, Emily, I'm not sure I like the sound of that..."

"Let's see what your attitude is when it shoots up the charts, shall we?"

"You think it's that good?" Mr. Galley asks, sounding more than a bit disbelieving.

"It's the same caliber and quality as *hostage* – in our opinion. And not only does it fit the six of them *perfectly*, they created it, *on their own*. Trust me... you can't get any more *Ransom*, than this song is."

We hear Mr. Galley exhale deeply, and then sigh, as if he's completely relieved.

"So… can we cut the masters here? Or do you want them back there?" Emily asks, winking at me.

"You think they're ready to cut the masters?"

"Nope. I'm absolutely *certain* they are. So is Willie."

"And what's this going to cost me?"

"Have we ever screwed you, Richard?"

A loud hearty laugh comes from the phone, which somehow, makes me relax.

"Whatever the kids want to do is fine with me. How long?"

"Ten days – two weeks at the most. You want me to bring them back with the master?"

"Yeah… maybe we can work on the album art and some promo stuff. Any idea what they want to title it?"

"HIGH SPEED RUSH!" Emily yells.

"Interesting. Well… I trust you, and the kids as well. Get to work and don't keep me in suspense! Later!"

"Bye Richard…" Emily replies, punching the button to disconnect the call.

I'm about to say something, when there is a knock on the open door. I turn and find Stanley and Emma coming in. As she passes me, a strange little smirk covering her face, she smiles, and says, "I only need a second, Joshua…" then turns and hands a single sheet of paper to Emily. It takes Emily about ten seconds to totally crack up.

Emma turns, winks at me, and disappears out the door with Stanley right behind her.

By the time I turn back around, Emily is out from behind her desk, and as I stand up, she stops right in front of me. The look in my eyes, is enough to tell her that the need to know what's going on is about to make me implode. With a big grin, she hands me the sheet of paper, then curls her finger, indicating she wants me to bend over – I'm actually seven inches taller than her. Once I do, with the goofiest smirk (which confuses me even more) I have ever seen, she gets right in my face, says just three words…

"nener-nener-nener"

…and as calmly as you please, turns and goes out the door.

Confused beyond all comprehension, I lift the page and read what's on it, only to discover that in only 23 days, *Begin Again* rules *all* the charts.

The Hot 100 – #1

The Billboard 200 – #1

Pop Songs – #1

Radios Songs – #1

Digital Songs – #1

And even the Canadian Hot 100 – #1

All of them – without exception.

Then, out of nowhere, a seriously bizarre thought occurs to me. What are the possibilities we could actually find ourselves *sharing the charts with our mentors*?

My entire body shudders, and my heart takes off – like a rocket…

'the best pop band in years... and now this – how depressing'

~ A Ransom Fan

Reality Check

Ariel Williams

Ten weeks after *Begin Again* completely trashes all the music charts, Lucky Guess releases the first single from *High Speed Rush*.

The response is less than stellar.

The six of us talk Richard into releasing *Bubblegum* first. The song is about how, as a band, we seem to be in a constant battle with our identity. The hook in the chorus is…

No matter where we are
We always seem to be
Wearing boot-cut jeans, and sneakers
With our mouths full of bubblegum…

And yes, *everyone* says the song is a borderline country crossover. The band loves it solely because Misty captures all our hearts, in a single song.

Our fans are disappointed. The song does make it onto the charts, but never gets above 50. When we check the blogs and comments on our website, and the Discovery Studios website, we begin to understand just how unhappy our fans are. While none of them are rude, they don't hesitate to share their feelings…

'jezzz guys! what happened to the band I fell in love with?'

'if this is the direction you guys are going, I just can't follow you'

'the best pop band in years… and now this – how depressing'

The six of us follow Mrs. Maxwell into Mr. Galley's office, and one at a time, plop onto his couch. When none of us says a word, he breaks up laughing.

"What's so funny?" Rhyan asks.

"The six of you… of course."

"We messed up, Mr. Galley… we get it." Vanessa offers.

"How, exactly, did you do that?" he retorts, as Mrs. Maxwell slides up onto the corner of his desk.

"We should have let you deal with the 'release' stuff – and kept our mouths shut," I offer.

"You guys stood up for a song you love – nothing wrong with that," Mrs. Maxwell says, smiling at us.

Then we hear an unfamiliar voice behind us – a female voice, with an odd British accent.

"Knuckleheads… I swear, you're all knuckleheads…"

We spin around and find Catrin Sharpe – who everyone calls Cadi – standing behind us. She's *AD's* Welsh bass player.

"Are the six of you so entirely caught up in yourselves, that you think your fans are going to like *every* song you record?" she says, crossing the room and stopping in front of us.

"Aren't we here to keep our fans happy?" Misty asks, the tone of her voice indicating her level of confusion.

"Well yeah… within reason. But if you only write for them, and never for yourselves, what do you think that will do to the band?"

When we all sit silently staring at her, she cracks up. Seconds later, a second voice comes from the direction of the doorway.

"Do any of you have a copy of *Journeys End?*" Emma asks, as she too crosses the room, stopping next to Cadi.

"Well yeah… of course," I quickly reply.

"*Along The Way* – What's the song about?" she shoots back.

I'm pretty certain that, from the looks on our faces, Emma realizes she got us. Mr. Galley pulls a CD from the rack behind him, tosses it to Emma, who laughs and tosses it to Joshua.

"It's on there," she says, sitting down on the arm of the couch, next to me, "number nine I believe. It never charted – heck it never even got any airplay…"

"But the five of us will play it in a heartbeat – because *we* love the song," Cadi says, finishing Emma's thought.

The strange silence that engulfs the room is suddenly broken by the sound of pages crinkling. Everyone turns in the direction of the sound, and finds a very solemn Misty, carefully turning the pages of her notebook, and scanning each one.

"I have three of those, Misty. You saw number two back at DS… a few years ago."

Misty looks at her, the emotion evident in her eyes.

"And how much of it ends up as part of… well… 'history'?" Misty asks, carefully closing the notebook.

"In my case, about eighty percent of it. But…" Emma hesitates until Misty makes eye contact with her.

"But?"

"But…" Emma smiles, pulls a brand new notebook from the satchel slung over her shoulder, and hands it to Misty, "I've never stopped writing."

It's as if in that single instant, we all understand – not just Misty. I look at Vanessa, who grins, and squeezes Misty's hand. When we look at the guys, all three of them wink at us.

"So…" I turn and look right at Mr. Galley, "what are you releasing next?"

"Any suggestions?" he asks.

"Not a one," Vanessa quickly blurts out, pretty much making our point.

"Well," Mrs. Maxwell says, "what we want to do, is give them your," she points right at Misty, "voice back. The one they all got addicted to…"

"Trying To Hold On…" Martin says, and immediately gets nods of agreement.

"Yep."

"Emily did say she believes it will chart…" Rhyan says.

"Chart? Seriously?" Cadi says, making Mr. Galley and Mrs. Maxwell laugh, "I've got twenty bucks that says it's in the top five a week after you release it."

"I agree," Emma adds. "I think your fan base will forget about *Bubblegum* – which, for the record, is a totally amazing song – the moment they hear *Trying To Hold On.*"

Finally, Martin asks the one question that's driving all of us nuts…

"Do you think *High Speed Rush* is gonna work? Are our fans gonna understand why we had to go there?"

We all watch as Mr. Galley stands up, and comes around his desk.

"I've been doing this crap for thirty-five years, guys, and I've pretty much seen it all. That song is, in my professional opinion, going to double your fan base. I also firmly believe it will in fact, hit #1."

Yeah… he gets us. Big time.

After thirty seconds of total silence, Cadi starts giggling. Emma is onboard seconds later. Once Mrs. Maxwell joins them, it's pretty much over – all of us are laughing almost hysterically.

This is also the moment my life drastically changes. The instant Josh takes my hand and gently squeezes it, my heart races. When, amidst all the laughter, we make eye contact, I simply know.

Ariel Williams is, for the first time in her life, about to fall for a guy… a guy she has known, all her life.

"NO FREAKIN' WAY!"

~ Joshua Miller

Irony

Martin Masterson

Just as if it had been planned, forty-eight hours after the label releases it, *Trying To Hold On* enters the Heat Seekers chart at #4. Twenty-four hours after that, Misty finds it on the Hot 100 – at #3.

And yeah, we all pretty much freak out.

Within hours, the blogs and forums run rampant…

'oh… thank… God!'

'faith… we just had to have faith.'

'please! for God's sake, RELEASE THE CD!'

'it's a miracle – I swear!'

Richard and Terri have us hang around for what they are calling 'promotional purposes' – I think it's because they knew what was going to happen. Within hours, they already have four interviews set up, as well as a quick spot on MTV.

I go in search of Misty, to tell her what's going on, and eventually find her in the basement, sitting on the floor of a totally dark, Studio Two. The moment I open the door, I hear the sniffles.

"Hey! You okay?"

"I don't know, Martin – I honest to God, don't know…"

I quickly take a seat beside her, pulling my feet up under me, and putting an arm around her shoulders. It takes less than a heartbeat for her head to land on my shoulder. For close to a minute, I sit quietly and listen to her softly crying.

"Sometimes… things go *too damn fast*, and I feel like my life is out of control. As dumb as it will sound, at this exact moment, Martin, I just want to be home…"

"At one point or another, all of us have had the same feelings, Misty. But why hide?"

"I don't want to screw this up for you guys…"

"Meaning?" I ask, gently lifting her head, and making her look at me.

"No room for falling apart, in this business…"

"*Oh bullshit*. That's the dumbest thing you have ever said to me," I quickly reply, forcing myself not to laugh.

"We're a band, Martin… it takes all of us. I'm not about to let you guys down by going to pieces because I can't handle it."

"You do realize what's gonna happen as soon as I tell Ariel and Nessa what you just said, right?"

"*Damn it*… you're the one person who is *supposed* to understand, Martin."

"And I do, actually. You're eighteen, Misty. Your entire life has always been school and the thriving metropolis of Ransom, Kansas. Then one day, a bunch of lunatics discover you can sing, snatch you right out of the middle of your life, and drop you in the middle of 'famous'…"

When she finally looks at me again, I can see she's relaxing… and listening to what I'm saying.

"If that alone isn't enough to warrant a 'total breakdown' – I'd like to know what does."

"For like the last two days, I've been petrified – and I'm not sure why. Being scared is one thing, but not knowing what you are scared of – well... that's called petrified. And when I look at the rest of you, all grins and giggles, and not at all concerned, it makes it worse."

"Okay... we are gonna squash this right now," I say, standing up and pulling Misty to her feet. "Time for a band meeting. Come on..."

Ten minutes later, having found Mrs. Maxwell's office empty, we lock ourselves in.

Once I get Misty to explain herself again, two things happen – neither of which I would have ever expected.

"If you ever," Vanessa blurts out, hands on her hips, her face as red as a fire truck, "pull that hiding out crap again, I will personally kick your silly little ass all the way back to Ransom. *Do you understand me?"*

Then, out of nowhere, Josh speaks up.

"Say the word, Misty – right here, right now – and this is over. We go back to Ransom and go back to being ourselves."

"No questions asked..." Rhyan quickly adds.

Ariel, her eyes full of tears, steps over and takes Misty's hands.

"None of this is worth your sanity, Misty. We're family – the six of us. You stepped up when you didn't have to, and look how far we've come – and at what we've accomplished."

"If continuing means letting you slip away from us," Vanessa adds, "we're done. Simple as that."

When Misty burst into tears, I put an arm around her and squeeze. Even as she is wiping the tears from her cheeks, we all hear the voice on the other side of the door, as a key is slipped into the lock…

"I know I didn't lock this damn door…"

When the door swings open, we find ourselves face to face with the most stressed looking Terri Maxwell, any of us has ever seen. The woman looks as if she's on the verge of collapse. The moment she sees all of the tear-covered cheeks in the room, she throws her hands into the air in complete frustration.

"My God! What the hell else can come up, to freakin' complicate this day?"

"Well…" Misty blurts out, a smile finally breaking on her face, "if you mean us, you're safe. We seem to have solved our little problem, all by ourselves…"

"Yeah," Ariel adds, "and sorry about hijacking your office…"

Suddenly, she relaxes. It's as if our response allows all of her tension, to flow out of her in a single instant. She looks from Misty, to Ariel, to Vanessa, and finally at me.

"You guys rock… I swear. I'm sorry… really. You sure there's nothing I can help with?"

"Nope. We have a handle on it," Rhyan replies, twirling a drum stick in one hand.

"Well then," she continues, crossing the room, and taking a seat at her desk. "Have a look at that…" she hands a single sheet of paper to Josh, and lays a second one on her desk.

It takes about ten seconds for Josh's response…

"NO FREAKIN' WAY!" he screams, leaping into the air.

Ariel instantly snatches the page out of his hand, and she too, almost explodes.

"Number freakin' One!" she screams.

Once I get the page and read it, I find out that *Trying To Hold On* has actually moved into the #1 position on the Hot 100.

"Okay," I say, laughing and looking right at Mrs. Maxwell, "what else is stressing you out?"

She shakes her head, rubs her temples, and then clicks something on her computer. Within seconds, there's a video playing on the plasma behind her. It only takes a second to realize we are looking at the Grammy nominations…

"The nominees for Best Pop Vocal Album are…"

We listen in silence as the woman reads off a list of names, the last of which, stops all our hearts…

"Audio Distortion – Begin Again"

Almost immediately, Mrs. Maxwell fast forwards the image, and when it stops, we again watch the same female announce yet another group on nominees…

"The nominees for Song of the Year are…"

Even as she is reading the names from the list, we all hear Vanessa and Ariel, as at the same time they mumble, *"oh… my… God…"*

"Audio Distortion – Begin Again"

I spin Misty around, grin at her, wipe the few remaining tears from her cheeks, and say, "This is about to get all kinds insane girl… You sure you're up to it?"

The other five pairs (counting a confused Mrs. Maxwell) of eyes in the room are on her immediately.

"Crap Martin! Are you freakin' kidding? I'd actually cut a MATH class to see this go down!"

The riotous laughter that follows is symbolic of what our lives are about to become…

Insanely amusing…

'…not pop, not rock, not country – just a good, old fashioned, kick-ass band!'

~ A Music Reviewer 

Once In A Lifetime

Joshua Miller

A week after *Trying To Hold On* makes #1, Richard releases *High Speed Rush* – and we all panic.

The response, however, is so over the top, if we hadn't lived it, we would never have believed it. Misty Maitland – *rock* singer? Who knew?

Reviewers are saying things like…

'…a new multi-talented, multi-faceted band'

…and

'…not pop, not rock, not country – just a good, old fashioned, kick-ass band!'

…and the one that got all of us

'…definitely NOT a fluke – Ransom is for real!'

The requests for interviews run rampant – Terri has to get help just to keep track of them.

Two days after the song is released, so is the CD. A week later, it's #12 on the album charts.

Go figure…

Anyhow, it's Friday afternoon, and we are again sitting around Terri's office, listening as she organizes what seems like an endless list of interviews. Rhyan is about to ask a question when Terri's phone rings. Now more than a bit frustrated, she grabs the receiver and answers the call.

"Maxwell. Yep... that's me. Who?"

There's a moment of silence, which gets our attention, and when we turn to look at her, Terri is the strangest shade of pale.

"I see. And you want all of them?"

There is another brief silence, which pretty much pegs everyone's heart rates.

"Well, I can easily arrange that. Can I put you on speaker? Cool... hang on."

We watch as she pushes some buttons, and then lays the receiver back on the base.

"Okay – they're all yours..."

"They are all there?" a deep male voice asks.

"Yes sir," Misty blurts out. "All six of us."

We hear a muffled laugh, followed by, "Well, Miss Maitland, good afternoon. My name is Charles Hampton and I'm... well... the goofy title they gave me is 'Time Acquisition Supervisor'."

"Man," Ariel blurts out, "that's about a mouthful."

Again, the same deep laugh.

"And," Vanessa adds, "how did you know it was Misty anyhow?"

"She has an unmistakable voice, of course," he replies.

"So, Mr. Hampton," Misty says, blushing and smiling, "what does a Time Acquisition Supervisor want with us?"

"He wants to talk you into introducing your mentors when they play their title song... on February 12th."

"The freakin' Grammys? You want us to introduce *Audio Distortion* at the *Grammys?"* Rhyan almost yells, looking as if he's going to faint.

Ariel's eyes are instantly full of tears, and Vanessa is right behind her. I find it interesting that the calmest person in the room is last person you would have expected.

"Who better for the task than *Ransom?"* Mr. Hampton asks. "It will probably be the most epic moment of the night."

Without missing a beat, Misty is all over it.

"Will you let me write our intro?"

"Of course. We will have to review it, and check it for time, but I fully expect you will want to write it."

"And we are just introducing their performance, right?"

"Yes ma'am," he quickly replies. "They have agreed to make the show their first live performance of the song."

"We'll do it, Mr. Hampton," Misty says, her face awash with excitement.

"Well now," comes from the phone, "that was even easier than Richard said it would be..."

Instantly, both ends of the connection are caught up in a burst of insane laughter.

Writing the introduction...

For the biggest band of the day...

And delivering it, *on stage*...

At the *Grammys*...

And she's only eighteen years old...

How totally freaking cool is that?

True Stars

Misty Maitland

I've rehearsed it so many times, it's burned into my memory. My heart is racing – not because I'm nervous or scared – but because this is our chance to give back to the people who made our fame possible.

The second the arena falls into darkness, I hear the voice in my ear, give me my queue...

"Any time you are ready, Misty..."

It's my stage... and I take full advantage of that.

"Ladies and gentlemen," I hear my voice say, as it echoes through the Staples Center, "my name is Misty Maitland..."

A single spotlight illuminates me, as I stand center stage, "...and most of you know me as the lead singer of *Ransom*. Tonight, however, along with the rest of you, I'm just a *fan*..."

A *huge* monitor behind me comes to life, displaying the image of an album cover, across the bottom of which are the words *Begin Again*.

"Just more than three years ago, I was a high school sophomore whose biggest concern was which college I would attend. Then, as strange as it was, my destiny was set, by the arrival of one amazing, if not slightly odd, lady...”

The image changes to one of Emily, guitar over her shoulder, and a fist in the air. I turn and glance up at it, and after a second's hesitation, I turn back toward the audience and continue.

“I was sitting under a tree, studying for a math test, generally minding my own business, when she walked past me, headed for the school's parking lot. I was singing away – which according to her, is what made her stop – to what was at the time, my favorite song. Without a word, she walked over, sat down across from me, pulled one of the buds from my ear, and stuck it in her own. For some reason, I just kept singing, right through to the end of the song. Emily never said a word – nor did Mrs. Perkins, our music teacher, who stood silently the entire time, watching. When the song was over, still never having said anything, she handed me the ear bud, smiled, then stood up and walked off with Mrs. Perkins. Two days later, I found myself, along with five other kids, in the school's music room, on our way to becoming a pop band...”

The image on the monitor begins changing at intervals, to the six of us inside Discovery Studios, working on our first CD. When the image stops on one of Emma and me, I again turn back to the audience.

“Then... I met Emma Greene – I mean Campbell. Sorry, Emma.”

There are a *bunch* of snickers in the audience, which makes me relax even more.

“She alone is responsible for where my career as a vocalist is today... *She* had faith in me... and convinced me to have faith in myself...”

As I again turn toward the monitor, the image changes to a video of me in the studio, singing *Destined To Be*.

"She took a fifteen year old kid, and taught her how to use *and* control, what everyone tells me is a 'gift'..."

The image again changes, this time to *Ransom* performing *hostage* live in concert.

"All through the wild ride our lives became, our mentors – the five members of *Audio Distortion* – were there, keeping six high school kids on track, and headed for stardom."

The lights come up on the stage, as the rest of the band joins me center stage.

"It's taken them thirteen years..." Rhyan says.

"An absurd amount of struggle and diligence..." adds Ariel.

"And an extended hiatus," comes from Joshua.

"But, tonight the members of *Audio Distortion* have, in our band's opinion..." I offer, and am quickly interrupted by broken and sporadic applause, whistling, and yells of agreement. "...finally gotten their due..."

The image on the monitor behind us changes to an exploded view of the *Begin Again* album cover, with two Grammy Awards superimposed over it.

"Tonight," I continue, my eyes now filled with tears, "the members of the Academy have allowed the six of us, the honor and privilege, of presenting to all of you, for their first live performance of this year's Song of the Year, *Begin Again*, from this year's Best Pop Vocal Album of the same name..."

The lights go out, and as the curtain behind us begins to rise, six voices simultaneously scream...

"AUDIO DISTORTION!"

The thunderous round of applause, and standing ovation that follow, is something that you only get to experience once in a lifetime...

"I've been on a number of flights –
including charters – with musicians on
them. You guys are by far, the coolest
band I have ever flown with..."

~ A Flight Attendant   

Payback

Vanessa Preston

A week after the Grammy's, we bailed. We told Richard and Terri it was time to get away from all of it... for a while.

They never batted an eye.

They're in the middle of planning our next tour – to support *High Speed Rush*. They were all ready to get an opening act, when Josh mention that we'd rather go on our own, if the label would support it. When Richard asked why, Misty – with a huge grin on her face – quickly replied, "Cuz then it's *our* audience. If I want to waste time, screwing with them, I can. If Josh wants to extend one of his solos, he can."

With a shrug and a laugh, he quickly agreed.

The day before we bailed, Terri introduced us to our 'support team' – a hyper guy name Preston, who is the lead set-up technician, and a cute, but deadly serious female, name Penelope. Everyone, however, calls her PJ. She's our road producer.

Anyhow, we made sure they had all our phone numbers, and insisted they could call any of us, at any time, and then Terri took us to the airport.

The flight home was weird only in that for the first time, people recognized us. The label's publicist got us VIP access to our boarding gate, and yet the moment we got there, we drew a crowd. The strange thing was, Misty simply took over. I don't think I've ever seen her as comfortable as she was during the thirty minutes we had to wait to board.

Even though we were secluded in First Class, Misty was the first one up, and headed for coach. Thing was, *everyone* onboard knew who we were, even if they weren't fans. Misty also took a moment to threaten each of us, insisting we *all* needed to at least make an appearance.

"It's about them," Misty said, pointing toward the back of the plane, "*the fans*. Without them, we don't get to do any of this..."

And of course, she was right – and we all knew it.

An hour into the flight, as I was about to take a turn talking to people, one of the flight attendants stopped me in the aisle.

"I've been on a number of flights – including charters – that had musicians on them. You guys," she pauses, and points toward the back of the plane, where Josh and Ariel are laughing and joking with some passengers, "are *by far*, the coolest band *I have ever* flown with..."

Yep... almost cried.

Then, to cap it all off, Josh did his patented 'sad, pathetic' face on the head flight attendant, in order to get his acoustic guitar from a closet up front. Once he had it, he and Misty sat on the floor in the middle of the coach section, and she gave what has to be the most amazing acoustic performance of *hostage* there will ever be.

And... if you've never seen a standing ovation on a plane in flight, let me tell you, it's a sight to behold.

The totally amusing part came when video of the performance turned up *everywhere* online – which of course we expected. Hazards of living in a digital world.

Even Richard said it brought him to tears…

So… having settled into the calmness of being back in Ransom, this morning Misty texted me and asked me come over to 'talk'. When I asked about what, her immediate reply was 'just get your butt over here' – which I did.

"What's up, Misty?" I ask, closing the front door of her parent's house behind me.

"I have a *totally* insane idea, and I want to spring it on someone. You're elected." Misty replies, turning and grinning at me.

I cross the room, step over the mess on the floor, and sit down opposite her.

"Why me?"

"Because…"

"Because…?"

"Yeah… because. Is that a problem?"

I laugh, and glance at the mass of papers spread across the floor between us.

"Nope… not even a little one," I reply. "You keeping up with the tour schedule?" I ask, picking up one of the numerous calendar pages lying in front of her.

"More like changing it…" she offers, turning and making eye contact with me.

"Is this going to get us into trouble?" I ask.

"Depends on your definition of trouble…"

This is when I see something – a single page amidst the mass of papers on the floor – which grabs my attention. Something that Misty *shouldn't have…*

I reach out, pick it up, and she just grins at me.

"*AD's* tour dates? And you have this because?" I ask, my heart beginning to race – for reasons I don't understand.

"Mostly because it supports my totally insane idea…"

As I hand the page back to her, the look in her eyes tells me that whatever we are about to set in motion, is going to be epic beyond anything in our lives so far…

"I'm onboard," I say, as 'matter-of-factly' as possible.

"Just like that?"

"Heck yeah. The last two things you got us into turned out to be phenomenal. Why would this be any different?"

She stares at me for a few seconds, takes a really deep breath, and lets it out slowly. Then… with just one sentence, she changes my world.

"*Ransom* needs to *open* for *Audio Distortion* on their *Begin Again* tour…"

The moment she says it, my heart speeds completely out of control, every hair on my body stands straight up, and I even feel my entire body shudder. She's right… *it is a totally insane idea.*

So insane in fact, that it could actually work!

Misty stares at me for a few seconds, and then, just as she is about to say something, I reach out and put a finger on her lips, and stop her. Once she concedes, I pull out my phone and type a text to the rest of the band…

'Misty's house. As quickly as you can. IMPORTANT.'

Twenty minutes later, the entire band is present…

"I'll stay awake for the entire tour, if that's what it takes..."

~ Rhyan Crossman 

Insane? (yes... yes it is)

Martin Masterson

Five completely frozen figures are sitting on the living room floor, at the Maitland's house, silently staring at Misty.

None of us would have ever conceived the idea she just presented us with – it's something that could only come from Misty's mind. The girl's brain is... well... different.

When Mrs. Maitland comes in carrying a tray of filled coffee cups, the eerie silence stops her in her tracks, and she stares at the five of us, as we stare at Misty.

"You couldn't measure this on the epic scale..." I mumble, which makes Misty look directly at me.

"Because there's no precedent..." she replies, grinning.

Math geeks... what can I say.

"Are you guys okay?" Mrs. Maitland asks, holding out the tray to Josh, who takes one of the cups.

"Okay?" Josh says, sipping his coffee. "Misty is about to take us light years past 'okay', Mrs. M..."

With a laugh, she continues passing out cups, and when the tray is empty, she stops and looks at us.

"Come on kids – you were *on stage at the Grammys* for crying out loud. How in the world do you top that?"

"Mrs. Maitland," I offer, grinning like a fool, "If Misty pulls this one off, no one will even remember our appearance at the Grammys..."

Shaking her head, and still laughing, she disappears into the kitchen.

"So," Misty says, sipping her coffee and then putting the cup down next to her, "you're all in on this? If we talk them into it, it's gonna be a butt buster for us..."

"I'll stay awake for the entire tour, if that's what it takes," Rhyan blurts out, making Ariel and Vanessa crack up.

I reach into my pocket, pull out my cell phone, and toss it to Misty.

"Call them and ask. Worst case, they say no. We can't spring it on the label until we know they are willing..."

With a smile, Misty tosses the phone back to me.

"This had to be done face to face, guys. Someone has to go to Fort Collins, knock on their door, and ask them."

"You and who?" Ariel asks, a devious little grin covering her face.

"Me?" Misty quickly blurts out, appearing nervous for some reason.

"It's *your* idea, girl," I say, reaching out and gently squeezing her hand.

She looks at me, and her eyes tell me what she's thinking.

"Nope – no way. We all know Josh is way better in 'weird' situations than I am."

When everyone turns and looks at him, Josh laughs.

"Yeah, okay. Nice set up. I'm up for it if you are, Misty..."

We look at Misty, and quickly realize that for the first time in a long time, she's scared.

"They will know it's your idea," I say, leaning over and hugging her. "None of us would have come up with it, in a million years. If someone other than you turns up to ask, Emma is gonna wanna know why…"

When everyone cracks up laughing, Misty lifts her head, and gently kisses me – right on the lips.

Yep… totally freaks me out.

"Should I book you guys a flight?" Ariel asks, opening her laptop.

"We can drive faster than we can fly," Misty says, wiping a few tears off her cheeks.

"COOL!" Josh blurts out. "I've been dying to drive this silly thing," he's jingling a set of keys to his new Jeep Cherokee, "somewhere, ever since I got it!"

Again, everyone laughs.

Although we're all psyched about Misty's idea, none of us has even the slightest clue how epic and life changing what we are about to do, will turn out to be.

Genesis Of A Tour

Joshua Miller

"Are you going to get out?"

We've been parked at the curb, in front of the Campbell house, for about ten minutes.

When Misty turns and looks at me, I get it.

"Look… if you can stand alone on the most important stage in music, then you can certainly march up there and knock on that door."

"What if…"

"Come on, Misty! The last four years of our lives have been one big 'what if'."

She smiles, and reaches out to touch my cheek.

"So come on. Let's go tell *Audio Distortion* that *Ransom* is the opening act for the *Begin Again* Tour…

"What happened to 'ask'?" she says, as she opens her door.

"Screw that. Your bold, take charge attitude has served us well so far… why mess with it?"

Together we go up the walk to the house, now laughing. When we reach the door, Misty pushes the doorbell button, and we wait.

Nothing.

Misty pushes it again.

Still, nothing.

We glance at the driveway at the same time, and see the truck and two cars that were there when we pulled up.

"Well..." I mumble, "If their cars are here..."

"Let's try something..." Misty says, pulling her phone from her pocket.

I watch over her shoulder, as she diligently types a text message...

Emma ~

Josh and I were hoping we could have a minute of your time, to talk to you about something kind of important. Let me know.

Misty

...and then sends it. In less than a minute she gets a response.

Of course! Give me a call!

As fast I read it, Misty is typing a response...

We were hoping we could do it face to face...

Again, Emma's response is instant.

When? I can try to meet you.

This time, Misty already has the response typed, and she simply hits 'send'.

Uh... how about now? We're on your front porch...

After a full thirty seconds of no response, we both start to get nervous. Then, without any warning, the door in front of us flies open, and we find ourselves face to face with a smiling Emma Campbell.

"What the…" Stanley blurts out, the moment he sees us.

"Come on in guys," Emma says, holding the door open for us. "What could be so important you'd come all the way to Fort Collins?"

We smile at her, step through the door, and the moment we are inside, see Cadi standing in the hall. She waves at us, and we follow her into the living room. Stanley and Emma are right behind us.

"Oh, and… how in the heck do you know where I live anyhow?" she adds, laughing.

Misty turns, faces her, and forcing a smile, says, "Terri told me."

"Well, sit down and tell me what's on your mind guys."

The three of them are quietly waiting for Misty to explain, when I realize her 'nerves' seem to have gotten the better of her. I take a deep breath, reach out, take her hand, and gently squeeze it.

"Remember what Terri told us…"

"What's going on, Misty?" Emma immediately asks. "Since when do I make you nervous?"

When Misty does nothing more than stare at her, the three of them exchange glances, then Emma gets up, crosses to the chair Misty is in, and kneels down in front of her.

"A long time ago, we decided that you would always see me as your *friend* – never as some big star, remember? I'll be seriously bummed if getting those," she points across the room at the two Grammys, "has changed that…"

Emma pauses, glances at me, and I wink at her.

"Whatever this is about, all you have to do is tell me – *tell us* – and we'll be here for you."

"We want to ask a favor of you – of *Audio Distortion,*" I offer, trying to give Misty some space.

"Sure," Stan replies, without hesitation. "Whacha need?"

"You guys have always toured independently..." Misty finally says, looking first at me, and then directly into Emma's eyes, "but we're wondering if this time, you might consider..."

When she pauses, and again looks up at me, with a pleading look in her eyes, I do what needs to be done.

"*Jeeezzz!*" I blurt out, losing it and finally laughing. "We came to tell you that *Ransom* is opening for *Audio Distortion* on the *Begin Again* tour this summer..."

"*What?*" Stan yells.

"O... M... G..." Cadi quickly adds.

"*You are going to open for us?*" Emma blurts out, visibly stunned. "Aren't you guys doing your *own tour* in support of *High Speed Rush?*"

"Okay..." Misty says, now smiling, and giving me one of her 'looks'. "He left off the part about talking you guys into it..."

All of them are totally speechless for a good twenty seconds. Eventually, Misty restarts the conversation.

"Yes, Emma," Misty says, wiping her eyes, "Richard has our tour pretty much set up. But, we feel we can still support *our* record, while opening for you guys. We'll just play fewer songs..."

"*Guys!*" Stanley offers, still in a state of stunned disbelief, "Are you nuts? *Ransom* has three songs in the top twenty-five at the moment, and one of those is number three! Why in God's name would you want to *open* for us?"

"This isn't about where we are on the charts..." I blurt out, looking right at Stanley.

"I have to believe your tour will be about more than *just* twelve shows," Cadi offers.

"Yes ma'am," I reply, in response to Cadi, "twenty-two actually. We'll just rearrange some stuff…"

After a moment of hushed silence, Emma looks Misty right in her tear-filled eyes, and an intense tension fills the room.

"Why?"

Misty smiles again, and finally relaxes.

"You – *all of you,*" she glances at Cadi and Stanley, "know why. Four weeks ago, at the Staples Center, in front of the entire world, the six of us finally understood why…"

The biggest smile spreads across Emma's face, and I'm certain her eyes cloud up. She pulls her phone out of her pocket and as the four of us watch, she dials. The call, which is on speaker, is answered on the second ring.

"Discovery Studios."

"Hang on a second, Em…"

Emma quickly dials a second number, and it too, is answered quickly.

"Morgan."

She pushes the buttons to make it a conference call, and when she turns to glance at us, she cracks up.

"Okay – official band meeting! Stan and Cadi are standing here with me guys. I have a question, and it's something we all have to agree on."

"What's up?" Emily asks.

"How do we feel about adding an opening act?"

Across the room, behind Emma, Stanley and Cadi are doing their very best not to break out in laughter, as we wait for a response from the phone.

"Someone in particular?" Willie asks, "Or just an 'opening act'?"

"Could be fun," Emily adds. "We've never done it before."

Cadi steps over next to Emma, tugs on her ponytail, points at us, sitting paralyzed across from them, and then leans over next to the phone.

"*Ransom!*" Cadi says loudly. "They actually want to *open* for us…"

"*No freakin' way!*" Emily blurts out even before Cadi finishes her sentence.

Just as quickly we hear "I vote *HELL YES!*" from Willie.

In seconds, everyone is laughing, and when I glance at Misty, I see the tears, cascading down her freckle-covered cheeks.

This is when I realize that we – the members of *Ransom* – are in fact about to discover the true levels of irrationality, and absurdity, the world of music has to offer.

And yes, if we actually pull it off, *this* could very well turn out to be the most epic tour of the decade…

Gentle Persuasion

Vanessa Preston

"You're totally nuts – the whole damn bunch of you!"

Mr. Galley is about as close to the edge as one can get, without falling over.

There are fifteen of us in the conference room – *Audio Distortion*, *Ransom*, Terri, Stephen – *AD's* road producer, Max – their lead set-up technician, and Mr. Galley.

"It's their crazy idea," Willie says, pointing directly at us, which makes everyone laugh.

"It can work Mr. Galley – we just need the chance to put some planning into it," Joshua says, as the rest of *Ransom* chime in our agreement.

"He's right, Rick," Stephen offers, "the kids are already playing at, or near, nine of AD's confirmed venues. Give me a day or so to rearrange…"

"Confirmed?" Mr. Galley asks, interrupting him.

"Yeah," Emma says, joining the conversation. "Our online voting ended yesterday, and Cadi has already figured out where we're going – or at least where we would like to go – and in the most logical order. We just aren't sure where we want to start."

The discussion goes on for about two hours – Mr. Galley pokes holes in their plan, and the five of them patch them, just as quickly.

The only point we enter into the discussion (it is *Audio Distortion's* tour), is when they are discussing venues...

"Wichita – Intrust Bank Arena... Wichita?" Mr. Galley blurts out.

"Sure!" Stanley replies, "It's almost smack in the middle of the country. We figure fans from Utah to Kentucky would rather get to Kansas, than NYC or LA..."

"Besides," Cadi quickly adds, "you'd freak if you saw how many non-specific votes there were for 'some place in the Midwest' – and the fans don't even know about them," she points without looking at us, "yet..."

Nine heads turn immediately, and look right at the six of us, and after a few seconds, the laughter starts. Mr. Galley turns his attention back to the page, and continues reading...

Once the discussion is over, a strange and perhaps eerie silence settles over the room. Mr. Galley is staring at the pile of paper on the table in front of him, and everyone else is staring at him. It's Mrs. Maxwell who eventually breaks the silence.

"Richard," Terri says, "the label has got to do this – simply because of who's involved. You know perfectly well, that once it's over, this will be the tour everyone will be talking about for the next few years..."

"Mr. Galley," Misty offers, a big grin on her face, "just give us the chance. We swear we'll make every other show on our tour, and every commitment you have for the band – even if it kills us. Just let us do this…"

As she talking, Mr. Galley's secretary comes in, goes directly to Stephen, whispers something to him, and then leaves. Stephen immediately pulls his phone from his pocket and turns it on.

"Sorry guys, the boss said to call him – as in right now… something about what we're discussing."

Even as he is dialing, I'm looking at Emily – who hasn't said a word since she got here. It's apparent, even to me, that something's wrong.

When Stephen is finished, he closes his phone, and with a twinkle in his eyes, and a gigantic smile on his face, turns and looks right at Cadi.

"Here's the thing about the internet, Cadi. When you set the site up to post the results of the voting, everyone gets to see it…"

Everyone turns and glances at Cadi, who looks totally confused.

"In this case, everyone includes the booking agents of the venues in the areas in question…"

"Oh… my… god…" Emma mutters, looking at Stanley.

"Which means?" Terri asks, looking as confused as Cadi.

"Six of the venues on that list, assuming, from the numbers Cadi posted, that they will be one of the show locations, have already contacted the office and are asking questions. Care to guess what the two most popular ones are?"

This is when Mr. Galley's little light bulb goes on.

"No kidding…" he mumbles, glancing at Emma.

"Stephen?" Cadi says, now more than a bit anxious.

"The fans figured out from your numbers, where the shows will most likely be, and have been calling the venues asking about ticket prices and…"

"What!" a totally exasperated Misty blurts out. "What's going on?"

Even as we all start laughing, Stephen continues.

"…and asking if there will be more than one show at each location. Walter just told me that both the O2 locations have indicated that based on queries so far, that they can easily support two shows and perhaps a third in London. LA and Toronto have both suggested two shows."

"damn…" Mr. Galley mumbles, shaking his head, and looking right at Emma – who we all know is pregnant.

"And…" Stephen quickly adds, pointing at the members of *Ransom* as he does, "Like Cadi just said, the fans don't even know about them yet…"

"If we merge the two tours, this will get completely out of hand…"

"We'll do as many shows as the fans will support, Richard," Emma quickly offers. "It's what we do – you've been around us long enough to understand that. And don't even start about the other thing…"

After a few seconds, he nods at her, laughs, then turns and looks at Max.

"You're certain your guys are up for a monumentally insane adventure of this magnitude?"

"Crap, Rick, are you kidding? I wouldn't miss this for the world! Besides, can you imagine how it's gonna look on my freakin' resume?"

"What the heck guys, let's go on tour, shall we?" Mr. Galley says, lowering his head, and rubbing his temples.

The room erupts in cheers and clapping, and it's the members of *Ransom* who are making the most noise. I however, turn and again look at the only person in the room who isn't happy – quite the opposite apparently. She's just sitting there, between Stanley and Willie, staring off into space.

I'm also the only person who seems to notice when she gets up, and quietly slips out the door...

Stumbling

Misty Maitland

The first weird thing I notice is that Vanessa seems to have disappeared. And even as I am contemplating what that may mean, I watch first Cadi, then Emma, disappear out the door and into the hall.

I join the others, who are all gathered around Stephen, discussing the specifics of the tour. After about fifteen minutes, both Emma and Cadi reappear, and in seconds, have Mr. Galley backed up into a corner of the room, and are into a heated discussion.

When I again glance around the room, I notice that Vanessa is still missing.

Although the urge to do so is about killing me, I choose not to butt into whatever is going on, and instead turn my attention back to the discussion in front of me.

That lasts about three minutes. Although we don't hear her phone ring, *everyone* hears Emma answer it.

It's a one-sided conversation...

"Vanessa? Where the heck are you? Doing what? Where are you – look at a street sign. MacArthur Park? You're in

MacArthur Park? You are the smartest kid I know! You stay right there, Vanessa, and keep an eye on her. If she moves, you call me back, immediately. Understood? We're on our way."

As she is closing her phone, she realizes we all heard her, and mumbles "damn... me and my big mouth." There are a number of snickers in the room, but the mood remains serious.

Seconds later, Emma, Cadi, and Stephen all disappear out the door, leaving the rest of us in stunned silence, wondering if our 'epic tour' has already been derailed...

Arbitrary Bonding

Vanessa Preston

Following Emily turns out to be absurdly easy – probably because she isn't expecting to be followed.

When I see her get into the elevator, I go down the stairs, and am peeking through the window in the stairwell door, when she crosses the lobby and goes out the front doors of the building.

Having spent an inordinate amount of time in the studios at Lucky Guess, I pretty much know my way around the immediate area. And, because Emily isn't your 'average' girl, picking her out of a crowd isn't all that hard either.

I follow her across the concourse, past Staples, and onto Wilshire Boulevard, where she immediately turns right, and seems to wander aimlessly. We follow Wilshire under the interstate, all the way to Good Samaritan Hospital where, for some reason, she sits down on a bus bench. I pull up, and pretend to read the playbills plastered all over a telephone pole, which I use to hide behind. When I look around the pole, I see her, bent over, her head in her hands... and know she is crying. I pull out my phone, and am about to dial, when Emily stands up, wipes her eyes, and continues up Wilshire Boulevard.

Once there is some distance between us, I step out and again follow her, wondering what it is that could have her so upset.

Three blocks, and a half mile up Wilshire, I can see the park – McArthur Park.

When we cross Westlake, and pass the LA Medical Center, Emily crosses Wilshire and when she reaches the intersection of Wilshire and Alvarado, she takes one of the paths into the park. But, she doesn't go far. A couple hundred feet into the park, she drops down next to a tree… and again, starts crying. This time, I'm dialing even before I stop walking. The call is answered on the third ring…

"Emma."

"It's me, Mrs. Campbell…"

"*Vanessa?* Where the heck are you?"

"About twelve blocks away," I reply.

"Doing what?"

"Following Emily… She's *really* upset about something."

"Where are you – look at a street sign."

"We followed Wilshire, under the interstate, and kept going until we reached the park…"

"*MacArthur Park?* You're in MacArthur Park?"

"Well… more like on the edge of it. She's sitting next to a tree, by herself, crying…"

"You are the smartest kid I know! You stay right there, Vanessa, and keep an eye on her. If she moves, you call me back, immediately. Understood?"

"Yes ma'am."

"We're on our way."

I flip the phone closed, and stand for a second, staring at Emily. That's when my heart takes over – I know that there is no way she should be sitting there alone.

I step onto the path, and head toward her, wondering how long it will take for her to notice me. Apparently, I'm stealthier than I thought. She doesn't turn around until I speak to her...

"Mrs. Faintree?"

"Awww... crap," she blurts out, turning and facing me. The tone of her voice makes me stop in my tracks.

"Sorry... I'll go away... I didn't mean to..."

"You're here, and we know you called someone, so come over here and sit down."

When I hesitate, she wipes her eyes and tries to smile.

"Jezzzz, I'm sorry, Ness, it just came out. I'm wound a bit tight at the moment."

When I still hesitate, she glares at me.

"Quit this, and come talk to me. You *did* just spend thirty minutes following me, didn't you?"

I finally concede, take a seat opposite her on the grass, and do nothing more than stare at her.

"Why?" she finally asks.

"Because you need someone..."

"How would you know that?"

This is when my internal struggle begins. Even though everyone suspects, no one has ever actually said it... yet.

"Well?" Emily asks, pressing me.

I suck in a huge breath, and make a decision.

"It's about me..." I reply, even as my eyes glass over, and the tears build.

"Huh?"

"hostage… Mrs. Campbell wrote the lyrics about me…"

The look on her face tells me she is definitely struggling with what I just told her. I give her a minute, and once she makes eye contact with me again, I continue.

"It's hard – but then you spent a whole year making the six of us see that hard, *is not* impossible. You, *of all the people I know*, probably understand *hard,* better than the rest of us."

The moment she starts to cry again, I get nervous. When she finally smiles right through the tears, I actually relax.

"I'm just scared, Vanessa. Too much, all at once, and I'm just not sure I can handle it all."

"You only have to handle one thing at a time. No one will expect more than that."

"Yeah, well… the problem is, which is most important?"

I reach up, wipe my own cheeks – which now have a few tears on them – and laugh.

"You know full well what is most important… and so do your *friends*…"

"So…" Emily says, fighting off a laugh of her own, "what happened… with the guy from the song…?"

"He went back to school the day before we flew out here. I'm going to try to sneak him into one of the tour shows after his classes are out."

"You and he are still…"

Again I laugh – I can't help it.

"Yeah… he's the only guy I've ever been in love with, and I couldn't just give up. What can I say?

"And do you guys… well…"

"Yes ma'am, we intend to try to make a life together, once we each find our direction. His priority is his education

– and he's totally committed to it. I need to get this whole 'rock star' thing out of my system."

This time she laughs.

"If he loves you, the way you apparently love him, you being a roc...."

All of a sudden, in the middle of her sentence, Emily apparently has some kind of revelation. I, on the other hand, am instantly and totally confused.

"Mrs. Faintree?"

"Will you quit with the 'Mrs.' crap and go back to *Emily*. Please?"

"Definitely! Calling you 'Mrs.' does feel a bit strange."

"Come on," she says, jumping up and brushing herself off. "Let's go make sure the rest of them aren't screwing up our tour!"

I laugh as she pulls me to my feet, and as we're turning toward the street, we see Emma and Cadi getting out of an SUV that has pulled up on the sidewalk. I immediately reach out and touch Emily on the shoulder, which makes her turn and look at me.

"Can I ask a favor?"

"Of course..." she replies, a definite smirk on her face.

"What I just told you... about the song..."

"Told me what? About what song?" she instantly replies, grinning at me.

"Thanks."

When we see Cadi and Emma running toward us, Emily laughs and yells, "Damn! Can't a girl sneak off, without the world coming to a freakin' halt?"

They stop dead in their tracks, side by side, about ten yards from us. I'm trying not to laugh as Emily takes my hand, and we race across the grass, right past them, to the still idling SUV. As she is opening the back door, I turn and see that the two of them are still standing there, looking at us like we're crazy.

"Girls..." Emily says, pushing me into the truck, "there are a bunch of GUYS sitting around a table, planning *our* tour. Do you seriously trust them to do that?"

I start laughing – really loudly. Seconds later, Cadi follows my queue. Then, being unable to stop herself, Emma joins in, shaking her head. The two of them are headed back toward the SUV when I hear a voice... *a male voice*... sitting behind the wheel, say, "I freakin' heard that, Emily..."

Fifteen minutes later, we walk back into the conference room, and being the professionals they each are, no one questions anything. It's right back to business.

It's strange... the things that will bring people together in times of stress...

100% Freaked Out

Misty Maitland

Opening night on our first major tour.

BankUnited Center, on the University of Miami campus.

10,000 people who came *just to see us*.

Intimidating to the tenth power.

The moment we take the stage, I have to *make* myself calm down.

And of course, the moment we start playing, we are *Ransom*. No more nerves, no more pressure. We simply do what we do best...

Make music!

And, our fans are amazing! Even between songs, you can barely hear. Five songs into our twelve song set, it's time for *hostage*. This will be the largest crowd we've performed it for, and yeah, I'm scared. I'm standing next to Vanessa when Martin puts a hand on my shoulder.

"It's just a song, Misty. You've sung it a hundred times – including acoustically, on a freakin' airplane, *in flight*. It's a big part of what they," he points through the darkness at the strangely quiet audience, "came to hear."

Vanessa takes both my hands, squeezes them, and then looks me right in the eyes.

"You do this with the same passion you did on that plane, and they're going to end up in tears."

"How did you guys know?" I ask.

As Rhyan runs across his drums once, Vanessa and Martin look at each other, laugh at the same time, and say, "DUH?"

That's all it takes to relax me. The second I hear Ariel's acoustic intro, I'm ready. When the others join her, I throw myself totally into the song...

And it is freaking amazing!

Martin and Vanessa were right. The moment the last note fades, and the lights go out, the crowd is so stunned, they actually forget to applaud – which makes me giggle. And yes, right next to the stage, you can actually hear crying...

An hour later, it's time to give them their memory. There's only one song they want to hear, that we haven't played yet – and they let us know it. At first it's just a few people near the stage...

'high speed rush!'

As it gets louder, I cross the stage to Josh and Vanessa, who are standing together, talking.

'high speed rush!' the crowd continues to chant.

I tug on Josh's shirt to get his attention.

"Is this nuts, or what?" he blurts out, grinning like the Cheshire cat.

"I can't believe we get to do this twice a week for the next three months!" Vanessa adds, laughing like a fool.

'HIGH SPEED RUSH!'

Now, at least two-thirds of the crowd is chanting.

"Time to let the world know who you are, Joshua Miller!" I blurt out.

"Huh?" he replies.

"Stretch out the intro – just keep playing until your heart says you are done, okay?"

"What a totally freaking amazing idea!" Vanessa says, jumping into the air.

"Don't worry Josh… we're a *band*. They'll," I point at the others, "know when it's time to play. This is going to be the most epic live version of this song, that there will ever be!"

Even before I stop talking, Vanessa is telling the others what I'm up to, and they all give us a thumbs up. Josh, who actually looks teary eyed, leans over, puts a hand on each of my cheeks, and gently kisses me.

"You are amazing…" is all he says.

Now, the crowd is chanting *and* stomping, and you can actually feel the building vibrate.

'HIGH (stomp) SPEED (stomp) RUSH (stomp)!'

When I finally glance at the lead tech, standing at the top of the stage stairs, I see a near-panic PJ, which of course makes me crack up. I flip on my mic, and go to work.

"Jezzzz guys! I wonder what song they want to hear?" I yell, as I head for the front of the stage.

Then, as if by magic, Ariel's voice rings out.

"I'm not sure that song is on the play list, Misty!" she yells into her mic.

The moment she quits talking, Josh unleashes himself…

And it's totally insane!

The guy turns a fifteen second lead intro into a seventy second brain-mangling lead riff that sends the crowd right off the chart!

Even as the lights come up and the rest of us join Josh, the crowd never lets up. The techs actually have to turn us up, which is crazy on its own.

Once it's over, we disappear off stage, and are met at the bottom of the stairs by PJ – who, for the first time since we met her, is actually smiling.

"I've been doing this for thirteen years guys, and that," she points out at the stage, "was by far, *the coolest* opening night I have ever seen."

Then, without warning, she hugs each of us. As we stand listening to the crowd get louder and louder, PJ finally laughs.

"You should probably go and give them what they want… before they wreck the place…"

Still very much in a state of shock, we go back up the stairs, out onto the stage, and set up to play our very first encore. After a brief discussion, we decide to play a song *we like*, and are surprised beyond all explanation, by the crowd's response. The moment Ariel starts the intro to *Bubblegum*, there's a massive round of applause. I only get two lines into the song before I have two-thirds of the people in the building singing along with me.

And yes, I cry the entire time.

Reality Check

Martin Masterson

Walking into the American Airlines Center in Dallas is all it takes to put the show in Miami into perspective. We're supposed to be doing our sound check, but instead, six figures are frozen in place, center stage.

"This place is freaking *huge*..." Rhyan mumbles.

"According to this," Ariel adds, holding up a sheet of paper, "it's *twice as big* as the arena in Miami..."

"And we sold it out?" comes from Josh, as he spins in a circle, taking it all in.

"Twice..." Vanessa mumbles, reaching out and taking Josh's hand.

"In ten hours, there's gonna be twenty thousand people in here," Misty finally adds, her voice cracking.

"*Hey!*" a female voice yells from somewhere behind us, making us all turn to look.

"You guys okay?" PJ asks, crossing the stage and stopping next to us.

"Yeah," Misty says, smiling at her, "we're just in the middle of our first reality check."

"It's just bigger guys – that's all. Adjust yourselves to the fact that it will be louder, and you'll be fine."

After a few seconds of silence, PJ smiles, and nods in the direction of the numerous technicians standing around, patiently waiting on us, and says, "They're ready when you are…"

"OMG…" Ariel blurts out, making all of us laugh.

"Sorry guys!" Josh quickly adds, as we all head for our instruments.

Once we're powered, we play parts of five different songs, allowing the guys on the sound board to establish levels, and the lighting guys to get their timing. Once the techs are happy, we power everything down.

"I think we're on top of this one," Curtis – the #2 sound guy – offers. "If this crowd gets louder than you, we'll be all over it."

"Are you gonna stick to your marks tonight?" Pam – the lighting supervisor – asks, following it with a little snicker.

"Yes, they will," PJ says, as she walks up.

"Well… there you go," Misty says with a smile. "I guess I'll be behaving tonight."

"In all seriousness, guys," PJ continues, looking directly at Misty, "this is a different environment than you've ever been in. I need to know you understand the ramifications of getting close to a crowd this size."

She pauses, takes a deep breath, looks at each of us, and then back at Misty.

"I know it's about the fans for you, Misty, but if you get too involved while you are down on the walkway, you will make Security's job damn near impossible, and it could end badly. They don't mean any harm, but things happen. Just please, please, pay attention when you're down there..."

She pauses again, as she points at the narrow, elevated deck, which juts out about sixty feet from the stage. The look in her eyes is enough to indicate her level of concern.

Misty immediately steps over, takes both PJ's hands, and with a smile says, "Derek and Chuck have already schooled me about safety, and I'll make you the same promise I made them. Tonight, we – or *me*, more specifically – will follow the producer's directions, to the letter. I'll slap a few hands, wave, and pay close attention to everything around me."

"Okay..." PJ says, stepping over and hugging Misty, "Go meditate or whatever it is you pop stars do before a show, and I'll see you in the Green Room ninety minutes before show time!"

As we file past her, the rest of us stop and give her a hug.

Twenty minutes later, not really knowing what else to do, the six of us end up sitting on some concrete barricades in the parking lot behind the arena.

"Am I the only one who finds all this totally bizarre?" Vanessa asks.

"Nope," Rhyan instantly replies. "I'm in the seat next to you on the 'crazy train'..."

"Very cool Ozzy reference, dude..." I mumble, cracking everyone up.

As we sit laughing and discussing the current level of insanity in our lives, a golf cart with a thirty-something guy and girl in it, pulls up next to us and stops.

"You guys do realize that they've already started lining up out front, at the main doors, right?" the girl asks.

"Seriously?" Vanessa blurts out.

"Yep. And if they discover you guys are just sitting back here... well..."

"I see..." Misty retorts, a devious little sneer on her face, "So maybe we should just wander around front and say hi."

When the two of them stare in stunned disbelief, one at a time, we start laughing. It takes a couple of seconds, but the girl is the first to recover.

"I'll bet the bunch of you, are just crazy enough to do that..." she says, laughing.

"As our lead singer likes to point out," I offer, putting an arm around Misty, "without them," I point toward the front of the arena with my free hand, "we wouldn't be doing any of this."

"Point taken," the girl replies. "How hard is it going to be to talk you into loitering someplace just a bit less public?"

"Oh... now I get it," Josh says, following it with a laugh. "You guys are Venue Security..."

"Yep," she replies, smiling at us.

"Well..." comes from Ariel, as we all slide off the cement blocks, "we did promise to behave..."

"We'll wander around back, and get our driver to take us to the hotel."

"There's a small crowd back there as well," the guy offers. "Mostly kids I think..."

"So?" Rhyan says, as we turn and start toward the building, "We're always up for signing a few autographs. Besides, we have you two to keep them from killing us..."

It's a short walk, and the moment we turn the corner of the building, we see them – about thirty kids, not one of them older than sixteen – surrounding the door we need to go in. When they see us, the moment the first one flinches, Misty steps up and takes charge. And just like *we* always seem to do, the kids immediately concede to her instructions.

"*Stop!* All of you."

It's as if we are in a movie – I swear. *Every single one of them* freezes where they stand.

"We're all going to *behave, and act respectfully, right?*" Misty says, making it sound more like an order, than a request.

Much to our total astonishment, again, *every single one of them* mumbles 'yes ma'am' as if they're talking to their mothers. It's actually kinda cool.

"Okay then, everyone sit down – and *no texting*! I see any thumbs typing, we're…" she points at the rest of us, "out of here. This is just between you guys and us. You can brag later…"

"Yes ma'am," they once again reply in unison, and immediately start putting phones into pockets.

Even as Misty is organizing them, I call Stephen and ask him to send someone out with a box of Sharpies, which arrive just as everyone finds a seat. Jessica – the tech who delivers them – falls out laughing the moment she sees what we are up to.

The kids ask question after question, and we take turns answering them, while at the same time, signing everything in sight – CDs, shirts, hats, and even a couple of pairs of sneakers.

And of course, eventually they ask permission to take some photos – to support their inevitable 'bragging' to their friends. We, of course, agree, and by the time all the phones are full of pictures, another forty-five minutes has elapsed, and we finally tell the kids we have to go. They are amazing, and after some hugs and high-fives, they all turn to leave.

Then, to our stunned confusion, Jessica yells at them.

"*Hey!* How many of you have tickets?"

About half of them raise their hands.

"Well..." Jessica says, turning to look right at the six of us, "everyone who didn't raise their hand, take out your phones and call your parents – and tell them you'll be right in front of the stage at the *Ransom* concert tonight... and they can pick you up out front after it's over!"

Total and complete insanity follows, as Rhyan picks Jessica up off the ground in a big bear hug, to the cheering of twenty-eight kids.

The thing I find totally intriguing, is that the guy and girl from the golf cart, stand silently watching – with the most amazing looks on their faces.

Fifteen minutes later, there's a line of kids – and six musicians – sitting on the edge of the stage, watching the crew setting things up.

When they get to watch us do a sound check, I'm pretty sure four or five of them probably exploded...

Prepared

Ariel Williams

The two shows in Dallas come off perfectly. Even our mentors are impressed.

Yeah, that's right. Willie and Stanley actually saw the second show. Seems our producer snuck them in, and they spent most the night, fifteen feet from center stage. The strange part is that not only did none of us notice them, but the two of them disappeared without a word after the show.

This morning, we stopped by the venue on our way to the airport in Dallas. Our crew was busily breaking things down and prepping it for shipping. Moments after we arrived, PJ, Preston, and Pam, all came to say goodbye.

Yep – totally freaked us out.

"Relax guys," Preston offered, "all the hardware will get where it's supposed to."

"But why don't we get to take *our* road crew?" Josh blurted out, his concern evident.

"Seriously?" PJ replied, actually laughing.

When all we did was stare at her, she quickly explained.

"You're going on *their* tour, guys. This one is on hold. And..." she paused and made eye contact with each of us, "Stephen, Max, and Terri..."

"*Mrs. Maxwell* is with them?" Martin blurted out in the middle of her sentence, making her crack up.

"Yes, she is. She's running their board for the entire tour. I think Stanley and Willie bribed her..."

"No freakin' kidding..." Rhyan mumbled.

"Anyhow, know this, guys – the six of you are just as important to them as their tour band is. This is going to be the experience of your lives – period."

"Yeah," Preston added, grinning, "jump in with both feet and make the most of it!"

We did the hug thing, and once we were finished, the six of us turned toward the exit. Just short of the door, we heard PJ... again.

"And remember this! *Nothing* intimidates you! No band on this planet is more qualified to open for *Audio Distortion*, than the six of you. *You are ready!*"

Without any warning all one hundred members of the support team broke into applause, whistling and cheering.

That's the moment the six of us realized that, no matter where this crazy ride takes us, these people – our entire production crew – are, and will always be, family.

We arrive in New York just after noon, and a large van is taking us to the charter area of the airport, to meet up with the members of *Audio Distortion*. The moment we get out, and I see the plane we're flying on, my heart stops and I find myself in the middle of yet another 'reality check'.

It's a shiny 767 with the words '*Audio Distortion – Begin Again Tour*' plastered across the body. As the others climb the stairs, I have to stand and stare at it for a good minute or so, just to be sure it all sinks it. Eventually, I too climb the stairs, and once inside, I drop into an empty seat, and let my mind wander... and absorb...

My moment of quiet contemplation is broken, when the two cutest little girls I have ever seen, burst into the plane's cabin, giggling and cutting up. As they rush over and introduce themselves to my bandmates, a single thought pops into my head...

Welcome to the 'Begin Again World Tour'

Fasten your seat belt...

"I'm gonna show you some really cool stuff..."

~ Bailey Morgan 

The Drummer

Rhyan Crossman

The drummer.

The quiet guy who agrees with pretty much everything, and simply makes sure the tempo is correct. The guy who is always lifting dumbbells, so he can make it through a twelve song set, and still be amped up.

So far, my story can be found scattered throughout the stories of the others. Although the five of them take the band in a bunch of different directions, I'm always right there, jamming away, with a big grin on my face. Who would have ever guessed that Rhyan Crossman – the football jock – would end up being famous?

On a sunny Tuesday morning, I and my bandmates, board a customized 767 for a charter flight to England, and within seconds of taking a seat, my life changes forever.

The moment I see her, sitting with the two little kids at the back of the plane, my life takes on a new and unexpected direction. I have no idea who she is, but I definitely intend to find out.

The first two hours of the flight are pretty calm. Willie and Stanley are ranting about the second Dallas show, Emma and Misty seem to be working on some lyrics, and everyone appears to be totally relaxed.

I'm lying on a small couch, eyes closed, contemplating the amazingly cute girl at the back of the plane, when I hear the voice...

"What's your name?" the squeaky little voice says.

I turn my head, open my eyes, and find the cutest little girl, wearing jeans, tiny little sneakers, and a flowery shirt, standing with her hands on her little hips, staring at me.

"I'm Rhyan," I reply, smiling at her.

"I'm Bailey!" she blurts out, grinning at me. "Are you in a band?"

"I sure am," I say, turning on my side, and letting my head rest in my hand.

"I bet you're in *Ransom*..." she says, scrunching her eye brows.

"I am."

"My dad says the girl talking to Aunt Emma," she pauses and points at them, "is the singer. What do you do?"

At this point, it's taking all my willpower not to start laughing. Then, to make that even more difficult, I hear yet another squeaky voice.

"Aunt Georgia says he's a drummer – like your dad!" the second little girl – who is dressed almost identically to the first one – says, as she comes to a stop in front of me.

"And who might you be?" I ask, biting my cheek to keep from laughing, and sitting up.

"I'm Melissa! That's my mom," she replies, pointing at Emily, who has the cheesiest grin on her face.

"And how old are you guys?" I ask, still fighting the urge to laugh.

"Four..." Bailey offers.

"*...and a half!*" Melissa blurts out, interrupting Bailey mid-sentence.

"But," Bailey adds, looking far too serious for a four-year-old, "I'm forty-three days older than her, so I'm really close to five..."

This is the point that I realize the three of us have become the single point of attention in the cabin. When I glance around the plane, I find that everyone – including the two flight attendants – is watching the three of us. And, still sitting alone, at the back of the plane, I see the brunette, feet up, laughing like she's crazy. The moment we make eye contact, she smiles at me and my heart races.

"I'm going to see my mom," Melissa says, turning and heading for the front of the plane.

"And what are you going to do?" I ask a still smiling Bailey.

She stands quietly thinking about it for a second, and then holds out a satchel that's been on the floor at her feet the entire time, which I take. Then, without any help, she gets her short little self, up onto the seat next to me, and holds out her hands for her bag. Once she has it, she pulls out an awesomely pink laptop – designed for little kids – opens it, and powers it up. As she waits, she looks up at me, smiles, and completely overwhelms my heart.

"I'm gonna show you some really cool stuff..." she says, and starts clicking away.

Over the next hour, I get the most entertaining education of my life – from a five year old.

L.A.F.S.

Georgia Campbell

I'm way too young to even think about 'love at first sight'. I'm in college, and have a list of priorities that drive most guys my age, completely nuts.

But, I gotta admit, the very first time Rhyan looked at me... well... I'm honestly not sure how to describe it.

Sure, I've had boyfriends, but none of them ever had the same effect on me that Rhyan seems to.

And I don't even know him yet...

At first, I get a bit worried. Although I catch him looking at me a bunch of times during the flight, he never makes any attempt to talk to me.

So, I make a plan.

The one really awesome thing my big brother taught me over the years is, if you want something, you can't wait on it – *you gotta go get it.*

With that in mind, I send the girls to go mess with him. Little do I know, that eventually, I will end up competing with Bailey, for Rhyan's attention.

Kinda comical, if you think about it.

An hour after she crawls up next to him, Bailey slowly nods off – hazards of being five – her little head coming to rest on Rhyan's lap.

Once I see my opportunity, I stand up, and cross the cabin to them.

"I'll take her," I say, smiling at him.

"Awww… let her sleep. She's fine…" he quickly replies.

The moment we make eye contact, I get the exact same rush… and the hair on my arms stands up.

"If you say so…" I reply, taking a seat across from him.

"I'd introduce myself, but according to Bailey, you already know who I am…"

Yeah… I blush. Big time.

"Kinda hard *not* to know who you are – who all of you are," I say, waving at the rest of *Ransom's* members.

"Fan are you?"

"Duh?" I blurt out, fully aware I'm blushing again. "Find a single girl between sixteen and twenty-one who isn't. Heck, I know of at least ten who would throw themselves at Josh, in a heartbeat."

The guy cracks up… but does his best not to wake Bailey.

"Strange… no one seems to want to do that to me…"

"It's a 'guitar player' thing. I wouldn't worry about it," I quickly reply.

What I wanted to say was… well… never mind.

"They," I point at my brother and Willie, who are talking to each other, "said you guys totally wrecked the place in Dallas – twice."

The guy actually blushes! I can hardly believe it.

"I guess – well, once we got past the terror of the size of the place."

I bite my cheek, and force myself not to laugh at him. He however, catches me, and calls me on it.

"What's so funny?"

"You do realize that the O2 holds 35,000 – right?"

The look of total panic on his face melts my heart. This is the moment I realize that they – all six of them – are just kids, like me. Six kids who, through sheer determination, managed to become amazingly talented musicians.

"And how would you know that?" he asks, jerking me back into the moment.

"They," I point in the direction of the front of the plane, "have played there before."

"And you know *that* because?"

When Bailey moves and rearranges herself, I stand up, grab a blanket from the overhead, and lay it over her. Then, completely out of the blue, I have an epiphany! *(yeah, I know… big words. sometimes, I just can't help myself)*

Rhyan has no idea who I am! He assumes I'm just someone they got to watch the kids on the tour. Once again, I have to force myself not laugh.

"I know a lot of stuff about *Audio Distortion*, actually."

"Do you now…" he replies, a huge grin covering his face.

We spend the next hour becoming friends. And even after such a short time, I somehow know.

I *will* marry Mr. Rhyan Crossman… eventually.

Oh… and no. I never do tell him Stanley is my brother…

Shazam!

Misty Maitland

The only thing that can stress us more than the fact we're playing in the biggest arena in England, for the first time, is the fact the place is *sold out!*

As we sit around the Green Room, waiting for them to call us to the stage, no one says anything. We just stare at one another.

Nope... this isn't going to work. No way can we pull this off, under this kind of pressure. We need to let go. We need to go back to being those six goofy kids from Kansas, who make music because *it's fun...*

I walk over, pick up Ariel's acoustic guitar and hand it to Josh. Rhyan, who has his sticks in hand, looks at me, wondering what I'm up to. I pick up a second guitar and immediately start a bass line (yeah, I can actually play a little – and it's an easy line) – one that every single one of them is intimately familiar with.

In a single heartbeat, Rhyan is playing on table tops, and empty boxes. Martin and Josh crack up laughing, and Josh instantly joins me. Martin almost runs across the room, turns on a small battery powered synthesizer in the corner, and starts playing – from memory.

Then… Vanessa too, breaks out laughing – *and singing!*

Yo! I'll tell ya what I want…
What I really, really want…

Then Ariel…

So tell us what you want…
What you really, really want…

In fifteen seconds, for the first time in well over a year and a half, the girls of *Ransom*, are about to 'go off'. Before any of us can stop ourselves, we are two verses deep in the *Spice Girls* song *wannabe*. When we reach the chorus, the three of us let ourselves out… totally.

If you wannabe my lover
You gotta get with my friends
Make it last forever
Friendship never ends

And, more importantly, the pressure pushing down on us only moments before, is simply gone.

When Ariel and Vanessa start the third stanza, the door suddenly opens, and there stands the lead technician, Rachel. She's about to say something, when the absurdity of what she sees sinks in, and she bursts into laughter.

"Ninety seconds, guys!" she yells over the singing.

We put down the instruments, while Ariel, Vanessa and I keep singing in harmony, right out the door and into the tunnel leading to the stage. By the time we reach the stage area, we're all laughing and shoving each other around. The stage crew is fairly certain we've lost our minds.

Then we see them – lined up at the bottom of the stairs, each holding up a hand. As we pass them, still laughing, we high-five each of them. As we start up the stairs, Emily grabs Josh's arm, and stops him.

"Just like Dallas," she says with a seriously sinister tone, "Kick ass, and take names…"

We hear Terri's voice the moment we power up our ear monitors,

"Thirty seconds – lights out."

Being last in line, I'm almost face to face with Emily.

"Oh, Emily…" I offer, following it with a devious snicker, as the entire arena goes dark, *That… is exactly what we plan to do…*"

We hear the arena announcer, even before we make it to center stage…

Music fans! Welcome to The O2!

Here tonight we have what may turn out to be the show of the decade!

Tonight, two of the greatest pop bands of this generation, will share the O2 stage.

The O2 is proud and honored to present, on their first trip to the United Kingdom…

RANSOM!

"Any time you are ready guys!" we hear in our ear pieces.

As Joshua is getting his guitar – the one he's had since he was seven, and that none of us has *ever* seen him use at a show before – I put a hand on his shoulder.

"She *did* say to kick ass, right?"

He laughs, puts the strap over his shoulder, and plugs up.

"Uh-huh."

"Well then, just like Friday night, in Miami, okay?"

"The same song?" he asks, confusion now covering his face.

"Uh-huh," I calmly reply, a noticeable smirk on my face.

"It's number nine, Misty, not first – on the set list I mean."

"And your point is?"

He laughs – so loudly it gets the other's attention, as they all look over at us. Then he leans over and gently kisses me.

"You got it boss! As long as I want?"

"Uh-huh. Stretch the last note, and Rhyan is right behind you."

"You guys still with us?" we hear in our ear pieces, from a very nervous sounding Terri.

I step over, grab a radio from one of the techs, key it, and say, "Yeah, we are. We're going to make sure all these people know that *Audio Distortion* has an opening act..."

"oh my god..." we hear in our ears, followed by a deep laugh.

As the others finish tuning, I flip on my mic, and into the darkness I yell, "HEY LONDON! WHAT SONG DO YOU WANT TO HEAR FIRST?"

"Oh damn! Someone get a light on her!" comes from Max.

Back from the darkness comes, *'hostage'* and *'The Way Home'* and *'Trying To Hold On'*, and we even hear *'Bubblegum'* at one point. Then, after fifteen seconds, it starts...

'we wanna rush!' 'we wanna rush!' fills the building in a thoroughly British fashion.

The Brits however, waste far less time than Americans do. It only takes another fifteen seconds before what sounds like everyone in the building is chanting – *and stomping!*

'WE (stomp) WANNA (stomp) RUSH! (stomp)'

And I am here to tell you, 35,000 people chanting and stomping in a totally dark arena is something that simply can't be explained in words...

Then Terri's frustrated sounding voice again fills our ear pieces.

"Jezzz... why is it none of you freakin' musicians can seem to follow directions?" which is followed by more laughter over our communication circuit.

At the exact same moment, Josh – who is standing alone at the front edge of the stage – unleashes himself, and Terri is amazingly on top of it.

"One and Six! Light the crazy guy with the guitar!"

Two spots are on Josh even before Terri stops talking. The rest of us wait, laughing like fools, on our assigned marks.

Fifty seconds later, as Josh stretches out the last note, all 35,000 people in the O2 are on their feet, and the place simply goes berserk – there's no other way to describe it. The crowd is so loud, that when the rest of us join Josh, you can barely hear us – which Terri fixes in a heartbeat.

Once the song is over... well... none of us will ever be able to explain the feeling.

After I mess with the crowd a bit, we play through our set. When we reach *hostage*, Terri kills all the lights except the two she puts on Ariel and me, center stage. The moment we're finished, all the lights go out again, and the applause is immediate. Once Terri brings the house lights up again, we find ourselves looking at yet another ovation...

Isn't music totally amazing?

Once we're done, we take a bunch of bows, and head for the stairs, where we find our mentors – pretty much all in tears. As we pass them, Vanessa stops, hugs Emily, and whispers something to her.

Then, following what has become our 'standard routine', the six of us go to find a quiet corner to slow down in.

PJ was totally right – it *was* the show of a lifetime...

"Can it get much more crazy or intense than this?"

~ Misty Maitland   

Realizations

Vanessa Preston

We end up halfway down one of the service tunnels, sitting together on the floor.

Martin has an arm around Misty, Josh's head is resting on Ariel's shoulder, and I'm lying on my back, with my head on Rhyan's thigh.

Rhyan is the first to break the silence.

"What did you say to Emily?"

"I told her it was totally for, and about, them…"

"Perfect!" Martin blurts out.

"No doubt," Ariel adds.

"Can it get much more crazy or intense than this?" Misty asks, her eyes still closed, and her head on Martin's shoulder.

"I have no idea…" I offer, sitting up and facing her. "But the five of us, will be eternally grateful that you were in the Green Room an hour ago…"

I watch as everyone sits up, and faces Misty.

"Yeah," Josh offers, smiling at her, "like it or not, Misty Maitland is in fact, this band's leader..."

"Even though you never asked to be, you keep doing stuff that says you are," Ariel adds.

"And we're all okay with that..." Rhyan adds, leaning over and putting a hand on her knee.

"Guys..." Misty starts to say, and is quickly interrupted by Martin.

"Just go with it dear... it will be easier for everyone."

As everyone breaks out laughing, we hear an all too familiar voice, as it resonates through the arena.

"HEY LONDON!"

"Was that Emma?" Josh blurts out.

"Yeah it was," I say, getting to my feet, "and it's only been ten minutes. Isn't there supposed to be a twenty minute gap between bands?"

"Pretty cool how we just snuck right up here, huh?"

"What the hell are they doing?" comes from Martin, who is now on his feet, pulling Misty to hers.

It takes us thirty seconds to make it back to the stage stairs, where we find three very confused crew members.

"What's going on?" I ask the guy nearest me.

"Like we know?" is his reply, as he laughs, and shakes his head.

"So London," Emma – who is standing at the very edge of the fully lit stage – says, *"Was it a good idea bringing Ransom with us?"*

Instantly, the entire place is again, totally off the hook. The six of us stand at the bottom of the stairs, our eyes full of tears, overcome. Seeing our stunned surprise, the tech next to me, puts a hand on my shoulder, and with a whimsical tone in his voice, says, *"Family* – eventually, you guys will get it."

Then, without any warning, we hear Cadi's voice as it echoes through the building...

"You guys..." she says, sounding totally British, and pointing directly at us – which of course makes Terri put a spot on us – "need to come back up here and give your fans another bow!"

At this point, the crowd is chanting *'Ransom, Ransom',* and it seems to keep getting louder. Not knowing what else to do, the six of us climb the stairs, go center stage, and with our arms around each other, take a couple of bows. As we turn to leave the stage, Emma hugs each one of us, and when it is Misty's turn, she looks her right in the eyes, and just loudly enough we can all hear her, says, "Live in the moment – it only gets crazier from here!"

As we descend the stage stairs, we have no idea that our moment of realization is about to occur.

We watch the lights go down, and hear Emma say, "Following them is going to be near impossible, but we'll give it a try..."

Seconds later, we hear the intro to *Being Noticed,* and when Emma starts the vocals, the stage lights come up. Fifteen seconds later, we get it...

By the time Emma makes it to the third line of the song, *35,000* voices are singing along with her. It's been thirteen years since the song was released, yet every single person in the building knows the words to it...

The crowd sings right through the first chorus, and by the second stanza, even though the band keeps playing, poor Emma is standing at the front of the stage, her mic at her side, tears streaming down her cheeks, listening...

It's in this single moment of perfect clarity, each of us, in our own ways, understands.

We all just 'get it'…

Yes, these 35,000 people supported our performance, but they are here for a different reason. Every single one of them would be here, even if *we* weren't…

They are here to see the band that, at some point, touched their lives…

They are here to see their heroes…

*They are here to see… **Audio Distortion**.*

Ooops!

Vanessa Preston

The European part of the tour rolls on every weekend during May, and into June. We inevitably end up doing two shows at each venue, which is totally cool with us. We learn so much from our mentors, that we are actually excited to put it to use in our shows.

Knowing that the *Begin Again Tour* will have to go non-stop through July and into August, Richard works in a break during the last two weeks of June, which works perfectly for us. We have some US shows to do…

Then, just before the break, between the second and third shows in Sydney, *Ransom* does the stupidest thing we ever have. Period.

And yes, it involves alcohol…

And… because the tour has become 'high-visibility', the entire world is going to find out about it.

We're all in really good spirits when we finally make it back to the hotel. In the lobby, we meet some Aussies, who seem totally cool, and are fascinated by the fact we are *Ransom*. Once our girls get some food to go from the restaurant, we head upstairs. The Aussies ask if they can hang out for a while, as none of their friends are going to believe they met us. With a laugh, we agree.

When we get out of the elevator, we find Georgia standing in the hall, outside Rhyan's suite. We probably should have noticed the disapproving look on her face, but we are all totally burnt and need to let go.

We just pick the wrong way to do it.

Once in the room, the Aussies pull a number of bottles from a backpack, and start pouring. None of us has the sense to stop them. In less than an hour, the nine of us are pretty much plowed.

Even poor Misty – who ends up vomiting, violently.

The only one with any common sense is Georgia. At some point the girl simply disappears, and not a one of us notices.

Misty getting sick is what sparks the stupidity. As she is heaving into a garbage can, one of the Aussies is holding on to her, trying to keep her from both falling over, and getting vomit everywhere. When she finally goes to straighten up, the buzz, combined with someone she doesn't know holding on to her, and maybe a bit of fear from being in this situation, screws with her judgment.

In a moment of freaked out concern, she thinks the guy is getting 'grabby' and that his hand is where it shouldn't be.

As she straightens up, she screams and tries to slap the Aussie who, looking totally stunned and confused, does his best to avoid it. Rhyan and Josh, instantly over react – again, probably because of the alcohol – and both try to grab the guy.

The next thing I know, fists are flying.

Even as Misty sits sobbing on the couch, Ariel and I are trying to separate the guys. Unfortunately, we're just as drunk as they are, and all we manage to do is get shoved around a lot.

Before our brains catch up with what we're seeing, Rhyan pretty much *throws* one of the Aussies out the door and into the hall. Ariel and I stand stunned, as we watch the poor guy, bounce off the wall and land on the floor.

Fifteen seconds later, all six of the guys are out in the hall, rolling around and being stupid, as Ariel, Misty, and I are screaming for them to stop.

Then… *salvation*. Three doors – one of which is directly across from us – fly open. While Stanley and Willie are trying to separate the guys, the concierge and three police officers come blazing out of the elevator. Between the police, Stanley, and Willie, they get all the guys under control.

Then… much to our dismay, Mr. Galley appears at the end of the hall. He immediately takes charge, telling the concierge that all the damages will be taken care of, and that he will make certain, no more stupidity occurs while we're here. Then he tells the police that we aren't interested in 'pressing charges' and the police are quick to convince the local guys that it's in their best interest to just call it a night.

The three of them are all for that idea.

As the Aussies and the police turn toward the elevator, we think we may have escaped complete disaster.

Then… *everyone* hears the irritated female voice.

"HEY!"

We turn and find Emily standing in the middle of the hall, wearing an oversized t-shirt, with her hands on her hips, and a face so red, she very well may explode. It's the first time any of us has seen her truly angry.

"That's a bunch of crap! How about you jerks, step up, and behave like *men? All damn six of you!*"

The really cool thing is that *every single one of them* gets it. As the Australians turn back toward our guys, Emily holds up her hand to the police, and we all watch quietly, as the six of them shake hands, and apologize to each other. Then, as the Aussies turn, and again head for the elevator, one of them hesitates, turns and walks directly over to Misty. It's the guy who freaked her out to begin with.

"I'm truly sorry, Miss. I never meant to..."

Misty suddenly throws her arms around his neck and hugs him, right in the middle of his apology. After a second, she lets go, takes a step back, and says, "I'm just as guilty as you are. I'm sorry too."

He smiles at her, turns, and heads for the elevator. As the elevator doors close, one of the cops mumbles *"amazing"*.

Once the hall is clear, a still visibly pissed off Emily, points at the room we were partying in, and without a word, all six of us file in. Pushing past Richard, and almost knocking him over, Emily follows us.

"So... you've found your 'rock star' personas, huh?" Emily says, in a voice so calm it scares me. "I do wish you could have done it after one of *your* shows... not after one of ours. I'm not really qualified to judge any of you, and I don't remember signing up to be anyone's babysitter, but I will say this. I want the six of you to think long and hard about this disaster, because while I'm spending tomorrow morning trying to smooth it out with the press, I will *damn sure* be thinking about the six of you."

We watch her turn and head for the still open door, pausing when she reaches it.

"Oh... and for the record, I'm *totally fucking disappointed in all of you...*"

That one cuts way deep, and we all feel it.

She's two steps outside the door when Mr. Galley starts talking.

"I can't take the chance kids. This whole thing is just too damn high-visibility. I'm gonna have to pull the plug, and you six are going to finish *your* tour..."

The moment she hears Richard's comment, Emily stops dead in her tracks, spins around, and comes flying back into the room.

"The hell you are, Richard! These six wannabe rock-stars came to us, and said they were ready to play in *our world*. They signed a damn contract, and committed to opening *on our tour* – and by God, they will finish what they started! *Even if it kills all of us!"*

Mr. Galley turns and looks at Emily, then glances at Emma and Stanley. Even before he can respond, Emily is on us again.

"Isn't that right...?" she says, glaring at us.

When no one says anything, she walks back across the room, and gets right in Joshua's face.

"Right?"

"Yes ma'am," he instantly blurts out.

Each of us repeats the 'yes ma'am' as she makes eye contact with us. When she's satisfied, she turns, says, "I'm going back to bed," and disappears into the hall.

Mr. Galley looks at the six of us, shakes his head, and says, "For some bizarre reason, that woman has an infinite amount of faith and confidence you guys..." Then he turns, and he too, leaves the room.

We stand quietly staring at Emma, assuming she has a few comments of her own. Instead, she turns and goes out the door, without a word. Stanley, however, does have a comment.

"Rehearsal at 10 am guys, final sound check is at 5 pm. Make sure you're at both, and are ready to work."

Then he too, disappears into the hall, pulling the door closed behind him. The moment we hear the lock click, all six of us drop onto the nearest piece of furniture.

Even as we sit staring at each other, I'm pretty sure we're thinking the same thing…

How, in God's name, are we going to recover from this?

Recovering

Misty Maitland

I swear… being hung over, totally sucks. It's one of those things that should be avoided at all costs.

When the alarm goes off at 8:00 am, we all get up, and go to our rooms to shower and dress. My head hurts so bad, I can't even see clearly enough to put on my make-up, or get my hair into the now standard pigtails.

When I step into the hall, I find Vanessa and Ariel looking just as miserable as I feel.

"Hey," Ariel says, taking one of my hands. "We're sorry. You shouldn't have had to endure any of that crap last night…"

"Well… if it was going to happen, better it happened with my best friends, right?" I reply, grinning at them.

The two of them take turns hugging me, while at the same time, Josh and Martin appear. When they see that Rhyan is still missing, they knock on his door. It takes a few minutes, but eventually he too appears.

The guilty looks on the guy's faces makes me speak up as we are headed for the elevator.

"No more apologizing, okay? It happened, it's over, we move on."

"Works for me," Josh and Rhyan say at the same time.

As the elevator doors open, Martin leans over and kisses me, but never says a word.

Not knowing what else to do, we find our driver, and head for the arena. Not fifteen minutes after we make it to the Green Room, so do Stanley and Emma. As we watch them cross the room, Stephen appears with a bottle of Excedrin, a gallon of orange juice, and six glasses. He puts it all on the table and turns to face us.

"Each of you takes four aspirin and drinks a full glass of juice. And for the rest of the day, I expect that any time I see any of the six of you, it will be with a bottle of water in your hand…" He pauses and points at a tub full of ice and bottles of water. "Understood?"

We nod our understanding, and then file over and do as told. Once we're finished, Stephen goes back out the way he came in. Moments later, Willie comes in with Melissa in one arm, and Bailey in the other. Following them is Georgia, who stops in front of Stanley.

"I was there…" she says, looking totally guilty.

"Excuse me?" Stanley says, glaring at her.

"Emily and Willie had the girls with them, and well…"

"Let it go, Stanley," we hear Emily say, and turn to see her coming in the door, with Mrs. Maxwell and Mr. Galley. "She didn't have to come tell you – she chose to."

This is when I notice Rhyan's concentration is on Stanley and Georgia.

"You're the boss…" Stan replies, giving Georgia another serious glare.

Then without warning, Joshua, and Rhyan, walk over and stop in front of Stanley, and Rhyan gives Georgia an odd look.

"It isn't her fault Mr. Campbell – we sorta coerced her into it," Rhyan says, his eyes instantly dropping to the floor.

"And not that it's much good as a defense, but she only had one drink, and didn't even finish it," Joshua adds. "Being smarter than the rest of us, she bailed before it got stupid."

"And I just spent thirty minutes, with twelve reporters, who would have liked nothing better, than to get the chance to hang the six of you out to dry..." Emily says, stopping right next to us. "They were using terms like 'unprofessional' and 'immature'..."

"*damn...*" Vanessa mutters, glancing at Mr. Galley.

"Yeah..." he says, *"Damn..."*

Then, much to our amazement, without any further explanation, Emily pours a cup of coffee, and sits down. Stanley quickly turns his attention to Rhyan.

"The only reason I'm not chewing my sister's butt, is because she answers to Willie and Emily on this trip. You clowns," he pauses and glances at Josh first, then Martin, and then returns his attention to Rhyan, "damn sure knew better. *She's eighteen...* and in case you forgot, *so is your lead singer.*"

When I see Georgia cringe, I know something's up. The moment Rhyan, who is so pale, he might be dead, turns and looks at Georgia, I get a good idea what it is.

"Your... uh... *sister?*" Rhyan blurts out.

Stanley turns and immediately looks at Georgia, who is now six shades of red.

"I never told him..." she mumbles.

In this single instant, all the pressure of the situation evaporates, and *everyone* breaks into laughter. I watch as Emma crosses the room and stops next to Rhyan.

"She..." Emma says, nodding at a still blushing Georgia, "really likes you. She told me so."

"*oh god*" Georgia mumbles, the blood again rushing into her face.

"Last night happened," Emma continues, "Move on. Just make certain stupidity doesn't over run the six of you again, okay?"

Rhyan moves his head up and down in response.

"Don't you..." she pauses, and makes eye contact with each of us, "*...any of you*, lose sight of your goal."

"Yes ma'am," we each say, loudly enough that all of them hear us.

"So, you rock stars ready to rehearse?" Emily blurts out, standing up, coffee in hand.

A bit stunned, the six of us turn and look at Emma.

"She asked, not me."

You can tell just by her facial expression, it's taking every ounce of her willpower not to laugh.

We shrug, look at Emily, and in unison say, "Yes ma'am."

Emily turns and heads for the stage. When we turn to follow her, Stanley steps in front of us, points at the tub of water bottles, and watches as each of us pulls out two – except Rhyan. He grabs four. With a perfectly straight face, Stanley points at the door, and we go single file, the same direction Emily did. Emma, Willie, Georgia, and the girls, bring up the rear.

Because we're opening, the stage is set up with our instruments, and as soon as we clear the stairs, each of us goes immediately to ours.

"Anything in particular you want to hear?" Vanessa asks, as we power up our instruments, and wait for someone to power the sound board and our amps.

As I make eye contact with each of my bandmates, I know we are all thinking the same thing – through the same pounding heads...

Please, God, don't let her say High Speed Rush...

"As a matter of fact..." Emily says, a devious little sneer on her face, as she picks up her acoustic practice guitar from a stand, at the back of the stage, and heads toward Joshua.

Willie, who is holding Bailey and Melissa's hands, tells them to go hang out with Georgia, who is sitting on the floor near the stairs, then points at Rhyan indicating he wants to use his drums. Rhyan immediately gets out of the way, and watches as Willie takes the stool, and starts a beat – which I recognize immediately. Vanessa too, knows what song it is, and with a grin, immediately starts the bass line. Within seconds, Emily jumps in on lead, and everyone with an instrument falls in.

Emma, with a big grin on her face (I now understand that we've been set up) grabs a mic from a stand, and starts clapping to the beat. I turn and look at Martin, and behind him see Bailey and Melissa – their little ears stuffed with cotton – clapping along, and dancing to the music.

Then, I hear my name...

"Misty..."

When I turn around, I find a still smiling Emma, her eyebrows raised, wiggling the mic she is holding. Taking the hint, I quickly get a mic of my own, and walk over next to her.

By the time Emily makes it to the first chorus, most of the roadies, and all of the technicians, are tapping their feet, and clapping.

As Vanessa thumps along on her bass, Emily and Joshua are trading rifts. Ariel, now smiling, is making it up as she goes – which is cool, considering the song was written for two guitars.

After two minutes of improvising, Emily points at Vanessa, who cuts the bass line and waits, as Emily and Willie, do a count and start at the beginning again. The moment Vanessa joins them, Willie stands up, and gives Rhyan his sticks. Martin is quick to cover the keyboards – and does a pretty good job of it – while Stanley generates the effects, and the background track, on his Roland.

Emma waits a couple of beats, and then starts singing – one line. When she looks at me, I catch on and sing the next line. From then on, we take turns singing alternate lines, doing our best not to laugh. When we reach the chorus, *everyone* sings...

It's a totally amazing experience, and is probably the coolest rendition of *Begin Again*, any of us has ever heard – mostly because it's totally improvised and impromptu.

Emily, being the amazing person she is, manages to make her point, using something as simple as a song. Once we're done, the four of them, and the girls, head off to find something to eat, leaving us to finish rehearsing.

When Georgia stays behind with us, Stanley doesn't say a word – which actually makes me smile.

Maybe, with His help, we have managed to dodge a huge bullet, and can move on, with a harsh lesson learned.

On Our Own

Martin Masterson

After the third show in Sydney, it's time for us to go our own ways for a while. *Audio Distortion* is getting some down time, and we are off to work on *our* tour.

At 9:00 am, we are aboard a charter, for a sixteen hour flight to Seattle.

We play two shows at Key Arena, and when Willie and Stanley sneak into the first show, Preston rats them out. Although we only catch one quick glimpse of them, standing in the crowd center stage, we know they are there. Accordingly, we unleash ourselves, and I am sure, give the two of them something new to rant about.

Then we shoot down to Portland to play a single show at the Aladdin Theater – as a benefit for a local private school. When we find out that 80% of the ticket proceeds are going to help keep the school open, we insist that whatever part would have been ours, goes as well. When we do that, the venue owner caves, and with a big smile, says, "Give it all to them!"

Because it's really small (only seats 600), it will be *Ransom's* first chance to truly interact with our fans. Even knowing we're going to cut up, PJ too, is psyched about the show. She sees it as a learning experience for all of us. Once it's over, we personally tell the manager, and the owner, we will come back and play their theater any time – at the drop of a hat.

Then it's on to Albuquerque – and a single sold-out show at The Pit – UNM's sports arena. This show gets us our first real 'review', from Chuck Stanner of Rolling Stone, who just happened to be in town. Although he doesn't smother us with accolades, he does outright say that we know what our fans want, that the show was excellent, and that he expects we, just like our mentors, have staying power and will be around for a long time.

Freaks us all out...

Once we finish the show in Albuquerque, we finally get a break. The following day, we pile into a van that PJ got us, and take our time driving home to Ransom. And, because we know our way around, we take the back roads, stopping to speak to everyone we encounter. By the time we make it home, we are once again, those six goofy kids from Kansas...

Oh... and because we didn't tell anyone we were coming, our parents – *all of them* – totally freak out.

For Shame

Rhyan Crossman

The moment I walk in, I know I'm in trouble. I drop my bag, and even though my parents hug me, it's obvious something is wrong.

"Mom?"

"Sit," my father says, pointing at the couch.

I do as instructed, and my mom sits down next to me.

"We've supported you, and your music, from the very beginning, and we are so proud of you, we can't put it into words. But..."

The moment Mom starts to cry, I somehow know what this is about.

"oh crap..." I mumble.

"It made your mother cry, Rhyan, and embarrassed me as well. This is a small community, and everyone knows about it. No one is pointing fingers, but there are some apologies that need to be made..."

"And they will be made – by the six of us. It's our mess," I reply, my head dropping into my hands.

"True... but..." my father says.

When I lift my head, I see that my mother has the TV remote in her hand. With a smile – which confuses me – she pushes some buttons, and the TV comes to life. It's quickly apparent I'm watching a recording, and even though certain words are 'beeped' out, it isn't hard to tell what's being said...

"Care to comment on the exploits of your opening act?"

"The nine kids who drank too much and ended up acting their ages, or the six 'pop music superstars' the media has created, and apparently have absurd expectations of?"

The reporters sit staring at Emily, apparently shocked by her response.

"So... which one are you asking about?"

When none of them says anything, Emily continues.

"So... not a single one of you has ever gotten drunk, and done anything stupid? I know I have. Fortunately the press hounds weren't in hot standby, ready to crush me."

"Damn it, Emily!" a woman in the second row yells, *"that isn't even remotely fair, and you know it. It was totally immature of them. Rhyan and Martin are both twenty-one for crying out loud, and know better."*

"The hell it isn't, Audrey. They're kids! Even at twenty-one. Were you overflowing with maturity at twenty-one? I know I wasn't. And before any of you says anything else, know this – I have put foot to ass over the eighteen year old drinking. I freakin' guarantee it will not happen again."

You can hear a number of muffled laughs in the room.

"Still, quite unprofessional," a guy in the first row
says, *"don't you think? Lots of kids look up to the six
of them."*

"Yes they do," Emily is quick to retort. *"And all
those kids are now saying the same thing you guys
are – 'how totally dumb was that?' I doubt they are
all going to run out and get trashed, just because
their favorite band was dumb enough to."*

Again, a lot of the reporters laugh.

*"Report it guys. I'm not asking you not to. But is it
really necessary to crucify them over this? Let them
have this one, and then judge them later, based on
what they learn from their stupidity."*

There is a moment of calm and quiet, as most of the
reporters scribble in their notebooks.

"Anyhow," Richard – who has been sitting next to
Emily the whole time – says, *"We have a meeting
we need to get to. Are you guys satisfied?"*

Most of the reporters nod in agreement, and start to
stand up. The female who actually challenged Emily at the
beginning of the news conference, smiles and says 'Yes'. As
she and Richard are headed for the door, Emily pauses, and
turns back to face them.

*"And... if you guys get the police report, you'll see
that all six of the knuckleheads apologized to each
other, and shook hands before the Aussies left. How
about you put that in your stories?"*

Then Richard and Emily disappear out the door.

For the first time in as long as I can remember, I cry. My
father takes a seat next to me, and puts an arm around my
shoulders.

"We owe her, Dad... all of us."

"You most certainly do," he replies, handing me a stack of pages, which turn out to be copies of some articles from magazines. The moment I start reading the first one, I get it...

> *So far, the Begin Again tour's opening act has fried the brains of well over 100,000 screaming fans. Even in the strictest sense, they have 'brought down the house' at every venue they have played. However, last night, for the first time, they stumbled.*
>
> *The thing is... if they weren't 'Ransom', no one would have noticed.*

The article goes on to explain what happened, what the police report said, and what Emily had to say about it. It's the last line and the name on the article that again, brings me to tears...

> *Having seen the amazing affect these six talented kids have on the members of their generation – as well as music fans of all ages – this reporter chooses to withhold judgment, until we see what they have learned from this experience.*
>
> *Audrey Clarke*
> *for MOJO Magazine*

Although it's not even remotely her responsibility, there's no doubt about one thing...

Emily Faintree probably saved *Ransom*.

Gratitude

Ariel Williams

Yes, we all found less than happy parents waiting for us.

And yes, whatever we got, we had coming.

My mother didn't say a word for a full hour.

Scared the crap out of me.

When she did finally speak, it wasn't to chastise me, she just had a request.

"Please, just promise me it won't happen again…"

"I promise…" I quickly reply.

"I don't mean drinking…"

"I know, Mom. I know what you mean."

Then she leaned over and hugged me tighter than she ever had.

Now the six of us are sitting around the table in the Crossman's garage, writing a note to Audrey Clarke. Once Misty (she does pretty much all our writing…) has it the way she wants it, she passes it around and each of us reads it – and then signs it. Once Misty signs it, Martin puts it into the overnight envelope, seals it, and hands it to Josh. He in turn, heads for his Jeep, to make the drive to Dodge City – the nearest place with an actual FEDEX office.

We hang around for six more days, talking to everyone, and of course, make more than a few apologies. You see, the world knows where we are from, and by default, everything we do reflects on Ransom.

As badly as we wanted to be home, by the time Wednesday rolls around, we're actually antsy to get back to the tour – and make music. We leave really early and drive the rental van to Denver, and are on a commercial flight to Vancouver by 3:00 pm.

And of course, once again, we all get caught up in the rush of being recognized. I think PJ booked us commercial, on purpose.

Yes, I think we're finally getting used to being 'famous'…

Making Peace

Joshua Miller

The show in Vancouver is just want we need, to get back on track. When we play *hostage*, Vanessa comes up with an acoustic bass, and joins Ariel and Misty. The three of them sit on the edge of the stage, their feet hanging over, and when she realizes what they're up to, Terri kills all the lights, and puts a single spot each of them. Martin, Rhyan, and I quietly cover them from the darkness, as for the very first time, *Ransom* performs a completely acoustic version of the song. Once it's over, and the lights come up – standing ovation, and tears everywhere. After they take a few bows, the girls come back and join us. I immediately ask Vanessa what made her think of doing it acoustically. With a goofy grin, she points at the top of the stairs, where *Audio Distortion* is yelling, and applauding, just as loudly as the crowd, and says "Cadi. It's her guitar…"

Because the next shows are in LA, there's lots of press coverage. In an effort to keep up, Terri makes us fly out the same night, only hours after the Vancouver show. It's blatantly obvious that LA is the show *Audio Distortion* is psyched about.

Outside the hotel, as we are getting into the limos, Rhyan speaks to Stanley, who smiles and directs Willie, Georgia and the girls into the second limo, with our girls, while we get in with Emma, Cadi and Emily – who look more than a bit confused.

"What did you do with my husband?" Emma asks, which makes Cadi laugh.

"He's in the other limo," Martin replies.

"I really need to say something to you, Emily," Rhyan says, looking more serious than I have ever seen him. "Everyone," he glances at Martin and me, "keeps telling me to let it go, but I can't."

Cadi and Emma look at each other, but keep quiet.

"What's up, Rhyan?" Emily asks, once the limo begins to move.

"I need to thank you… from in here," he puts his hand over his heart.

"So do we," Martin and I quickly add.

"For?" she replies, looking genuinely confused.

"I've done my share of stupid crap in my life," Rhyan offers, a goofy smirk on his face, "and yet my mom has always been there. Even when I was totally wrong, she stood by me. That mess in Sydney – well… it really kinda hurt her."

"Coming from where we do," I add, "the one thing you try not to do, is… well… give Mom reasons to be disappointed."

Emily is starting to get teary eyed at this point, and both Cadi and Emma see it.

"Anyhow, my mom recorded what you said to the press the next morning – bad language and all."

The three of them laugh at the same time.

"She showed it to me, and was crying the entire time."

"You didn't have to do that, Emily," Martin adds, "you could have stepped back, and let us fend for ourselves – it was after all, *our* disaster."

"Anyhow," Rhyan finishes, "although it took a while, we do honestly get it now." He pauses, looks at Emma, grins, and says, "We've refocused on the goal…"

"Okay guys," Emma says, poking Rhyan in the side and trying to lighten the moment, "if you learned from the experience, it's all good. And, on the plane, you can tell the girls we said so, okay?"

"Yes ma'am," we reply in unison.

Emily is covertly wiping the tears off her cheeks when, with a seriously devious sneer, she asks, "So, are we going to totally destroy Staples…?"

"Oh…" I quickly reply, winking at the three of them, "you guys have no idea what's to come…"

"Los Angeles is *definitely* going to know we're there…" Rhyan adds.

Merging

Misty Maitland

The crowd in Staples is so loud, that we actually have trouble hearing each other. It's easily the most intimidating crowd we've play for as well. As we take the stage, Terri is quick to make adjustments for the noise levels, and as the lights go out, we hear the arena announcer...

Ladies and Gentleman!

Welcome to Staples Center!

Here tonight we have what is now being called the 'tour of the decade'!

Tonight we have old school and new school. Two of the greatest pop bands of this generation, are going to share the Staples Center stage.

Staples Center is proud and honored to present, giving their first live performance in the City of Angels...

RANSOM!

The moment the announcer stops talking, we go right into *The Way Home.* Song after song, the audience is totally into our performance. When we play *hostage*, Ariel, Vanessa and I do the acoustic thing again, sitting on the edge of the stage. This time however, because of how close the crowd is, there are six really big guys standing between us and them.

Finally, eight songs and fifty minutes later, it's time – time to play the one song every audience seems dying to hear – and it's not really a 'pop' song. But, it does say a lot about *Ransom*.

This time, I make my bandmates wait – to see how wound up the audience will get. Yeah... I'm getting the whole 'working the crowd' thing down pretty well. After ninety seconds – which is an eternity to a pumped up audience – we hear Terri in our ears.

"Guys... please don't wind them up too much."

Josh, Ariel, and I all laugh at the same time. I point at Rhyan, who does a short run across his drums to let them know we are still here. The second he stops, we turn Josh loose...

We tear through *High Speed Rush*, and for the first time, we make a change. On the fly. And yeah, ad-libbing in the middle of a show is... well... *a total rush!*

Just before the break in the middle of the song – the part where Josh and Ariel go after each other – Josh leans over and pretty much yells in my ear...

"Go tell Rhyan that at the break, it's all on him – tell him to go till his freakin' arms fall off!"

I'm so excited, I can hardly stand it. On my way to Rhyan, I tell Ariel to watch him at the break, and she nods her understanding. The twinkle in our drummer's eyes when I tell him to cut loose, is so bright, it almost lights the stage.

Ariel, Vanessa and I sing the third chorus, and the very second the last word fades, Rhyan Crossman – the goofy

Riley Morgan

jock from Ransom, Kansas – let's Los Angeles know he's in town. And once again, Terri Maxwell shows us why she's the best in the business. In the blink of an eye, the Staples Center is totally dark, and two spots from opposite directions land on Rhyan. Then we hear her *and* Stephen in our ears... *at the same time.*

"oh... my... god..." comes from Terri.

"Totally freaking awesome!" Stephen screams over her.

Fifteen seconds...

Terri has the mic pickups on his drums cranked so high, you can *feel* him playing.

Thirty seconds...

The crowd is getting into it.

Forty-five seconds...

The longer he plays, the louder, *and* rowdier the crowd gets.

Sixty seconds...

The building begins to resonate from all the clapping, screaming, and whistling.

Ninety seconds...

The five of us stand staring at him, completely lost in the amazement of the moment.

Who freakin' knew?

When he reaches two minutes – which is a long time for a drummer doing a solo – Rhyan gives in. Josh and Ariel are right there to pick up the song, and Vanessa and Martin are right behind them. The moment the last note is played, the entire arena again goes dark, and we get the most insane response we ever have, from any crowd. When the stage lights come up, a sweat-covered Rhyan jumps up, runs to the front of the stage, and throws his sticks *way out* into the crowd. When he turns to look at us, Ariel spins him back around, as Vanessa snatches the mic from me, and turns to the crowd.

"HEY, LA! CAN THIS LUNATIC PLAY THE DRUMS, OR WHAT?" she screams, easily as amped as Rhyan is.

As the crowd continues screaming, the six of us take a bunch of bows, and finally, we head off stage. The crowd, now totally over-amped, continues to chant *Ran-som, Ran-som* over and over. *Audio Distortion* is waiting for us at the top of the stairs.

"How the hell are we supposed to follow that?" Emily blurts out.

The woman looks so scarily serious, that the six of us freeze where we are standing. When we start looking at each other, all on the verge of panic, the five of them break into almost hysterical laughter, and are quickly joined by Stephen, Terri, and Mr. Galley.

"I freakin' told you, didn't I Richard?" Emily says, glaring at him.

"Told you *what?"* I yell, still concerned that we may have overstepped our bounds, and are in some kind of trouble.

"She told me that the six of you are a *headlining act...*" Mr. Galley replies, even as the crowd's chanting gets louder.

"And," Terri quickly adds, "that *Ransom* has no business *opening* for anyone!"

I burst into tears, I can't help it. Everything rushes out of me all at once, as I – and my bandmates as well – finally understand what the members of *Audio Distortion* have been doing. As I glance around, at the rest of *Ransom*, at the members of *Audio Distortion,* and all of the support people around us, I realize that *our family*, and *their family*, are about to become *a family.*

"I gotta go somewhere and wind down..." a jumpy Rhyan blurts out, breaking my concentration.

"Yeah," Ariel adds, laughing and taking his hand, "me too!"

After we exchange some hugs, the six of us cut between some equipment, and slip into one of the service tunnels, taking seats on the floor, just like we always do. I lay back and put my head in Martin's lap, Josh does the same thing, his head landing in Ariel's lap, and Vanessa and Rhyan sit facing each other, cutting up and poking each other.

"Thanks guys…" Rhyan says, in the middle of his antics.

"It's was Josh's idea," I offer.

"And you freakin' killed it!" Vanessa blurts out, leaning over and kissing him right on the lips.

When we all snicker, Rhyan blushes, and Ariel comments.

"Don't worry, we aren't gonna tell Georgia she did that…"

Everyone laughs at that one.

After a couple of seconds of silence, Rhyan spins around, leans back, and lets his head come to rest on Vanessa's thigh.

"The weird thing is, she'd laugh if you did tell her. That's how she is…"

"We know…" Ariel says, giggling. "We've been talking to her."

"You guys have known me since I was like six, and you know I've never been serious about any girl. Until now."

He pauses, and we hear him take a really deep breath.

"Georgia pretty much owns my heart…"

"And for the record," Vanessa adds, reaching out and taking his hand, "you pretty much own hers too."

"Yeah…" Ariel adds, muffling a laugh, "she made *that* pretty clear."

As we are all laughing, one of the roadies sticks his head around the corner, and with a big grin, says, "You guys might wanna come watch this…"

"Huh?" Martin replies, as I sit up.

"Stephen says they're up to something…"

"They?" Ariel asks, as Josh too, sits up.

"*Audio Distortion…*" he replies, and then disappears.

As we are standing up, we hear the announcer…

Ladies and Gentleman.

It's time for the old school part of our show.

The Staples Center is proud and honored to welcome to our stage, fresh off two Grammy Awards, the pop band that critics say, 'simply doesn't seem to go away'…

Music fans, young and old, we give you…

AUDIO DISTORTION!

By the time we make it back to the stairs, the five of them have taken the stage, and are plugging up. Then, out of the darkness, we hear Emma…

"Hey Southern Cal!"

The crowd once again, goes off – even though they can't see who said it. After a second, a single spot lands on Emma.

"So… how the heck do we follow that last performance?"

Instantly, the crowd is again chanting *Ran-som, Ran-som* over and over. In less than a heartbeat, the stomping begins. And… the members of *Audio Distortion* are laughing like they're nuts.

"Hey Misty!" echoes out of the darkness, as the light on Emma goes out, and a new one hits Emily. *"I think your fans want an encore!"*

"Opening bands don't do encores!" Cadi says, following it with a laugh, while at the same time, the stage lights come up.

"Says who?" Emma blurts out, now laughing herself.

Then, Stanley, Willie, Cadi and Emily, leave their instruments, and walk over to Emma, and together they join the audience chanting....

"Ran-som, Ran-som!"

The thing is, they're doing it into Emma's open mic.

"RAN-SOM, RAN-SOM!"

I burst into tears – deep sobbing tears. I couldn't have stopped them if I wanted to. Ariel is right behind me. Seconds later, Terri hits the five of us – standing on the stairs – with a spotlight, while at the same time, a hysterically laughing Stephen push us, one at time, out onto the stage. Once the fans see us, they again go totally nuts.

When we stop center stage, Emma hands me the mic, and gently wipes the tears off my cheeks. The crowd, now totally caught up in the interaction between the bands, has gone quiet.

"We... uh... well, we don't really have a song to play..."

As I say it, Martin leans over and whispers in my ear...

"Who I Am. You know the words, we know the music, and it isn't part of their set."

I turn and smile at him, then look back at Emma.

"Can we play Catrin's song?"

"Which one?" she shoots back.

"Who I Am ..."

"YES, you can!" Cadi yells, with a huge smile on her face.

The audience breaks into applause, some high-fives are exchanged, and *Audio Distortion* gives us *their* stage. The situation is so completely insane, none of us can believe it's happening...

Yeah... you guessed it. The encore turns out to be the highlight of the tour so far, for the members of *Ransom*.

"MY DADDY ROCKS!"

~ Bailey Morgan 

Acting Like Kids

Ariel Williams

Our second night at Staples, takes crazy to a whole new level.

We're all set to play *Right At The Light*, which is one of our more up-tempo songs, when Willie wanders out onto the stage as if he belongs here. I quickly glance at Josh, who shrugs his total confusion, and when I look at Vanessa, she too is shaking her head.

Twirling a drumstick, Willie casually strolls over to Rhyan, who puts his hands in the air as if to say 'what'?

"I need to borrow your drums for a bit, dude..."

Everyone onstage – techs included – break out laughing. Rhyan jumps up so fast he knocks the stool over. Willie, shaking his head, rights the stool, takes a seat, and does a run over Rhyan drums.

This is where Misty Maitland takes the 'frontman' thing to a whole new level. After spending eight weeks together on the road, one of us, finally gets the nerve to take a shot at one of them...

"Uh... Mr. Morgan," Misty says, a really devious grin on her cute little freckled face, as she glances at the rest of *Audio Distortion,* standing offstage, "this song is pretty fast... you sure you can keep up?"

The entire arena goes completely stupid – and the 'amped' meter simply explodes. In one single sentence, Misty Maitland, our once timid, bubble-gum chewing, lead singer, perfects the art of 'working the crowd'. A month earlier, the five of us would have freaked out, and panicked, at her comment, but instead, we're all laughing, and whooping it up, right along with the crowd. Then, Willie Morgan, master drummer, and all around awesome guy, almost falls off the stool, as he gets to his feet, and in front of 17,000 fans, raises his arms, and gives Misty the 'we are not worthy' bow. When she and I make eye contact, it's easy to see she's having fun with it, but it's also apparent it's taking all her willpower not to freak out.

We get reorganized, and the six of us go to work, while Rhyan disappears off stage somewhere. The results are amazing in that, Willie is so intuitive, one would think he is part of our band!

Once we finish the song, and take a few bows, it's Willie's turn to be freaked out. During the song, Terri brought Vicki (Willie's wife, who just flew in) back stage, and Rhyan hatched a plan of his own – with a little help from the woman of his dreams.

Because they take the kids out and let them dance and cut up during *Crazy Road*, Bailey and Melissa are standing with Georgia, at the bottom of the stairs. The moment she sees her mother, Bailey goes goofy, and giggling, jumps into her arms. That's when Rhyan's light bulb goes on.

He steps over and asks Victoria if he can borrow her daughter, then asks Bailey if she wants to surprise her dad. Again, the child goes loopy. He tells Georgia to take her around to the side of the stage behind the speaker stacks, and wait. Knowing Willie's In Ear Monitor is on a different channel, he takes a radio from one of the techs and says something to the five of us – and we take action.

As Rhyan comes back onstage, clapping and urging the crowd on, at the same time, Vanessa pulls her mic from the stand, and disappears between the stacks.

A totally unsuspecting Willie, stops and gets a hug from Rhyan, who turns and heads for his drums. As Willie crosses the stage toward the stairs, bowing to the crowd, and putting his hand over his heart as he does, he sees Victoria – who Terri pretty much shoved into the lights seconds earlier – standing at the top of the stairs. Then, as if seeing his wife for the first time in two months isn't enough, the entire arena hears Bailey's amazing five-year-old voice as she screams *"MY DADDY ROCKS!"* into Vanessa's open mic, then runs out from between the speakers, rushes across the stage, and jumps into her father's arms the moment she is close enough.

Even with all the other totally bizarre stuff that has happened to us over the years, on this completely insane ride we've been on, this single moment will live forever in my heart.

Once we finish our set, Willie meets us at the bottom of the stairs. Each of the girls gets a kiss and a hug, and he hugs the guys so tightly, I think he almost pops Josh. Then he turns and joins the rest of *Audio Distortion* as they get ready to take the stage.

The strange thing? He never says a word to any of us.

Sometimes, as I'm learning, there's simply nothing to say.

Accidental Superstar

Martin Masterson

Although we are learning to 'play the game', make no mistake – the members of *Audio Distortion* are way better at it.

It takes them less than an hour to prove it.

Audio Distortion is between songs as the six of us approach the stage stairs, having abandoned our hiding place in the service tunnel. All the lights are down, and because we know the order of their set list, we know what song they are setting up to play. Every time they play it, we make a point to stand together with our arms around each other. Why? Because the six of us believe it is the very best, and most deeply touching song, our mentors have ever recorded. It touches each of us, in its own way.

Tonight, however, it's going to touch one of us, in a way she would never have imagined.

The first hint something is up, is Emma walking out of the darkness, coming down the stairs, and stopping right in front of Misty. She smiles, and then hands her a mic, which Misty takes, her face awash in confusion. First she looks at me, then turns and looks at Vanessa, who is on the other side of her, then back at Emma.

"You're going to need that…" Emma says, loudly enough that the mic – which is apparently *powered* – picks it up, and sends it echoing through the arena. The moment Misty hears it, she glances at the mic, and pretty much panics.

"Missssssssty!" Cadi's amplified Welsh accent says, as it too, resonates through the eerily quiet building, while at the same time, she and Emily start the intro to *Destined To Be. "Come sing for us…"*

"…right about now…" Emma finishes, doing her best not to laugh.

Misty simply bursts into tears, and actually starts shaking. Stanley, who appears out of nowhere, takes her hand, pretty much pulls her up the stairs, and points her at center stage, as the rest of us, all totally zoned, stand speechless, and watch. Terri quickly adapts, and puts a single spotlight on Misty. Now realizing she's kind of trapped, Misty makes herself cross the stage, as the stunned and almost silent audience, watches. The spot follows Misty across the stage, and opens out to reveal Cadi and Emily, who are cross-legged on the floor, instead of on their stools. When she reaches them, Misty stops, and stands staring at them.

After a few seconds, both of them still strumming away on their guitars, Cadi giggles, and Emily points at the floor between them, and says, "Sit right there," which the audience of course, hears. Misty quickly complies. After a few more seconds of silence, never having missed a chord, Cadi adds, "You know the lyrics, Misty. Emma has heard you sing the song."

Again, poor Misty, who is kneeling at an angle to Cadi and Emily, with her back partially to the audience, can't seem to say anything. I find myself wondering what is going on in her head – *and in her heart* – as all this is happening. When Willie, who is sitting at his drums, in the shadows behind the three of them, laughs, it brings Misty out of her daze. At the same time, a bunch of voices in the crowd start yelling *"you can do it!"* and *"go for it!"*

When Emily smiles, points out into the darkness of the arena, and says, "The audience is that way," Misty takes a huge breath, wipes her cheeks, and when Willie joins in, she turns to the crowd and simply turns her heart completely loose. It is by far the most amazing thing any of us have ever seen the girl do.

And yes, for the first time in my life, a song brings me to tears.

Or maybe… it's the singer…

The bizarrely incredible thing is, when the song is over, the crowd's reaction is *exactly* the same as it was the night before – when Cadi did the vocals.

Full on sobbing, with tears again streaming down her cheeks, and shaking like a leaf in a high breeze, our cute, soft-spoken, freckled-faced lead singer, who always has her hair in pigtails, gets a show-stopping *standing ovation from 17,000 people.*

I swear… *crazy and incredible* have become the adjectives of choice, when describing any given night, on the *Begin Again Tour…*

"You've shown them that 'famous' can actually be normal, and that 'superstars' are just people..."

~ Patricia Hill

Vice Principle

Giving Back

Misty Maitland

It took me a full week to get past the intensity of singing with Cadi and Emily. I spent over an hour on the phone, crying and telling my mother about it, right after the show. It will always be, the highest point in my music career.

Once we make it to Toronto, I'm ready again. We do two shows, both of which came off perfectly. And... the members of *Audio Distortion*, find out about our secret stress reliever.

In the middle of a building lobby, Vanessa and Ariel started singing, and I of course, joined right in. For some reason, the three of us can harmonize *wannabe*, by the *Spice Girls*, almost perfectly. It's actually kind of weird. After we finish, Cadi steps over, and whispers in my ear...

"Emily has a plan cooking..."

...and then walks away.

Eventually, we'll find out exactly what that means.

The shows at MSG turn out phenomenally. On the second night, the cutting up and silliness, continue when, without warning, Willie stands up and walks off stage, leaving the rest of *Audio Distortion* looking totally confused.

When he reaches the bottom of the stage stairs, Willie smiles at Rhyan, hands him his drum sticks, says, 'restroom', and then disappears into the tunnel. Seconds later, Bailey and Melissa appear, ready to do *Crazy Road* with their parents, and Rhyan follows them onto the stage, laughing almost hysterically. The girls go right to Emily, and Emma stops Rhyan – with her mic on, of course.

"Where's our drummer?"

"He handed me his sticks," he holds them up, "mumbled something about the restroom, and disappeared," Rhyan quickly replies.

I'm pretty sure *every single person* in the building starts laughing.

"Well... it's on you then, Rhyan," Stanley says, as the lights go down, and he starts the intro. "Take a seat dude..." The five of us, and Willie, who is actually standing right behind us, all start laughing and high-fiving each other. Then almost as an afterthought, Stanley adds, "...and you better not screw up."

Yes, we have pretty much become a 'family', and the tour now seems to be 'the act', instead of 'their act' and 'our act'.

Every single one of us is having an amazing time, and we have gained a clear understanding of the single thing the members of *Audio Distortion* have been stressing since this started...

It is 'all about the music' – and the fans.

Four days later, we're home. *Wichita.*

Richard makes us go early, because he knows how crazy it's going to get. We find it interesting that our mentors all seem okay with taking a back seat to us. They give us the lead at all the interviews, and when we do a local TV show, they make *us* play a song, when the station expected they were going to.

Then Emily comes up with the most amazing idea I've ever heard. After borrowing some minivans from the TV station's employees, we head for the local schools.

While our mentors have to find a covert way to get into the high school, the six of us take the easy way into the middle school – right past the office, and right into the cafeteria. It takes less than fifteen seconds for some of the older kids to recognize us. Well... actually, a bunch of girls recognized Rhyan and Josh – which totally cracks us up. Ariel immediately takes charge...

"You guys wanna have a chat?"

About a hundred voices scream 'yes' at the same time.

"We're all gonna behave, and be respectful, right?"

This time she gets a 'yes ma'am' – which cracks up the three ladies behind the steam table. We each take a couple of tables and after the kids crowd around us, we answer question after question. Even the lunch ladies get into it at one point.

Then... the autographs start. Notebooks, backpacks, shirts, shoes – basically, whatever is handy. One of the lunch ladies has us sign a clean apron, really big, and tells us she's going to wear it every Wednesday, so that the kids will all remember the day we stopped by.

After about forty minutes, I see them – standing near one of the entrances. A guy in a shirt and tie, and a lady in a business suit.

'Gotta be the principle' I think to myself, as I turn and head for them. As I get closer, they both smile, which lets me relax a bit.

"Hi!" I blurt out, holding out my hand, "Misty Maitland. I'm the..."

"Seriously?" the woman says, as she takes my hand, and starts to laugh. "As if the lead singer of *Ransom* needs to introduce herself *anywhere* in the state of Kansas?"

Yeah… I blush. Then the guy reaches out and takes my hand.

"Dillion Marsh – I'm the Principle. She's," he points at the woman, "Patricia Hill – our Vice Principle."

"We're sorry for disrupting your day…"

"Yeah, okay…" the guy mumbles, as the female again starts laughing. "Name another number one pop band that would drop in and have lunch with a bunch of middle-schoolers, just for something to do?"

After I blush again, and Ms. Hill stops laughing, Mr. Marsh continues.

"That," he points at the kids, still talking to the rest of the band, "is the quietest, and most well behaved they have *ever* been in the cafeteria. The six of you have done what I think is an amazing thing."

"Yeah," Ms. Hill adds, "You've shown them 'famous' can actually be normal, and that 'superstars' are just people…"

About this time, my cell phone rings and its Emily telling me that Richard wants us back at the hotel. We say our goodbyes, and head for our borrowed van. Twenty minutes later, having returned the vans, we pile into the limo, and are on our way to the hotel.

The following night, Josh and Ariel pull off the party of the tour – which includes pretty much *everyone* in Ransom, as well as everyone we graduated with. Even though they're all psyched to see us, the fact *Audio Distortion* is just hanging around, talking to everyone, seems to have captured all their imaginations.

We expected to give away a bunch of copies of our CD, but when Emily turns up with enough signed copies of *Begin*

                                    Riley Morgan

Again, to make sure everyone there gets one, we pretty much freak out. Even our parents – *all of them* – are impressed with our mentors.

And... it turns out that Bailey and Melissa are the most popular girls in the room for most of the night.

Friday night, we pull off what is easily *Ransom's* best show of the tour. I suppose there's something to be said for playing 'at home' – for *family and friends*.

Saturday night's show... well... this one definitely goes into the 'absurdly cool' file. And of course, Emily is totally to blame – as you might recall, she had some kind of 'plan'...

"Okay guys," Emily whispers, as the six of us stand quietly between the equipment stacks. "You ready to do this?"

"I can't believe we're actually *going* to do it," Ariel says, giggling.

"It's going to be totally amazing!" Emma blurts out, sounding absurdly excited, too.

"What's Richard gonna say?" Vanessa asks.

"Do we care?" Cadi replies, laughing.

"Vanessa has the drums – which by the way, is amazing," Emily continues. "Emma easily covers the keyboards. There isn't really any lead, so I've got rhythm, and Cadi has bass. Everyone has a mic, and knows who's singing what. This is so totally going to blow their minds..."

"Man..." Ariel mumbles, sounding seriously nervous, "I wonder if my mom is still out there."

"She most certainly is – all your moms are," Cadi says, laughing.

"Yeah..." Emily adds, "as soon as you guys finished your set, Terri sent someone to make sure they didn't leave the VIP section."

"She is *sooo* going to freak out! Thanks guys…"

The moment Ariel stops talking, Terri appears around the corner, and with a big smile, says, "Richard knows something's up, and may wet his pants at any moment. Let's freakin' do this ladies!"

We go single file, out onto the dark stage, and plug things in. The crowd is milling around, waiting for the crew to get the stage ready for *AD's* set, and isn't paying any attention – well… until Vanessa does a run across Willie's drum set. And yes, the drums are just one of a number of instruments the girl can play!

"HEY!" Emily screams into a mic in front of her. *"YOU GUYS WANNA SEE HOW THE GIRLS DO IT?"*

In the blink of an eye, the crowd goes completely nuts, and everyone on the floor, rushes toward the stage.

I walk to the very edge of the stage, and Ariel is right next to me. The moment we start the harmony, the others start jamming. When the lights come up – thanks to Terri's devious little self – the six of us pretty much launch the entire arena into orbit with a brain-numbingly loud cover of *wannabe* – just because we can.

By the second chorus, we have what is probably *every* female in the building, singing along with us. I find it totally amazing that so many people would know the words to a twenty year old song! When I glance across the stage at the stairs, I see Richard shaking his head, and laughing. And right next to him, are the five most awesome guys I know, clapping, whistling, and cheering us on.

Yeah, I'm pretty sure that Wichita is going to remember when the girls of *Audio Distortion* and *Ransom*, cut loose one Saturday night in July…

Red Rocks

Joshua Miller

In order to explain Red Rocks from *Ransom's* perspective, we have to go back to our first night in Staples.

Emily put us on the spot, and made us come back for what was our first encore. None of us will ever be able to explain the emotions that were generated by the crowd's response to Misty's performance of *Who I Am* that night. It was a very important stop on the road to our band's destiny.

The six of us totally committed our souls to that show – partly because we were still a bit spooked, and worried, about our 'incident' in Australia, and partly because we knew how important the show was to the five of them.

Anyhow... it all comes down to a conversation that occurred at the bottom of the stage stairs, only seconds after the show was over...

The very moment Emily looked at me, her eyes filled with a bizarrely devious look, I knew it was about to get weird. Everyone watched as she raced across the thirty feet separating us, and without warning, *jumped* – forcing me to catch her. *Everyone* – including Emily's husband – fell into hysterical laughter. Then, as if I'm not already embarrassed enough, the crazy woman planted a kiss on me, that made them all laugh harder – and made me blush shades of red, no one knew existed.

The very first comment came from a five year old…

"Mommy!" Melissa blurted out.

Vanessa quickly followed with…

"O… M… G…"

Finally, my ever-quiet girlfriend (yeah, that too, eventually comes out) expressed herself…

"NO SHIT!" escaped Ariel's lips, and then she instantly blushed, and covered her mouth when she remembered the kids were standing there.

After a second, I relaxed my grip on Emily's waist, and she slid to the ground. She took turns hugging each of my bandmates, and Emma too, took the time to not only hug them, but to thank them.

"You guys sooo totally rocked!" Emily said, and was immediately backed up by everyone else. "We have six more shows, and by God, I expect the *exact same performance* at every one of them. Understood?"

"Yes ma'am!" the six of us said, simultaneously.

Then, for a second time, Ariel spoke up.

"Uh… excuse me…"

"Yes, Ariel?" Emma asked, stepping around Emily, and looking right at her.

"I'm pretty sure we only have five shows left… well, with you guys I mean."

Emma laughed, glanced at Emily, and rolled her eyes.

"Which show are you guys planning on skipping?" Emma asked, quickly turning and looking at Richard, who was blatantly clueless.

"We thought…" came from Martin.

"Thought what?" Cadi interjected, grinning herself.

"Well… it seems reasonable to think you guys will do the last show on your own… with your fans…" Vanessa offered.

"*Man!*" Stanley said, trying his very best not to laugh, "you guys are kinda dense!"

"Apparently," Willie added, also giving in to his laughter, "you guys haven't noticed that *your* fans, and *our* fans, are one and the same…"

Poor Ariel was going to lose it – I could tell. Slowly but surely, the tears started trickling down her cheeks. Martin, stepped over, and with a grin on his face, and put an arm around her shoulders, and gave her a squeeze.

"Why?" she muttered, "why are you guys doing all this?"

"Because, you need to understand one very important thing, if you intend to make this a career," Emily said, fighting back her own emotions, "and we intend to make sure you do."

"*It is…*" Stanley said, stepping up next to Emma, and putting his arm around her.

"*And always has to be…*" Willie added, as he stepped up on the other side of Emma, and put the arm his daughter wasn't in, around her.

"*All about the music…*" Emma finished with a smile, as Emily turned and joined them, putting her arm around Willie.

"Besides," Cadi added, as she stepped to the end of the line, and put an arm around Stanley, "*We are, and always will be – no matter what paths we travel, or what complications life throws at us – Audio Distortion.*"

The thing that will make us remember that moment, was the show's reset crew – *close to fifty of them* – when they instantly broke into applause, and cheering.

I think *Audio Distortion* even got to Richard that night...

Oh... and the lesson in all this?

When *Ransom* plays Red Rocks, with the biggest pop band in the world, tomorrow night, it will be, **'all about the music'!**

"Did you actually jump the fence too?"

~Ariel Williams

Red Rocks

Ariel Williams

How does one explain this place?

I'm twenty years old, and here I sit, on what is probably the most important stage in music. As I listen to the wind whistle through the rocks around me, I close my eyes and let it all sink in.

How did six kids from Ransom, Kansas end up at Red Rocks? What are the astronomical odds of that happening?

Music is in our hearts – it has been since we could walk. My mind slips into a memory of Vanessa and me when we met in dance class, in second grade. Even as I am smiling, a gust of winds blows across the stage, and I feel my hair catch it.

Fourth grade – the day I discovered a guitar in the music room. I remember telling Nessa "I'm gonna learn to play that – I swear."

Suddenly, I feel a presence. I open my eyes, pretty sure someone is going to chew me out for jumping the fence to get in here, and instead discover Vanessa sitting down next to me.

"Do you believe in destiny?" she asks.

"You mean, like we were always going to end up here?"

"Yeah."

"Maybe… I guess. I was just thinking about the day I told you I was going to learn to play guitar…"

"In the music room – fourth grade," she blurts out.

After a couple of seconds of staring at each other, we both start laughing, then she leans over and hugs me.

"Are you scared?"

"No," I reply, "even though I get the feeling I'm supposed to be."

"Good!" comes from a female voice behind us.

When we turn to look, we find *Audio Distortion's* bass player crossing the stage toward us. With a smile, she takes a seat next to us, and we sit silently.

"Did you actually jump the fence too?" I eventually ask, which gets a snicker from Vanessa.

"Oh please," Cadi says, in her totally cool Welsh way, "I simply asked someone to unlock the bloody gate."

"What does this mean, Catrin?" Vanessa asks, turning to look at her. "What does our presence here mean?"

"Yeah," I add, "what *does* it mean? We're just a bunch of kids from Kansas. Lots of other acts – with far more time into making music – never make it here…"

"Yet… here we sit…" Vanessa finishes, shaking her head.

"You guys crack me up… I swear," Cadi replies. "This isn't about 'a bunch of kids from Kansas'. It never has been. Since the day Emily heard you play together, it's been about five insanely talented *musicians.*"

"There are six of us…" Vanessa mumbles.

"Yes there are. And without our favorite redhead, the five talented musicians might have still made it. But…" she pauses and looks at each of us, "the five of you wouldn't be the incredible people you are today, and I don't believe the trip would have been anywhere near as amazing as it has been."

"That's how the five of you feel about each other, isn't it?" I ask.

"Yep. Everything we've been through – *good and bad* – over the last thirteen years, is what makes *Audio Distortion* what it is. A long time ago, Stanley's dad told us that we needed to make sure that the *members make the band*, and that we if ever let the business *or* the band, change us, we'd be done."

"Don't let it consume you…" I mumble.

"To answer your question, I think that *Ransom's* presence here means they understand. Music is what you do – what you are amazingly good at. But, it's *not* your life. Your families, your friends, each other, and even Ransom, Kansas – that's your life."

"Fit music into our lives, not our lives into music," Vanessa says, leaning over and hugging Cadi.

"You guys totally rock!" Cadi blurts out, as she stands up. "Now, come on, Emily has a total crap load of stuff we all need to sign."

I stand up, pull Vanessa to her feet, and as Cadi goes down the stage stairs, we simply jump off the edge.

"Hey… can we jump the fence on the way out?" Vanessa asks, as we take off at a run, toward the main gate, leaving Cadi – who breaks up laughing – to bring up the rear.

"It's about the passion. It's about the
six of us, pouring every ounce of
ourselves into **everything** we do
tomorrow night…"

~ Misty Maitland 

Red Rocks

Martin Masterson

Emily, Emma, and an old friend of theirs named Matt, go all out on the 'giveaways' for the attendees. Matt and his guys – who are without a doubt, digital imaging geniuses – create the most amazing t-shirts ever. *Begin Again* on the front and *High Speed Rush* on the back – with our bright smiling faces circling each cover image. Matt even takes our signatures digitally, and puts them under our photos.

Then he, Richard, Stephen and Terri, come up with the most bizarre idea we've ever heard of. Once the label signs off on it, Matt comes up with a beautiful DVD case with the title *Red Rocks Live – Them and Us* on the front insert, and an explanation of how the concert came to be, on the back. Emily has us put one with each of the shirts for the attendees. The six of us are of course, confused, wondering why we are giving away empty DVD cases. Knowing Emily and Emma, that's probably exactly what they wanted. And yeah, we're smart enough to know we aren't being told everything...

Totally lost in thought, I hear footsteps behind me, and turn to find Misty walking down the center aisle toward me.

"Hey!" I say, as she reaches the bottom, and stops below where I'm sitting, my feet hanging off the edge of the stage.

"I wondered where you went," she says, giving me the cutest smile.

"I'm still trying to absorb all this," I say, reaching over, taking her hands, and pulling her up onto the stage.

"No kidding..." she mumbles, as she turns around and sits down next to me, taking my hand and squeezing it.

"Do you have any idea how much history we are in the middle of?"

Misty is about to show me just how deep her love of music actually goes...

"Neil Young, Jimi Hendrix, Fleetwood Mac, Rush, U2, Dave Matthews, Coldplay, Phish – every single one of them played here... on this stage...."

When I turn and look at her, she again smiles, and gently kisses me.

"I'm just trying to figure out how I got here..." she finishes, laying her head on my shoulder.

After a few seconds of silence, we feel the stage moving, and turn to find Victoria and Bailey coming up the stairs. Bailey runs across the stage, and almost throws herself onto Misty, who breaks up laughing.

"You're here..." Victoria says, taking a seat next to me, "because you've earned it."

"Mrs. Morgan, we're..." I start to say.

"Hey!" she blurts out, cutting me off.

"Sorry..." I mumble, as Misty laughs. "I keep forgetting."

"You call my husband Willie... you can certainly use my first name."

"We're here because *Audio Distortion* brought us," Misty says, as she tickles Bailey, who begins giggling.

"True. And knowing them as well as you do now, do you think for a second, you'd be here if they didn't believe you've earn it?"

Misty and I glance at each other, being unsure how to respond.

"You guys rock! You're amazing musicians and your love of music shows every time you touch an instrument. There are millions of fans out there, that will tell you the same thing," she pauses, and looks at Bailey, who is now exploring the stage. "Thing is..." she says, never taking her eyes off her daughter, "*Ransom* is *Audio Distortion* seven years ago..."

"What do you mean?" Misty asks.

"Making awesome music... trying to find your way in a complicated world... and trying to stay true to yourselves," she replies.

When we look at her, stunned beyond the ability to comment, she just laughs. She again looks at Bailey – who is trying to climb on some equipment – and shakes her head in apparent frustration.

"That child has no fear... I swear," she mumbles, then calls to Bailey. *"Come back here young lady – before you hurt yourself."*

As Bailey, giggling like a five year old, runs back across the stage, Vicki stands up, and we turn to face her.

"Since the day Willie and Emily brought you home with them, the six of you have been trying to find a way to get even with them. For the last three months, you've been trying even harder. Tomorrow night is your chance guys..."

"Oh... we plan to make it the best show we've ever done," I offer.

She looks at me kind of funny, as if disappointed in my response.

"It's not about 'the best show ever', Martin..." Vicki starts to say.

Then, just as she has done so many times over the last five years, it's the youngest member of *Ransom* who actually *gets it*...

"*Passion*. It's about the passion. It's about the six of us, pouring every ounce of ourselves into *everything* we do tomorrow night..." Misty says, her eyes locked to Vicki's.

With a huge smile, and very glassy eyes, Vicki kneels down, leans over and gently kisses Misty on the forehead.

"*You*... are the most amazing young woman I have ever met, Misty Maitland."

Then she stands up, takes Bailey's hand, and heads across the stage.

Misty and I sit quietly staring at the empty seats in front of us, for close to a minute, until finally, she breaks the silence.

"Tomorrow night, fifteen hundred people are going to see, *and hear*, a Misty no one has seen or heard before..."

After a few seconds of thought, with a laugh, I add, "...and if she's *anything* like the Misty we discovered, the day she figured out *High Speed Rush*, it's going to be amazing, on a scale that hasn't even been designed yet."

Finality

Misty Maitland

The fans are in their seats, the stage is set, and we – all eleven of us – are standing together at the bottom of the stairs backstage. While our mentors all seem absurdly calm, the six of us are wound tighter than we have ever been. In fact, when Josh and Martin – who are holding my hands – feel how badly I'm shaking, they both get concerned.

"Hey… come on now."

"I'm fine… well… sorta…" I reply, just before Vanessa steps between us and points at Stanley, who is holding Emily's hands and talking to her.

"…in Papa Roni's all those years ago, when, with a mouth full of pizza, you told us what you'd done, *you* have been this band's *leader*. So go out there, and lead."

Five pairs of eyes instantly look at me.

"Guys… come on."

"Seriously?" Ariel blurts out.

Josh, who is still holding my left hand, quickly adds, "Yes, you are. Without you, we would not be standing here. We may still have become a 'band', but we wouldn't be *Ransom*.

Each of us knows it... and in her heart, Misty Maitland knows it too."

We stand watching Emily do her thing – for close to forty minutes. When, without warning, she decides we are going to do question and answers, we watch the rest of *Audio Distortion* break out laughing. Both bands end up on the edge of the stage, while the twin sisters Emma discovered in New York, spend over an hour taking microphones to audience members.

All in all, it's an amazing experience, and is the closest to any audience we have ever been. We, of course, are totally stoked that at least half the questions are for, or about, us...

Finally, almost two hours after the scheduled start of the show, as Emily suggests to the audience that maybe we should play some music, the six of us, now totally relaxed, and comfortable with how things are going, make a decision.

"I say do it," Rhyan blurts out.

"Yeah... me too," Vanessa adds.

When I glance at Josh and Martin, they just laugh.

"You guys are going to jump in, and back me up, right?"

They nod their response, and I turn back toward the front of the stage.

"Excuse me, Mrs. Faintree," I say, trying not to laugh.

Cadi looks at me, and then at Willie, who smiles and says, "Uh-oh...!"

"What can I do for you, Misty?" Emily says, turning back to the audience. "Whenever teenagers call you *'Mrs.'* they're usually up to something..." she whispers into her mic, generating more laughs.

"I think you need to tell the audience exactly what belongs in those empty cases you've avoided talking about..."

Emma spins to her left, and looks at Josh, who is standing within feet of her. At the same time, the entire audience goes completely quiet.

"Oh come on!" Josh says, as the rest of us start laughing. "We've been around you guys for the last eleven weeks. You didn't seriously think you could digitally record the performance without us finding out, did you?"

The audience is quickly filled with 'wow's' and 'no way's' and so many deep breaths, it actually sounds like one big one. As I turn back to look at Emily, I hear Ariel giggling behind me.

"Yeah guys… we know about the DVDs," she says.

"How in the…" Stanley starts to say, looking at Cadi and Willie.

"We learned from the best," Vanessa offers, now also grinning.

The place erupts in applause, and I realize that Victoria was right. Tonight is all about the 1500 people in the seats. I watch as a smiling, and slightly teary-eyed Emma, steps aside, and holds out her hand to indicate Joshua has the stage.

"Folks," Josh says, as he passes me, "tonight's show is being recorded digitally, in its entirety, in high-definition. It started the moment Emily sat down and started talking."

"Once the technicians get it cut together, and edited…" Rhyan adds.

"Everyone here gets a copy," Vanessa finishes, and is rewarded by another huge round of applause.

As my bandmates are talking, I'm carefully watching the faces of the members of *Audio Distortion* – who it seems, have conceded a silent defeat.

"Although they will eventually be for sale," Cadi says, turning and smiling at me, "the ones you guys get will be signed – *by hand* – by at least one member of each band. One hundred and fifty of them will be signed by all eleven of us, which means, each of you has a one in ten chance of getting one. It will all be totally random, so hopefully you are happy with what you get. Just make sure you send in the postcards."

Again, there is a massive round of applause. Once it dies down, Emma turns to the audience.

"Give us five minutes, and we'll see if between the eleven of us, we can rock this place!" she yells, turning and pointing backstage, and waiting until the six of us go ahead of her. At the bottom of the stairs, we turn to face her.

"You didn't seriously think being recorded would freak us out, did you?" Josh asks, still in a joking and jovial mood.

When Emma's facial expression doesn't change, Ariel is quick to ask, "We didn't piss you off, did we?"

Emily laughs, and is followed by Willie.

"No," Stanley says, "you didn't. Definitely freaked us out, though."

"How?" Emma asks, looking right at me.

"Common sense, mostly. And of course, because we pay attention – something our *'mentors'* taught us," I reply, a little smirk on my face. "And, after Rhyan found some of the equipment, we beat it out of Richard."

When none of them says anything, I step up to Stanley and Emma, and take each of their hands.

"Guys," I say, feeling the tears come, "this is going to be the highpoint of our careers – and all of us know it. We'll keep playing together, and if we're lucky, we'll have half the career you guys have had. Tonight, we intend to pour every ounce of ourselves into this show... for you guys..."

"And for them..." Ariel adds, pointing at the audience, and fighting her own tears.

"We're here, because of the five of you," I continue, "and although we all know that some debts simply can't be repaid, we intend to make absolutely certain you never forget us..."

After a few seconds of intense silence, standing behind everyone, Rhyan mumbles, "...and when we play *High Speed Rush*, someone had *better* get a shot of me shredding."

The eleven of us are laughing when Terri and Stephen walk up.

"Okay guys," Stephen says, shaking his head and laughing as well, "You're like seventy-five minutes off. How about you make some music?"

A full ninety minutes late, we actually start the show. The sun has dropped behind the mountains, and the colors on the horizon are amazing. And of course, the lighted theater is a sight to behold.

The members of *Audio Distortion* made it quite clear to *everyone* involved, that this wasn't going to be a standard first act/second act show. Instead, just as the DVD covers says, it's *us and them. Audio Distortion* plays two songs, then we change, and *Ransom* plays two.

We take turns cranking out music, for over an hour. While one band is onstage, the other is out loitering in the crowd, talking to people, and generally experiencing our fans. It's beyond amazing, and the crowd seems pretty astonished as well. Josh even has a woman burst into tears, the moment he sits down next her!

Eventually, *Audio Distortion* sets up to play the last song of the night – *Journeys End*. This is when the most perfect moment I have ever experienced occurs.

Emma is finishing a bottle of water, Emily and Cadi are wiping their faces, when, completely unannounced, Leonard and Vicki – each of them carry a guitar, and being closely followed by Melissa and Bailey – walk to center stage, and stop between Emily and Cadi.

Emma tosses the plastic bottle, takes a few steps in their direction, and the second they start talking, we understand why – her mic picks up what is being said.

As Melissa moves next to her mother, Leonard says, "Here…" and hands Emily her Ibanez, "I think you need this."

"And you'll need yours as well," Vicki says, handing the Taylor to a very confused Cadi.

The entire audience, as confused as we are, has gone eerily quiet.

"Guys," Emma offers, *"Journeys End* isn't acoustic…"

"This isn't an ending, Emma," Vicki replies. When she turns and smiles at her, *everyone* can see the mass of tears building in her eyes. "It's just a break. I honestly don't believe it will ever end…"

Then Leonard…

"This," he says, staring right at his wife, *"is what the five of you do. What you are all amazingly good at…"*

Then, *everyone* hears Melissa's squeaky, yet amazingly cute, British accent…

"Mummy…"

"Yes dear?" a now emotional Emily says, squatting down next to her daughter.

Emma quickly bends over and holds the mic right next to them.

"Will you play the band's song?"

Almost immediately, Emily starts crying.

"Which one, baby?"

"We Are!" Melissa – *and* Bailey, who is standing next to her, holding her hand – yell at the same time.

Yeah… I'm guessing that at least half the audience simply bursts into tears. Everyone knows Leonard – and probably Vicki as well – coached her, but it is nonetheless, heart-stopping. Leonard turns, looks right at Emma, and takes her free hand.

"Every single one of your fans has at some point over the years, seen you guys play *Journeys End* live – on TV, or video, or at a show. You brought this amazing group of people," he waves an arm to indicate the audience, "here *free* for a reason, Emma. You've interacted with them, like no other crowd…"

He pauses, spins around, and faces the rest of the band.

"The five of you need to go right up to the front of this stage," he says, in as totally a British manner as I have ever heard, "and make *this* the show of your lives, and *of their lives*," he points at the audience. "Share with them, what only one other crowd has experienced…"

"Give them," Vicki says, stepping over and kissing Leonard on the cheek, picking up Bailey, and then looking at the five of them, *"all* of *Audio Distortion*…"

As the stunned and silent crowd watches, without a word, Willie stands up from his drums, pulls his mic out of its stand, and starts toward the front of the stage. Stanley is right on his heels, also with mic in hand. Cadi unplugs her bass, takes it off, and hands it to Leonard. Emily does the exact same thing. As the five of them go and sit down on the edge of the stage, the crowd gives them a standing ovation.

Leonard and Vicki – *and the 1500 people standing in front of us* – have just made this show an affirmation of the intense bond, the five members of *Audio Distortion* will always share… with each other, and with their fans.

Even as the last note fades, the audience is again on their feet, applauding – a soft, heart-warming applause. Stanley turns and tries to get us to join them onstage, but we just grin at him, shake our heads side to side, then walk around the front of the stage and into the crowd, and join in the applause.

This is Audio Distortion's moment...

With a little help, they manage to get off the stage, and then arm-in-arm, the five of them take a final bow together. Once the stage lights go out, they turn to head backstage, to the continuing applause of an amazing audience.

It's as perfect a 'final show', as any band could ever possibly hope for, and we are incredibly honored to have been a part of it.

"Over the last few years, the 'pop stars'
have taken over, and I'd like to find
Misty again – just for a while."

~ Misty Maitland 

Going Home

Misty Maitland

I know I keep turning up a lot in this story, but at some point, my five best friends made me the pivot point of the band. Even when we are separated from each other, I always seem to be the one keeping track of everyone.

'Mother Hen' – that's what Nessa likes to call me.

So… we quickly and silently disappeared within hours of the show at Red Rocks. It was *Audio Distortion's* night – period. When it came to doing the interviews, we told Richard and Terri to schedule them without us – unless Emma specifically asked us to be there. I sat down and wrote *Ransom's* statement about the tour, the Red Rocks show, and our part in it. Once they each read it, my bandmates signed off on it.

We all have apartments in LA, and for about two months following the tour, leaving them became not only completely comical, but almost impossible as well.

Eventually, under the close scrutiny of Vanessa (who has never tolerated pushy reporters very well) I sat some of them down near the pool at my apartment, and explained things to them…

"I'm not answering questions guys – I have something to say. This has all become childish, and completely absurd. You need to let it go. No matter how much you hound us, or tell the world we are 'stuck up and uncooperative'," I pause and look right at the reporter who made the comment in one of his articles, "our position isn't going to change. We've said everything we intend to, about the *Begin Again* Tour. Keeping us under siege isn't getting you any brownie points…" I hear a bunch of snickers in the group, "for the next time we find ourselves in front of you. At this point, we're all considering going home to Kansas for a while, just to get away from you guys…"

There is a strange hushed silence as the nine reporters all sit staring at me, their eyes telling me they are torn between letting it go, and trying to press me. Eventually, the notepads begin to close.

When Patty Princeton – an independent who has always been more than fair to us in her articles over the years – makes eye contact with me, I smile, nod at her, and she stands up.

"Okay then, Misty Maitland – I know you said you aren't answering questions, but maybe you can throw us a bone…"

I shake my head, and start laughing.

"What's the question?"

"Is *Ransom* going to record again anytime soon?"

She catches me totally off guard, and I laugh again.

"I'll answer that one, Patty. We're going to take a break from all this – and try to find ourselves. Over the last few years, the 'pop stars' have taken over, and I'd like to find Misty again – just for a while. As far as a new record…" I pause and look right at Vanessa, who gives me a huge smile,

"*...yes.* In fact, all the experiences of the last six months of our lives will be the inspiration for our next CD."

"Can we print that?" a male reporter blurts out.

"Sure," I reply, making Vanessa laugh.

"Any idea on a time frame?" Patty asks.

"I'm already writing," I offer, and Vanessa interrupts me.

"you're always freakin' writing..." she mumbles, making all of them crack up.

"To answer the question, no. It's going to take some time. But, because you all seem to be accepting of what I'm saying, give me some email addresses and I promise to keep you guys up on what's happening."

All of them are instantly scribbling on pieces of paper.

"And yes, Keith," I say, directing it at the guy who asked if he could print my comments, "if it's in an email, you can print it. Just please stick to what I say – I'd rather not have Richard chewing my butt..."

"Will what you send us, have been 'approved'...?" Patty asks, her smirk telling me exactly what she's asking.

"Richard is our producer, and Tami is our press agent. They aren't my mom and dad. Besides, they trust me enough to know what I can say, and what I shouldn't. As long as you guys are fair with us, I see no reason I can't be up front and fair with you."

"And *that*, Misty Maitland, is why *Ransom* will stay at the top... no matter how long it takes you guys to record your next CD. Damn shame some other bands can't figure that out..." Patty blurts out, as she walks over and holds out her hand to me.

Just to confuse her, I stand up and instead of taking her hand, I hug her.

Believe it or not, that morning was the end of the press's siege of *Ransom*.

Three weeks later, I wake up from a sound sleep, overcome by the strangest sensation. My head is on Martin's chest, his arm is wrapped tightly around me, but I am being consumed by a need to get away – to be somewhere other than in Los Angeles.

"Hey…" I whisper into his ear.

When he doesn't answer, I gently bite his ear lobe, which makes him laugh.

"You make it freakin' impossible to ignore you, I swear…"

"I need to go home."

"Okay… you want to shower first?"

"Not back to my apartment… *home.*"

The moment I say it, his eyes pop open, he turns onto his side, my head slipping off his chest and onto a pillow, and he props his head up with his hand. After he stares at me for a couple of seconds, he reaches out and pushes the hair out of my face.

"You okay?"

"I just need to go home. I need to hug my mom, and sleep in *my* bed – as goofy and childish as that probably sounds."

"*Seriously?* Childish? I must be a big baby then… because I've been thinking *the exact same thing* for like a week."

"Really?"

"Yeah. I want to… no wait. Truth is, I *need* to walk down Parks Street and cross the empty lot to the school. I need to sit on the bench at the Dairy Queen and watch people go by. I need to stand in the middle of the Hopper's field, and see nothing but corn in every direction…"

He pauses, and I watch, his big, beautiful, brown eyes glass over and a couple of tears hang in the corners.

"I need to remember *Martin's* life…"

"Are we driving or flying?"

"It's October you nut. I'm not driving over the Rockies in October."

"So… fly to Dodge City?" I ask, rolling out of bed and heading for the bathroom.

"That works," Martin yells, as he too, gets out of bed and goes to make coffee.

An hour later, I'm sitting at the kitchen counter, sipping my coffee, and thinking about calling the others to tell them what we are doing. Then, yet another instance of destiny inserts itself into our lives, when my phone rings.

"Hey, Ariel!"

"We're going home. Are you and Martin coming?"

I'm so weirded out, I can't even respond.

"Misty?"

When Martin looks at me, and sees the confusion on my face, he laughs, takes the phone, and puts the call on speaker.

"You freaked her out, Ariel. What's going on?"

"We're going back to Ransom for a while. I asked her if you guys wanted to come with us."

"Hang on a sec…"

Martin spins my laptop around, and seeing that I haven't booked our seats yet, he goes back to the phone.

"Everyone is going?"

"Yeah. And Rhyan is bringing Georgia – to meet his mom and dad."

"You booking the flights?"

"Uh-huh."

"We're in. I'll get Misty out of her daze, and we'll pack some stuff. When we leaving?"

"Shooting for tomorrow morning."

"Cool. Email the info, and we'll meet you at the airport."

"Awesome! See you tomorrow."

The moment she hangs up, Martin walks around the counter and wraps his arms around me from behind.

"Weird yes... but definitely not the weirdest thing that's ever happened to us."

"But it's close..." I mumble, as I gently kiss the back of his hand.

Thirty-eight hours later, the six of us are sitting at the picnic table, next to the Dairy Queen, in beautiful, downtown, Ransom, Kansas. And... for the first time in well over a year, my heart slows down and relaxes.

"So guys," Mrs. Weston – who owns the Dairy Queen – says, as she puts our food on the table, "Any of you need a part time job?"

Ariel and I crack up. The very first job we each had, was working for Mrs. Weston.

"I can help out for a couple hours a day," Ariel says, reaching for one of the burgers on the tray.

"Me too!" I add, pulling the lid off a cup of hot chocolate.

I swear to you... there's something about being *home*...

Riley Morgan

"Yeah... well... I'm from Kansas. Get me off the stage, and out of the lights, and this is what you get..."

~ Vanessa Preston 

Freedom

Vanessa Preston

Three days after we got home, I slipped into the Honda Civic I keep at my parent's house, jumped on the interstate, and didn't stop until I was in Lawrence.

Now I'm sitting in a parking lot, staring at an apartment building, wondering if what I am about to do, is a good idea.

He has no idea I'm here.

And yeah, I'm scared.

But, I need to know – to get my life, *and my heart,* back...

I get out, climb the stairs to the second floor, and knock on the door with C2 on it. After a couple of seconds, the door opens, and the moment I see her, the weight of the entire world is lifted from my shoulders.

"Hi! I'm looking for Chris – my name is Vanessa."

For some reason, I'm not upset, or freaked out, or any of the other things I was expecting to happen.

"*o...m...g...*" the girl mutters, as she stands staring at me.

"Oh relax," I blurt out. "I'm harmless... honest."

"He said you guys were..."

"And we are," I quickly reply, opting not to contradict anything Chris may have told her.

After a few seconds, she recovers, and invites me in.

"Crap! I'm sorry. Come on in..." she says, pulling the door all the way open.

The moment I step in, the first – and most prominent – thing you see in the room, it a giant poster of *me*... on stage, playing. It makes me smile, and yeah, I get teary-eyed.

"Chris isn't here – he's helping some underclassmen at the lab, who were having issues with an assignment..."

"Sounds like Chris," I reply as I stop in front of the poster, and lay my fingers on the glass covering it.

"I can tell you how to get to the lab... if you want?"

"When's he gonna be back?" I ask, spinning around to look at her, and being instantly overcome by a feeling of guilt, the moment I see her face.

"Uh... probably like an hour or so..."

"Hey! What's with the face?"

The moment I say it, the tears start.

"Please tell me I haven't done something really stupid..." she says in the most pleading tone I have ever heard.

"Are the two of you happy?"

She nods her head up and down.

"Then... I'd say you did something pretty freakin' smart."

She almost smiles, and then reaches up and wipes the tears off her cheeks.

"I was busy doing what I do," I say, turning and pointing at the poster, "and he's been busy living his life. Honestly, you are freaking, about nothing."

As she slumps into a chair, I cross the room and stop next to her.

Riley Morgan

"He said you guys were 'thinking about things' – and that you weren't sure you would ever fit into each other lives."

I laugh, and kneel down in front of her.

"He's probably right. We've each found our passion, and unfortunately…"

When she lifts her head, and makes eye contact with me, she still looks guilty.

"Are you a doctor too?"

"Not quite… but close…"

"Cool. I bet you guys always have things to talk about."

She sits staring at me, as if she's done something wrong.

"So here's the bottom line, Melody…"

"How do you know my name? I didn't tell you…"

I laugh, and point at a white coat, with her name and 'MD' on it, and she finally lets go. After we laugh for a few seconds, I continue.

"I'm a loud, obnoxious, out-spoken, pop star, but I do pay attention to things around me. Chris is my very first love – and he will always be. But… sometimes with life, it's more about the journey, than the destination. No matter where our lives take us, I will always be close to him. I'm hoping *you* will be able to live with that…"

She smiles, and points at the poster. "He asked me once, if I wanted him to take that down…"

"…and it's still there," I reply smiling.

"I'm just hoping to fit into today. Yesterday belongs to you and him…"

I lean over and hug her, then with a smile, ask, "So… can I hang around until he gets here?"

"Are you kidding? No one is going to believe I hung out with the bass player of the biggest pop band on the planet…"

"Well…" I say, standing up, and without warning, sitting down in her lap, and pulling out my phone, "let's get a little evidence, shall we?"

She is at first, totally confused. But the moment I start taking pictures, she cracks up. I get her email and send them all to her, and watch as she looks at them on her phone.

"I can actually show these to people?"

"Duh?" I reply, laughing.

"Well… I don't want to cause you any problems…"

"All I ask is that you keep them on *your* phone – don't send them out, and no 'posting' them anywhere. Who you show them to, is up to you."

"My little brother is *sooo* totally going to freak out…" she says, still staring at one of the photos.

"Fan is he?"

"You have *no* idea…" she mumbles. When she lifts her head, she has the biggest grin, and as she points at the poster again, says, "Ask Chris how many times he's tried to talk him out of *that!*"

"Cool – give me his address, and I'll send him signed copies of our CDs, and a signed poster of the entire band, big enough to cover a freakin' wall!"

"You know, Chris is right…" she says, putting her phone down, and looking me right in the eyes.

"About?"

"You *are* just a girl… like the rest of us. Well… except that you can play a guitar amazingly well."

"Yeah… well… I'm from Kansas. Get me off the stage, and out of the lights, and this is what you get…"

For the first time in as long as I can remember, my soul is at peace. Chris is apparently happy, and now I too, can try to find the heart I'm supposed to belong to. I have time…

Riley Morgan

Melody and I spend the next half hour, becoming friends. We're talking about the *Begin Again* tour when her phone vibrates, and she gets a text message. Once she reads it, her nervousness returns.

"Chris will be here in about five minutes."

"Hey... relax. Here's what's going to happen. He'll open the door, see me, say 'Hey Ness,' and go about his business."

"Seriously?"

"I have ten bucks that says so..."

She giggles, holds out her hand, and says, "You're on!"

Five minutes later, the door opens, Chris comes in, closes the door behind him, looks at me, smiles and says "Hey, Ness!" Then he walks over, kisses Melody, and asks, "Hey babe, how did rounds go today?"

The girl is right there at the edge of 'freak out'. Even the slightest breeze will probably send her over. When she looks at me, then at Chris, then back at me, the only guy I've ever been in love with, laughs, and pokes me in the ribs.

"Damn it, Ness... did you make that stupid bet again?"

Within seconds, we're all laughing – almost hysterically. And poor Melody is crying as well. I know that a new chapter of my life is starting. And the funny part is, I know that amidst all the silliness going on right at this moment, there's a song in it somewhere. It takes all my willpower not to pull out my phone and dial Misty...

It's weird... how I just can't seem to escape music...

Losses

Ariel Williams

"Hey!" I yell at Misty, who is sitting under the oak tree, outside the school's music room.

"Hey!" she yells back, without looking up from what she is doing.

Once I reach her, I take a seat next to her on the grass.

"Kinda cold to be sitting out here under a tree."

When she doesn't respond, I know she's lost in her lyrics again. This time, however, I know I need to interrupt. When I put a hand on the one she is writing with, she stops, and looks at me.

"Mom and I are going to Salina. Grams is way sick. Not sure when I'll be back."

"Is she...?" Misty asks, her eyes clouding up.

"Yeah, probably..."

"Oh my God, Ariel... I'm..."

I reach out and put a finger on her lips.

"Don't. We've known for a while. Grams even told me she's ready. I just hope God doesn't let her suffer too much."

"I can go with you…"

I smile, then lean over and kiss her cheek.

"I'll be fine. Mom and I have a handle on this. You need to keep doing what you are doing."

"Do the others know?"

"Yeah. I told Josh and he told them. I wanted to tell you myself."

"Keep in touch, Ariel… we're all here if you need us."

"I know that you goof. See you soon, okay?"

"Yeah… I guess…"

With that, I stand up and head for the car, where Mom is waiting for me. It will take us two hours to drive to Salina.

Lots of time to think…

"The first two records were written for the fans. I want to write **for and about us**, this time. I want them to know who the six people on the stage really are…"

~ Misty Maitland 

Sharing

Misty Maitland

For the last six months – even while the tour was still going – my heart has been telling what the next CD will be about.

The six of us. *Our lives.* The ones we live outside the spotlights, and off the stages. The ones, that are just like everyone else's.

At the moment, Martin and Josh are reading lyrics I just finished. The song – assuming they decide to make it one – will be about how 'home' pulls on each of us, no matter where we are.

"If you guys don't think it will work, just say so…"

"Are you joking?" Josh asks. "I'm about to cry here…"

"This is so freakin' *us*, Misty…" Martin adds.

"Sometimes… when I write, I remember what happened with *Bubblegum*…"

"Screw that," Josh blurts out. "If you write ten ballads, that's what *Ransom* will record."

"Besides, I know you remember what happened opening night in Miami…" Martin says, smiling at me.

His reference to the crowd's response to the band's first encore, allows my heart to totally relax.

"The first two records were written for the fans. I want to write *for and about us*, this time. I want them to know who the six people on the stage really are…"

"Can we put this to music?" Martin asks, holding up the pages he was reading.

"Yeah," Josh quickly adds, "Can we?"

I laugh, pull a stack of pages out of my notebook, and hand them to Josh.

"Look those over too. And you guys can do whatever you want with them." I close my now raggedy notebook, put the giant rubber band back around it, and turn toward the door.

"Hey!" Martin yells at me. "Where you going?"

"To Salina. Ariel and I are going to help each other. See you guys in a couple of days."

And so begins *Ransom's* third record – the title of which is still a mystery.

The sad part is, Ariel loses her grandmother, two days later.

Caroline June Williams will, however, live on, as part of what I believe is going to be *Ransom's* best record yet…

"You are such a big baby... I swear. I
will blackmail you – and you know it."

~ Georgia Campbell   

Committing

Rhyan Crossman

Yeah... the drummer is back, so hang on...

We spend the holidays in Ransom, and on Christmas Day, all our families get together at my parent's house.

It...

Is...

AMAZING!

To see us, you'd never know where the last six years of our lives have taken us. We are once again, six kids from a small town in Kansas.

And Georgia... well, she too, is amazing. When I offer to send her home in time for Christmas, she runs out and tells my parents I'm trying to get rid of her! Talk about comical? Everyone – including my grandparents – fall in love with her instantly.

On New Year's Eve, she talks me into doing something I told her about when we first got involved – during one of our 'tell the truth' conversations.

At the moment, we're lying in the middle of the Hobb's wheat field, staring up at the stars, and her head is resting on my chest...

"It's almost midnight..." Georgia says.

"I'm honestly not comfortable with this..."

"You are such a big baby... I swear. I *will* blackmail you – and you know it."

"And you are a pushy, pain in the ass..."

"Uh-huh... I am. Now, we are going to do this, so get used to the idea."

"Why? Why is this so important to you?"

"Because," she says, sitting up, and then straddling me. "A *full year* is more than enough waiting. *And...* a girl likes it when the first time is something she's going to remember. *And...* my mind has already decided that it's going to be *incredible...*"

Yeah... even at twenty-two, I'm nervous. Sure, I've done it before – there are at least a few girls who will tell you I'm nowhere near an angel. But... well... Georgia is different.

"Rhyan..." she says, "this *is* going to happen – unless you jump up and leave. I love you – *with every ounce of my being* – and this is just part of it. It's not like I'm losing my virginity in a wheat field – although, thinking about it... that would have been pretty cool..."

Even in a moment as tense as this, the girl can make me laugh.

"So will you please, quit being a 'proper gentleman' and just take advantage of me – before I go and tell your parents you won't?"

Yep. Georgia Campbell is the most amazing woman in the entire world.

And yes... on a chilly New Year's Eve, inside an oversized sleeping bag, in a wheat field on the outskirts of Ransom, Kansas, I make love to the woman of my dreams – for the very first time.

And she's right – *it is incredible!*

What she doesn't know, is that very soon, *she* will have to 'get used to' being called Mrs. Crossman...

"Yes, we know how important it is to
you, and only you are going to be able
to find it... But you know damn well,
the harder you try, the more it will
elude you..."

~Rhyan Crossman 

Helping Hand

Misty Maitland

"Noooo!" Ariel blurts out.

"Yeah… I know. It just isn't working," Martin adds.

"I can change the lead line – if that's the problem," comes from Josh.

After a few seconds of silence, they all look at me.

"I don't know guys… I honestly don't know."

They all shrug, and seem to let it go.

"Can we put this aside… and maybe finish one of the others?"

"Well yeah!" Vanessa says, dancing across the studio, her guitar still over her shoulder, and then wrapping me up in a hug when she reaches me.

"Hey!" Rhyan says, "Martin and I have an idea for *Being Drawn* – to pick up the tempo."

When I don't say anything, Martin adds, "You did say it needs to be faster, right?"

When I still remain silent, the five of them walk over and circle me.

"It's just a song, Misty," Vanessa says.

"Just like a hundred others you've written," Ariel adds.

"And it will come to you," Martin says, leaning over and kissing me.

"You just need to let it," Josh finishes, putting a hand on my shoulder.

Finally, Mr. Head-Over-Heels-In-Love sees through me.

"Yes, we know how important it is to you, and only you are going to be able to find it – in there…" Rhyan pauses, and gently taps on my heart. "But you know damn well, the harder you try, the more it will elude you. And…" he pauses, and glances at the others, "we all know what you need to do. We're just waiting for you to quit being hard-headed, and do it."

"Just go ask her. Even if she helps, it's still your song… *and our song*," Ariel says.

Then… fate and destiny – again. My phone rings, breaking the tense silence of the studio. Josh picks it up and answers it.

"Yeah? Oh hey! No… I was just closer. Hang on."

"It's for you…" he says, handing me the phone.

"Well duh? It *is* her phone, Josh…" Vanessa blurts out, making everyone laugh.

"Hello?"

"I'm pretty miffed with you at the moment…" I hear Emma say, just before I burst into tears. Then, almost immediately, she adds, "And you better knock that crap off, and talk to me…"

"My brain can't get there, Emma. I keep trying, and it's… it's… '*empty*'. And the frustration is making my heart hurt…"

"Been there, done that. Will probably be there again, eventually."

"What do I do? How do I fix this?"

"Sometimes, it can't be fixed. Some songs simply aren't meant to be finished, Misty."

Again the tears come. I can't help it.

"You're on a plane here in three hours. Just you. And leave your notebook there…"

"What?" I blurt out, totally confused.

"No questions. You're going to trust me, and do as I say, okay?"

"Yes ma'am," I reply, not knowing what else to do.

"Let me talk to Martin."

I hand him the phone and sit stunned, listening.

"Yeah, Emma? Uh-huh. Yep. You got it! And thanks… from all of us."

He closes the phone and looks at Josh.

"Take her home, let her pack some clothes, and take her to John Wayne – over in Irvine. Emma says she has a seat on a Southwest flight to Fort Collins at 4:00 PM."

As Josh puts his guitar away, Martin steps over to me.

"You need to do this, and you know it. Don't lose yourself to this, babe. I've gotten used to having you around…"

Ariel and Vanessa both let out snickers, and when I look at them, the look on their faces, finally makes me smile.

"How did she know?" I ask, as I wrap the rubber band around my notebook, and hand it to Martin.

"I told her…" a female voice, coming from the studio speakers, says. When we turn to look, the lights go on in the booth and we see a teary-eyed Terri Maxwell, sitting there staring at us.

After a second, she stands up, and comes down into the studio.

"I'm sincerely sorry, Misty..." she starts to say, just before I put a finger on her lips, and hug her.

"Never be sorry for looking out for me. At times, I'm not as smart as I think I am. Hazards of being the youngest..."

She smiles and returns the hug. Then I turn to face the others.

"At least I have an amazing family looking out for me... and keeping me on track."

When I turn to find Josh, he's standing at the door, twirling his key ring, with a goofy smirk on his face.

"See you guys in a couple of days..."

I cross the studio and go out the door, with Josh right behind me. The thing that occupies my thoughts all the way to the airport is, Martin never said a word when I handed him the notebook...

Being Released

Misty Maitland

When I land in Fort Collins, no one is there to meet me – which for some reason, cracks me up. I only have a carry-on, so I skip baggage claim and head right for the Avis counter. I give them my credit card, the studio's account number, and once they verify it all, they rent me a car. I stand quietly, watching the girl – who, from the look on her face, no doubt recognizes me – finish the paperwork, and realize this is the first time I've ever done this on my own! How weird is that?

Once we're done, and I've signed the contract, she hands me a set of keys, and tells one of the lot guys to show me where the car is. Just before I walk off, I reach over, take her pen, grab a piece of blank paper off the desk, and write 'To Millie' and sign it really big. Then I hand it to her. Almost immediately she blurts out, "How did you…" and even before she finishes, I tap on her name tag with the pen, laugh, hand the pen to her, and turn to follow the guy.

At times, 'famous' can just be so insanely amusing…

Forty minutes later, I pull up in front of the Campbell house, and notice that there are four vehicles in the driveway. I grab my backpack, get out and head up the walk toward the porch. I'm half way there, when the door opens, and the two cutest little kids come down the steps and race up to me, each latching onto a leg when they reach me. I burst into riotous laughter – no way could I have stopped it. Within seconds, I'm on my knees, with two little people hugging me endlessly, and laughing like the entire world entertains them.

Finally, I hear male laughter. I turn and find Stanley standing on the porch, with Melissa by his side.

"HI AUNT MISTY!" she screams, then races down the stairs and gets in on the hugs.

"Guys!" Stanley yells, still laughing himself, "Let her get into the house! Come on back up here – all of you..."

The kids let go, race back to the porch, and I watch as Melissa helps the little ones back up the stairs, and into the house. Stanley comes down, holds out his hand to me, and pulls me to my feet.

"Does she really remember who I am? Or did you guys tell her..."

"Ask her that question," Stanley quickly replies. "And for the record, I was going to pick you up... but I was overruled."

I laugh, take his arm and let him lead me back to house. Inside, I am totally shocked to find both Emily and Cadi, sitting in the living room with Emma.

"See... she *can* get here on her own," Emily blurts out, making me laugh. "Give me my five bucks, Cadi..."

She holds out her hand, and Cadi puts a $5.00 bill in it, then they all start laughing.

"I take it the two that jumped me in the yard are Carson and Shannon?"

"Yep," Emma replies. "They haven't seen each other since they were born, so Emily came to visit."

"I heard they were born minutes apart…"

"Sixteen," Emily says, smiling at me.

"Which one is older?"

Emily snickers, and Cadi laughs.

"We've decided we aren't saying…"

After a few more minutes, the kids come rushing in. The little ones go to their mothers, and Melissa comes and sits next to me.

"So… you remember me?" I ask, putting an arm around her shoulders.

"Duh?" she quickly replies, rolling her little eyes. "You and Aunt Georgia fed me bagels when my mom was busy on the tour…"

I look at Emily, more than a bit shocked, and she just grins and shrugs.

"And…" Melissa adds, laying her head in my lap, "I really like that one song you sing – Mom says it's called *hostage*."

Yeah… that one gets me. And they all see it.

"Okay you guys, time for bed."

"Awww Mom!" Melissa blurts out.

"Where are you sleeping?" I ask her.

"With my mom. Shannon has to sleep in the crib…"

"Wanna share a bed with your aunt?"

The girl's eyes light up the entire room, and my heart finally lets go – of everything.

"She'll talk you to death," Emily says, a big smile on her face.

"Second door on the left, top of the stairs," Emma says, also grinning like she's guilty. "Good luck…"

I take Melissa's hand, and as we head up the stairs, I hear the three of them laughing. Thing is… Misty Maitland's entire world is for some reason totally perfect at this moment. And… even if Melissa talks for hours, I will enjoy every single word she says…

Just because…

"They're her freakin' lyrics — we'll just blame it all on her!"

~ Ariel Williams   

It Needs To Be Faster

Joshua Miller

"This will work!" Vanessa says, scribbling on the sheet music in front of her. "Misty can fit the lyrics when she gets back."

"I agree," Ariel says. "Josh?"

"It works really well," I say, grinning, "as long as the drummer doesn't mess it up…"

"Is it just me," Rhyan says, as the girls crack up laughing, "or is it weird that we're doing this without our lead singer?"

"Yeah, it is sorta," Martin says, "but she needs to find her way past that song. It's really driving her nuts. Hopefully Emma can give her some direction."

"You think they went through all this?" Vanessa asks, waving her arms to indicate the studio. "*AD* I mean…"

"Of course they did," we hear a deep voice that we all recognize, say, through the studio speakers. Seconds later, Richard and Terri walk in, and find seats.

"So… all bands go through this, huh?" Ariel asks.

"Creating?" Terri says, "Of course."

"Some bands are better at it than others," Richard offers. "The six of you tend to be just like Emma and the rest of them…"

"Meaning?" Martin asks.

"You've reach the plateau – the point where you're having fun with it, instead of stressing over it. You *all* live and breathe music – yet it doesn't control you."

"The more I watch you guys, the more jealous and amazed I get," Terri says.

"Huh?" Vanessa says.

"This album is going to recapture your fans – *all of them* – because it's so deeply personal. You are putting *yourselves* out there for review and comment – and your fans will. Trust me."

"You've been keeping up?" Martin asks.

"Of course," Richard says, laughing, "You're one of my top acts at the moment, and I need to know where your music is going."

"Misty is afraid the songs aren't upbeat enough – like the fans are used to," Martin says.

"Your fans got past that with the last record. They understand that you're *musicians* and that you have things to say…"

"And," Terri adds, following it with a laugh, "I heard at least three songs that sound pretty upbeat…"

"I hope you guys are right…" Rhyan mumbles.

"So… how many are you short?" Richard asks.

"We're still working on two that we want to use, and then there's the one that's making our lead singer crazy…" I offer, glancing at my bandmates, who are trying really hard, not to laugh.

"Well, let us get out of here then. You will let Terri know when it's time to record, right?"

"How come you didn't ask 'how much longer?'" Vanessa asks, carefully scrutinizing Richard, as he stands up.

"I don't need to. You guys are well past that. I know you are as anxious to get the music to the fans as the label is. I also know that with the six of you, it has to be *right* first…"

"As soon as Misty gets back…" Martin says.

"Yeah, yeah… In the meantime, create something, please? You're tying up my studio!"

Laughing, the two of them disappear out the door.

After a few seconds of silence, Vanessa starts a beat on her bass – one that none of us has heard before, and almost instantly, Rhyan is backing her up. Ariel turns and looks at me, and I just shrug. Then Martin has what the five of us have decided to call 'a Misty moment', and he rushes over and grabs her notebook – which for reasons none of us understand, she left behind. He opens it, rummages around the pages for a few seconds, and then apparently finds what he's looking for.

"Keep playing, Ness! Keep playing!"

He rushes over to me, and keeping everything covered except three lines, holds up the notebook for me to read.

We're always moving at the speed of life
Never slowing down
Eventually we will discover

Ariel, who is getting into the beat, grabs his hand, moves it out of the way, and reads the rest of the lyrics. Then, just as we have so many times over the last six years, out of nowhere (or perhaps it's actually out of our hearts) *Ransom* finds a song. With a wickedly devious look in her eyes, Ariel pulls a pen out of her pocket, scratches out the next line of the lyrics, and adds her own…

Terminal velocity has been reached

"Faster!" I blurt out, as Martin runs back to his keyboard.

"How much?" Vanessa immediately asks.

"It has to be the same tempo as *High Speed Rush*…" Ariel says, pulling her guitar around in front of her, and cranking the volume.

Within seconds, Rhyan and Vanessa are shredding, and when Martin jumps in with a blazing keyboard cover, Ariel and I and get busy.

What none of us notices, is that there are at least twenty people in the 'box', watching us, and nine of them, are members of two new bands…

What's going through my mind is, 'what's our lead singer gonna say about us writing a song in her absence'?

As if she's reading my mind, as we reach what we figure will be the end of the song, Ariel strikes her last chords, then steps over and whispers in my ear…

"They're her freakin' lyrics – we'll just blame it all on her!"

We become aware of our audience the moment Rhyan yells and throws his sticks into the air, and everyone in the 'box' breaks into applause.

And there, near the back, is one Terri Maxwell, fist in air, and a look of total satisfaction on her face.

Maybe she's right…

Maybe *Ransom* isn't done just yet…

Maybe… we *are* about to kick butt, one more time…

Continuing Evolution

Misty Maitland

I wake up to find that the sun is up, and Melissa is nowhere to be found. When I think about how she talked herself right to sleep the night before, I grin.

I sit up, swing my legs over the edge of the bed, and as I am about to stand up, a thought occurs to me...

'I haven't slept that soundly in...'

...and I realize I honestly can't remember the last time. With a big grin, I get up and head for the bathroom.

Once I'm showered and dressed, I'm staring at myself in the mirror, and again, I smile. Time for something else I haven't done in a while. I wander down the hall and when I reach Emma and Stanley's room, I peek in. Seeing no one, I walk over to her dressing table and just as I suspect, lying on one side is a stack of hair bands. Emma does love her ponytails. I grab two that are the same color and head back to the bathroom. It takes me about three minutes to actually 'find' Misty – something I've been trying to do since the tour ended. Even though my hair has gotten longer, the moment I have the pigtails pulled up tight, there she is...

Misty Maitland – from Ransom, Kansas.

And the funny thing is, without make-up, and with the pigtails, although I'm almost twenty-one, I still look fifteen.

Laughing, I head downstairs. When I wander into the kitchen, I find Georgia and the kids, sitting at the table.

"Aunt Misty!" Melissa yells.

"Hey bunk-mate!" I yell back, making Georgia crack up.

As I walk toward the coffee maker, Georgia offers her assistance.

"Cups are in the cabinet above it. Sugar and stuff is in the canisters."

"Cool. Where is everyone?"

"Downstairs."

"Are they working?"

"They have been for about a month. Some of it sounds pretty cool, too."

"What about their drummer?"

"He comes and goes. He and Vicki are pretty busy during the summer."

I fill a cup, add some fake sugar, and turn to face her. After a few seconds, and a couple of sips, I walk over and sit down next to her.

"You okay?" she asks.

"Who knows? Been talking to your boyfriend, have you?"

She blushes really badly, which cracks me up.

"After the incident in the wheat field, I can officially call him that. It's a rule where we come from..."

She laughs, leans over, and hugs me.

"He and the others are just really worried about you. My brother and Emma are too – they've been there, Misty."

Riley Morgan

"I don't know why this song…"

"Because," I hear from behind me, "it's going to be the title song."

When I turn around, Emily is standing there with a coffee cup in her hand.

"Mummy!" Shannon blurts out. It's the first time I hear the true deepness of her British accent, and it makes me laugh.

"It gets way bad when her dad is around," Georgia says, using her coffee cup to hide her grin.

"You've read it?" I ask Emily.

"Yep. Lyrics and music."

"And you can just tell?"

"What do I do for living, Misty?" she says, walking over and filling her cup. When I glance at Georgia, she has the goofiest grin on her face.

Once Emily has her coffee, she turns back to face me.

"Come on down stairs and listen to what we are working on, and we'll discuss your 'song', okay?"

I shrug, stand up, and follow her into the hall. Just before we disappear, we again hear that cute little British voice.

"Bye Mummy!"

Emily opens the door to the basement and waits for me to go through it.

"Shannon sounds *soooo* much more British than Missy… Her accent is totally amazing."

"Yeah… I blame her father."

As we descend the stairs, I'm laughing at Emily's comment. The moment we reach the bottom, I fall instantly silent. I knew Emma and Stanley had a studio in their basement, but I'm not even close to prepared for what I find.

"Oh... my... God..." I mumble, which makes all of them look at me.

Stanley pulls off his headphones, laughs, and says, "Welcome to Campbell Studios."

"This is amazing!" I blurt out.

Emma and Cadi laugh, and Emily puts a hand on my shoulder.

"Yeah, Emma had it built during her 'stuck and confused' period."

"One of them..." Stan adds, generating more laughter.

"So... do you want to hear something cool?"

"Of course!" I reply, taking the nearest stool.

The four of them play parts of a few different songs that they're working on, but never say what they intend to do with them. At one point, I hear a melody so amazing, it reaches in and touches me.

"I might have to steal that," I blurt out, giving them my 'innocent' look.

"Well..." Cadi says, glancing at the others as she puts her guitar away, "you could. But we know your producer..."

"Yes we do!" Stanley adds, with a laugh.

"Come on – let's get some fresh air, and some sun," Emma suggests.

"Outside is an excellent idea," Emily says, as she heads up the stairs with Cadi right behind her.

Ten minutes later, everyone is in the backyard, laughing and joking. Shannon and Carson are giggling, and rolling around in the grass, and Melissa is begging her mother to teach her to play a small guitar she has.

This is the second time, in as many days, that I realize I am totally and completely relaxed. Nothing matters. Not the label, not the CD, and most importantly, not that silly song.

"Hey," Emma whispers, breaking my concentration, "where you at?"

"I'm in your backyard, happier and more content than I've been in a really long time."

She smiles, and puts a hand on one of mine.

"How did you guys get here?" I ask.

"Life, of course," Cadi replies.

"Are you done?"

"Done?" Stanley asks.

"With the whole 'famous' thing."

"Don't know…" Emma says, as she pokes straws into juice boxes for the kids.

"From what I just heard, you haven't let go of music…"

"Yeah…" Emily says, shaking her head, "like *that* will ever happen."

"We've reached the place we want to be. A place where we make music, because *we want to* – period," Emma says, as Carson – juice box in hand – drops into her lap.

"And it's the music *we* want to make," Cadi adds.

"What we do is endless, Misty. It doesn't stop or pause. It simply keeps going, and changes as it does."

The very moment Emma says it… well, my brain takes off. Everything everyone has been telling me for the last four months forms as one clear thought in my head, and *I get it.*

"Don't *look* for it… *wait* for it… let it come to you…" I mumble, causing all of them to go quiet, and look at me.

"Just… be… patient…" comes out of my mouth, without any help from my brain.

Although I'm staring at Emily, who has taken a seat across from me, I don't even see her. Instead, I'm seeing sheet music, bars and notes, and lyrics.

And then, just like it did with *High Speed Rush*, the answer is simply there, in my mind, *and* it makes total and complete sense.

"Do you have a fax machine?" I ask, not even looking at Emma. At this point, I'm even afraid to blink, for fear the image in my mind, will fade if I do.

"Of course," I hear a voice say.

I open my phone, hit speed dial #1, and Martin answers on the first ring.

"Hey babe!"

"I need you to fax me the six pages of music and the three pages from my notebook..."

"Huh?" he replies.

"Martin..." I start to say, before Emily takes the phone.

"You need to do this, Martin. No questions." She pauses, and then says, "Yeah, I'm pretty sure that's the song she's talking about. Emma will give you the number."

She hands the phone to Emma, who rattles off a number, then says goodbye, closes the phone, and hands it to me.

After a few seconds of silence, it's Georgia's voice that brings me back to reality.

"Well?"

Just her tone makes me smile, and I glance at Emma, who is smiling as well, because *she gets it*. She's been right where I am at this exact moment, a bunch of times over the years.

"It's endless..." I mumble, locking eyes with her. "It's... *continuous*..."

Emma lets out a small laugh, and takes one of my hands.

"It simply keeps going, and changes..." I offer, squeezing her hand. "It... *evolves*..."

The four of them sit staring at me for a few seconds, and then Georgia again breaks the silence.

"And?"

"The band... *Ransom*... it's a *continuing evolution...*"

"I told you it was the *title track*, didn't I?" Emily says, leaning over and hugging me so tightly, all the air rushes out of me.

"And *that* is a totally kick-butt title, for this particular CD! Come on," Stanley says, pulling me to my feet, "let's go check the fax machine..."

"It's **her** song. She has damn near every minute of the last six months of her life in it."

~Martin Masterson 

Disbelief

Ariel Williams

It's been four days, and since her cryptic call to Martin, we haven't heard a peep out of Misty.

Truth is, we're all going nuts.

Josh is so stressed, he suggests calling her, right in the middle of a recording session. It's actually rather comical. Our concern is split – although it's more about her finding her way past the song, a good bit of it is about how she is going to react to the fact we wrote one without her.

We need two more songs for the record. We're figuring to use the one we wrote, and hopefully, the one that has been Misty's nemesis for close to six months.

Yeah… we're all pretty sure she's had a 'Misty moment', based on her call to Martin asking for the music and lyrics. In my heart, knowing Misty Maitland the way I do, I have no doubt she's going to bring back an amazing song.

"How in the heck does she do this?" Martin blurts out, actually banging his head on the conference table, and making the rest of us crack up.

"It's what she does, Martin. You need to quit screwing with her lyrics, and be patient," Vanessa says, slugging him.

"Yeah," Rhyan adds, "give her an hour with the song, and she'll make the lyrics work…"

Martin, who has been rearranging the lyrics to what we have titled *Terminal Velocity*, lifts his head, and turns to look at Joshua.

"Uh-uh – no way dude. I'm on their side," Josh says, pointing at the rest of us. "We play it for her, and like Rhyan said, get out of her way and let her do her thing."

About this time, the door to the conference room opens. Richard, Terri, and a girl we don't know, walk in. Richard stops at the far end of the table, drops the CD he's been listening to on the table, sits on the edge of it, and just stares are us. Terri goes and gets a bottle of water from a small refrigerator across the room, and the other girl, simply drops into a chair, without a word.

"Misty called," Richard finally says. "She's on her way."

"Finally!" Martin and Josh blurt out simultaneously.

"I've heard what she's been working on…"

"And," the unknown female says, "I hope you guys aren't tired of the whole 'famous' thing yet."

Richard turns, looks at her, then back at us.

"Guys, she," he points at the girl, "is Ashleigh Burns. She's your new publicist."

"Your new record," comes from Terri, who crosses the room and stops next to us, "is titled *Continuing Evolution*."

"She did it!" I yell, jumping up from the table.

"Yes, she did," Richard says, pulling out a chair, and finally sitting down. "I've worked with a lot of lyricists over the last thirty-five years, and your singer is in the top ten. As God is my witness, she may be as good as Emma…"

 Riley Morgan

"You guys need to get into the right head-space before she gets here. You are about to record the mother of all ballads," Terri says, as she too, takes a seat at the table.

"OMG!" Vanessa yells, as she too, stands up. "She wrote it as a ballad? How totally freakin' cool!"

"Guys," comes from a spooked looking Ashleigh, "I'm pretty new to this game, but I'll bet money the song will *enter* the charts at number one, forty-eight hours after the label releases it." After a pause, and a strange facial expression, without looking at us, she pretty much mumbles, "Her voice is unexplainably amazing..."

That's the moment the five of us get it, and after we glance at each other, we all start laughing. I walk over, straddle Richard, and sit down on his knees. Then I grab his cheeks and gently kiss him.

"You guys are just too funny," Rhyan says, walking up and hugging Terri from behind, and picking her right up out of her chair.

"Is our lead singer going to steal the limelight?" Josh asks, between laughs.

"Oh crap!" Martin blurts out, acting as if he's going to faint, "Say it isn't so!"

During our antics, poor Ashleigh is looking at us like we've totally lost our minds.

"Uh... excuse me," she finally says, and waits for us to give her our attention.

Rhyan lets go of Terri, I get off Richard's lap, and we all turn to face Ashleigh.

"Josh's comment is more accurate than you know. And..." she pauses, looks at Richard, then down at the table top. "I've seen bands that couldn't handle it..." she finishes, so quietly, you almost can't hear her.

"Put her on stage by herself, if that's what it takes," Vanessa says.

The stunned look on Ashleigh's face makes us start laughing again.

"I told you, Ash. Didn't I tell her, Terri?" Richard says, shaking his head, and trying not to laugh himself.

"It's *her* song," Martin says, taking a seat across from Ashleigh, and waiting until she looks at him. "She has damn near every minute of the last six months of her life in it."

"Yeah," Rhyan adds, stopping behind Martin, "and you're right – she has an amazing voice. If all she needs to tell this particular story is that voice, we're good with that."

About this time, Richard's phone rings, he pulls it out and answers it.

"Hey. Yeah, all five of them. Okay, they're on their way."

He closes the phone, and with a devious little smirk on his face, looks at the five of us.

"When I said Misty was on her way, I neglected to tell you she was on her way from the airport."

Once again, laughter.

"She's in Studio Two. I've closed the entire studio area, until you guys are done down there. She wants to talk to the five you alone. Take this," he hands me the CD he brought in with him, "so she can hear it. I'll be in my office."

Single file, the five of us head for the door, and just to be a clown, Rhyan stops next to Ashleigh, leans over, and kisses her – smack on the lips – before she knows what's happening.

Five minutes later, we find our lead singer sitting cross-legged on the floor of Studio Two, with the most amazing grin on her face.

Yep... whatever happens now, it's going to be epic...

Moral Support

Martin Masterson

We're in Studio Two for all of twenty minutes. As soon as we read what Misty has done with the song – which she titled *Continuing Evolution* – we're psyched. Without a word to Richard, we pile into Rhyan's Expedition, and eight hours later, walk into Discovery Studios.

Willie has a full schedule, but we beg enough, that he agrees to let us work at night. Ariel explains to him that this record *has to be recorded here...* at Discovery Studios, and that *Willie Morgan has to engineer it*. Once he hears the first three rough songs, he understands.

On the day we plan to record *Continuing Evolution*, much to our surprise, we find Colbie Caillat sitting in the Morgan's kitchen, drinking coffee with Victoria. Poor Misty turns a shade of pale, that makes us think she may actually faint.

After some introductions and a pretty cool conversation, we excuse ourselves and tell Willie we'll be in the lower studio, when he has time to squeeze us in. He asks which songs we want to get down, and Misty says, "Just *Continuing Evolution* today."

Willie's eyes get big, a grin spreads across his face, and then, to our total surprise, Colbie has a comment.

"That's the ballad, isn't it?"

Six heads turn and look right at her.

"Guys! We're in the same business, remember?" she says, making Victoria crack up.

"It is... and it's freaking amazing," Willie says, his grin getting bigger.

"Well... fit them in right now. I want to hear this song..."

"You're giving us your time?" Vanessa blurts out.

"Sure! Vicki says it's easily a number one song, and I want to hear it." She pauses and sips her coffee, looking right at Misty the entire time.

It takes us close to three hours, but we finally get to the vocals. Misty is off the chart nervous, and we all know why. Being the amazingly astute woman she is, and realizing she's the problem, Colbie walks into the studio, and up to Misty, who is on a stool with a mic in front of her. She gives Willie the signal to cut the mic, then leans over and whispers something to Misty. Then she walks over, closes the door to the studio, and sits down on the floor with her back against the door. After a few seconds she closes her eyes.

Misty takes a couple of really deep breaths, closes her eyes, and after about fifteen seconds, raises her hand to tell Willie she's ready. Willie starts the music track, and we all stand watching as, once again, Misty Maitland unleashes herself...

Validation

Ariel Williams

We're once again, sitting around Richard's conference table. There are six people other than the band present – Patty Princeton, our favorite independent reporter, Dixon James, the one reporter who has always had a problem with us, but that Patty begged Misty to invite, Casey Hill, from Rolling Stone, and of course, Richard, Terri, and Ashleigh.

The reporters, thinking they are going to get to hear a couple of songs from the finished CD, are a bit stunned when Richard starts it at the beginning, and lets it play through. The three of them are scribbling on their notepads the entire time. Forty-five minutes later, they sit staring at us, with the strangest looks on their faces.

"You guys can have a copy, if you'd like," Richard says, a devious smirk on his face, as he slides them across the table.

Three heads go up and down in unison, as they each take one.

"*Drawn Home* goes to air Friday," Ashleigh says. "Three weeks later, *Just Because* follows it. The CD is on sale three weeks later."

Now, here's the comical part – as they pick up the copies of the CD, they all immediately tear off the shrink wrap, walk around the table, put the CDs down in front of Vanessa who is at the end, and with the cheesiest grins, all say *"Please?"* in unison.

It's the first time in six years that *reporters* have asked for autographs...

Guess that says something about the record.

The Press

Misty Maitland

It's my mother who calls, and in deep sobbing tears, tells me the reviews are out. We have no idea if they are good or bad, as I can't get Mom to stop crying. So naturally, we expect the worst. What we discover totally freaks us out... even our producer and our publicist. It's Terri who comes up with all the publications, and spreads them out on the Richard's desk...

...and, once again, Ransom shows us why they are superstars. This time it's taken them sixteen months, but the results are... well... I'll let their fans decide. This reporter will say that it's the most personal record she has ever seen a band put out. And... as do many of their fans, I sincerely hope that Misty Maitland never stops singing...

Patty Princeton
Independent Music Writer
For MOJO Magazine

Because she put it 'on the wire' Patty's story appears in the music section of at least four major newspapers as well.

Then we find…

> *…I walked into the break room, put the CD in the player, and punched the button for track number six. Four minutes and thirteen seconds later, there were eleven adults in tears. Thank you, Ransom. No matter what comes next in your Continuing Evolution, we know it will be beyond incredible.*
>
> *Casey Hill*
> *Rolling Stone Magazine*

…and even as we sit and stare in total disbelief, Ashleigh finds the one that will forever hold meaning for the six of us.

> *Most of my readers know what I've said about Ransom over the years. I now find myself in a position to take some of it back – because it's the right thing to do.*
>
> *Stuck-up? Not hardly. They are actually the most personable musicians I've met of late.*
>
> *Uncooperative? Yeah, they can be. But there are reasons, and I had the privilege of hearing eleven of them. It's all about the music for them – and everyone and everything else is non-relevant when they are creating. Including whiny reporters…*
>
> *Tears? Hell yes. Misty Maitland caused them…with nothing more than her voice. I'd compare her to her mentor, Emma Campbell, but honestly, that wouldn't be fair to either of them. All we can do, is hope that Misty will continue to share her voice, and her talent as a writer, for many more years.*

And yes, Continuing Evolution has converted me.

*I **am** a Ransom fan...*
Dixon James
Notes Magazine

The moment I finish reading, I burst full out into tears. I simply can't help it. First Vanessa hugs me, then Ariel, then the guys. It takes me a full five minutes to regain control of my emotions, and just about the time I do, Richard's fax machine jumps to life.

"Well crap..." he mumbles, as he steps over to it, and waits for it to finish what it's doing. Once it does, he picks up the page that comes out, breaks into laugher and hands the page to me.

'Congrats Guys!' it says in someone's handwriting, below which, are the signatures of the five most amazing people I have ever met.

Can this strange journey we are on, get any more insane?

"It's not fun anymore, Richard."

~Ariel Williams 

Another Tour

Joshua Miller

Headliners.

That's what we have officially become, although none of us is sure how we feel about it.

Thirty shows in nineteen weeks – twelve of which are outside the US. Suddenly, it's work.

We aren't sure how we feel about that either.

Richard makes us take an opening act – and they're actually pretty good. Once we get them past the whole star-struck thing, they're a blast to hang out with too.

When we play Pepsi Center, Stephen lets on that our mentors are back stage, watching. Misty wastes no time in getting them to come out and take a bow. Then... in her usual devious manner, she gets Emma to sing *hostage* in her place. The audience of course, loves it.

The highlight of the each show is performing *Continuing Evolution*. The song bares our souls, and tells the audience how we feel about our fame. *And...* hearing 15,000 voices singing the chorus...

On this extraordinary path
We're traveling together
With family and fans alike
Our lives are and will always be
One continuing evolution

...at each show, simply can't be explained with words.

As has become the rule, we play the last show in Wichita, once again to a sold out arena. We hang around for a couple of days, to do the necessary interviews, and once we're done, the six of us again disappear – back to Ransom. Thankfully, the press leaves us alone, and gives us some space.

One at a time, we each slow down, and absorb the idea of privacy – from the world, and from each other. After three months, we realize that the same questions are circulating in each of our minds...

Have we had enough of the fast lane?

Do we have any more to give?

Is Ransom done?

Richard and Terri (mostly Richard) get nervous when, one at a time, we each let our apartment leases go, pack our stuff, and send it back to Ransom. Rhyan is the last to go, and once that happens, Richard asks us to come and talk to him.

"So..." he says, looking as depressed as I've ever seen him.

"We're even with Lucky Guess, right?" Martin asks.

"Of course. The CD and the tour covered your contract," he replies, his voice almost cracking.

When no one says anything for a few seconds, it's Ariel who finally speaks for us.

"It's not fun anymore, Richard."

"We knew it would be work – would be a job," Vanessa adds, "but you have to like your job, to be good at it."

"We're going to let go of music for a while," Misty says, her eyes clouding up. "We're afraid it may be getting away from us."

"Yeah," Rhyan adds, "like Stanley said, 'the members make the band – you can't let the band make the members'."

"So, *Ransom* is done?"

"Not fair," Misty quickly replies.

"Yeah," Terri says, grinning, "she's right, it wasn't."

"You know how to find us, Richard. And you, of all people, should know that when we are ready again, this is where we will come," I offer, giving him a glare.

"Sorry guys… I'm just… well…"

"We get it – we're feeling the same things. But it's time…" Misty says.

"If we don't slow down, we will lose ourselves…" Vanessa adds.

"Let us go be us for a while…" comes from Martin.

"Fair enough," Richard says, standing up. "We're," he points at Terri, standing next to him, "here… even if you just want to talk."

"Good luck guys…" Terri says, as we all swap hugs.

Forty-five minutes, and a ton of tears later, we're sitting on a plane, waiting to go home.

It's the quietest flight we've ever been on…

Reflections

Misty Masterson

Fourteen months.

That's how long it takes us to come to terms with the fact that yes, perhaps *Ransom* really is done.

During this time, Martin and I get married, and manage to keep it a private thing. Although I've been writing, it isn't with any real enthusiasm. Something is missing...

Rhyan never set his drums up at his parents. He spends a lot of time in Fort Collins – for obvious reasons. His mind and heart are elsewhere now, and although he has played a bit while helping out Willie and Vicki at the studio, it hasn't been much.

Ariel and Josh have been traveling – a lot. I think that over the last year, they've only been home for two months. On their last couple of trips, Vanessa joined them. I think she is finally trying to live 'life after Chris'. In all honesty, I can't remember the last time I saw any of them with a guitar in hand.

Truth is, we're all busy finding ourselves, and finding ways to let go of the 'superstars' the world made us into.

This morning I called a band meeting – while our travelers are actually in town. Just before noon, everyone shows up at our house. We sit them down in the dining room and serve up lunch, which I hope will take the edge off what I'm about to suggest to them.

"We need to go tell them *Ransom is done* – we owe them that…" Then, as an afterthought, I add, "…unless you guys are ready to go back to it."

Silence. It's one of those eerie, strained silences. The kind no one wants to break…

"She's right," Vanessa finally says, between bites.

"Yeah… *as freakin' usual*…" Rhyan adds.

"Your responses are telling me that *Ransom* is in fact done. True or false?" I ask, making eye contact with each of them.

"I keep thinking back to the last tour…" Josh says.

Instantly, the others agree with him.

"But touring is only part of it, guys. What about the writing… the creating? Do any of you miss that?" I ask.

Again, a strange silence. But this time it's more like they're considering my question – which is what I think I was secretly hoping for.

"Okay…" I continue, "Our lives are on hold, and Friday we are going to Fort Collins to tell them we're done, and we're going to get on with our lives."

Although I can tell not a single one of them is convinced, everyone nods their agreement.

'This' I think quietly to myself, grinning, *'should be an interesting adventure. What, can 'music' throw into our path to complicate it, this time?'*

                                        Riley Morgan

Caught Up (again)

Ariel Williams

"Their cars are here," I say, pointing at the driveway.

"I hear voices," Rhyan says, going down the steps and around the end of the house.

When he doesn't reappear, we follow and find him standing next to a gate on the side of the house.

"HEY!" Vanessa yells, "Anyone home?"

"Pull the latch, it isn't locked!" Emma yells.

When the gate opens, and we see the five kids scattered across the grass, being the smartass he is, our drummer has a comment.

"Damn! You guys have replaced us?"

Stan and Emma start laughing, which of course makes us laugh. When after about fifteen seconds, Misty sees the bizarre looks on the kid's faces, she speaks up, directing her comment at them.

"He was kidding guys... honest."

"You're... well... you guys are..." a little blonde, who can't be more than five feet tall, pretty much forces herself to say.

Realizing what's happening, Misty laughs, walks over, and kneels on the grass, directly opposite her.

"Misty Maitland, at your service," she says, holding out her hand.

"*No freakin' way...*" the only guy mumbles, as he goes about as pale as a person can get.

"And," Stan interjects, relieving the tension of the moment, "why is *Ransom* in my backyard?"

After a second, Josh starts laughing. Then Rhyan. Then me. The other three girls on the grass with the blonde, put their hands over their mouths at the same time, as if trying to stifle outbursts. We watch as the first girl takes Misty's hand, shakes it, and says, "Sally – *major* fan".

Misty smiles, turns to the girl next to her and again holds out her hand.

"Patty..."

Misty moves on to the next kid.

"Melinda..."

When Misty gets to the skinny brunette next to Stanley, all the girl can seem to do is stare, and shake her hand. The lone guy, who is on the other side of Stan, says, "She's Randi – when she can talk." Then he extends his hand, which Misty takes. "Pete."

"Well," Misty says, "it's a pleasure." Then she turns and looks at us. "The guy with the big mouth is Rhyan – our drummer. The tall, cute guy is Josh – lead guitar. The ponytail belongs to Ariel – rhythm guitar. The rowdy looking one, with the braid is Vanessa – bass guitar. And the really cute geek in the back is my husband, Martin – keyboards."

When Randi suddenly starts crying, I quickly walk over and sit down next to her.

"Hey! Come on now…" I say, taking one of her hands. "We're trying to get away from the whole 'superstar' thing. Can you guys help us out?"

The five of them sit staring at me.

"You guys are musicians, right?"

Five heads go up and down a few times.

"So are we," I offer. Then I point at Emma and Stanley. "So are they. This isn't bands and fans. This," I make a big circle in the air to indicate all of us, "is a bunch of musicians, talking. Cool?"

As the kids make themselves nod again, my bandmates all find seats, and of course, Carson races over and climbs into my lap. For some reason, the child latches onto me every time he sees me.

"They got an invite to play at a festival," Emma says.

"Oh man!" Martin blurts out, "Seriously? Which one?"

Playing an outdoor festival is something we've always wanted to do, but have never been asked.

"The Garden Party – on the Isle of Man," Stan replies, with an interesting grin on his face.

"Wow! Totally cool festival. Martin and I went last year, just to watch," Misty offers.

"They had a thing called 'Undiscovered Talent'" Martin adds, grinning, "and the two bands were totally off the chart."

Stan laughs, and hands Martin a single sheet of paper.

"no way…" Martin mumbles, as his grin fades, and he becomes serious. He hands the page to Misty, then looks at Stanley, and says, "Maybe we have been replaced…"

"You guys must totally rock," Misty adds, now quite serious as well, "to get this invite. They're *very* selective about who they invite to this particular event…"

"Actually," Patty says, seeming to have relaxed, "we have no idea why we got it. We were talking to Mr. Campbell about it."

"And... there's no way we could go all the way to England anyhow," Melinda adds, looking a bit dejected.

"We're just a garage band, guys," Pete says. "How would a festival in England even know about us?"

"Where'd you play last?" I ask.

"A frat party at UC Boulder..." Randi offers. "About two weeks ago."

"Well, it's possible someone saw you, and told them. *Every* party has video at it..."

"Like Melinda said, there's no way we can get to England. Besides, we've never written a song – we just cover stuff."

Now... back to 'life and music' for just a moment. What, you ask, could 'music' possibly throw into 'life's' path, to side track our plans to give it all up? Well... as weird as it is, the moment Misty turns and looks at Joshua, I know *exactly* what the girl is thinking.

"Each band at the festival only plays three songs," Misty says. "How much time you got?"

The five kids again slip into a stunned silence. When they look at Stanley, he shrugs, points at Misty, and says, "She asked – not me."

"It's in seven weeks. How can we possibly write songs in seven weeks?" Sally asks, looking genuinely perplexed.

"Heck, how can we *learn* them in seven weeks?" Pete blurts out.

Realizing what's happening, I actually laugh. Although we might want to think we're done, and that we came here to tell our mentors we've had enough, this single moment proves we're full of it. When I glance at the others, I can see they too, get it.

"I bet we have a few songs we've never used," Vanessa offers, fighting off a laugh. "You guys want to 'borrow' them?"

"Wow…" Stanley says, handing the letter back to Pete. "Seems like you guys are going to have to step up, and decide just how badly you want to do this."

"Even if we come up with the songs…" Melinda starts to say a second time, and is instantly cut off by a *very* serious looking Emma.

"Oh… *no way*… you're not using *that* excuse." She reaches over, pulls Stan's phone out of his shirt pocket, and dials. The call is answered immediately. We only hear one side of the conversation.

"Vicki – it's Emma. One time offer – yes or no. Does the studio want to sponsor a band to attend The Garden Party in England?"

"Oh man…" Vanessa mumbles, looking right at the five most confused faces I've seen in forever, and fighting back the same laugh that Misty is. "You guys are *sooo* in it now…"

"In seven weeks…" Emma says, winking at me.

I lose it, and once I start laughing, Misty and Vanessa are right behind me.

"I dunno – let's ask them…" Emma pulls the phone away from her ear and looks at the kids.

"The owner of Discovery Studios wants to know if you guys will be ready, should they decide to sponsor your trip to the festival…"

As the five of them look at each other, I turn and look at Misty and Josh, and the second we make eye contact, I know we're all thinking the same thing. I smile, nod at them, and almost in unison, the two of them pretty much yell, *"They most certainly will be!"*

As strange a moment as it is, the six of us realize *we just adopted a band*. Even as I am lost in the moment, I again hear Emma's voice.

"Are you guys willing to put your entire lives on hold for at least a month, just to play a festival? Is it *that* important to the five of you?"

Four of them turn simultaneously to look at Sally.

"It's *finals week*, guys..." she says, looking a bit pathetic.

"You have a 3.9 GPA, Sally," Stanley says, fighting off a laugh, "and I can assure you CSU will still be here when you get back. I'm thinking I can pull some strings, and get them to let all of you take your finals after the fact, if necessary."

Suddenly, our ever-quiet drummer has a comment...

"This is a chance for you, guys – an important chance," he says, staring the five of them. "You don't have to do it. If you are happy with the part music plays in your lives right now, don't mess with it. But... if you feel there's something more out there for you to discover, *don't hesitate*. You know we were with these guys," he points at Stanley and Emma, "on their last tour. Of all the stuff – good and bad – that we learned from them over those three months, there's a single thing that will always outweigh all the rest. If you take this step, remember this..."

He pauses, looks at me, I see his eyes cloud up, and I know exactly what he wants to hear. When I glance at Josh, he knows too.

"*It is...*" Josh and I say together.

"*And always has to be...*" Vanessa and Martin chime in.

"*All about the music...*" Misty and Rhyan finish.

I watch as Emma pushes some buttons on her phone, and then says, "They can hear you."

"Go home and talk to your parents," Vicki says, "and whoever else you need to. If you decide to do this, be absolutely certain about it. It isn't going to be easy. There will be a charter at Municipal at 9:00 AM tomorrow, and it will bring all of you here..."

"Which aircraft are you using, Vic?" Stanley asks.

"Why?" she asks.

"There are eleven of them..." Emma says, fighting a laugh.

"Wow... pretty big band," she replies.

"*Ransom* is babysitting them," Emma forces out, as she loses the battle with her laughter. In a matter of seconds, we're all laughing.

"Can't go wrong with help like that. We'll figure out something. Maybe Devin can fly the big plane..."

"We'll get there on our own, Vicki – just don't forget us at the airport," Misty says.

"That works. Text me your flight info. The rest of you are bringing your clothes, and your toothbrushes – nothing else. If the five of you *really* want to make a statement, Discovery Studios is in – with both feet. See all of you tomorrow."

Without waiting for a response, Vicki disconnects the call, and Emma closes the phone.

"So..." Stan says, grinning like the Cheshire cat, and staring at the five kids. "What are you going to do now...?"

I look at Josh, who is so totally trying to fight off a laugh, and then at Rhyan, who quickly does his 'adjusting the halo' thing. Even as Vanessa and Misty start laughing, I lean over and hug them.

In a matter of twenty minutes, 'music' won. 'Life' is once again on a back burner. We came to call it quits, and bail, and music simply won't let us. It lives inside each of us, and now it's giving us a chance to pass it on.

Time to quit fighting it, and just go with the flow, right?

New... And Old

Rhyan Crossman

"OH MY GOSH!" Bailey screams, as she tears across the lobby, and jumps on me, forcing me to catch her. While I was a bit embarrassed when it was a seven year old who had a crush on me, now that she's nine and still freaks out every time she sees me, I'm actually kind of honored.

"You guys got an invite to the Garden Party?" Willie blurts out, the moment he sees the members of *Saturday Afternoon* – which we discovered is their band name.

"Willie Morgan!" Victoria says, slugging him, and making everyone laugh.

"Ouch! Hey... I didn't mean it like..."

"It's okay, Mr. Morgan," Patty says, with a silly grin, "we don't get it either..."

Victoria walks over and hugs Sally.

"Long time since that afternoon on the stage, huh?"

"Yes ma'am," she replies, smiling.

Victoria points at the six of us, and says, "You guys take a hike. I need a moment with these five."

Grinning, we file out the door, and onto the back deck, with Bailey hot on our heels.

Less than thirty minutes later, Willie appears, and finds me giving Bailey a piggyback ride. The look on his face tells me he intends to mess with me.

"I'm telling your girlfriend about this…" he calmly says.

"Oh please, Dad," Bailey blurts out, as she slides to the deck. "Aunt Georgia knows I have a crush on her boyfriend…"

The six of us crack up.

"Vic needs you guys, in the studio. And for the record, what you are doing is absolutely phenomenal."

As Misty passes him, headed for the studio, she stops, kisses him on the cheek, and says, "Like how phenomenal a certain pop band was…?"

Then, out of nowhere, Bailey has yet another comical comment.

"I'm sooo telling Mom other girls are kissing you!"

As I follow my bandmates (yeah, no matter what we think, we are in fact still a band) toward the studio, I realize that what we thought was an ending, has turned itself into beginning. *Music* is once again controlling our path.

And personally, I'm totally cool with that…

Controlling Interest

Misty Masterson

We've been sitting on the deck, working on sheet music, and letting *Saturday Afternoon* work on their 'songs' by themselves.

They've actually done really well so far, considering how hard we've been pressing them. Josh even compared them to us, when Willie and Emily brought us here, all those years ago.

Watching Bailey and Rhyan is almost magical. They're both drummers – and over the years, Willie's daughter has become quite the talent. I happen to be looking at them, when Bailey says she's going inside for something, then disappears through the door.

"Have you heard her actually play?" I ask Rhyan.

"Heck yeah! She's better than I was at her age…"

"Well…" Ariel says, giggling, "Look who's teaching her."

Even as we're laughing, the door opens again, and standing there holding Riley – Bailey's younger sister – is none other than Emma Campbell. Right behind her is a smiling Bailey.

After we stare at her, in stunned silence and confusion, for a few seconds, she puts Riley down and takes a seat next to me. Riley is quick to squeeze in between us. Bailey continues to stand in the open doorway.

"How's it going so far?" she asks, almost in a whisper.

When no one says anything, she laughs.

"Hellooo?"

"Oh… uh… not bad," Ariel finally offers.

"They're actually really good musicians," Josh adds.

"Here," she says, handing each of us one of the pages she's holding. "Opinions?"

We sit quietly reading, for about thirty seconds, and Josh is the first to comment.

"I need a guitar…" he says, standing up.

"Me too…" Ariel adds, jumping up herself. "And we'll need you too, Rhyan…"

As Rhyan, who is sitting next to me, stands up, all I can seem to do is mumble 'amazing' without looking away from the page in my hands. When Josh and Ariel reach the door, Emma stops them.

"Hey… you guys remember when it was your turn, right?"

"Yes ma'am," they each reply.

"The songs you gave them, they can learn. But this one…" she taps on the page in my hands, "This one they have to create. Help them, but don't do it for them. If it's going to come from their hearts when they perform it…"

I interrupt her midsentence.

"…they have to own the song," I offer, turning to look at her, with a big smile on my face.

"Exactly!" she replies, also grinning. "So… any comments on the lyrics?"

Ariel and Josh glance at each other, then at Rhyan – who does nothing more than shrug – and then at me. Somehow, I know what they want me to say.

"The few bars you have at the top tell us you wrote it pretty much as a ballad, but having heard them play, I'm betting they," I turn and glance at Ariel and Josh, "think it needs to be a bit faster..."

When Emma does nothing more than grin at us, I get a strange rush and wonder what she is thinking.

"And you?" she asks, looking me right in the eyes.

"I gotta agree, with them. Although Sally's voice will easily carry any ballad, for what they're about to do, a ballad just isn't going to work..."

"If they're going to get to this particular crowd, they gotta rock, Emma..." Josh finishes for me.

"Well, get to it then. I'll come listen in a bit."

"Huh?" Ariel blurts out.

"There's something else going on here guys, something I'm not in a position to talk to about. What I'm hoping is that with your help, I can fix a couple of things, all at once."

Suddenly, the one person standing quietly, and listening to every word, has something to say. Bailey walks over, and stops in front of Emma.

"Even if it doesn't work, Aunt Emma, thanks for trying..."

Emma leans forward, hugs her, and picks up Riley.

"You guys," she says, pointing at Josh, Ariel, and Rhyan, and at the same time, putting a hand on my knee, "get to work – and you didn't get those," she points at the pages we're holding, "from me. Bailey, go tell your mom to meet me in the booth."

"Yes ma'am," we all – Bailey included – say at once, which is, in its own way, a bit comical.

Within minutes, the three of them – with a little help from me – are establishing a tempo for what is going to be *Saturday Afternoon's* very first song.

Full Ownership

Misty Masterson

Watching them day after day is an experience all by itself. I honestly believe they're even more driven than we were, our first time here.

They get going, and roll along for a bit, then something comes up, and slows them down. They try to work it out, and when it seems they're lost, Josh or Ariel scribbles something for one of them, and the kid runs with it. I sat silently watching as Melinda was intently trying to get her solo correct, and just about the time I *thought* she was getting frustrated, across the room, Josh played *four chords*. The second their eyes met – well… you should have been there. Josh laughed, winked at me, and then got up and went out the door. Ten minutes later, Mindy had her solo on paper, and was working through it on her guitar. When she finally played it all the way through, I got goose bumps…

They – the five of them – *will* own this song, just like we have always owned *hostage*…

Three weeks in, they're ready to try it. Willie is nowhere to be found, so Rhyan and Josh man the booth, while Pete and the girls give it a shot. Although they manage a complete play-through, it's kind of weak. After a second try, they decide to work on it a bit more. When they play the two songs we gave them, the six of us are astounded, and we get them to play both a second time – for their sponsors. Vicki and Willie are all smiles.

Then, about two hours later, it happens.

Out of the blue.

No warning.

I'm sitting in the kitchen talking to Vanessa and Ariel. Martin is just outside the door, at the bottom of the stairs, and as he turns to go up them, the entire house is filled with music. Even as we are standing up, Martin mumbles *"no freakin' way…"* and disappears up the stairs. The three of us are right on his heels. The moment the vocals start, and Sally's astonishingly perfect voice fills the air, every hair on my body stands up…

By the time we make it to the studio, they are through the first chorus and are into the second stanza. As we approach the door to the studio, the door next to us flies open, an arm comes out, and Rhyan jerks me into the booth. The others are quick to follow.

The first thing I notice is that although the blinds are closed, the board is lined up, and is recording.

"They changed something…" Vanessa whispers.

"Yeah…" Josh adds, "But what?"

We stand listening in stunned silence for another thirty seconds, before our drummer figures it out.

"Damn! *It's Patty!* Listen to the percussion!" Rhyan blurts out, following it with a laugh.

"It's… I mean *she* is faster… but…" Martin offers.

"She's playing with *both feet* guys!! She's got a second bass drum! How totally freakin' ingenious!" comes from *our* drummer, as he pulls the chord and lifts the blinds, letting us see into the studio.

Sure enough... Patty now has two bass drums side by side, and her sparkly high-top sneakers are pumping away on the pedals.

I laugh and say, "Tell me they don't own this song..." then I turn and open the booth door. "Follow me..." I add, as I step into the hall and turn toward the door leading onto the deck.

The moment I open it, Pete and the girls fill the air. First, Emma, then Willie, and finally, Vicki all spin around on the grass and look in our direction. I walk over and stop at the railing, and just smile at them. My timing is perfect when the second chorus...

Each time we do it...
It's all about the music...
Each time we live it...
We live it for the music...
Each time we give it...
It's always for you...

...comes blasting out, as Sally and Randi belt out the vocals.

Then, as my bandmates file out onto the deck behind me, Miss Melinda Kelly cuts loose in a fashion that makes even Josh turn to look. Once the insane lead guitar riff is over, they settle in and finish the song. Sure, it still needs some work, but five kids who have never written anything, have managed to create, and play, *their* song, start to finish.

And it's incredible...

As I stand watching Emma, Willie, Vicki, and the girls come up the stairs, I realize that I'm not even close to being finished with music.

I'm pretty sure that music isn't even close to being finished with us, either...

Total Collapse

Martin Masterson

"Three days ago, I would have sworn they were ready..." Willie says.

Emily, who arrived unannounced, early this morning, is staring out the kitchen window.

"And," Willie adds, "none of them will tell me what the hell is going on."

"How's their last song coming?" Emily asks, without looking away from the window.

"They're *really* close. Another day of practice, and they would have had it. Now," Misty pauses, and points out the window at the five of members of *Saturday Afternoon* sitting together on the grass, staring at the lake, "this is all we get. I swear... I just don't get it. And, just like Willie said, none of them are talking."

"After you and I talked Monday," Willie says to Emily, who continues to stare out the window, "I thought it was just stress – which is why I made them take yesterday off. They did pretty much nothing, all day. They slept a lot, and

Sally wandered off somewhere by herself for about two hours, but not a single one of them did anything musical."

"When they sat down for dinner last night," Vicki adds, "this is what we got. For some reason, they seem completely disinterested – which I'm not buying…"

"Me either!" Misty blurts out, in the middle of Vicki's sentence.

"Emma tried talking to them," Vicki continues, "but they were pretty much the same way with her. We talked, and she felt pressing them would serve no purpose. I took her and Stanley to the airport late last night. Emma said that if, in some fashion she can help, she'll come back – no questions. Stanley is seriously bummed, but not knowing what the problem is, he felt he shouldn't press them either."

"Honestly, Em… I'm out of ideas," Willie adds, following it with a deep sigh.

Emily finally turns around, looks at me, then at Josh and the others. They immediately shrug, indicating they have no clue what has caused our newest band, to fall into a silent oblivion.

"Have you guys done what you can – as far as the music is concerned?" Emily asks.

"We honestly think so, Emily. I'd just really like to know *what is going on,*" Josh says, shaking his head. The rest of us mumble our agreement to his comment.

"I'm telling you," Ariel says, with so much force and conviction, it makes Emily smile, "they *can* do this. I'm pretty sure they'll wreck the place, with little or no effort…"

"Well, you guys may as well get back to your lives. Thanks – from the heart – for stepping up."

"In a heartbeat, Emily. Every time…" I offer, smiling, and then hugging her.

"Come on," Vicki says, "I'll take you guys to the airport."

The ride to the airport is quiet – mostly because we're all totally confused. The fact our first attempt at mentoring seems to have completely collapsed, is wearing on Vanessa. She sits listening to *Saturday Afternoon's* three songs over and over on her iPod, every so often mumbling 'damn it' and shaking her head.

Vicki decides to send us home on their charter, but we insist on paying half the costs – it isn't like we can't afford it. The flight is very subdued – mostly because each of us knows that our previous decision to give up recording and performing really isn't an option. We just spent five weeks proving that...

"How come you didn't tell them?" Vanessa asks, with a cute little smirk on her face, as she gently pokes Misty in the ribs.

"*Me?*" Misty retorts, fighting off a laugh. "Why didn't *you?*"

"I cancelled our flight to Italy," Josh says, directing the comment at Ariel.

"Probably for the best..." she replies.

"So..." Misty offers, closing her notebook, "what are we doing then?"

"We?" I ask, glancing at Rhyan.

"You are all such pains in the ass! I swear!" Misty blurts out, sounding totally exasperated, which of course, cracks everyone up.

What none of us realizes is that music is about to take over our lives again, and the next three weeks are going to define the path *Ransom* will travel for the next few years.

Spur Of The Moment

Misty Masterson

"Seriously? What was wrong?"

We (the six of us) are sitting in my mom's dining room, listening to Ariel – who is wound tighter than a clock spring – talking to Vicki. It's been three days since our 'band' faded away on us, and since we've been home, it's all we can seem to talk about.

"Catrin? Cadi *did it?* Totally amazing. Uh-huh. When? Cool. Yeah, we can, but don't tell them, okay? You rock, Vicki! Talk to you soon. Bye."

She spins around, and is so excited, we all expect she very well may pop at any moment.

"Misty," she says, looking at me, "book a flight to England, and get out your passport. We're going to a concert!"

"No way!" Rhyan blurts out. "They're going after all?"

"Yeah," Ariel replies, "Cadi somehow managed to find the problem *and* fix it – and she did it in like thirty minutes. Vicki says Cadi turned up, got in everyone's – meaning our band – face, and after fifteen minutes alone with Sally, everything was hunky dory. She also said it was so weird, that if she hadn't seen it, she wouldn't have believed it…"

I immediately notice her use of *'our band'*, which makes me grin like a fool.

"And *we're* going?" I ask.

"Uh-huh. Vicki says *Audio Distortion* is going to be there when *Saturday Afternoon* performs, and she needs our help to set up them up…"

"Set *who* up?" Vanessa blurts out.

The devious smirk on Ariel's face, more than answers Vanessa's question.

"She gave me the name of the guy we need to find when we get there," Ariel says, waving a piece of paper at me.

"What about…" I start to say.

"Never mind us," Josh says. "I told Carl I'd help out at the shop until he hires someone."

"And I'm going to be helping the new music teacher at the school," Martin adds, grinning.

"Besides," Vanessa says, poking me in the ribs, "you know it wouldn't be fair to the other bands playing if our band *and Audio Distortion* turned up. Let them all have their day."

"My only excuse is that I'm sick of flying…" Rhyan says, laughing.

I glance at Ariel, who laughs, then at Martin, who leans over and kisses me.

"Heck! Let's go to the Garden Party!"

'Extraordinary' isn't even close to explaining what Ariel and I are about to experience.

"I was beginning to think we might need a lawyer."

~ Ariel Williams 

It's The Cops

Ariel Williams

Our first shock is a British Airways agent waiting for us just inside the terminal at Heathrow. Once she verifies who we are, she takes us on a winding route through the airport, eventually going down some stairs and ending up on the tarmac at the southern end of the airport. There we find a smiling guy standing next to a helicopter with its engine running. He introduces himself, and explains he's been sent to take us to the Isle of Man.

Not knowing what else to do, we climb aboard.

The second shock is the cop waiting for us on the helipad at the airport in Castletown.

"HI!" he yells over the noise of the helicopter, "Jameson Parks. Welcome to the Isle of Man."

He leads us to his car – a police car no less – puts us in the back, and climbs in behind the wheel. In seconds we are moving through a gate and out onto city streets.

"I've booked rooms at the Glen Helen Inn, in St. Johns. It's considerably closer to the festival site, is quite nice, and you will be able to avoid the crowds that will be at most of the big hotels."

"So… you *are* the 'Jimmy' we're supposed to meet?" Misty asks, making him laugh.

"Most definitely."

"Thanks goodness," I say, following it with a sigh, "I was beginning to think we might need a lawyer."

Again he laughs – a deep, friendly kind of laugh.

"You mean no one told you I'm the Constable?"

"No sir. Vicki said 'Jimmy' – who is one of the festival's organizers – would be meeting us."

"That would be me. My Sergeant – Ted – is my associate in the music business. He is going to be meeting us at the inn, and once you are settled, we thought we might take you two to dinner, and explain our plan…"

Misty totally cracks up, and for the first time since being at Discovery Studios, seems completely relaxed.

"Rock and roll cops! How come we don't have any of those back home, Misty?"

"Dinner sounds great," Misty says, "and I can hardly wait to hear how much trouble we are going to get into with this plan of yours…"

Sneaking Around

Ariel Williams

The festival is amazing! I'm jealous that we've never been asked to play one. There are about 2500 fans here, but the *atmosphere* – not the size of the crowd – makes it electric.

We're sitting on the grass, about fifty yards from the stage, in the middle of the throng. Here's the interesting thing. While I do get recognized from time to time, everyone on the planet recognizes Misty the second they see her, especially when she has her hair in pigtails.

Yet, not a single one of the people around us says a word, until we do. Turns out they do recognize us – but understand that we're fans today, not famous. The cool thing is, we make a number of new *friends* – even exchanging email addresses with a few.

The two opening acts and the two headlining bands are all excellent. I even have a couple of CD's by the headliners. Now, as the sun begins to set, it's time for what we came to see.

Undiscovered Talent...

As they light the entire site and the stage as well, we watch Ted, mic in hand, as he goes center stage to announce the first band.

Ladies and Gentleman...
Boys and Girls...
Dogs and Cats...

You can tell the audience is psyched for this, by their response to the intro. *This* is what a lot of them came to see...

Every year since our inception, we've
managed to bring you some new and
amazing, Undiscovered Talent! This
year is no different. In fact we believe
we've outdone ourselves this time...

The crowd again gets loud.

The Garden Party is pleased, and proud to
present, this year's Undiscovered Talent!
The first band comes to us from
Birmingham, England. Give a warm
Garden Party welcome to, Terminus G!

As the crowd breaks into energetic applause, four kids take the stage. It's evident they're nervous, but they take full advantage of their chance to shine.

Once they finish their set, they take a bow and head off stage, far more confident than they'd been thirty minutes before. The crowd's response is so positive that Jimmy sends them back out for a second bow – which is totally cool.

As the stage lights go down, we see the silhouettes of *our band* as they take the stage.

"I'm not watching this from way back here," Misty says, putting her stage pass around her neck. "Come on, Ariel..."

She's up and headed for the stage even before I can respond. I pull out my pass, and as I am putting it around my neck, I lean over and speak to the couple next us.

"Pay close attention – this next band is going to totally destroy the place…"

I'm up and following Misty before they can say anything. About halfway to the stage, we hear Catrin's voice…

*Our second Undiscovered Talent comes
to us all the way from Fort Collins,
Colorado. The moment we saw their video,
we knew you needed to see them. The
Garden Party is pleased, and proud to
present, on their first trip to the United
Kingdom, Saturday Afternoon!
Let's make them feel welcome!*

The Brits go completely nuts, and it gets so loud I have to put my fingers in my ears, as I weave my way through people. We're just short of the stage entrance, when a single spotlight lands on Sally.

"Hey United Kingdom!" she screams, which amps the crowd even more.

Once the applause dies down, much to our surprise, shy, timid, Sally Wright actually works the crowd a bit. I tug on Misty's sleeve to get her to stop, so we can watch.

"We're going to tell you guys, up front, we had a lot of help getting here. Eight weeks ago, I was sitting in an advanced calculus class, when our keyboardist texted me, to say we'd been invited to play here. Since then, it's been non-stop crazy. Anyhow, they gave us thirty-five minutes to put smiles on your faces, and get you tapping your feet, so let's see if we can pull that off!"

She turns and looks at Melinda, who is laughing her head off, and gets 'thumbs up'. She turns back to the crowd and yells, *"You guys ready?"*

The second the crowds start screaming, they go to work.

They play their first song – one we had already written – and the crowd's response brings all the girls to tears. Once the crowd stops to breathe, Sally introduces *their* song...

"Okay... so, this next song is going to pick up the pace. The awesome woman, who wrote it, is an amazing song writer, but she wrote it as a ballad. With the help of some other kick-butt musicians – *you guys know who you are! –* we managed to turn it into *our* song! We've decided to title it, *'All About The Music'*, and we hope it touches all of you."

The moment she quits talking, the spotlight on her moves to Melinda, and she jumps into the screaming lead intro, and within seconds, they have a thousand people fist-pumping in the air, to the rhythm. Then, Sally's amazing voice fills the cool evening.

They tear through (it's really fast) the song, and everyone in the crowd gets totally lost in it. By the second chorus, some of them have picked up the lyrics, and are singing along. By the third chorus, *everyone* is singing...

When they reach the end, the lights on the stage dim, Pete slows the tempo way down, and the other three stop all together. Sally takes a deep breath, and the moment the spotlight hits her, she sings the last chorus, in perfect pitch, and pretty much 'a cappella', followed by a few closing notes from Pete keyboard...

> *Each time we do it...*
> *It's all about the music...*
> *Each time we live it...*
> *We live it for the music...*
> *Each time we give it...*
> *It's always for you...*

When the stage goes dark, the applause that follows is so thunderous, you'd think the kids are the festival's main act...

Fun With The Producer

Misty Masterson

We're standing close enough that we can see Jimmy and Cadi, standing at the top of the stage stairs – and Cadi is in tears. Pete and the girls have done exactly what Ariel said they would – they totally wreck the place! Five kids, no one has ever heard of, just gave a performance that easily rivals any of ours, and it was incredible. I have goose bumps on pretty much all of my body.

Once the crowd calms down, and the applause dies out, Sally once again turns on her mic.

"Okay, so… were there any feet tapping out there?"

Even at fifty feet from the stage, I can clearly see all the tears streaming down her face, under the stage lights, but the girl keeps it totally together.

"Anyhow, we have another song we're supposed to play. But, if you guys don't mind, we want to cover an old song, instead."

The crowd screams and whistles their approval, and its apparent Cadi is trying to figure out what they are up to.

Nothing like changing the playlist, to screw with the show's producer.

While the kids are getting ready, Jimmy turns and says something to Cadi, as Ted, who has managed to sneak up behind her, wraps his arms around her, and in the middle of a sentence, lifts her off the stage. *Everyone* who sees it, cracks up, and once Ted puts her down, a laughing Jimmy kisses her smack on the lips.

"Come on… let's get back stage – we have a set-up to make happen," I say, tugging on Ariel's shirt.

"You think it's going to work?"

"Oh heck yeah!"

We get past the security guy, and I briefly make eye contact with Jimmy, who gives me a covert nod. As we wander around backstage, looking for two specific cases, things on the stage again heat up.

"So, this song was written by our high school music teacher," we hear Sally say, "and some of his friends, way back when. It even made it to number three on Billboard," she continues, "the year it came out, and I'll bet most of you will recognize it. The reason we want to play it tonight is, even as old as the song is, it speaks for *every undiscovered talent around the world*. The bands that will never be famous, but keep playing, *just because we love music…*"

Most of the crowd is now pressed up against the barriers in front of stage, and it seems that every single one of them has a video camera or phone recording. Remembering how fast we spread online, I'm pretty certain that by tomorrow morning, *Saturday Afternoon* will probably own the internet…

Then, Ariel and I find ourselves pretty much freaked out… by an intro we instantly recognize, four lines of lyrics, and Sally's amazingly powerful voice…

On a quiet night
I was cleaning tables
Watching the band
Knowing they're able

...and within seconds, the night air is filled with the sound of a thousand pairs of hands, clapping in time to the music. It's so amazing, that for a moment, Ariel and I forget we're supposed to be 'hiding', and we wander out where we can see.

By the third line of the song, *everyone* is singing along, and even with her mic, you can hardly hear Sally. When, they reach the first chorus, there are two thousand beautiful voices, all singing in unison...

We're here!
Under the lights
Hoping we'll get noticed...

And yeah... we both burst into tears...

Music... is just so amazing.

The Set Up

Misty Masterson

When Emma, Emily, Stanley and Willie make it through the security gate, and go up the stage stairs, and never even notice us, Ariel laughs and high-fives me. I still can't believe that Vicki would set them up like this.

For the first time since they played *We Are* at Red Rocks, *Audio Distortion* is about to play again. Ariel and I are going to help put them on the spot – and get a little retribution at the same time.

Even as they are swapping hugs with Sally and the others, Ted signals us. First *Saturday Afternoon* comes down the stairs to the continued screaming of the crowd, and then our mentors follow. When Emily reaches the bottom of the stairs, she sees me holding her Ibanez, and next to me, Ariel holding Cadi's Taylor. She stops so suddenly, Cadi runs into her from behind. Then, Stanley and Emma see us – and true to who they are, both crack up laughing.

"Here," I say, even before the shock of our presence sinks in, as I hand Emily her guitar, while at the same time, Ariel hands Cadi the Taylor.

"You're going to need those…" Ariel adds, following the comment with a devious little smirk.

"Hey Garden Partiers! Has this been an amazing afternoon or what?" suddenly blasts from the speaker stacks, making all of us jump.

The place again erupts, even as people are gathering their things to leave.

"While that was technically, the last act of the night," Ted says, a single spotlight hitting him front above, as he walks to the front of the stage, "Jimmy and I have decided to try to pull off the impossible…"

The very moment he says it, Emma figures it out. When she glances at me, the amazing twinkle in her eyes, and the big silly grin on her face, make my heart soar. Then, Jimmy appears at the top of the stairs, mic in hand, grinning like a criminal, and is immediately hit by a spotlight.

"Everyone here knows what group originally recorded the last song…"

The very instant the words leave his mouth, my brain clicks, and I understand! Pete and the girls changed their last song on purpose! *They're part of the set up too!*

"…and believe it or not," Jimmy continues, "for the first time, in a very long time, all five of them are together at the same time – right here, *at our festival!"*

The entire crowd goes so quiet, I swear, you can hear the crickets in the grass. Every single head is once again, facing the stage.

"Oh man! No way!" Stanley blurts out, still laughing.

Emma, staring right at me, mumbles, "Oh, dear husband, but there is a way…"

"So, as a bonus," Jimmy continues, "to what has already been an unbelievably amazing night…" he walks down the stairs, and stops right in front of Emma, "how about we talk the amazing *Audio Distortion,* into sending this crowd home with something to talk about for years…"

The moment he quits talking, the lighting guys hit the five of them with a spotlight. Then, as they're standing there, staring at each other in a completely goofy manner, I make my final comment…

"Right about now!"

When the four of them immediately look at Cadi, her eyes are full of tears, and she quickly tries to defend herself.

"I had nothing to do with this! I swear!"

Everyone immediately looks at Ariel and me.

We crack up laughing, and at the same time, yell, *"Vicki!"*

"I may have to strangle my wife…" Willie mumbles, as he glances at Emily.

Emily laughs, and looks at Emma, who also laughs, and looks at Stan who, still laughing, shrugs and looks at Willie, who does nothing more than shake his head, and laugh.

"What the heck, guys?" Willie offers.

Then… *still staring directly at me,* Emma sticks her arms out in front of her, and I – *as well as everyone else* – know we have them.

Emma just started the STAR…

Everyone watches as Emily, her guitar pushed around behind her back, steps up next to Emma, a huge grin on her face, and extends her arms as well. Stanley steps into the circle and takes Emma's left hand with his right, and Emily's right, with his left. In seconds, Willie joins them, and with a laugh, takes Emma's right hand in his left. Then, when she doesn't immediately move, they all turn and look at Cadi, who is full on crying at this point.

"Well?" Willie blurts out, making most of the stage crew crack up.

Cadi, tears trickling down her cheeks and a huge smile on her face, lets Jimmy take her Taylor, then immediately steps over and puts her left hand into Willie's right, then takes Emily's left hand with her right – completing the five-point star. The five of them close their eyes, take deep breaths, and scream (so loudly it hurts my ears) ***"TURN IT UP!"*** in unison.

In a single heartbeat, the five of them become their alter egos – *they are Audio Distortion.*

No matter how many times I see them do it, it still totally amazes me…

Every *AD* fans know about it, so the very moment they yell, the crowd is totally off the hook, realizing that yes, *they're actually going to play!* I'm certain they are making more noise than any crowd ten times their size. It's totally and completely incredible… and I can't stop crying.

Then it starts. Somewhere way back in the crowd. Softly at first…

'cra-zy, cra-zy, cra-zy'

Then it gets progressively louder…

'Cra-zy, Cra-zy'

By the time it makes to the front of the stage, you can actually feel it…

'CRA-ZY, CRA-ZY, **CRA-ZY, CRA-ZY'**

The lighting guys immediately bring up all the stage lights, and even the stage crew starts chanting with the crowd. Emily, once again laughing, pulls the strap over her head, and hands the acoustic guitar back to me.

"We're gonna need different equipment for the song they want to hear," she says, looking at Jimmy.

"Here," a female voice behind me says. When I take a step to the side, there stands Melinda, holding out her well-used Gibson Firebird to Emily. Just as quickly, Randi offers her Fender Deluxe to Cadi.

"The rest of our stuff is still on stage," Patty quickly adds, looking at Stan and Willie.

Emma shrugs, takes the mic from Jimmy, and says, "Come on guys…"

The moment they head up the stairs, Ariel and I rush over and jump the barricade so we can get right up front. Within seconds, we feel someone pushing into us from behind, and turn to find Ted and Emily's husband, Leonard. The moment they are close enough, Bailey and Melissa go up on their shoulders.

"You people… *all of you,*" Emma says to the crowd, "are totally incredible. From the bottom of our hearts, thank you!"

Even as they go about tuning up and getting ready, we – and everyone within 100 feet of the stage for that matter – hear what has to be the greatest compliment any musician has ever received…

A youthful female voice, with a *deep* British accent, screams, *"My mum's the lead guitarist!"* which is immediately followed by a bubbly, little-kid voice, screaming, *"And my dad's the drummer!"*

So… is it possible to over-use the word *'amazing'*?

Confessions

Ariel Williams

It's such a beautiful day, Misty and I decide to walk the three and a half miles from the inn to the festival site. It takes us about an hour and a half to make the walk, and I'm pretty certain that every single person we pass speaks to us.

When we arrive at the site, with the exception of the stage, it's almost impossible to tell there was a concert the night before. All the trash is gone, all the lights are packed away, and there is a huge crew hurriedly disassembling the stage. It's no wonder the locals support the festival so enthusiastically.

Halfway to the stage area, we see Emma, sitting on the grass, and next to her is Nick Sharpe – Cadi's husband.

"damn," I mumble, looking at Misty. "With what has been going on, do you think it would a good idea to interrupt them?"

"Not much choice – unless of course, we *aren't* going to tell her."

"Yeah, Jimmy said we had twenty minutes…"

"Come on…" Misty says, heading toward Emma, with me right behind her.

"Hey, Emma!" Misty calls out.

She and Nick spin around and face us.

"Good morning, ladies," Nick says, smiling at us.

"Hi guys!" comes from Emma.

"We're going to the airport – Jimmy got us a helicopter ride to Birmingham. We're flying home from there," Misty says.

"Heck, I was totally surprised you even turned up," Emma replies.

"I told you… didn't I?" I blurt out arbitrarily, giving Emma a 'look'.

She breaks up laughing, knowing exactly what I mean.

"Yes, Ariel, you certainly did!"

"Can we talk to you for a minute, before we go?" Misty asks.

When I glance at Nick, Emma catches on.

"Mr. Sharpe…" she says, in a joking manner.

"Yeah, yeah… run the guy off… I get it," he replies, laughing and getting up. "I'll say bye before I leave…"

"Before *you and your wife* leave…" Emma retorts, making him laugh again.

As he heads down toward the stage, Misty and I sit down.

"We need to tell you something," I offer, "and we want you to hear it from us – face to face."

"It's what we came to tell you at the house, before all this," Misty waves her hand, indicating the festival, "started."

"But, well, we're not sure what it means anymore," I add.

"Okay... so tell."

"We think we're done..." Misty says.

"Seriously?" Emma blurts out, grinning.

"Well," I quickly add, "after eight years, three CDs, and three tours, we're sorta losing interest... if that makes sense."

"We need to try and figure out our real lives... not that making music isn't 'real'. We want to see if maybe, we can be... well... normal," Misty adds.

"Oh how totally cool!"

"That's it?" I blurt out, confused by her response.

"So what? You expected me to try to talk you out of it?"

"Well..." Misty mumbles, also looking confused.

"How many times has *AD* faded away over the years?"

With just a single question, she makes us instantly understand.

"Look... when the six of you tell the world – tell them you're 'taking a break'. *Do not* say 'quit'."

When our confusion spills over on to our faces, Emma cracks up.

"When *we* did that," Emma continues, "right after the *Journeys End* tour – we almost messed up. A lot of our fans were both crushed and angry..."

She lets us process for a moment, and then continues.

"*AD* got really lucky. Don't make our mistake guys – *don't alienate your fans*. When you talk to the press, tell them this break is about finding yourselves – not that 'you're done'. Your true fans will understand, and will wait patiently."

"But... what if we decide..." I start to say, just before Emma interrupts me... with a *real* laugh.

"What's so funny?" I ask, truly confused by her response.

"You guys are! If you really believe this is over, why the heck did you let yourselves get caught up in all this?" She waves her hands, indicating the festival.

"That's that problem… none of us has a good answer to that question. I mean… it was sorta automatic. They needed help…"

"And they aren't the last band you will encounter, that might need help… need direction."

The moment she says it, we get it – she's talking about *Ransom*. She's talking about what happens next, for the six of us.

"Should I tell you how this will play out?" Emma asks.

"Uh-huh," we say at the same time.

"You're going let life, *and music*, take you where they want to. And, at some point in the future, the urge will strike you – maybe one or two of you, maybe all of you at the same time – and before you know it, you'll be *making music again*. It's part of who you guys – *all six of you* – are!"

As the understanding spreads, one at a time, we lean over and hug her.

"For the record, the six of you will *never* be normal…"

She pauses for a moment, and then continues.

"So, what did your producer say when you told her?"

"Pretty much the same thing you did," I offer.

"*'You're not quitting, you're taking a break,'*" Misty says, mimicking Terri, which makes all of us laugh.

"It's all about the music, ladies. Did you honor all your obligations?"

"Uh-huh. We even gave her some songs we finished and some we were working on, but sorta lost interest in. We told her she could do whatever with them…"

"What's the new plan for the members of *Ransom* then?"

When I look at her, again confused, she laughs.

"What?" she asks.

"Well… if we're 'taking a break', we aren't technically *Ransom* anymore… are we?"

"Have the five of us, ever *stopped* being *Audio Distortion*?" Emma shoots back, as a challenge.

I watch as Misty smiles, wipes what are apparently a few tears, off her cheeks, and finally says something.

"Point made."

"So?"

"Actually, we've decided to go back to school," Misty says, "before we're the oldest ones there."

"Awesome! Back home?"

"Well… not all of us," I say, grinning.

"So… quit with the suspense already!"

"Martin and I are going to University of Kansas," Misty says. "We're going to register when I get back."

"Vanessa has been invited to attend the School of Music, at the University of Leeds – right here in England," I add.

"Wow! How cool is *that*? And you, Ariel?"

"Rhyan and I are going to be at CSU…"

Although she tries not to, Emma lets out a laugh.

"Gee… I wonder why CSU…"

"You can't tell your husband yet, but Rhyan asked her to marry him…" Misty says.

"Rhyan wants to talk to her dad, before they tell anyone," I add.

"So… that leaves Joshua."

"This is the weird part…" Misty says, glancing at me.

"And?"

"He says he has a plan, but he won't tell us what it is."

"Well crap, more suspense," Emma retorts.

"We were kinda hoping you could find out…" Misty says.

About this time, Jimmy walks up from the parking lot.

"If you girls still want a ride, it's time to go."

When we stand up, Emma does the same. We do hugs, and as we are walking off with Jimmy, Emma yells at us.

"You better never forget…!"

"Like that could even happen?" Misty yells back, laughing.

We pile into Jimmy's police car, and slowly roll down the dirt road, headed for the airport.

Three hours later, we're on a British Airways jet, going *home*.

Where, I wonder, will *life* – and music – take the six of us now?

Being Normal

Martin Masterson

For three years, the six of us lose ourselves in life.

Misty and I move to Lawrence and throw ourselves completely into school. I'm after a Master's in music, and Misty has found her path is Language Arts. If nothing else, we figure we can teach one day.

Vanessa disappears to England – and I mean, *disappears*. At one point, we have to ask Emily to go make sure she's still alive. She gets so far into school, and her new boyfriend, she pretty much loses the rest of the world.

When Rhyan marries Georgia, Josh is Rhyan's Best Man, Emily is Maid of Honor, and Misty is a bridesmaid. What makes the ceremony even more amazing is, Mr. & Mrs. Campbell got married in the exact same spot.

That leaves Ariel. She's the one confusing element of the story. Well… she and Josh. Although we all suspect one has something to do with the other, none of us can prove it.

Shortly after the girls came back from the festival in England, something occurred between the two of them. Within days, Josh packed up, moved to LA, and went to work for Terri. His contact with the rest of us became less and less frequent, until finally, after a year and a half, I was the only one he talked to, and that was only occasionally.

Josh seems to have slipped into his own world, and sadly, there doesn't seem to be any room for *Ransom* in it.

Misty made the comment that, whatever is going on, it very well may be the end of *Ransom*…

Ariel has stayed single – which is kind of weird to all of us. According to Rhyan, who sees her every day at school, the line of guys chasing her and asking her out, is endless. And yet, she always makes it clear she has no interest in a 'boyfriend'.

So… it seems as though we have actually let the band go – and there hasn't even been a discussion.

Rhyan sent me an email last week, and his wife – who has a special insight into the anatomy of bands – makes a pretty good point about *Ransom*…

If Audio Distortion survived all the silly crap they went through, and are still together twenty years later, Ransom can certainly find a way past their problems. They just have to make the effort…

The more I think about it, the more I realize Georgia is right.

We just need to make the effort…

And… as strange as it is, it's our now nearly-British bass player that will send us down the road to doing that…

"Step up, Vanessa. Call them. Be the
one who gets Ransom back together…
I dare you…"

~ Leonard Faintree 

Stepping Up

Vanessa Preston

Three years, one month, and sixteen days.

That's how long I've been in England.

That's how long it's been since I gave up my other life.

The one, that unlike the others, I thought would never end.

Being a student isn't all that bad. Studying music is amazing, especially where I am doing it. And... it's every kind of music.

I've written a concerto, helped score a musical, and am learning how to score a movie. All this, from a bass player, from Ransom, Kansas.

Truth is, I can't imagine my life without music in it.

I have a boyfriend – of sorts – which I am pretty sure is... well... let's just say a broken heart at twenty-eight, isn't quite as severe as when you're twenty. Yeah, I'm probably in love, but sometimes, even love isn't meant to be forever.

And yeah, I know... I'm one weird female.

Anyhow, when I got up this morning, I was overcome by an odd sensation to get away – from school, from London, from this part of my life. So here I am… on a train… going to see the one person who will understand where my head is. After all, she's a guitar player too…

My train gets into Southport around 5:00 am, and even though it's cold (and there is still some snow on the ground) I decide to walk the 4 km (about 2 miles) to the music hall. The Faintree's live right behind it…

It's 6:20 when I let my butt drop onto the front steps of the building, and for some strange reason, I'm overcome by a need to cry – which is what I'm doing when Emily comes around the corner to unlock the doors.

"Vanessa?!" She stops dead in her tracks, and stands staring at me. "What in the world are you doing…" she starts to ask, and then stops midsentence when I lift my head and we make eye contact.

"Jeeez! What's wrong?" she blurts out, climbing the stairs and taking a seat next to me.

When I don't say anything, she wipes the tears off my cheeks, wraps her arms around me, and I immediately let my head come to rest on her shoulder. After a few moments, she stands up, and then pulls me to my feet as well.

"I'm freezing – let's go talk where it's warm."

She leads me into the Hall, and right to the small lunch room, where we find a guy making coffee. The moment he sees my tear-covered face, he smiles, nods at Emily, and heads for the door.

"Let me know when it's done!" he says, disappearing into the hall.

"Sit," Emily says, pointing at the table. I pull out one of the chairs, and do as instructed. Emily takes the one next to me. "So?"

I'm about to say something, but when we make eye contact, I burst out in laughter.

"Okay… so you're crazy. Anything else you want to share?" Emily says, trying her best not to join in my laughter.

"Sorry," I reply, sucking in a deep breath, "I was thinking about a conversation in a park… forever ago…"

"So… let me repay the favor. What's going on? Why aren't you at school?"

"I left…"

"You what?"

"No, I didn't quit. I just needed to get away…"

"Jezzz… way to freak me out," she says, making me laugh again. "Guy thing… school thing… or life thing?"

"Life thing… mostly," I reply, standing up and going to the coffee pot. I grab a cup, turn to face Emily, and say, "You should probably tell…" I nod in the direction the guy went.

"Mickey – he's our maintenance guy."

"Mickey," I continue, grabbing the pot and filling my cup, "that the coffee is done."

"Stick your head into the hall and yell 'coffee'…"

With a grin, I do as she says, and seconds later, Mickey comes in grinning. I turn and sit back down at the table.

"I'll be out of your hair in a moment," he says, quickly filling a cup he brought with him.

"I graduated you know…" I say, sipping my coffee.

"Already?"

"Yeah… a term early. I love music… what can I say?"

"So… life?"

"Professor Aston got me into a Master's program…"

As Mickey is headed for the door, I pause, and speak to him.

"Hey – nicely done!" I hold up my coffee cup.

"I learned from a pro," he replies, pointing at Emily, and then he disappears out the door.

"So... kind of 'schooled out' are we?"

"No... more like... well..."

This is where our shared love of music comes out. Somehow, Emily just 'gets it', and all I ever said was 'well...'

"All you have to do is call them, Ness..."

"I dunno..."

"Okay... up to you," she replies, again laughing.

"And... the guy thing?" I offer, sipping my coffee.

"Uh-huh..."

"A broken heart at twenty-eight, is a lot different than the one you have when you're twenty..."

"Were you in love?"

"Not sure, to be honest. Thought I was... but my attitude about him leaving is making me question that."

"So... what's next?"

"I'm open to suggestions."

"I made one... you decided against it."

About this time, Melissa and Shannon come wandering in to say goodbye to their mother, on their way to school.

"Hey, Vanessa!" Melissa blurts out, then rushes over and gives me a hug. "What are you doing here?"

"Stopped by to talk to your mom. I think I may be going back to the States for a while."

"You finished school already?"

"Yep. Got a diploma and everything."

Riley Morgan

"Well, we gotta get to school, but I hope you'll have time to talk before you go home!"

"Definitely!"

They each hug me, and then vanish out the door. Seconds later, Leonard walks in, goes directly to the coffee pot, and pours a cup. We sit staring at him, wondering why we didn't even get a 'good morning'. Once his cup is full, he comes over and takes a seat at the table with us.

"These knuckleheads," he pauses, and points at Emily, "screwed around for about the same amount of time before one of them decided to step up and say something."

I feel the tears building in my eyes, as a smile starts to form on my face. Leonard slowly sips his coffee, and continues to stare at me.

"You aren't an 'on paper' kind of musician, Vanessa. You never were. For that matter, none of you are," Leonard says, that serious, chiseled granite look, embedded into his face.

My smile has turned into a huge grin, and a tear is tricking down my cheek, as I too, sip my coffee. While Leonard and I continue to stare at each other, Emily stands up, walks to the counter and pours her own cup of coffee. Once she has the sugar and cream in it, she turns around just in time to see her husband pull his phone out of his pocket.

"Step up, Vanessa. Call them. Be the one who gets *Ransom* back together... *to make some music...*" he says, sliding the phone across the table to me.

We sit, eyes locked, staring at each other for a good fifteen seconds.

"*I dare you...*" Leonard adds, a devious sneer on his face, knowing he's about to win this one...

Back Together

Georgia Crossman

So... here's where I make an appearance.

It's five after one in the morning, when the phone rings, and my heart takes off.

I hope it isn't about Dad...

"Hello?"

"oh my god... I am sooo sorry, Georgia..." I hear a female voice say – a voice I know I should recognize.

When the giggling starts, for some reason, I too laugh.

"Vanessa? What the heck?" I blurt out, as I turn on the lamp next to the bed.

"I forgot about the time difference..."

"You're still in England?

"Yeah. I'm at the Faintrees..."

"Are you okay?"

"I will be. Can I talk to your husband... just for a sec?"

Again I laugh.

"Here…" I say, hitting my husband's shoulder, "your bass player needs you."

He rolls over, rolls his eyes, and takes the phone.

"Have you lost your mind?" he blurts out, as he puts the phone to his ear. Then… his facial expression changes – to deadly serious – and he goes quiet for a moment.

"*No way*. When? One of us will pick you up. I'll call them. I don't know. I'll ask Emma for help. You rock, Ness! See you when you get here."

Rhyan lies there, staring at the phone in his hand, looking as if he can't believe what he just heard. I laugh, take the phone, and put it back in its stand. Then I turn off the light, roll over, and put my head on my husband's chest.

"It's about time. I was thinking I was going to have to get Stanley and Emma to kick someone's butt to make this happen. Seems good old Emily saved me the trouble…"

"No…" Rhyan mumbles, "…it was actually Leonard."

I laugh, and kiss him on the cheek.

"I'll have to remember to thank him…"

Yeah, I know exactly what that conversation was about, based solely on my husband's reaction. Let's remember, I grew up with one band, and I'm married to a drummer.

Finally… after three years, *Ransom* is about to get back together.

And, knowing the six of them the way I do, I'm pretty sure it's going to be off the charts…

Complications

Rhyan Crossman

I'm sitting in my truck, in front of the Campbell's, when the text message comes in. I flip open my phone, and the moment I see who sent it, I laugh, and open it.

When you guys start recording, you better come here to do it!

I laugh, and quickly type a response.

How is it that a twelve year old knows what I'm doing, before I do?

I have to give the kid credit – she's crazy smart. And quick, too.

It's a girl thing, Uncle Rhyan :-)

I'm headed up the walk toward the house, when Emma and the twins come out the front door.

"Hey brother-in-law! What's up?"

"Seriously?" I blurt out, climbing the steps and laughing at the same time.

"Well... yeah... 'seriously'. Did I miss something?"

"HA! So it's not a girl thing… *it's a kid thing…*" I mumble, as we sit down on the steps.

"Okay… now that I'm confused…"

"Oh man… sorry. Guess you haven't talked to Emily lately.

"Nope. I did send her a song to work on though."

"Okay… so…"

When I hesitate, she prods me a bit.

"So… what?"

"What would *you* think about… I mean… well… Do you think we waited too long?"

The woman is so amazingly intuitive, she immediately 'gets it'. As the reality of what I'm suggesting spreads through her, she shudders, almost spills the cup of tea in her hand, and in an instant, the biggest grin covers her face.

"Totally freaking amazing – and about time! That's what I think!"

"How do you know what I'm talking about, Emma?"

"It's a girl thing, Rhyan," she replies, which makes me laugh. "Are you going to?"

"Well… I've talked to Ariel, and she's in. Misty and Martin – who I kinda thought would be the hold-outs, are totally psyched about the idea."

"Should I assume Emily is behind all this, based on…"

"Nope…" I say, interrupting her, "guess again."

"Well… why did you ask me if…"

It only takes a heartbeat for her 'light bulb' to come on. The look on her face makes me laugh – again.

"No kidding…" she mumbles.

"Hey…" I offer, slipping my arm around her shoulders, "you *did* predicted this would happen, remember?"

Emma laughs, and kisses me on the cheek.

"So, what do you want with me?"

"Our lead guitarist..."

"Joshua doesn't want to participate?"

"We're not sure... he hasn't responded to any of us yet. How else should we interpret that?"

"I dunno. But I bet we can find out..."

She pulls her phone from her pocket, and I momentarily get nervous.

"You're not going to have Terri give him grief about it... are you?"

"Oh please...!" she blurts out. "Are you guys still in grade school here, or what?"

Her phone autodials and she's talking the instant the call is answered.

"Cadi... I have a task for you..."

Secrets

Ariel Williams

"We need to talk to you... if you have a few minutes."

Rhyan and I are standing on the Campbell's front porch, looking at Emma. Paige and Peyton each have hold of one of Rhyan's legs.

It's been two weeks since Rhyan asked Emma for help, and with no word from Josh, I made the decision to come clean. Just as Josh spent years telling us, sometimes, it has to be only about the band...

"Of course, come on it."

She pulls the door open, the twins go tearing back into the house, and we follow. Once Emma closes the door, we follow her toward the kitchen. The twins, however, stop at the door to the basement.

"Momma! Let's hear a song!" Paige blurts out, trying to open the door.

"In a bit guys. I need to talk to Ariel and Rhyan..."

"We can talk downstairs," Rhyan says, laughing, and watching the kids try to open the door.

"Okay... and you guys can give me an opinion as well."

Once we're downstairs, Emma loads a track into the mixer, and hits play. It only takes a few seconds, before Rhyan and I are lost in the music.

"Wow! Totally cool cut. Are you guys working on a new record?" I ask, strumming a guitar next to me.

"Hard to say. I'm thinking we probably are..." Emma replies, laughing.

"So tell her," Rhyan says, putting a hand on my knee.

Emma immediately cuts the volume in half, leaving it loud enough the twins can still hear it.

"Tell me?"

"I'm the problem with Joshua..."

"Huh?"

I take a deep breath, let it out, and then let Peyton climb into my lap, as the track ends.

"Josh and I were... well..."

"o...m...g..." Emma mumbles, fighting off a laugh. "And you actually managed to keep it a total secret! How insanely cool is that..."

"It's always been about the music for Josh – since the day the band started. He didn't want anything to interfere with that. I understood, and was okay with... our... relationship, I guess – the way it was. I'm telling you now, because all of this has moved past him and me, and has become about the band, and we're hoping you can make him see that..."

I stop, take another deep breath, and glance at Rhyan, who gives me a nod and a smile.

"Anyhow," I continue, "when we took the break, Josh... well..."

"He asked her to marry him – the day after she came back from England," Rhyan blurts out, trying to save me.

It's such a sudden and total shock, there's no way Emma can control her facial expression.

"And you said no..." she mumbles, her eyes now locked to mine.

"Uh-huh. I love him, Emma – honest to God, I do. But it was just too sudden – I wasn't ready."

"Pretty much the only person he's talked to since that day is Martin," Rhyan says, squeezing my hand. "We were all totally surprised when he went through with the 'best man' thing at our wedding, to be honest..."

"Yeah..." Emma says, "I remember a couple of people mentioned his odd behavior..."

"Even his contact with Martin has faded, but Martin refuses to let it go. They grew up two houses apart, and that's a hard bond to break."

"None of them knows about any of this. Only he," I glance at Rhyan, "and I know what really happened. I think Josh isolated himself because he believes the rest of the band *does* know what happened."

"Well... you do realize that hiding it, isn't the solution... don't you?"

"Well damn..."

"What?"

"I told her you'd say that," Rhyan replies, laughing.

"Oh, and keeping secrets has served you well so far, hasn't it?"

Emma is looking right at me when she says it, which of course, makes me laugh.

"We all want to play again... we just aren't gonna do it without Josh. Unless I can find a way to fix this..." I finish, and let the thought hang.

"So…" Emma says, a definite glimmer in her eyes, "if I can pull it off, will you go talk to him?"

"In a heartbeat. I thought about it more than once over the last year or so, but each time I remembered the look in his eyes that day… and my heart wouldn't let me. I've been asking myself what if I hadn't…"

Emma quickly interrupts me.

"Come on, Ariel, you made the decision that was best for you, at that point in your life. It took me almost four years to figure out where I was supposed to be – you just gave yourself the chance to do the same thing."

"Once things slowed down, I decided to follow your advice – what you told Misty and me, on the grass at the festival…"

"You let life and music, take you where they wanted to…"

"Uh-huh. Pressing him, and making a big deal out of it wouldn't have served any purpose. I let him go his way, and hoped that eventually, things would work themselves out. After a year, I started to worry, and tried to get him to talk to me. After the second year, I figured *Ransom* really was done – and that it was kind of my fault…"

"We did okay, Emma," Rhyan says, putting an arm around my shoulders, and giving me a gentle squeeze. "We got famous, made some really good music, and maybe even inspired some people. But if this is really…"

"Don't you dare say it, Rhyan Crossman!" Emma blurts out.

"But…" I start to say, and then she glares at me, making me stop after one word.

"Do you want it to be over?" she asks.

Rhyan laughs and then with a big smile, says, "When Misty and Ariel told us what you said to them at the festival – about 'quitting' – we all sorta laughed it off. But… here we are. Music is again biting us in the butt, telling us it's time to create..."

"But... we're definitely gonna need some help, Emma," I add. "We *aren't* going to do this without Josh..."

"Okay..." she replies, with an interesting glimmer in her eyes. "If *Audio Distortion* can recover from all the crap we've been through, you guys should be able to get past this. You said Misty and Martin are onboard, right?"

"Yeah," Rhyan says. "Misty said *she* was thinking about calling everyone."

"And we know Vanessa is in, because she started all this..."

I let out a laugh, and say, "Yeah, at like 1:00 AM..."

"Huh?"

"She called me at one in the morning," Rhyan says, also laughing. "Seems Leonard dared her to do it..."

Emma cracks up, and we're right behind her.

"So... all we have to do is tag team Joshua..." Emma mumbles, as she picks up a now sleeping Paige from the floor. "Come on," she says, the look in her eyes telling me she already has a plan of some kind forming in her mind, "let's put these guys to bed."

Rhyan picks up a sound asleep Peyton from my lap, and as we follow Emma up the stairs, I'm overcome by a feeling that somehow, all this is going to work out...

Called Out

Joshua Miller

I've done my share of stupid crap over the span of my life, but there's only one thing, I'd give anything to fix.

Unfortunately, I've let it go for so long, and have screwed it up so badly, I'm not sure if it can actually be fixed at this point. It's become easier to avoid the problem, than to face it. And, in the process, I, Joshua Miller, may have in fact killed *Ransom*.

She kept trying, but at first the pain was too great – I simply couldn't stand it. I had to block it – and the cause – completely from my life.

Dumb.

Eventually, she did what any normal and sane person would do – she gave up. Actually, they all did...

Now... where once there were five best friends, there's just a big empty hole.

And I have only myself to blame.

So, my life has become being an engineer for Lucky Guess Records. Hey, it's a good job, and I learn something every day, but it isn't being in a band, with my best friends.

Although Terri has continuously questioned me, she never really pushes.

Sometimes... I'd give anything if she would... just once.

So... instead of being a lead guitarist, I sit alone, in an empty studio, playing music from my past. And, as if God is taunting me – trying to point out how stupid I'm being – every night, I hear her playing... and laughing... just like she always did.

And yes, I spend a lot of time crying.

Being stupid sucks... and it makes being in love painful.

Anyhow, it's yet another Friday night, and with no one recording tonight, I'm once again alone, playing my guitar. The moment the lights go on in the booth, I pretty much freak...

"Why don't you write something new, Joshua?" a female voice that I recognize as Terri's, says. Seconds later the blinds go up.

"So what... you're spying on me now?" I blurt out, in a way more demanding, and defensive tone, than I intended.

I'm *in charge* – remember? I get to go where I want, when I want. And what's with the attitude?"

"Nuthin'..." I say, again with a defiant tone – and I'm not even sure why – "The place is yours, I was leaving anyhow..."

I get up, put my guitar into its case, and at the same time, hear a frustrated sounding Terri behind me.

"Yeah...well... don't let me run you off. I just came by on the off chance an *old friend* might want to talk. I'll run along and you can go back to feeling sorry for yourself – or whatever it is you call this."

In the five seconds it takes me to turn around, she's gone – and I am again alone. My butt drops into a chair, and yes, the tears come. Being 'stupid' has again bitten me in the butt. It's as if I can't control it any longer. After thirty seconds of... well... feeling sorry for myself, I hear a new voice.

"Joshua, come in here please..."

I lift my head, and standing in the booth, staring at me, is Emma Campbell. When I don't immediately respond, she's all over me.

"You *are* going to have to deal with me, Joshua. I'm not leaving until you do. And neither are you..."

When I do nothing more than glare at her, she laughs.

"Yeah... like you'd even try that," she says, shaking her head. "Just get up and come in here."

Being at a loss, and at this point, both confused and embarrassed, I get up and go into the booth, turning off the studio lights as I go out the door. When I step into the booth, Emma points and says, "Close the door," which I do. She in turn, lowers the blinds on the window.

"*Ransom* needs their sixth member. It's time," she says.

When we make eye contact, she looks far more serious than I think I have ever seen her, and something inside tells me not to screw with her – which turns out to be one of the smarter ideas I've had in the last few years.

"I'm not interested, Emma," I reply, as calmly as I can, hoping beyond hope, that I can talk my way out of this.

"Your eyes are telling me that's a load of crap, Joshua, and I'm pretty sure *not even you* believe it..."

That idea is instantly shot to hell – and the fact she is actually trying *not* to laugh at me, tells me she knows it. I watch her reach up and punch a couple of buttons on the console next to us, and the moment I hear the music, I also feel the emotions.

"How did you..."

"Are you serious? You're really going to ask that? Terri just snuck up on you, not fifteen minutes ago for crying out loud – with little or no effort," she replies, shaking her head and laughing again. "And… like she said, *she's in charge* and *does* have free run of this place."

I sit staring at her, totally embarrassed, and more than a bit bewildered. After a few seconds, I finally understand. Emma Campbell – with a little help from Terri Maxwell – is about to *make* me find my way.

"I know, Joshua. She told me. And, just for the record, none of the others knew."

"Knew?"

"Yeah. They know now. I made her tell them. When six people – no wait, when six *friends* are as close as you guys *were*, secrets only serve to screw things up – like this one has."

In the blink of an eye, my entire world comes right back into focus, and I totally relax. The fact it isn't a secret any longer, somehow releases me.

"You've kept yourself isolated for close to three years, and you sit down here almost every night, after everyone is gone, and you play. *And*… instead of creating new stuff, you play *old songs*… songs that remind you of your life when you were *happy*…"

"Apparently not *everyone* was gone…" I mumble, and then smile.

"You want to know what I think?"

"Well…" I reply, wiping my tears, and feeling more relief than I have in forever, "we both know you're gonna tell me, no matter what I say, so go ahead."

"I'm pretty sure that if you hadn't been such a huge idiot, she would have married you – eventually. She just wasn't ready, when you asked."

As I sit staring at my hands for a moment, I realize that the 'confrontational' Joshua is gone. Instead, I'm now just a guy with a problem, who is carefully thinking about what I'm going to say next – not wanting it to come out wrong...

"It freaked me out, Emma. In my heart, I honest to God thought she was going to say 'yes'. I will never be able to explain what I felt the moment she said 'no'..."

"And you totally freaked me out by asking the way you did, Josh," a female voice says, filling the dark studio. "I felt completely trapped, and it took all my willpower not to burst into tears. Heck, our entire relationship was still a secret, and neither of us even said the word 'marriage', until you asked..."

In one single instant, the weight of the world is lifted from my shoulders. I know I'm going to lose it, as I stand up, and pull the shades up. The moment I hit the button for the studio spotlights, I find Ariel sitting alone on the floor, in the middle of the room, looking at me.

"And..." I add, blubbering through my fast-falling tears, as I put a flat palm on the glass between us, "because I've been such a total ass – *to all of you* – I honestly had no idea how to fix it..."

"So... you sit down here, driving yourself nuts instead?" Emma asks, putting a hand on my shoulder.

"We have to *talk*, Joshua – that's how *friends* fix things," Ariel says, standing up, walking to the window, and when she reaches it, putting her palm directly over mine on the glass. "You and I," she says, looking me right in the eyes, "were *way more* than friends. You wouldn't come to me, so Emma said I needed to come to you. It's time to fix this..."

I'm out the door, and into the studio, even before she stops talking. All I want is to hold her... to wrap my arms around her, and just hold on to her. The moment I do, she kisses me with more passion than I have ever experienced.

I know then, Ariel Williams is the only woman I will ever love. Period.

"Before you say anything, listen. I'm here because of *us – not the band*. I told the rest of them the same thing. We need to fix 'us', before..."

I put a finger on her lips, stopping her midsentence, and she just smiles, and hugs me tighter. It's a good ten minutes before we realize we are alone.

Emma has disappeared.

Now, I owe her a second huge debt. But, my heart knows that there is no better person on earth, to be indebted to...

Riley Morgan

Home

Ariel Williams

Once we close up the studio, we go to Josh's house, and we talk – until the sun comes up. Just being with him… feeling his touch… and hearing his voice, brings my entire world into perfect balance.

This… is where I'm meant to be.

At 7:00 AM, he tells me he has to go to work – Terri has a group that needs some studio time, so he agreed to work with them on the weekend. He tells me to get some sleep, and that he'll be back around noon. I laugh.

"Yeah right! I'm going with you. I want to see what it is you do…"

An hour later, I'm sitting next to him in the booth, watching him work his magic on the mixing board, for a new 'girl group' that the label is working with. The patience he shows, when explaining things to the girls – who range in age from seventeen to twenty – is amazing. When their studio time is up, their manager tells them it's time to pack it up – and Josh simply takes over.

"You," he says to the manager, "sit down and shut up. You," he points at the youngest of the group, "park your butt on that stool, and run your lyrics in your head for a minute."

"Josh," the manager says, "we can't afford…"

"You let me sweat that," he says to her. Then he spins around and finds the girl on the stool staring into the booth. *"Lyrics, damn it!"* he blurts out, making the girl blush, and the other three giggle. "We are close here," he turns his attention back to the manager, "and trying again later, isn't an option." He spins back toward the studio, and looks at each of the girls through the window, then, with a devious sneer, says, "Terri wants this track down before any of you leave here, understood?"

"Yes sir!" comes from four mouths simultaneously, and the girls are back in 'work mode' just that fast.

"Good…" he mumbles, as he starts adjusting things on his board, "you're cutting into my 'girlfriend' time…"

Fifty minutes later, after four more takes, Josh plays back the finished track for the girls, and watching how giddy they get, makes me giddy as well.

Josh takes the finished product on a stick, up to Terri who, shaking her head and grinning, high-fives him.

"We're going to meet the rest of the band," he tells her. "As Emma so eloquently put it, 'it's time'."

"Your job is still here when you want it back, Josh," she replies, hugging him. "Go make some music…"

We exchange hugs, Josh hands her a set of keys, and we head for the door. Just before we go out into the lobby, Terri has one last question…

"I take it you will be using your original label?"

"Duh?!" I blurt out, not giving Josh a chance to reply.

As we make our way to Josh's truck, it's all I can do to contain myself. Two hours later, we're flying up the interstate, headed for Fort Collins... *to make some music!*

"I'm about to put **Ransom** back in touch with the music world..."

~ Georgia Crossman 

Getting In Touch

Georgia Crossman

They've been at it for thirteen weeks – continuously.

No matter how many times I see it, watching a band 'create' is still totally amazing to me. Even as I watch the six of them, I see Stanley and the others, so many years ago.

Martin and Misty are staying with us. Ariel and Josh are staying at her place. And Vanessa has taken over my brother's extra bedroom.

Four weeks ago, Stanley and Emma – and the rest of *Audio Distortion* – went to Tahoe for a summer music camp, my brother organized. The day after Emma and the kids left, *Ransom* took over her studio…

"Faster?" Vanessa asks.

"No… it isn't tempo," Misty says, scribbling on a page in front of her.

"Is anyone besides me wishing we had kept a couple of the songs we gave Terri?" my husband blurts out, making them all laugh.

"Georgia?" Martin says, making everyone look at me.

"I keep telling you guys, I'm not a musician…"

"Yeah, but you're a *fan*. What's wrong with it?" Vanessa says, indicating the song they're working on.

"I'm not sure… but Misty is right, it isn't tempo. I was bobbing my head by the first stanza."

"Gotta be the lyrics then…" Misty mumbles.

"No…" I say, scrunching my face up, "it isn't."

They *all* look right at me, and although I *do* know what the problem is, I'm going to make them figure it out.

"So?" Ariel asks.

"The lead singer needs to take a break…" I offer.

Understanding what I mean, Misty smiles, and hugs me.

"I'm going for a walk," she says, as she goes up the stairs.

Seeing a chance to do some 'steering', I follow her.

"Me too…"

Ten minutes later, the two of us are walking along a quiet side street. Eventually, Misty breaks the silence.

"It's different this time…"

"I can tell."

"Just by watching, huh?"

"Yep. You're all different people now. Life has changed each of you."

The very moment I say it, her facial expression changes, she stops walking, and turns to face me.

"We're *different*…" she mumbles.

"Well yeah," I reply, smiling. "Time changes everyone."

"…and…" she says, stepping over and sitting down on the curb next to us, now appearing lost in thought, "by default… *Ransom* has changed."

"It has to, Misty. You do remember the last record, right?"

"Continuing Evolution…" she says, turning and looking at me. "Duh?"

I laugh, and lean into her, which makes her lean to her left and laugh as well.

"So? Something has captured your thoughts…" I offer, hoping the seed will grow…

"You did silly – with just one sentence."

"So… explain," I say, fighting a smile, already knowing she's gone where I was trying to lead her.

"I – well, *all of us* actually – have been writing as if it's three years ago. As if we just came off the tour, in support of the last record."

"Ohhh…" I mumble, as a new idea forms in my head.

"We've been away from music for three years, Georgia… we need to get back in touch with it – *before* we try to finish this record…"

"How?" I ask, hoping she'll be open to my solution.

"I don't know… I need to think about it…"

"Will the songs you have so far, work for a record, or will you have to go back and rework them?"

"Good question."

Time to give the six of them some direction – in a roundabout fashion. I laugh, which confuses Misty, pull out my phone, and dial. It's answered on the second ring.

"Maxwell."

"Hey, Terri – I have a question."

"Georgia?"

"Uh-huh. Kinda cool that you recognize my voice."

"So, Mrs. Crossman, what's your question?"

"Does Lucky Guess have anyone on tour at the moment?"

"Well... yeah. Do you need tickets?"

"Nope. *Ransom* does."

"Huh?" she blurts out, probably as confused as Misty looks.

"They need some motivation..."

She laughs – as if my comment is somehow totally comical.

"Motivation, huh? *Shot In The Dark* is opening an arena tour for *No Purchase Required.* If those two together can't motivate you, you're probably dead..."

This time, I crack up – which further confuses Misty.

"Georgia?" she whispers.

"Where are they now?" I ask Terri.

"I dunno, let me check..."

I hear her put the phone down, and then hear typing. At this point, Misty's curiosity gets the better of her.

"What the heck are you up to, Georgia Crossman?"

When I look at her, she's grinning like she's crazy – which is a good thing.

"I'm about to put *Ransom* back in touch with the music world..."

"Friday and Saturday – Pepsi Center..." I hear from the phone.

"No way! Denver? How convenient is *that?"* I blurt out.

"Full passes?" Terri asks.

"Both nights, if you can," I reply.

"Done. Go to the business office – next to Will Call – on Friday and tell them you need to speak to Tina Marcus. I'll let her know you're coming..."

"New producer?"

"Stephen's protégé. She's very good at what she does."

"And Terri…"

"Yeah?"

"You just need some passes – no names. Let's see how Tina handles things."

"I told you… she's good. You want to get in unnoticed, she's your girl."

"Cool."

"So… are they writing?"

"Of course. Why do you think they need to be motivated?"

"And?"

"No comment."

"You suck, Georgia Crossman! Tell them I said hey, and that we're ready when they are. Enjoy the shows, and let me know if you need anything else."

"Later, Terri. And thanks!"

I close the phone, turn and look at Misty, who is still grinning like a criminal.

"Been down to the city lately?"

And together, we sit on a curb, in a quiet residential neighborhood, laughing as if we haven't a care in the world.

Learning Experience

Rhyan Crossman

So... has anyone figured out what my wife does for a living?

Didn't think so.

Master's in psychology, with a minor in education.

She's a counselor at the same junior high school she – and her brother – went to.

So... make sense now?

The woman is always three pages ahead of everyone, no matter what book we're reading. Even as she sat quietly watching us in the Campbell's basement, she already knew what our problem was.

Her solution is simply incredible.

Tina – the show's producer – freaks when she sees who's waiting for her in the arena's business office. I'm pretty sure I hear her use a couple of choice adjectives in front of Terri's name at one point. But, Terri is right – the girl is frighteningly good at what she does. *And...* she knows about *everything* that happens on her tour.

She manages to not only get us in undetected, but backstage as well. Once the bands discover us, they freak. It takes Misty forty minutes to convince them we are just here for the show...

Shot In The Dark opens right on schedule, and honest to God, completely destroys Pepsi Center – in just over an hour. We're *all* so stunned by both the performance, and the crowd's response, none of us can seem to say anything. Tina stands a few feet away, and does nothing more than grin at us.

The seven of us (we made Georgia come) last about fifteen minutes backstage. When we make our way into the crowd, the security guys at first think we're crazy. Then, during the encore, they see my wife, *up on my shoulders*, singing at the top of her lungs, her fist pumping to the beat, and they *know* we are.

The fans near the stage are incredible. Even though a lot of them recognize us, they let us be *fans*. At one point, Vanessa and Ariel are dancing away with a bunch of kids, center stage.

Finally... *No Purchase Required* takes that stage. As they are tuning up, I make eye contact with Misty, and the moment I see her tears, I understand. We are *then* – three years ago. This is *now*. Misty Maitland's eyes tell me she's found a way for us to fit into *now*.

And the one thing the five of us have learned over the years is, when Misty gets going, get out of her way...

The next ninety minutes are so far off the chart, none of us will ever be able to explain it – which is totally cool. We don't need to... *we just lived it.*

A YouTube Star

Misty Masterson

It's 3:20 in the morning, and the six of us are sitting in a booth, in a Denny's, about two miles from the arena. The place is packed with other concert-goers, who are wound just as tight as we are. My mind has been racing out of control for at least the last two hours. Georgia and Martin have been watching me carefully, worried that... heck, I don't know what they are expecting.

I'm ready to be in the studio – and the urge is so acute, I have to concentrate to control it. Just as Georgia said in the van on the way here, *rushing isn't what you do*. She's right of course. I need to slow down and refocus. Thing is, for the first time in my life, I'm not sure how to do that.

Then, fate gives me exactly what I need. Even as my mind races, I hear the bubbly female voice next to me...

"uh... excuse me," the voice says, almost in a whisper.

"Yes?" Ariel – who is on the end – says in response.

"Not to be rude, but aren't you..."

The moment she says it, I laugh. I can't help it. She of course gets embarrassed, and goes quiet.

"I'm sorry..." I say, winking at her. "It's just that you sound *a lot* like me..."

The girl standing next to her, laughs, shoves her playfully, and says, *"See!* Even she hears it..." which makes the first girl blush a brighter red than I have ever seen.

"Man..." Vanessa offers, looking from the girl, to me, and back again, "she even blushes like you do..."

The people at the table next to us suddenly start laughing – telling us they, along with a number of others, were quietly eavesdropping. When we start laughing as well, the two girls seem to relax.

"And yeah," Josh whispers to the first girl, "we are..."

Then, from the table next to us, a different voice.

"Rumor has it, you guys were actually on the floor, center stage, at the show tonight."

"Yeah..." Martin says, fighting a laugh, "every so often, we turn into *fans* – can't help it."

The entire end of the restaurant goes completely quiet, and when no one says anything for a good thirty seconds, a new voice joins the conversation.

"There's already, like fifty videos of her," a guy, in the booth across from us, points right at Georgia, who falls into almost hysterically laughter, "on his," the guy then points right at Rhyan, "shoulders, all over YouTube."

The eruption of cheering and clapping is almost deafening. When I push Martin over and clear the end of the bench, the girl who started it all, stands looking at me, as if she can't believe it. Ariel quickly pushes Josh in a ways, and lets the other girl sit down next to her.

In just a single night, Georgia did exactly what she said she was going to do – back on that curb in Fort Collins...

She put Ransom back in touch with the music world...

Being Sneaky

Martin Masterson

We have eight complete.

After our epiphany at Pepsi Center, they truly are *Ransom* songs.

We have no idea what we are going to call the record, and we still don't have a title song, but we're not worried. It will come to us...

I'm standing at Stanley's Roland when Misty's phone rings. Vanessa immediately picks it up, and when her facial expression changes, I start toward her.

"You should probably answer it, Martin," she says, handing me the phone. When I see whose name is in the caller ID, I have to agree with Ness.

"Hey, Emma!"

"Been to any good concerts lately," she asks.

I break up laughing – no way around it.

"Jezzzz..."

"Tell my sister-in-law, she's the talk of MTV News."

"*What?*" I blurt out.

This time, it's Emma who cracks up.

"Oh yeah… the last line they used when they aired the numerous video clips, was *'does Rhyan Crossman know what his wife is up to?'* I swear, Stanley about died laughing…"

"They know we were all there!" I almost yell, suddenly feeling a bit irritated.

"Oh relax, Martin!" I hear Emma say. "Sometimes, you are just so weird, I swear…"

About this time, Misty comes back from the bathroom, and quickly notices I'm on her phone.

"What are you yelling about?" she asks.

"My wife is back. Do you want to talk to her?"

"Yep – I certainly do. And will you do me a favor, Martin?"

"Sure…"

"Remember what it is we do for a living… okay?"

"Yeah… I get it," I reply, laughing and handing the phone to Misty.

"Hey!" Misty says. "Yeah, it was a riot, but it did what it was supposed to – according our drummer's wife…"

She goes quiet, and when her facial expression changes, Josh, Vanessa, and I turn our full attention to her.

"Seriously?" Misty blurts out, following it with, "Heck yeah! When?"

She turns to the table, grabs a pen, and starts writing.

"Uh-huh, you bet! Tell them thanks for thinking about us. We'll be there. What? Sure. Who wrote it? *Oh man. Seriously?* Okay… but it kinda sucks. See you in a week. Bye."

With the biggest, cheesiest grin I have ever seen on the woman, my wife says, "They want us to come to Tahoe, sneak into the studio, and surprise their students…"

"Oh... how insanely cool!" Vanessa says, laughing.

"No kidding," Josh quickly adds.

Misty walks over to me, puts a hand on mine, and with a smile says, "She also told me to calm my husband down," she pauses when we hear the others laugh, "and that she has something she wants me to read. She wouldn't say who wrote it, or what it is..."

"So..." Josh says, putting his guitar in a stand, "when do we leave?"

"Leave?" we hear from a female voice, as Ariel and Rhyan come down the stairs, pizza boxes in hand. "Are we going somewhere?"

When all we do is crack up laughing, the two of them simply shake their heads...

Messing With Fans

Vanessa Preston

Our van rolls to a quiet stop in front of the studio, and we see Cadi standing at the door, smiling. We get out of the van as quietly as possible, and Cadi meets us.

"Guys, this is going to be epic beyond comprehension. *They have no clue!*" she almost whispers.

"'They' who?" Ariel asks.

"*All of them!* Only Emma, Vicki, and I know you guys are here. The school's principle and one of the donors are here – having lunch, as we speak."

She leads us inside, and directly to the studio. In seconds, we are plugged up, powered up, and ready to go.

"So… you just want us to rip *High Speed Rush*?" Josh asks, trying his best not to laugh.

"As painfully loud, and insanely fast as possible," Cadi replies.

Then, Vicki appears at the door.

"OMG… they are cooking burgers and talking! I can't believe we are going to pull this off!"

"So?" Cadi asks.

"Say the word, and the people on the other side of the lake will know *Ransom* is here…" Josh replies, which is quickly followed by an *'oh heck yeah'* from Rhyan.

They laugh, go out the door, closing it behind them, and in seconds, appear in the booth. The second Cadi points at us, Josh wakes up the entire state of California – and probably most of Nevada.

Even before we make it to the first chorus, the door flies open and there stands a full on crying Bailey. Seconds later, kid after kid, after kid – all of whom are huffing and puffing – comes into the studio, and they line the walls. When the last note leaves Josh's guitar, we get the most sincere round of applause *Ransom* has ever received – period. All six of us are right there at 'emotional'… along with the eighteen kids lining the walls. Then, just like she does every time she sees him, Bailey races across the room, and Rhyan catches her, when she jumps into his arms.

Although none of us really understand the relationship, we all feel the power of it. Even Georgia – who is standing in the booth, tears covering her cheeks, watching.

After thirty minutes of excited questions – which are more about *making* music, than about *our* music – Vicki shuts them down. To our complete surprise, not a one of them complains. They simply say 'yes ma'am' to Vicki, 'thank you' to each of us, and then file out the door, laughing and joking among themselves.

"Wow…" Ariel says, pointing at the last few kids.

"No kidding," I quickly add.

"They have been completely lost in music since they got here," Vicki says. "Stan hit the jackpot with this bunch…"

"I hope we get to hang around," Martin says. "I want to talk to a couple of them…"

"We were hoping you could work that in – we know you guys are busy…"

"Busy hanging out at Discovery Studios," Rhyan says.

"I smell food…" Josh says, sounding so serious, we all crack up.

"Yes you do!" Vicki says, laughing. "Keep in mind that it's my husband who's cooking."

"Come on," Cadi says, as we fall in behind her, and head for the backyard.

This is just another step on the path to getting *Ransom back in touch with the music world…*

A Notebook

Misty Masterson

Being patient is just about killing me, but I'm doing it. I know that Emma will talk to me when she is ready.

In the meantime, we are all lost in helping the kids.

Josh is jamming away on the grass with the guitarists.

Rhyan and the drummers are pounding away on some empty buckets, which actually makes me laugh.

I'm working with the three vocalists, while Ariel and Vanessa are working on sheet music with another group.

When we hear the classical piano, coming from the lower studio, we know where Martin is. I'm the only one who knew that he loves classical music – until today. He plays through a few bars, and then there is silence. I look up and see Emma looking at me from across the yard, and my heart races…

Then, as I am getting my hopes up, there is again music from the lower studio – the exact same notes Martin played moments earlier – but somehow different. Within seconds there are at least ten people crowded around the studio door.

As the music continues to play, I look up and see Stanley racing across the yard, so excited, I half expect him to explode. He goes right past me, and into the studio. Seconds later, as the music continues, Emma wanders by, almost in a trance.

"Hey, Emma," I say, but she keeps going, not stopping until she reaches the studio doorway.

Finally, my curiosity gets the better of me, and I step inside the studio. What I find, not only astounds me, but explains all the mystified faces around me as well.

What I thought was my husband showing off, turns out to be him and a young girl, *playing together!* I watch as the girl plays four bars, and then Martin plays four. They go back and forth and back and forth continuously, for at least two minutes before they stop. The really spooky part is, the entire time, it sounds *as if one person is playing* – they are that in tune with each other.

Once it's over, and the girl – whose name is Anna – goes to join her friends, the four of us are trying to make sense of what we just witnessed. Once we give up trying to explain it, Emma, grabs my hand, and takes me outside. She stops, looks around, and then turns to face me.

"Are you guys close?"

"Huh?"

"Your record, silly. Are you close?"

I laugh.

"Well yeah, sorta. We have eight we think are ready. Vanessa and Ariel have one they are almost done with, and the guys like it. Two more and we have the CD."

"What if I told you I know where you can find those two songs...?"

"Huh?"

"Is *Ransom*, but more importantly, is *Misty*, open to some help?"

"Are you kidding? Heck yeah!"

"Cool. Come with me, and prepare to be freaked out…"

As she cuts a path across the grass, it only takes a second to figure out we're headed for her kids, and the girl who has been watching them – Carla Mitchell.

Carla, and her brother Randall, live with Nick and Cadi. The way we heard the story, Nick's heart made him bring them home with him, when they lost both their parents, to an automobile accident. I almost cried the day Emma told me about it.

"Hey!" Emma whispers, as she kneels down next to Carla. The twins jump up and throw their arms around their mother's neck, which makes me smile. Strangely, however, Carla – who seems lost in her own little world – doesn't say a word, or even look at us. I kneel down next to Emma, and watch as she taps Carla on the shoulder, and the girl almost jumps out of her skin, then turns to look at us.

"Oh man! Sorry…" she says, immediately looking back at the lake, "I didn't hear you come up…"

"What's the matter?" Emma asks.

Because I've already followed her gaze, I know what it is that has completely captured the girl's attention. The visual image alone, reaches in and gets a firm grasp on my heart.

"Remember the other day, when I said I was jealous of Bailey and Melissa?" she asks, still not looking at us.

"Uh-huh…" Emma replies.

She turns, looks at us, and has the goofiest, most carefree smirk on her face. With one hand she points toward the lake, and says, "I'm even more jealous of them…"

As Emma turns to follow her finger, Carla says, "How amazing is *that*?"

What Emma finds is, Shannon and Carson sitting Indian style, a couple of feet from the water's edge, holding hands, and laughing.

"Insanely amazing, actually," I offer, giggling. "I think I'm jealous right along with you…"

Carla, looking confused, and maybe a bit embarrassed, spins around, looks at me as if she just realizes I'm here, and says, "Hi, Miss Maitland!"

"Hey, Carla," I reply. Then I turn to the twins and ask, "And what are you two cuties up to?" poking each of them in the tummy.

"I want Carson," Paige blurts out, as she steps around me, and tries to take off that direction.

"I told you, Paige, your brother is busy…" Carla says, laughing, and grabbing her.

"Who's that, Momma?" Peyton asks, pointing at me.

"That's Misty. She sings, like your mom does."

He gets up, walks around in front of me and with his hands on his little hips, says, "My momma sings good!" which makes Carla and me laugh.

"I want *Carson*, Momma!" Paige says again, squirming and trying to get away from Carla.

Just the look in the child's eyes – even at five years old – is enough to tell me what's going on. I let out a laugh, look at Emma, and say, "The girl is actually jealous!"

"Let her go, Carla."

"Yes ma'am," she replies, standing Paige up.

The child is gone in a flash, which cracks us up. She races down to the water's edge and falls into her brother's lap. The really cool part is, Shannon breaks up laughing and then starts tickling, and playing with her.

"And that," Carla says, pointing at them again, "is even cooler…"

"Where's your notebook?" Emma asks, the question directed at Carla.

"Huh?" she replies, turning and looking at me, instead of Emma.

"Notebook? The thing you've been carrying with you for like six months?"

Suddenly, Carla puts two and two together, and I watch as the strangest look spreads across her face.

"Seriously?" she blurts out, still looking at me.

"You said you'd trust me…" Emma offers.

Even before she finishes the sentence, the notebook is in *my* hands. It's as if she knows I'm the one who is going to read whatever it contains.

"We'll get this back to you, before you go to bed," Emma says, as she stands up. Then she hands her a smaller spiral notepad, with a pen attached. "This is in case you just absolutely need to write something…"

Carla blushes – pretty badly.

Emma turns and calls to her son…

"Carson! Get your sister away from the water!"

Laughing like a total nut, he stands her up, and the three of them start toward us.

"I'm going to take them with me, so you can have a break."

"It's okay…" Carla starts to say.

"Hush. Go find someone – *your age* – to talk to for a bit."

She laughs, and says, "Yes, ma'am."

"Come on, Misty," Emma says, picking Peyton up, "let's go do some reading, shall we?"

I'm not even close to prepared for what I am about to discover.

"The girl has a way with words, Ness…
a strange, powerful way…"

~ Misty Masterson 

Composing

Misty Masterson

I'm composing lyrics – and I completely lose track of time. Seems *everyone* is trying to figure out where I went. When Ariel and Vanessa find me, I'm under a tree, at the far edge of the studio property – alone, and in tears. My friends pretty much freak out, the moment they see me. In the blink of an eye, Vanessa is next to me, her arm around my shoulders.

"Wanna talk about it?" she asks, assuming my tears are because I'm upset.

"Yeah… and why'd you run off anyhow? Why didn't you come find one of us?" Ariel quickly adds.

"You guys are just *sooo* totally amazing…" I mumble, and then smile at them.

After a second, I hand Ariel the lined pad in my lap. She takes it, confusion covering her face, sits down in front of me, and starts reading. A minute, and four pages later, I see the first tear as it escapes her eye.

"Where… I mean… how…" she tries to ask.

I hold up the notebook, and still smiling, say, "Carla."

"Oh my God..." Ariel says, returning her attention to the pad of lyrics.

"The girl that lives with Nick and Cadi?" Vanessa asks.

"Uh-huh," I reply, wiping my tears – again. I open the notebook to a specific page, turn it around, and hand it to her. "The girl has a way with words, Ness... a strange, powerful way..."

We sit together, Ness reading the notebook, Ariel reading my conversion of what I found into workable lyrics, for at least another thirty minutes, before the Calvary shows up.

So... what would be your immediate response to finding three thirty-year-old women, sitting under a tree, in tears?

Yeah... that's kinda how they reacted...

Telling A Story

Vanessa Preston

We make Emma and Cadi promise not to say anything about what they found, when they happened upon the three of us, under that tree. Misty, having copied a lot of stuff from Carla's notebook, gives it back to her during dinner, and she has to force herself not to cry again.

The next morning, Willie drives Misty the ten miles to the airport in Truckee, so she can rent a car. Before she leaves, she tells the five of us that she just needs some time, and is going to drive back to Fort Collins. The look in her eyes is enough to ensure none of us question her.

Not even Martin has ever seen her get like this over writing.

As we ride quietly in the back of Vicki's van, on the way to the airport in Reno, we all know that when this record is finished, it is going to be *Ransom's* greatest accomplishment – much like *Audio Distortion* playing at Red Rocks.

Misty gave me copies of the lyrics she came up with, and even as I read them, melodies form in my mind. It's going to be a ballad – slow, methodical, and meaningful. We are about to tell an intensely personal story, so we have to be careful.

Once we're on the plane, we get energized. The five of us take up one side of First Class, although Misty's seat is empty. We change seats continuously, comparing notes and music, and as we fly from Reno to Fort Collins, *Ransom* writes the music to what we are certain is going to be the title song, to our next record... although Misty hasn't titled it yet.

'Epic' doesn't even begin to describe the adventure, the six of us are about to embark on. The really amazing thing is, sooner than any of us know, *six* of us, will become *seven* of us...

You see, Carla Mitchell is about to embark on her own heroic journey – one that will influence *millions* of people, in every corner of the world.

One that starts with words in a notebook...

Uncooperative

Martin Masterson

It takes us ten weeks to finish our record. Misty and I offer to go rent a place, but Georgia threatens us when we do. The Campbell's twins have become addicted to Vanessa – and it works both ways. On more than one occasion, when we've used the studio to get something down, Paige and Peyton follow Ness to the basement, and sit quietly on either side of her, swaying to the music as we play. It's actually kind of amazing.

So… we're down to Misty's vocals on the last song. And of course, she's being a pain – but we love her anyhow. We're sitting in the Campbell's studio, discussing it…

"No… I told you guys, I'm not doing it. Not until the kid signs off on us using it."

"Yeah, yeah," Rhyan says, making everyone laugh.

"Terri sent the contract. Go get her to sign the stupid thing…" Josh says, shaking his head.

"I'll go with you, if you want me to…" Ariel adds.

"Do you think I need to call Cadi and Nick first?"

"Why?" comes from behind us. We turn around, and find Stanley sitting on the stairs, staring at us. "You don't think they already expect this?"

He gets us – big time.

"Well…" I start to say.

He laughs, and shakes his head.

"Emma is waiting to take you to the airport. Go talk to her, Misty – just you. The kid doesn't need the pressure of the six of you all at once."

Misty makes eye contact with each of us, and gets a nod of agreement.

"Okay… see you when I get back," she says, standing up and heading for the stairs. Stan stands up and lets her go by, and halfway up the stairs, we hear, "Wish me luck!"

Seconds later, we hear the door close.

Stan turns to face us, and with a grin on his face, says, "No luck involved this time…"

"This is going to be the **Ransom** record the world will remember forever..."

~ Misty Masterson 

Permission

Misty Masterson

I will always be mystified by the fact that high school age teenagers still recognize me. It's probably true that I don't look thirty years old – I got really lucky in the looks department – but I am, nonetheless. And, let's keep in mind, *Ransom* has been on a back burner for about three years.

Yet, only a block into the subdivision, I pick up a tail. By the time I park in the Sharpe's driveway, I have a crowd of six or seven teenagers following me. When I get out and close the car door, a couple of them get so giddy, I think they may explode on the spot. I swear, I gotta quit with the pigtails…

I climb the steps, knock on the door, and wait. Seconds later, the door opens, and there stands who has to be, Carla's younger brother – the resemblance is unmistakable.

"NO WAY!" the kid yells, so loudly it makes my ears ring.

From somewhere behind me (at the end of the driveway I suspect) I hear a female voice almost scream, *"I freakin' told you it's her!"* Seconds later, Nick appears at the door, and he too, starts laughing.

"Carla! It's for you!" he yells into the house.

A few seconds later, Carla comes around the corner, and ten feet from the door, she stops so fast, Cadi walks right into her.

"Hey, Carla!" I say, grinning.

"Mrs. Masterson? What are you doing here?"

"We need to chat... and you know about what."

When Carla just stands there, staring at me, I laugh and add, "Besides, your aunt is a friend of mine..."

"OMG... I'm *sooo* sorry... I didn't mean to be rude," Carla blurts out, turning a really cute shade of red.

Nick and the boy start laughing, as Cadi opens the door and motions for me to come in.

"Guess the neighbors recognized you..." Nick says, pointing at the group of kids still standing at the end of the driveway.

"It's these!" I blurt out, tugging on one of my pigtails. "I swear – I gotta find a new hair style..."

"Don't you dare!" Cadi says in instant response, making Nick crack up. "Just like mine were, they are your *signature* – the world *expects* Misty Masterson to have pigtails... *damn it!* Besides... what are you going to do about the freckles?"

Carla and her brother both try to stifle their laughs, but fail. Then, as Carla looks around me, a couple of the girls at the end of the driveway are quick to wave at her, in an attempt to get her attention.

"Oh man... they're going to think..."

"No, they won't. I *never* ignore fans. Once we're done, you can invite them in, and we'll all talk."

"I'll take care of it," Nick says, and goes out the door.

"Come on," Cadi says, "let's get something to drink and, sit down."

"Can I come?" the boy asks.

"Sure!" I reply, putting an arm around his shoulders. "Who exactly are you... and how is it you know who I am, anyhow?"

The poor kid actually blushes, which makes Carla laugh.

"My name is Randall – I'm Carla's brother," he says, smiling at me. "And... *everyone* knows who *Ransom* is, Mrs. Masterson." We turn toward the kitchen, and just short of the doorway, pretty much as an afterthought, Randall mumbles, "...and to be honest, your pigtails *are pretty awesome...*"

As Carla does her best not to laugh again, I give Randall a gentle squeeze. We follow Cadi into the kitchen, and as she goes about filling glasses with iced tea, Carla and I take seats at the table. Randall grabs two of the glasses, and puts one in front of each of us.

After Carla and I stare at each other for a few moments, I pull my notebook out of my backpack, and the moment she sees it, Carla giggles. I open it to a specific page, pull out a stack of loose pages, and lay them on the table, all under the close scrutiny of Randall. I close the notebook, and slide the pages over in front of Carla, who picks them up, and immediately looks confused.

"I can't read music," she says.

"It's about the lyrics, Carla."

She turns her attention back to the pages, and puts all of them down on the table in front of her. She glances at me, I smile at her, and she picks up the first page, and starts reading. Fifteen seconds later, although her facial expression never changes, the tears come. Poor Randall gets nervous and confused.

"Sis? What's wrong?"

"Nothing, Randall… just hush for a second," she replies, as she picks up the second page, and continues reading. After a few more ticks of the clock, she picks up a third page, lifts her head and looks at me.

"You got all *this*, from what you read in my notebook?"

"Uh-huh. I tried to keep it as non-personal as I could – and still tell *your* story. So… whacha think?"

She hands Cadi the pages she's holding, reaches up with both hands, wipes her tears, and then holds them out to me. It's the perfect response to my question, and it makes my heart race. I watch as she picks up the remaining pages – which are a second song – and continues to read. When she finally finishes, and looks at me, my heart simply takes off. The magic in her eyes, tells me this is *sooo* going to work…

"What do you think of the title?" I ask, glancing at Cadi, who now has tears in her eyes too.

Cadi hands the first page back, Carla, who lays it on the table. I reach over and put my finger on the top of the page… on the title…

Being Saved

…and Carla immediately bursts into tears. She stands up, steps over to me, and hugs me tighter than anyone ever has – in my entire life.

"So… can we use them?" I ask, as she stands staring at me.

Talk about confused?

"Huh?"

"It's *your* writing, Carla – *your* words, *your* feelings, and *your* life – I've just rearranged it into a song. We want to record them both for our next CD, but we need your permission to do it."

"We?"

"*Ransom*, silly. Martin and Josh wrote most of that music. Once they were comfortable with it, they sent me to get permission. I haven't actually sung the entire song yet – just parts of it."

"*Why?*" Carla, who is again crying, asks.

"Because, I know they are going to be amazing songs – especially the first one. Maybe even the best songs *Ransom* has ever recorded. And, if I did get a complete vocal track down, and couldn't use them, my heart would be so totally broken. So… here I am."

Carla turns and immediately moves toward Cadi, who is on her feet instantly, and has her arms around her the moment she stops moving.

Yeah… I'm pretty much freaked out…

"Did I…" I start to say, but am interrupted by a laughing Nick, who has managed to sneak back in, undetected.

"No, Misty, you didn't," he says, laying a hand on my shoulder. "It's just too much, too fast – that's all."

"We just told her they want her to be in the video they're going to make for *The Time It Takes,*" Cadi says, smiling at me, and giving Carla another squeeze.

"A video? You guys are making a *video?* OMG!" I blurt out, suddenly excited. This of course, makes them crack up laughing – even stressed out Carla.

"Carla," I offer, reaching over and putting a hand on her back, "sit down and let me explain this. It's really nothing to get stressed over, honest."

Carla turns and sits back down, facing me. I slide a proof copy of the CD liner over in front of her.

"That's a rough of what the insert will look like…"

She interrupts me midsentence, and when I see her slowly running her fingers over the scripted letters of the title – *Taking Chances* – I know why.

"No way…" she blurts out. "You're using the second song, for the CD's title?"

"Yep… assuming you go along with it. It kinda speaks to what we are doing… all of us – you and Randall included, don't you think?"

Her smile gets even bigger, when she sees her name, in block letters, under each song.

"Just your name, in those two places," I say, touching her fingers. "Simple. The lawyers say we have to do it this way, any time someone other than a band member contributes to a song. It's really not that big a deal. We all love the way the songs look on paper, and *all of us* are really hoping you'll say okay, so we can record them – the suspense is killing us!"

"Okay," she instantly blurts out, grinning, and still running her fingers over the sample of the CD insert.

Finally, I pull out the contract, slide it over in front of her and put a pen on top of it.

"Sign that on the line above your name."

When she hesitates, and looks at me, I glance at Cadi and Nick, and quickly add, "They have to sign it too, as your guardians."

"Aunt Catrin?"

"Up to you kid. We," she turns and looks at Nick, "will support whatever you decide."

Carla picks up the pen, again looks at the page, and when she still hesitates, her brother – who up to this point has been strangely quiet – says, "I swear, Carla, if you don't sign that, I will *soooo* totally kick your butt!"

As everyone is laughing, Carla gets up and hugs Randall, then sits down, and signs the page. When she's finished, Cadi takes the pen and signs, and once Nick does the same, I start to restack the pages. This is when the ever vigilant

Randall, completely freaks out. Seems he is paying closer attention than any of us realize.

"NO FREAKIN' WAY!" Randall yells, as he instinctively reaches for the page that got his attention.

Cadi, realizing what it is that has Randall so excited, starts laughing. When Nick sees which page Randall pulls out, he too, starts laughing. Finally, the now completely confused Carla takes the page from Randall and looks at it.

It takes her a couple of heartbeats to figure it out...

"oh... my... god..." she mumbles as the tears again begin to flow. She glances at Cadi, then at Nick, and then looks right at me, and asks, *"Seriously?"*

"Yeppers!" I reply, reaching out and wiping her cheeks. "Did you think we were just gonna let you donate your life to our record?"

I open my notebook, pull out the check Terri sent with the contract, and slide it over in front of her. When Randall sees it, he turns an interesting shade of pale, and drops into a chair next to him. After a few seconds of silence, I reach over and put a hand on Carla's arm. When she looks at me, I wink at her.

"So... are we good?"

"Duh?" she quickly replies, finally smiling.

"Awesome..." I say, putting the contract into the envelope Terri gave me, and sealing it. "I'll let your parents explain the whole 'royalties' thing later. How about you go get your friends and we can hang out for a while?"

Still looking very confused, she shrugs and stands up.

"Call Marsha – they're next door at her house, waiting," Nick says, leaning over and kissing her on the cheek.

She pulls out her phone, makes the call, and ten minutes later I find myself in the Sharpe's family room, surrounded by two guys, four girls – all friends of Carla's – Carla and

Randall, having a completely informal chat about music. When one of the girls refers to me as a *'totally amazing pop star'*, I'm sure that for the first time in years, I actually blush.

Then, the discussion turns to the reason for my visit, and instantly, I'm no longer the center of attention. The very moment I say "Carla helped me write a song..." all six of them look at her, and I hear a couple of *'omgs'* and at least one *'no way'*. Carla, of course, turns at least three shades of red, and rolls her eyes at me. The ever-quiet Randall is quick to back me up, and through some sort of strange teenager magic, *instantly* produces the CD insert that I left on the kitchen table, and shows it to them.

And so begins Carla Mitchell's amazing journey...

Once our visitors leave, Cadi insists that I stay the night, which I readily agree to.

"I appreciate this. I want to be fresh when I show up at Emma's tomorrow."

Cadi looks me in the eyes, and with a big smile, says, "You're going to rough the vocals, aren't you?"

"*Everyone* is going nuts at this point. They all – the label included – want to hear it..."

The moment Carla appears in the kitchen doorway, I know she was listening. The same magical look is in her eyes, but she never says a word.

So I do.

"Can I take your daughter to Fort Collins with me?"

"I have school," Carla says, never breaking eye contact with me.

"I think a 3.8 GPA warrants missing a day of school... when necessary," Nick says from behind Carla.

The girl has her arms around his neck so fast, I almost miss it. Cadi laughs, holds out her hand, and I give her a fist-bump.

Riley Morgan

"Well... long day tomorrow. I need to get to sleep."

"I have a question, Mrs. Masterson," Carla blurts out, as I am headed for the stairs.

And that is?"

"The extra room has two beds in it and..."

"On one condition," I say, interrupting her, and making Cadi and Nick laugh.

"Yes ma'am?"

"You start using my first name, right now."

When she looks at Cadi and Nick, they laugh and walk away. She turns, looks at me again, and with a smile, says, "Misty it is..."

Thirty minutes later, we're safely tucked in, and the moment the light goes out, I hear Carla's voice.

"I have one question," she says, "then I'll go to sleep."

"Ask away."

"I understand about Aunt Cadi and Uncle Nick 'taking chances', I even get me and Randall, but how does the title apply to *Ransom?*"

"This record is the most *emotional* thing we have ever done as a band, Carla, and although it's completely new to us, we're all *totally* into it. We've always done the bubbly, pop stuff, a couple of loud rowdy songs, and the last record was about us – the band members. This record is going beyond all of that. This time, we've written about the things found in hearts... yours, Randall's, Nick and Cadi's, and all of ours..."

She doesn't say anything in response, and just before I roll over onto my side, I laugh. She, of course, hears me...

"Did I miss something?"

"For the first time since we started all this, *Ransom* has made a record about something of substance – something *important.* This, Carla Mitchell, is going to be the *Ransom* record the world will remember forever..."

Again silence. I let her dwell for a moment, and then, say the one thing I know *needs* to be said – even though I know how she is going to respond to it.

"And it's mostly your fault..."

In a matter of seconds, just as I expected, I hear the soft sobs...

Finished Product (sorta)

Carla Mitchell

My turn.

Yep, I too get caught up in this story. It does, after all, end up being a very important part of my life, and directly affects how my future unfolds.

The morning after a simple signature changes my entire life, Misty and I leave Flagstaff, and drive the 800 miles to Fort Collins. I have to tell the girl to slow down, at least five different times. Yeah… she's totally wound tight.

We stop for breakfast in Albuquerque, and again in Pueblo, for lunch. She asks me at least three different times if I want to drive, but not yet having my license, I figure it probably isn't a very good idea, considering it's a rental car. She just laughs and sticks out her tongue at me.

Now, twelve hours later, standing on the Campbell's front porch, I reach out and ring the doorbell. Seconds later, the door opens, and the look on Aunt Emma's face is priceless – and I'm actually relaxed enough to take advantage of it.

"No, Aunt Emma, I haven't run away to join a pop band…"

Misty starts laughing *so* hard…

"And you're on my porch, on a *school day*, because?"

"Let me into your studio, and I'll show you," Misty says, before I can respond. When I glance at her, she has the coolest look in her eyes.

"Well… come on then," Aunt Emma says, opening the door all the way, and waving us in.

A few steps down the hall, we pass the study, and seeing Uncle Stanley sitting at his computer, Misty sticks her head in, and says, "Can I borrow you for an hour or so?"

As if by some bizarre kind of magic, the moment she starts talking, the twins appear at the end of the hall.

"Hi Carla!" they say at the same time.

At first, I chalk the simultaneous response up to chance. With an odd look on my face, I kneel down in front of them.

"Sure!" Stanley says, in response to Misty's question. "Does my wife know?"

"Hi!" Misty says to the twins. "And yes, Stan, she knows…"

"Hi!" they reply… again, at the same time.

Okay… maybe it isn't 'chance'. Misty and I turn and look at Aunt Emma, who immediately laughs. About this time, Uncle Stanley appears behind the twins.

"It's their new thing… talking at the same time," Aunt Emma offers, in response to our comical facial expressions.

"Go find Carson for me," Uncle Stanley says to the kids.

"Okay Daddy!" they reply, in almost perfect unison, and disappear up the stairs – side by side.

"That's… kinda…"

"Spooky?" Aunt Emma says, finishing my thought.

"Uh-huh," Misty agrees, fighting off her own laugh.

"So… what do you want me for?" Uncle Stanley asks.

Misty snaps out of her momentary lapse, smiles, and tosses him a memory stick.

"I want to put some vocals over that."

He looks at it, and then says, "Misty, Willie is…"

"It's not about perfect – it's about getting a feeling for it. Willie will get his chance later. I just need a *complete* copy of the song…"

Suddenly, Aunt Emma's eyes double in size.

"Is that…?"

"Uh-huh…" Misty replies, grinning, and jabbing me in the side.

"So… it's official I take it?" Uncle Stanley asks.

"Yes sir," I reply, smiling. "She made me sign some stuff yesterday."

"Made you?"

Aunt Emma's comment makes Misty crack up.

"Sheeesh! You know what I mean!" I reply, rolling my eyes at them. "I *sooo* wanted to do this…" I reach out and take Misty's hand, "but honestly, I never expected it to be *this* big of a deal…"

"Hey Dad!" comes from the top of the stairs. "Did you want me? Or are they just messing with me again?"

The moment he says it, I break out laughing.

"Getting even with you, are they, Carson?"

"Carla!" he yells, and races down the stairs, to hug me.

"Can you keep an eye the twins for a bit?" Uncle Stanley asks Carson.

"It's okay Mr. Campbell – I got it," I quickly offer.

"Think you can keep them quiet for three full minutes?"

"Let's find out," Misty says, and reaches for the knob on a small door next to her.

Although I know that the Campbell's have a studio in their basement, I've never seen it – and I'm not even close to prepared for what I find at the bottom of the stairs. It's completely and totally amazing, and shows just how deep their love of music really is.

Less than an hour after Misty starts working, the rest of *Ransom* shows up. Heck, they do all live in Fort Collins for the time being, so I'm not really sure why I was surprised.

It takes Misty just over three hours, and eight tries, but when she's done... well... you have to *hear it*, to understand. The truth is, I'm beginning to believe that Misty's voice is easily as good as Aunt Emma's. *And...* from the look I see on her face a couple of times, while Misty is recording, I think maybe Aunt Emma believes it too.

The eight of us sit quietly in the Campbell's living room, while Uncle Stanley does his digital thing in the basement, putting Misty's vocals over the music file that's on the memory stick. It takes him a bit to get it the way he wants it, but forty minutes later, without any warning, the entire house is filled with *Being Saved* – in its entirety. Seconds after it starts, Uncle Stanley walks in, grinning, and holding a remote.

Aunt Emma and I are in tears by the second stanza, and the members of *Ransom* are all about to fly off the chain – I swear. It's apparent from the look on Uncle Stanley's face, that he knows how big this is going to be. At one point, while Uncle Stanley and Aunt Emma are gesturing back and forth, I catch him mouthing what I think is the word *'grammy'*, while Aunt Emma grins, and shakes her head up and down.

As Uncle Stanley starts the song for the third time, Aunt Emma leans over, and whispers in my ear...

                                          Riley Morgan

"Remember what you said about 'such a big deal'?"

"Uh-huh..."

"Hang on kid..."

She kisses me on the cheek, then turns to Misty – who is sitting next to me – and gently squeezes her hands.

Thing is, even though I'm only sixteen, and all this is completely new and foreign to me, my heart is telling me that Uncle Stanley and Aunt Emma are *both*, totally right...

This song is going to make *Ransom* even bigger stars than they already are, and will put them right back on the music world's front page.

As I sit watching the six of them listening to the song, I find myself wondering just how amazing their lives are going to get.

Can you say *'superstars'*?

Being Noticed

Carla Mitchell

Wyndom Parker turns out to be a totally amazing guy.

Once I looked him up online, I understood why Aunt Cadi and the rest of *Audio Distortion* were so totally freaked and excited about him making their video. His list of award winning videos is huge…

Although he's kinda business like, and knows exactly what he wants, the man is also infinitely patient.

Especially, with kids.

We're at Aunt Emma's house, working on the video for *The Time It Takes,* and although the other kids are too young to care, I know what's going on, *and* how important it is.

And yes, I'm pretty much petrified.

After four failed attempts to get the beginning scene shot, Mr. Parker pulls me aside and tries to calm me down.

"You need to relax, Carla – and let the cameras do the work. Honestly, 'acting' isn't really required. Just be Carla…"

Then he turns and claps his hands to get everyone's attention.

"Okay, so I'm off for fresh air, and some coffee. The technicians are going to McDonald's. Anyone want anything?"

As he is talking, I'm watching the two camera guys, messing with their equipment. For some weird reason, even before they are finished, I know exactly what they're doing... and wonder if it's for my benefit. I hide my smile, then turn and add my order to the others.

Once the techs are done, Mr. Parker speaks to them, and seconds later, they disappear out the back door. The moment we're alone, Aunt Emma takes charge.

"Look... this is supposed to be 'natural', but we really need to practice it. You guys up for that? It will take them at least thirty minutes to get to McDonald's and back."

"Yeah... I was thinking the same thing, Aunt Emma," I quickly offer, glancing at the two cameras, still pointed into the kitchen.

"So... first thing," Aunt Emma says, tossing the short script into the sink, "is to lose that. Now, how do you remember it, Carson?"

"I took Carla to show her Shannon's picture, and we came back because the twins wanted a snack."

"Carla?"

"He's right. I carried Peyton down the stairs, and Carson had Paige's hand so she wouldn't fall. When we walked in, you and Aunt Cadi were standing by the coffee pot, talking."

"Then I asked if we could have a snack, and..."

"And I was asking about the song," Aunt Cadi adds.

"That's exactly what we are going to do, guys. You four go to the top of the stairs, we are going to listen for you coming, and we'll see if we can get the timing right, okay?"

"Yeah," the four of us say at the same time.

We turn, head into the hall, and then climb the stairs, with Paige giggling the entire time. At the top, Carson yells to his mom.

"Here we come!"

The second Paige jumps off the last step, her shoes slapping the tiled floor, we hear Aunt Cadi start talking.

"So... the song..."

Knowing we need to walk in at a specific moment, I slow the kids down, and keep listening.

"I think it's amazing..."

"And your inspiration?"

Right on cue, the four of us turn the corner and stop just inside the door – Peyton in my arms, Carson next to me, and Paige standing in front of Carson. He reaches out, stops her, and says, "Can we have a snack, Mom?" Aunt Emma gives Aunt Cadi, a really strange look, and of course, they both start laughing. Aunt Emma turns and points at us, and says, "Standing right there, actually..."

The whole situation is so corny, the four of us are doing our very best not to laugh. But... the second Paige starts to giggle, the rest of us join in. Aunt Emma walks over, scoops her daughter up, leans over and kisses Peyton, and says, "That was awesome guys!"

Just watching how excited the little ones are, gets me wound up too. As Aunt Cadi passes me, she too laughs, and winks at me. Seems Mr. Parker was right... all I had to do was relax, and have fun with it.

We go through it three more times before the techs turn up with lunch. Carson goes and lets them in, and as he is digging out some paper plates for lunch, Paige attaches herself to the younger of the guys, which totally cracks me up. Ten minutes later, Mr. Parker shows up, and gives Aunt Cadi her coffee.

"Okay… so let's see it?" she blurts out, pouring the coffee into a regular mug.

"Huh?" Aunt Emma says, turning and looking at her.

"Oh please… you aren't *that* tricky, Emma," she replies, and then glances at Mr. Parker, who laughs, and heads for the living room.

I grab my cheeseburger, some fries, and follow them into the living room, where I find Mr. Parker in front of a laptop, clicking things. The moment Aunt Emma sees me, she rolls her eyes.

"You too?" she asks.

"Come on, Aunt Emma, that guy," I point at the one Paige has adopted, "pointed one camera at a specific spot, and put tape over the red light, before he left. How obvious is that?"

I give her a devious little grin, and stuff more food into my mouth.

"You, young lady," Mr. Parker says, smiling directly at me, "are astute beyond your years. I've pulled this many times, on kids your age, and you are only the second one to figure it out."

Yeah… he makes me blush.

We watch quietly as Mr. Parker accesses the video that the cameras captured over the forty minutes they were gone. The look on his face tells us we must have done good. Then, Carson turns up behind me.

"You guys tricked us, didn't you?"

One of the techs laughs and says, "Sorta…"

Then, to everyone's surprise, he lifts the hand that doesn't have food in it, and says, "Pretty cool…" and gets a high-five from the tech.

"Break it all down guys… we have what we need," Mr. Parker says.

He turns, looks at Emma, and says, "The stuff we shot earlier with Stanley, and the kids, is good for the rest of the video." He turns and looks at Aunt Cadi and me. "You guys are okay with us turning up at your house Tuesday, right?"

I smile and nod. Aunt Cadi swallows what's in her mouth, and says, "Of course. Her brother is so completely over-amped…"

"Seriously!" I quickly add, laughing.

"And Nick?"

"He's Nick. He'll play along…"

"Very cool…" he mumbles, turning his attention back to his monitor.

"So?" Aunt Emma asks.

"Mrs. Campbell," the second tech says, as he comes into the room, the twins hot on his heels, "this song is so incredible, I fully intend to make sure the video does it total justice."

When we all look at Mr. Parker, he grins and says, "He's my editor too – best one in the business."

After a second, the same tech glances at me, then looks back at Aunt Emma, and says, "And, I've been directed by higher authority to ask if the five of you will consider signing a copy of the CD when it comes out."

"Well of course, silly man," Aunt Cadi replies.

"How old is this higher authority?"

Again he looks directly at me, and I get a weird kind of rush.

"Fourteen," he replies to Aunt Emma's question.

After a second of quiet hesitation, Mr. Parker laughs and says, "Go ahead and ask her, Chris."

The tech again hesitates, and this time, looks at Aunt Cadi.

"What?"

When he turns and again looks at me, I get the same weird rush – and even goose bumps.

"Can I ask you something?"

"Me?" I blurt out, even as I am trying to swallow what's in my mouth.

"Yes ma'am," he replies, and again looks at Aunt Cadi. "With your permission of course."

Aunt Cadi, with a big smirk on her face, shrugs, and he quickly looks back at me.

"Did you really write the lyrics to *Ransom*'s new song?"

All three of our mouths hit the floor at the same time…

"oh my god…" I whisper, suddenly very nervous.

"Ha!" Aunt Emma blurts out. "That didn't take long. And yeah, she did, actually."

My head immediately turns toward Aunt Emma and I mutter, "Thanks a lot, Aunt Emma," so quietly, you can barely hear it. Aunt Cadi, of course, lets out a laugh.

The interesting thing is the look in Aunt Emma's eyes – telling me that even though I've been scared to death of this moment, I'm going to be okay…

"I guess I sorta did… but it was mostly Misty."

"She told us, she only rearranged what you gave her," Chris replies.

"She told you? Man! What a blabber mouth…"

"It's okay… honest," he quickly replies, while everyone else is laughing. "We're going to be shooting a video for them too, so we got to hear the finished song and – honest to God – it made me cry."

Even before he finishes his sentence, I'm looking at Aunt Cadi, who of course, laughs – again.

"You have her number, call her. This is your deal, kid."

In the blink of an eye, my phone is in my hand, and I'm headed for the front door. Misty answers on the second ring.

"I take it you heard..."

"Uh-huh," I reply, feeling the tears coming.

"I bet you want to hear it..."

"Please..." I force out, knowing I'm about to cry.

"Hey! Come on now. It came out amazing. I'm emailing you a link to our server. I'll text you a login and password. Just download it, and hit play. Call me back and let me know what you think, okay?"

"Uh-huh," I again force out. I disconnect the call, and then almost tear the front door off the hinges when I burst through it at a full run. I manage to slip between my Aunts, and am halfway up the stairs before either of them can say a word.

"Hey!" Aunt Cadi yells.

"Be right back!" I yell back, and disappear around the corner, down the hall, and into the room Aunt Cadi and I are using. I grab my laptop, which I left on earlier, and start clicking things. I watch as the email program starts to download the file, and at the same time, I turn and head back to the stairs. When I reach the bottom, Aunt Cadi – who looks seriously concerned – grabs my arm and stops me.

"Hey kid... what's going on?"

The moment she finishes her sentence, *Being Saved* comes out of the laptop's speakers.

And yeah, I start crying. Again.

"I said 'I heard...', then she laughed, sent me a password and login, and told me where to go download it..."

Aunt Emma takes the laptop, goes into the living room and quickly plugs it into the external speakers. As the music fills the room, we hear Carson.

"Mom!"

Aunt Emma disappears into the hall again, and seconds later, comes back around the corner carrying Peyton, with Carson and Paige right behind her. The moment they stop moving, Misty starts singing...

They are gone
Oh God how I miss them
But I gotta be strong
Because I'm needed

When He took them
I was filled with fear
When He sent you
I saw your tears

And my heart knew

I'm being saved
From the pain and confusion
I'm being saved
By your gentle intrusion

Into my life...

...and my face is immediately covered by a *huge* smile and there's a mass of tears, streaming down my cheeks. Aunt Cadi too, is full on crying. Although I've known all along, it takes only a heartbeat for the two of them to realize, the song is *about* Uncle Nick. We listen to it once through, all the while watching the twins slowly swaying to the music.

"Can we hear it again," I ask, the moment it stops.

Without a word, Aunt Emma reaches down and clicks play.

As I stand listening, I realize that it's a *real song* – not a 'possible' song, or a 'work in progress', like the last time I heard it. *This* could be played on any radio station – right now. And… hearing just how *amazingly perfect* it is, I finally understand why *Ransom* insisted Mr. Morgan had to record it for them.

Then… it sinks in… *I had a lot to do with it.*

As if she is reading my mind, Aunt Emma, her face covered with tears too, puts an arm around my shoulders and gently squeezes.

"Get ready, Carla Mitchell, your life is about to become a really *'big deal'*…"

Aunt Cadi steps up on the other side of me, puts an arm around me as well, and says, "Nick is going to freak…" then kisses me on the forehead.

"Good!" I blurt out, laughing and hugging my Aunts. "After all this, I think he deserves a good freaking out… you know?"

I am *sooo* ready for whatever is next…

Lesson Learned

Martin Masterson

We're sitting on one side of the conference table when, without warning, *Audio Distortion* comes strolling in. Being the big clowns they are, Cadi, Emily and Emma immediately come around to our side of the table, and kick Vanessa, Misty and Ariel out of their seats. Laughing, they get up and take seats on the other side, with Stanley and Willie. Poor Terri looks completely mystified.

"Interesting gathering," Stan says.

"We're as surprised as you are," Rhyan replies.

"We have a small issue – well, actually the eleven of you do," Terri says.

"Oh crap... have they been stealing our songs?" Willie blurts out, making every one laugh.

"Not exactly," Terri says.

"Oh come on, Terri!" Vanessa says, "We told you how we feel about it. Bringing them into it isn't going to change our minds."

"What did we miss?" Cadi asks, glancing at Terri.

She immediately turns and looks at Misty, and even as I'm laughing, I try to save her.

"We told her we aren't releasing, until after you guys do. That's all."

Emma starts laughing – and in seconds, the rest of them are as well.

"You brats think we might get another nomination," Emily says, glaring at us, "and you're holding back because you don't want to screw with it."

"Is that true?" Stan asks.

"It's our song. We can release it when we want." Ariel says.

"Uh… excuse me? I think your *label* has some say in that?" Terri says, looking confused herself.

"Screw the awards," Emily blurts out. "Let the fans decide. They're the ones buying tickets and CDs."

Joshua's facial expression changes, as if Emily's comment is somehow accusatory, and has hurt his feelings. And yeah, the rest of us are truly confused.

"You don't think we can hold our own against you guys on the charts?" Cadi asks.

Busted.

The six of us turn interesting shades of red, which makes our mentors start laughing again – one at a time.

"I say release them both," Emma blurts out, in the middle of her laughter. "Lucky Guess Records will be at the top for a while. You all know how I feel about 'awards'. Heck, I haven't dusted off the Grammys I have, in like five years."

"Uh… wife dear…" Stanley says, trying to control his ongoing laughter. "They aren't where you think they are…"

Everyone looks at him.

"Huh?"

"One is in Paige's headboard – with Papa Bear, and one is in Peyton's toy box – the one in the dining room."

The eruption of laughter is exactly what we – the members of *Ransom* – need to ease the moment. When we realize that Emma is still staring at Stanley, quite intently, the room again goes quiet.

"*What*?" Stanley blurts out, "They asked if they could hold them, and they just never gave them back!"

"What does the label want to do?" Cadi asks, making everyone turn and look at Terri.

"*Ransom* is ready to tour. Lucky Guess wants to release them first, and get them rolling."

"Cool," Stan and Willie say at the exact same time, and I catch them winking at each other.

"And what does *Ransom* want to do?" Cadi continues, turning to her left, and pretty much glaring at Josh.

He glances at each of us, making quick eye contact, then turns back to Cadi, and says, "Whatever you guys want to do is cool with us..."

Once again, Emma starts laughing. She grabs Josh's chair and spins him around until he is facing her.

"This isn't about us, Joshua. You – *all six of you*," Emma pauses and makes direct eye contact with each of us, "want this *so* bad, you can taste it. You think we haven't been right where you guys are now?" She turns, and again looks right at Josh and with a big grin, says, "My eyes looked just like yours... once."

"The day we walked away from Red Rocks, we were even. You don't owe us anything guys..." Emily adds, smiling, and poking Rhyan in the side.

"Now," Stanley says, standing up, and making eye contact with each of us, "we're just a couple of pretty good bands."

"More importantly," "Willie quickly adds, "we're even better *friends*. I'll be really pissed off if you guys let this world..." he waves his arms to indicate the record company, "...screw that up – *even slightly*."

"So quit feeding us crap, and tell us what the real bottom line is. Tell us what *Ransom* wants to do," Cadi demands, grinning like she's crazy.

After a second of hesitation, we watch Misty, tears trickling down her cheeks, stand up, make eye contact with each of us, then look right at Stanley, and say, "We *need* to do this, guys. It's probably going to be our last shot, and each of us knows it..."

"I seriously doubt that, Misty," Emma replies, getting a few snickers. "But, you're right. You guys need to go after this full speed..."

"It just seems... well..." Vanessa manages to get out, also very emotional.

"What's your timeline, Terri?" Emma asks, sticking her tongue out at Vanessa.

"Tuesday next week, we release *Lucid Dreaming*..."

"That's my favorite cut of the entire CD..." Stanley offers, looking right at me. I know it's because of all the retro-style keyboard work in the song.

"Two weeks later," Terri continues, "the title track – *Taking Chances*. Two weeks later, *Being Saved* goes to air, and the CD is on the shelves. The following Friday, they open at Staples."

"And then?" Emma asks, leaning forward and winking at Cadi – I think.

"After the third stop of their," she points at me, "tour, we release *Manic Melody*, with a lot of hype. Two weeks later, *Moving Too Fast* goes to air. Then we wait for a response. If the AD fans do what we expect," she pauses and lets out a little chuckle, "MTV has already agreed to release the video for *The Time It Takes*, unannounced on Video Premiers, two weeks later. *One More Time* goes to air the day after the video premier, and the CD is on the shelves the same day.

What happens next, cracks all of us up. The strange thing is, it's not a member of *Ransom* that, based on Terri's explanation, asks the question that's now simmering in everyone's mind.

"Hey! What about..." Cadi blurts out, making the strangest face.

"Figures *you'd* ask," Terri replies, giving Cadi the silliest grin, as the rest of us do our best not to laugh. "That's the sketchy part. Our vice president wants to release *Ransom*'s video the following week, on the same show."

Suddenly... it all sinks in, and we sit staring at her, pretty much in disbelief.

"You want to *promote a competition?"* Emma asks.

"You never said anything about that, Terri," Misty blurts out, the look on her face telling us just how uncomfortable the idea makes her.

Seeing our apprehensive dispositions, Terri takes a deep breath, and does her best to explain...

"I'm going to say one more thing, then the eleven of you will have to make a decision. I know you're musicians, and it's all about the music for you, but you guys have to remember one thing – *this is a business*. That's what Prichard sees... numbers. It's what he does. *And...* as all of you have discovered over the years, he's insanely good at what he does..."

"Okay..." Cadi says, for some reason appearing to be the only one who is totally relaxed. "Go ahead – share..."

It's as if she knows something the rest of us don't.

"Tom Case and Heather Parks over at MTV have seen both videos," Terri says, never breaking eye contact with Cadi.

Everyone is staring at Terri, trying to sort out what she's telling us, but for some bizarre reason, my eyes are locked on Cadi – who is sitting next to me. It's as if the woman is somewhere else... not here with us.

"When Cameron and I sat down with them," Terri continues, "and he explained his idea, they said the same thing, at the same time – *'What an insanely phenomenal idea!'* Then Heather – who you guys know is Program Director – looked me right in the eyes and said, *'My God, Terri... you do realize that, if you pull this off, between them, they'll own this network... for at least a month!'"*

The moment Terri stops talking, a seriously devious smirk slowly spreads across Cadi's face, and there is a very questionable twinkle in her eyes. She leans forward, looks at Emma – who is on the other side of me – and they wink at each other.

"Do it!" Emma suddenly blurts out, breaking the eerie silence that has fallen over the room. "Call Prichard right now, and tell him we're *all* onboard."

Before anyone else can say anything, Terri is up and out a door that is directly behind her. Emma finds nine stunned faces staring at her, as if she has lost her mind. With a laugh, she defers to Cadi...

"How about you explain this one, Mrs. Sharpe..."

As Cadi stands up, she reaches over and gets a high-five from Emma. The rest of us are staring at the two of them in puzzled confusion.

"I want the nine of you, for just one second, to consider something..." Cadi offers, making eye contact with each person at the table. *"What if...* there's actually a 'tie' when all this is over..."

You can smell the wood burning, as nine minds engage – simultaneously.

"And not just with the Grammy thing. Assuming both bands get nominated, we may end up in the middle of a different award show as well, this year..."

"The VMAs..." I mumble, looking at Misty.

"Oh...my...God..." Vanessa mutters, as reality sinks in.

Then Rhyan...

"No freakin' way! This is gonna be totally insane!"

"No kidding!" Emily blurts out, turning and looking right at Emma.

"Very nicely done, Cadi..." Stan says. Then he turns to Emma and asks, "When did *you* figure it out?"

"The moment Cadi's eyes lit up. Like Terri just said, *'this is a business'*, and I know what she..." Emma grins and points at Cadi, "...does for a living!"

After a couple of minutes of intense contemplation, I begin to get a clear understanding of what Emma and Cadi are trying to tell us. Even if neither band wins any awards at all, based solely on *our history*, the fact both bands are being considered *at the same time*, will probably overwhelm the entire music world. The Video Music Awards happen in September, and if either band – or perhaps *both* – gets a VMA nomination, a Grammy nomination is almost guaranteed. If one group actually *wins* a VMA, the eleven of us will be *everywhere* for the five months between the two shows.

And... because all this will be happening while *both bands* are on tour, – well... can you say *'epic'*?

'Sold out' is going to be a total understatement.

Ransom: Start to Finish

As I look from one face, to the next, each one sends the same message...

Regardless of how this all ends, *the ride is going to be extraordinary!*

Four Minutes

Carla Mitchell

Because the *Being Saved* video plays such a huge part in so many lives, *Ransom* decides I'm the one who should tell you about it – about how making it, affects me, *and* my brother. Although Misty is there the entire time, giving us emotional support, she feels that because we lived it, Randall and I are the ones who should share the experience.

My Aunts, of course, knew what Mr. Parker was planning, even as we were shooting the *Audio Distortion* video, a month earlier. I find out the day Mr. Parker shows up at our house, unannounced. He never even comes into the house, but instead, asks Aunt Cadi if he can have a word with me.

"Will you walk with me?"

"Well… yes sir, of course," I reply pulling the door closed and following him down the steps.

"Do you have a place here – that is your sanctuary?" he asks, turning to look at me.

"You mean where I go to be alone?"

"Exactly."

"Sure. But we'll have to hike through the woods…"

"Perfect. I need to escape my life for a bit."

I shrug, turn the corner around the house, and head for the trail that leads out of our backyard, and up onto the ridge. Mr. Parker is right behind me.

"I bet asking you to use my first name, will be too weird, right?" he says, as we wind our way through the trees.

"Probably," I reply, trying not to laugh.

"So… care to guess why I'm here…?"

"Not really sure… to be honest with you," I reply, as we start up the steep part of the trail.

"Miss Mitchell…"

The same moment I hear it, I feel a hand on my shoulder, which makes me stop walking, and turn around.

"Sorry… but that's kinda weird too."

"So… you made my point! If you will call me Wyndom, I will call you Carla."

"Fair enough," I reply. "Should I keep going?"

"Depends."

"On?"

"Why I'm here…"

This is the moment my teenage lightbulb comes on, and I get the strangest rush.

"no way…" I pretty much whisper, as reality sinks in.

"Ah!! She has figured it out!" Mr. Parker blurts out, trying his best not to laugh.

"I'm *soooo* not sure what to say…" I mumble, still staring at him.

"Speak from your heart, young lady. It will usually lead in the right direction…"

"The *Being Saved* video…" I barely whisper.

"Yep! The last time, it was about *all of you* – the families. This time, it's going to be all about Carla Mitchell – and her younger brother. If you already know in your heart, you can't pull it off, all you need do is tell me that. No pressure and no hard feelings."

I once said that Wyndom Parker is an amazing guy. He's just proven it again.

"Do Misty and the others know what you're going to do?"

"Yep..."

I turn and continue up the trail, and without a word, Mr. Parker follows me. After a six minute climb, we end up on the small ridge behind our house, looking out over the neighborhood. I go to a specific spot, and take a seat against some large rocks, facing east. Mr. Parker – who still hasn't said anything – takes a seat next to me.

"Pretty awesome sanctuary..." he offers, after close to five minutes of silence.

"Yeah..." I reply, turning and smiling at him. "Pretty much just me and God..."

We sit quietly for a couple more minutes, and then Carla Mitchell makes the biggest decision of her life.

"I take it I have to be *in* it?"

"No... I can use an actress."

"But the band... and you too, I bet, want me to be."

"Yep."

"Is that the best idea?"

"Depends."

"You're as frustrating as Aunt Cadi... I swear..."

He laughs and says, "Catrin is right, you're bright beyond your years, young lady." Then, kind of like he's challenging me, he adds, "If, of course, you have an idea, better than the person who lived the story, delivering the message the song carries, I'd love to hear it."

"Guess I'm not going to be able to talk my way out of this one..." I reply, leaning over and putting my head on his shoulder.

We spend an hour on that ridge talking. By the time we get back to the house, I actually understand every step of what he plans to do. He says no to coming in, kisses me on the cheek, says 'thank you', and gets into his car. He disappears down the road, even before I get into the house.

Inside, I find Uncle Nick, sitting on the couch with his insanely huge laptop (he's a computer dweeb, you know?) in front of him, typing away. Aunt Cadi comes out of the kitchen, a glass of something in hand, and all she says is "Hey," then turns and heads for her office. The whole situation is so totally goofy, I break out laughing.

"Will you guys *please* ask questions? You're my *parents* for crying out loud!" I pretty much yell in frustration.

Aunt Cadi pulls up, turns around, and asks, "Okay, what did Wyndom have to say?"

"He told me how to find my motivation when he puts me in *Ransom's* video."

"He's putting you *in* the video?" Uncle Nick asks.

I roll my eyes, shake my head, and laughed again.

"Come on... you both knew. But it's kind of cool that you tried to be surprised."

Aunt Cadi walks over and hugs me, without spilling her drink.

"So... you told him you'd do it?"

"Do you think I can?" I ask. "I mean, this is kind of important – especially to Misty and the others. It's not like that small bit in Aunt Emma's kitchen..."

"I think Carla Mitchell can do *whatever* she puts her mind to," Uncle Nick says loudly, standing up, and hugging me too. "I also think it's totally incredible... well, if you're going to do it..."

I look at Aunt Cadi first, then Uncle Nick, and for the very first time, I am overcome by an urge to call them Mom and Dad... and I know *Mom and Dad* would totally understand...

"Yeah, I told him I'd do it..."

"Your mom and dad will be remarkably proud of you, kid."

The moment he says it, the tears come. What happens next is totally automatic... it just comes out.

"Yeah... I know they are – *they just told me so.*"

The looks on their faces as I reach up and wipe my cheeks, tell me they understand. I step over and hug Uncle Nick as tightly as my arms will let me. Then, I turn and hug Aunt Cadi too.

"So... how's it going to be set up?" Aunt Cadi asks, trying to lighten things up. "Or did he tell you to keep it a secret?"

"It's kind of weird actually. He kept saying 'acting won't be required'. Apparently he's going to take me to some places that are part of what happened. He's going to sit me down, and all he wants me to do, is think about how that place relates to what happened, and where my life is now. And... I guess... he's going shoot lots of video of it all..."

When the two of them exchange a 'serious' glance, I pretty much know what they are thinking.

"Come on guys... it's been over a year. My heart isn't fixed yet, but I think this might help. Misty texted me and said that if I do it, she'll be with me, every single second. Can't ask for a better babysitter than the lead singer, right?"

"Well," Aunt Cadi says, reaching out and touching my cheek, "we will support you however we can. But... based on how amazing *our* video came out, I'm thinking you'll be in the best hands you could be."

"I'm supposed to tell you he wants to put Randall in a couple of parts too – with me. He says it's up to all of us to decide."

"What do you think?"

"I think I'll need him…"

"Well… go upstairs and talk to him, and see what he says. We'll go with what you two decide."

I get another hug, and a minute later, am lying across my brother's bed, listening to him tell me how 'insanely cool' the whole situation is.

Here's how nine days of our lives eventually turn into the *Being Saved* video…

Mr. Parker offers to let Aunt Cadi come along, but she says no. I think it's because she's worried she will be a distraction.

Mr. Parker, Randall, me, and two video technicians fly from Flagstaff to Salt Lake City. I find it interesting (and kind of amusing) that both the techs are female. Misty is waiting for us at the airport with a rented van.

They start with me, sitting alone on the curb, at the intersection where the accident actually happened – in Salt Lake City. Just being here is intense to a level I will never be able to explain. And yes, I do end up in tears, but I don't fall apart. After they get what they need, Mr. Parker explains that when they edit it, they are going to overlay an image of the newspaper article about the accident on the scene.

Next, we get on a plane and go to Seattle. Early in the morning, they shoot video of me and Randall, sitting together on the curb, in front of our old house. The fact *none* of our old friends turns up, kinda stings, and I of course, end up crying.

　　　　　　　　　　Riley Morgan

This is where my awesome little brother steps up.

Without prompting, Randall reaches over and puts his arm around me, the moment the tears come.

Our next stop is the cemetery where Mom and Dad are buried. When Mr. Parker sees the look on Randall's face, he pulls me aside and says that when they start shooting, I should try to get him to talk, but not to push him. He also explains that they aren't recording the audio – he just wants us to appear to be talking in the shot. I stand on my tiptoes, kiss him on the cheek, and say, "No problem."

We sit on the grass between the headstones, facing each other, and seconds after the tech calls out 'shooting', I look at my brother and even before he says it, I know.

"I'm gonna cry, Sis... I can't help it."

"Go ahead silly – I'll be right behind you," I reply, pulling my hair back and smiling at him.

"They're here you know..."

"Yep... I feel them too."

He smiles, and a couple of tears trickle down his cheek.

"Do you think they're okay with all this?"

"You mean making the video?"

"Uh-huh..."

"I'm positive of it. It may help a lot of people you know..."

Now, for all you people who have your doubts about the 'afterlife' and things like that, here's one for you to dwell on.

"Yeah..." Randall says, smiling through his tears, "you're right. Especially Mom..."

The moment my brother finishes his sentence, a massive breeze comes up out of nowhere, and the two of us are suddenly showered with maple leaves from a tree that is within a few feet of the graves. It's so sudden, and so bizarre, that both the techs, and Misty, all suck in huge breaths the moment it happens. Once the leaves quit falling, Randall leans over, hugs me tighter than he ever has, looks me in the eyes, and says, *"That,* was our mother..."

"Uh-huh," I reply, kissing him on the cheek. *"Absolutely!"*

Another fifteen seconds pass, and when no one says anything, we turn at the same time, and look to find them all in some kind of stunned trance, staring at us. Carrie – who is actually the camera tech – isn't even looking at her cameras! Misty is frozen, and has tears trickling down her cheeks. When Randall and I start laughing, and jump up, it sorta brings them all back.

Our next stop isn't all that hard, in part because by the time our adventure reached this point, we were mostly just pissed off – at the world in general.

Mr. Parker puts us on the steps of the court house downtown, which is where Grandma finally managed to get custody of us – just in time to keep us out of foster care. Because it's Saturday, and no one is really around, Mr. Parker and Misty recruit ten people who happen along, to be extras. Misty gets tickled when nine out of ten recognize her. All of them get excited when they discover it's a *Ransom* video they are going to be in.

Mr. Parker does some explaining, and when they start shooting, each of the extras walks past us, down the steps. One of them – a younger guy – actually steps between the two of us. I know Mr. Parker is using the scene to show how invisible the two of us had become at that point in our lives.

Now, the totally cool part. Carrie pulls me and Randall aside, and shows us on her laptop, how Chris – the guy who will edit it – will put a transparent Uncle Nick into the scene, directly behind us, digitally.

From here we head for Grandma's house in Spokane. As we are coming down out of the mountains, Mr. Parker asks if I'm up for helping him get a 'weird' shot. I laugh and say sure. We watch him diligently, for about fifty miles, looking this way, then that way, taking in everything we pass. Finally, Misty looks at me, shrugs her shoulders, and then makes a circle around her ear with her finger. I can't help it – I burst out laughing.

Mr. Parker does eventually find what he's looking for. We leave the highway, and drive about three miles to get to it.

It's a huge boulder, sitting all by itself, on the side of a hill. Mr. Parker gets out, spends twenty minutes looking at things, and then shows the girls where he wants the cameras. Then, he smiles at me, points at the boulder, and says, "Bet you twenty bucks you can't get to the top of it..."

I laugh, look at Misty, who is trying her best not to laugh, then turn and head for the rock. Halfway there, without looking back, I yell, "Jezzz, Wyndom, the bribe isn't necessary – all you have to do is ask..." Thirty seconds later, I'm sitting Indian style on top of the huge rock. When they all start laughing, I again yell at Mr. Parker.

"I still want the twenty bucks!"

A few seconds later, he says something to Randall, who nods and comes to the base of the rock.

"I don't know what it means, Sis, but he says to ask how you felt, the very *last* second, before you saw Uncle Nick..."

I smile, and tell him, "Go on back and tell him I'm ready."

Seconds later, Carrie yells 'shooting', and I let my heart loose. It's easy to tell that this shot is for the part of the song that tells how totally alone – and perhaps a bit unwanted – I felt, when we first got to Gram's house...

Even as I sit on top of a huge rock, in the middle of nowhere, lost in a mass of confused emotions, I find myself wishing I could get inside Wyndom Parker's head – just once – so I can find out how he comes up with this stuff...

Once we make it to Grandma's house, Mr. Parker gets a bunch of shots of both of us, wandering around, sitting on the front steps, and at the dining room table, with Grams. Once Mr. Parker has what he needs, we visit for a bit, then thank Grandma, say our goodbyes, and fly to Fort Collins.

They spend a full day, taking shots of Misty and me, in Aunt Emma's studio, as if we're working on the song. Mr. Parker keeps asking me questions, from out of the shots, trying (according to Misty) to get specific reactions from me. A few times Misty and I crack up, and once... I actually lose it, and start sobbing. Mr. Parker chases everyone off, comes and sits next to me, and then apologizes. Once I calm down a bit, he takes the time to explain why he did what he did. He's just a bit freaked by my response...

"If *any of this*, helps someone else find their way, then how we get it doesn't matter. I know you mean well..."

The man leans over, kisses my forehead, and then walks away. I'm not at all sure what to make of it.

Once we're done at Aunt Emma's, it's back to Flagstaff. Apparently, Mr. Parker wants a very specific shot, which will require driving from Albuquerque, home. Even Misty is a bit confused.

Anyhow, Mr. Parker and the techs fly out the same day they are done at the Campbell's. Misty, Randall, and I spend the night, and fly from Denver to Albuquerque the next day, and spend the night there. At first light, Mr. Parker and the girls turn up at the hotel, ready to go. The moment Randall and I see the huge truck that Carrie is driving, we smile at each other. Uncle Nick drove to Spokane in his big four-door Ford, when he came to get us the first time.

Then we see the inside of it – and discover there are cameras *everywhere!* I'm pretty sure the entire inside is covered from every possible angle. Turns out, Randall and I

Riley Morgan

are riding with Carrie and Jane – the techs. Misty and Mr. Parker are going to follow us in a separate car.

We drive along, laughing and joking, and basically just being us. Then, about forty miles from the Arizona state line, Mr. Parker gets serious again. He has Carrie pull over, and explains what he wants *me* to do...

The shot he's after is of me, in the front passenger's seat, taken over my shoulder as we pass the huge sign that says 'Welcome to Arizona'. Carrie and I find it amusing, when after each shot, we stop, Mr. Parker looks at it, and then makes us turn around and drive past the sign again. We do this *seven times* – until Mr. Parker gets the *exact* shot he wants. When he finally does, and I see his face, I understand just how important the shot is to him.

And, for some strange reason, this is also the point where my little brother's emotions catch up with him all at once. When I see him trying to hide his tears, I climb into the back seat with him. Without a word, he puts his head in my lap, and doesn't move again, until we reached our next stop.

Flagstaff High School.

Mr. Parker, seeing how washed out he is, tells Randall to relax, and that he can finish the rest of the shots without him. My tough-guy little brother isn't having it, and again, he steps up. He tells them he agreed to do it and that if he is supposed to be in a shot, *he will be.*

With the principle's permission, and after classes are out for the day, Mr. Parker sits us on the grass in front of the main building, with the name of the school right over our heads. When I see my brother again get emotional, I lean over, wrap an arm around him, and squeeze the poop out of him. Randall breaks up laughing.

Then, even as we are lost in laughter, completely spur of the moment, Mr. Parker decides to use one of Randall's friends, and my two best friends, to spice up the shot. He tells them he wants to try something, to see if it will work, and that he needs them to walk into the scene from different directions, and then sit down next to the two of us. Assuming the cameras are off, they all agree. Thing is, Carrie keeps the cameras rolling the whole time! It's a brilliant idea, and it makes the entire scene perfect. Our friends are, of course, totally freaked when they find out they're actually going to be *in the video*...

See what I mean about getting inside his head?

Seconds after Carrie yells 'out' there's a loud round of applause from the rest of the students who gathered to watch. Once again, I start crying, but my two best friends jump on me, start tickling me relentlessly, and eventually have me laughing like crazy, instead of crying. Later, Randall tells me he saw the principle, and a couple of teachers, standing in the crowd, clapping just as hard as the students.

Finally Mr. Parker takes us home. We're both ready to be there. Once we get our hearts, *and emotions,* back under control, they take a number of shots of the two of us on the front porch with Aunt Cadi, and walking across the backyard, into the tree line, together.

The shot that will always be most important to me is the final shot of the video – and with the exception of his ghost image at the court house, it's the only scene Uncle Nick is in – even though the song is about him. Although I thought it was a bit strange, Wyndom explained it to Misty and me...

"The lyrics tell a story, girls – a story about a very special man, and his relationship with the storyteller. I knew at some point, I had to put Nick in it, but my heart told me that it would have the greatest impact, if I made the audience wait..."

The final scene is of Uncle Nick and me, sitting together under the ash tree. Uncle Nick has his arm around me, he says something, and then without any warning, I lean over and kiss his cheek. For the second time, the crew gets lost in the moment. When no one says anything for a full thirty seconds, we look in the direction of Mr. Parker, and his facial expression is enough to tell me the shot is perfect.

Once he's done, Mr. Parker stands in the driveway next to the big truck, and has a short talk with us. Then he hugs me, shakes Randall's hand, gets into the truck, and drives away.

This time, I don't have to prompt my *parents.*

"So...?" comes out of Aunt Cadi's mouth, the moment the door closes.

"It was a lot harder than I thought..." Randall replies, and immediately goes up the stairs, to his room. Uncle Nick is quick to follow him.

Aunt Cadi takes my hand, leads me into the family room, and we sit down.

"He'll be okay," I say, "he just needs some time I think."

"And Carla? Is she okay?"

I lean over and hug my aunt as tightly as I can.

"Yeah... she is. For the first time since my parents died, I'm really okay. Thank you, Aunt Catrin... for everything."

Uncle Nick suddenly appears at the door.

"I think this is beyond me..." he says, looking frustrated.

"I got it," I say, standing up and heading for the stairs. At the door I stop, hug Uncle Nick, and then turn the corner. I get five steps before I realize I forgot something. I turn around, stick my head back around the corner, and find Uncle Nick sitting down next to his wife.

"Just before Mr. Parker left, he said we are the two bravest kids he's ever met, and that when he shrinks our lives down to four minutes, he's going to do it with respect, and hopefully, make us proud."

Then I'm off up the stairs to rescue my little brother.

Now, more than ever, I believe what I told Randall at the cemetery. Mom and Dad do totally approve of what we've done, and that we gave it our very best.

So... if you think I was weirded out about the finished song, watching me for three weeks, while they edit the video, is – according to my parents – *'incredibly entertaining'!*

Riley Morgan

Survival

Martin Masterson

The battle is on – *Ransom* versus *Audio Distortion.*

Since they premiered *AD's* video four weeks ago, it has pretty much ruled MTV, which is of course, making the six of us all kinds antsy.

We opened our tour at Staples with two shows. The following Monday, I caught Misty checking the list at VH1, to see how far up the chart *The Time It Takes* had made it.

Number 3...

Go figure.

The following week, we do two shows in The Pit – at the University of New Mexico. Both are sold out. At breakfast Saturday morning, I find Misty – this time Ariel and Vanessa are looking over her shoulder – checking the video charts.

Number 1.

Misty changes to the Billboard 100 and finds *The Time It Takes* at the top of that list as well. *Being Saved* is #3, and *Taking Chances* is up to #19. Then... Vanessa puts her finger on the screen – on top of *One More Time* – which, in only a week, has already made it to #14.

Yeah... like we expected anything less.

This week, poop hits the proverbial fan – because tonight, they're releasing *our* video.

We're back stage at Erwin Center, on the University of Texas, Austin, campus. At the moment, 10,000 fans are listening to *Between Classes* open the show. The six of us are sitting in front of a TV in the Green Room staring in stunned disbelief, as the host of The Music Meter tells his viewers that not only does *Being Saved* own the top spot on the video charts, but it managed the feat less than an hour after it premiered. It's both amazing and bizarre!

When Stephen and PJ come to check on us, the looks on our faces make them both break out in laughter. Then, as if this cake even needs any icing, at the end of the show, the host tells the viewers that *Being Saved* has completely crushed a thirteen year old record for number of play requests after a premier.

Five hours later, we're sitting around our hotel suite, doing nothing more than staring at each other, when Emma and Cadi call Vanessa's phone. The girl literally bursts into tears in the middle of the conversation. An hour later, it's Emily's turn to call my phone and congratulate us, and I have to admit, I get all kinds emotional. Finally, Willie calls Josh, and when he says, *'it's all about the music, guys'* over the speaker phone, everything floods out of us – and realization sinks in.

We did it. We actually did it...

Once the call is finished, a solemn looking Misty stands up, says, "It's just beginning guys – let's hope we can survive it..." and then disappears down the hall toward our room.

The VMAs happen twenty-two days later, and yes, just as Terri predicted, the nominations come.

For both bands...

Being Saved trades places with *The Time It Takes* three times over the next three weeks. It's this back and forth competition that makes the six of us finally understand Misty's comment, the night of the premier.

'*...let's hope we can survive it*' was meant to mean *Ransom and Audio Distortion – not* the six of us.

Crazy – Squared

Misty Masterson

So, the *Taking Chances* Tour...

Emma and the guys played the 'seniority card' on us when it came to opening acts. The moment we suggested *Saturday Afternoon*, Emily and Stanley, simultaneously said, "Sorry... they're booked," so fast, Joshua, Martin, and Ariel, all fell out in laughter. So, based on Terri's suggestion, *Ransom* ends up taking *Between Classes,* who totally freaked when they got the invite.

At our second show, as I stood off stage watching, I swear I had a flashback, and saw the six of us, nine years ago – the first time we opened for *Audio Distortion*. It was actually a pretty amazing feeling.

Between Classes jumped into the tour with the idea that opening for a 'major act' meant an absurdly massive production. When they discovered it's just the band, the technicians, and one really big monitor, they were actually disappointed. They did what they were supposed to, but they seemed to lose their 'spark' – and their show seemed kind of flat.

Well… until opening night at The Pit, when, with one simple gesture, Vanessa relit their fire. The crowd, which was totally caught up in their music, began chanting 'BC-BC' as soon as they left the stage. Vanessa took it upon herself to call them back out on stage, and while they were expecting to take a few more bows, within seconds, Ness had the crowd chanting **'one more song!'** and *Between Classes* found themselves doing an encore – *their very first one.* The response of the crowd added fuel to the fire Vanessa started, and they once again became the motivated musicians we originally met.

After the show, behind closed doors, Martin told the five of them that, if they wanted to *make music*, they were welcome to stay, but if it was about 'theatrics and flash' they were really on the wrong tour. He politely explained that *Ransom's* fans come to *hear,* not to see. The only reason we had the big screen, was for the video. Although they listened to what he had to say, later that night he told us he had his doubts.

Much to our surprise, the very next night, the kids turned up for their set, in their *street clothes* – and didn't even bother with make up! They all seemed way too subdued when they took the stage, which caused some immediate concern. The lead guitarist plugged up, and went directly to a mic, even before they were introduced, and told the crowd, "We're the new guys on the block, and we're still learning. Hopefully, once we're done tonight, you will remember us tomorrow."

To this day, it's probably the most amazing thing we've seen on any tour. The moment they lit the stage and the kids started their first song, they were *Between Classes – a band.* The music, their personal interaction, and getting it right, were all that seemed to matter to them. For forty-five minutes, it was only about the music – *their music.* This time when Josh sent them back out for an encore, it was because

Riley Morgan

the crowd was still chanting *'BC-BC'* – a full ten minutes after they'd left the stage!

As for us, performing *Being Saved* is easily the most incredible four minutes of each show. Although I understand the intensity of the song's message, I still find it astonishing how many lives the song seems to have touched. More than once, people in the crowd have asked who the girl in the video is, and each time I smile, and reply, "She wrote the lyrics."

So… this is where the *Taking Chances* Tour gets kind of interesting…

Because *Ransom* and *Audio Distortion* are on tour, none of us can attend the VMAs in Los Angeles, for what the media is touting as 'the battle for pop music supremacy'.

Thanks to Stephen Riggs – our show's producer, and our very good friend – the six of us are going to remember the end of our show the night of the VMAs, forever.

Before the tour started, the six of us agreed to forego encores for the entire tour. We've never understood all the theatrics involved. The crowd chants, the band waits a few minutes, then comes back and plays one more song. We decided we'll play twelve songs, and call it a night, and we tell each crowd this when the show starts. So far, they've all been really accepting of it.

And… because the song totally amps every crowd, and the audiences have come to expect it, we play *Terminal Velocity* last.

So… it's the night of the VMAs, and the show has been totally phenomenal – both ours *and Between Classes*. They came off stage after their encore, so amped they were bouncing around, and cracking up the stage crew.

Now, our set complete, we're setting up to play *Terminal Velocity*, (Josh and a couple of techs are realigning some of the amps, partly because he's nuts, and partly because this song has to be as loud as possible) when the giant monitor behind us, comes to life, and is filled with a live feed of the VMA's.

And none of us has even the slightest clue.

Our first hint that something is up, is the crowd falling totally silent. The second is how bright the stage becomes. Realizing it must be the monitor, I spin around just in time to see Avril Lavigne and Taylor Swift standing together in front of a mic, as Avril says, "...and this year's MoonMan for Best Pop Video goes to..."

The very moment I grasp what I'm watching, my legs go rubbery, my heart stops, and the tears come.

The entire arena is so quiet, you probably *could* hear a pin drop, as Taylor tears open the envelope she's holding, shows it to Avril, and then yells, ***"Ransom – Being Saved!"***

That's all it takes. As the crowd erupts into total insanity, I drop to the floor, my legs no longer able to support me, and burst into full on sobbing. Martin rushes across the stage, and is next to me in heartbeat. Vanessa and Ariel are also in tears, and are in the arms of Josh and Rhyan.

The strange thing is, winning the award isn't what will be with the six of us forever – it's the response of our opening act, and the 21,000 people filling the arena.

Ransom's fans...

It takes us a full thirty minutes to recover, but eventually, the crowd gets to hear the most powerful rendition of *Terminal Velocity* that *Ransom* has ever pulled off. After the show, Stephen, still a ball of nerves, tells us that the crowd response was the most insane thing he's ever seen, in the thirty-five years he's been in the music business.

We come out of the VMAs so far past what we expected, we're fairly certain God had something to do with it...

Best Video With A Message – *Being Saved*

Most Share-Worthy Video – *Being Saved*

Best Editing – *Being Saved*

Best Direction – *Being Saved*

Best Pop Video – *Being Saved*

And, Miss Carla Mitchell is famous – whether she wants to be, or not. Once we get them, I even make her take home the Best Pop Video MoonMan, and put it on her dresser – just because. Of course, Cadi and Nick think I've lost my mind...

As my amazing friend, and mentor, Emma Campbell, is so fond of saying...

'*Welcome... to the exponentially convoluted world of music*'

Sneakier

Joshua Miller

With the pressure of the VMAs behind us, our last ten shows turn out to be incredible. Knowing we cleaned up at the awards show, our fans go completely off the chain at every venue. Each night, when we play *Being Saved*, the crowd brightly lights each arena, with *thousands* of glow sticks – of every imaginable color – and keep them swaying in almost perfect unison for the entire song. It's so amazing, poor Misty ends up giving into her tears, every time.

Tonight is a special show – our last show of the tour. And we're playing it at home – in Wichita. Sure, we've played here before, but it's different this time – mostly because of the VMAs.

This time, it's about *Ransom* representing every music lover in the state of Kansas…

Anyhow, we're down to the last song, of the last show, of the *Taking Chances* Tour, and yeah, we're all a bit emotional.

"Okay guys!" Misty says, standing at the front of the stage, looking out into the crowd, "as you know, we aren't doing the whole 'encore' thing on this tour – which I should point out, has been the most amazing tour of our careers. So, just like we've done at every other show, we're going play *Terminal Velocity* as our last song, get all of you to sing along, and then call it a night."

Even as Misty is talking, I glance to my left and see a young girl – *maybe* all of sixteen and with a huge, childish grin on her face – appear from between the speakers, and without a word to anyone, she casually strolls across the stage, and even *waves* at Rhyan. When she reaches the grand piano, she slides the bench back and sits down.

Okay, so… let's discuss strange and bizarre. The fact that, not a single member of the stage security team turns up to stop her, should be a massive hint. But, the truth is, the six of us are so totally perplexed, none of us considers that.

Misty, mic in hand, glances at me and I shrug. Even though she is visibly stunned by the girl's presence, she looks directly at her, and with her mic on, asks, "And you are?"

Blatantly fighting off a laugh, the girl pulls the piano mic over, turns and looks right at Misty, and says, "Oh… I'm Anna," following it with a giggle. Then she looks right at Martin, and adds, "Hi, Martin!"

"No freakin' way…" Martin instantly blurts out, the look on his face telling us he definitely *recognizes* her.

I think this is the point that Misty at least, catches on. Now laughing, she starts toward the piano, with Vanessa right behind her.

"I see…" Misty says, playing along with whatever is going on. "Are you going to play this thing?" she asks, putting a hand on the piano when she reaches it.

"That's the plan…" Anna replies, again giggling. "As you guys know," she pauses, and looks right at Martin, who is now standing next to Misty, "I *can* play a little piano…"

That's when my brain puts two and two together. Anna… knows Martin… plays piano. Summer Music Fest at Discovery Studios…

When Misty quickly glances in the direction of the Sound Supervisor, standing at the top of the stage stairs, the guy holds up his hands, and shrugs his shoulders, as if to say 'I have no clue'.

"I see…" Misty says, again turning her attention to Anna, and trying her very best not to start laughing again.

Keep in mind, this is all happening in front of 18,000 fans that, now as curious as we are, have fallen eerily quiet.

"What song are you going to play?" Martin asks, also trying to keep a straight face.

"It's a *really* old Motown song…" Anna replies, "but I'll bet you this dollar," she pulls a bill out of her shirt pocket, pops it open, and then lays it on the top of the piano, in front of the three of them, "that it will have all of you," she pauses, and points at everyone on stage, "dancing, before it's over."

"Oh really?" Vanessa asks, now giving in to her laughter.

The once-quiet crowd goes completely off, as Rhyan and I join the others in laughter. The thing that touches me is the magnetic personality of this young girl. Sure, she has hijacked our show, but at this exact moment, she owns the entire building – and everyone in it.

"Uh-huh… really," Anna replies, as she pulls a finger down the length of the keyboard, bringing the piano to life. "You won't be able to help yourself – it's that kind of a song."

Again the crowd breaks out into cheers and whistles.

"So…" Vanessa asks, completely losing her struggle to stay serious, "Do you sing too?"

"Nope," Anna quickly replies, as she hits a few keys on the piano, as if checking the tuning. She leaves the six of us – and the audience – hanging for a couple of seconds, then says, "I have her," and lifts one hand and points at the back of the stage, "for that. She's pretty good too!"

Anna puts both hands back on the piano, and runs over the keys, as six heads turn, and look in the direction she pointed.

The very instant we see Sally, mic in hand and an absurdly huge grin on her face, coming out from between the speakers next to Rhyan, we know what's going on – and more importantly, who is behind it all.

You see, *Saturday Afternoon* is opening for her band!

"Ladies and gentleman, Miss Sally Wright, lead singer of…" is as far as Misty gets, before the entire arena goes complete nuts.

"And… I brought some help," Sally says.

"Can I borrow your drums, Rhyan?" fills the arena, as Patty appears next to him wearing a mic headset, and twirling a pair of drumsticks.

The very second Martin hears Patty's voice he spins around, and finds a grinning Pete, already standing at his keyboard, pushing buttons.

Rhyan, ever the consummate smartass, laughs and asks Patty, "Do I have a choice?"

"Nope," she immediately replies, laughing. "Move."

Rhyan loses it, and laughing, almost falls over, getting out of her way. Patty takes his seat, and does a run over his drums.

"Damn!" Ariel blurts out, "They've hijacked our freakin' show!"

Her comment gets yet another round of cheering, whistling, and screaming. Although they have no clue what, the crowd senses that something *seriously cool* is about to happen.

Anna gets up, walks around the piano, and stops next to Ariel. With a smile, she pulls the plug on her guitar, unhooks the strap, then takes it and hands it to a full-on laughing Vanessa. She then turns to me, and does the exact same thing, this time handing my guitar to Rhyan. Then without a word, she takes our hands and leads us to the front of the stage, points at the edge it, and says, "Reserved seating." Even as the crowd laughs, and again cheers, a teary-eyed Ariel sits down, her legs dangling, within feet of the audience. I quickly join her, hold out my hand, and she immediately puts hers in it.

"Okay... so," we hear Anna say, "This song is *really* old – like forty years even..."

When I turn to look, I see Anna crossing the stage back to the piano, stopping to get a high-five from Sally as she passes her. Seconds later, Randi and Melinda appear, and plug up. Now as if all this isn't strange enough, two guys who appear to be Anna's age, wander out onto the stage – one with a sax, and the other a trumpet – and the crowd goes quiet again for a moment. I spin Ariel around so she can see it too, and after she laughs, she whispers "This should be interesting," in my ear, and then gently kisses my cheek.

"But..." Melinda continues, now in front of one of the mic stands, checking the tuning of her guitar, "...*everyone* on earth has at least one really old song that touches them in some way. That's just how music is, right?"

Again, the crowd responds with cheers and whistles.

"A song that, no matter where they are when they hear it..." Patty adds, tapping on a cymbal, and stomping the foot pedal on the bass drum, "will make them remember something from their life..."

Then out of nowhere, Vanessa mumbles, "*Wannabe...*" which is picked up by Misty's mic. Ariel instantly squeezes my hand, and smiles at me.

"Exactly!" Sally says. "That song makes the six of you remember something, every time you hear it."

The next thing we know, Sally is standing next to Ariel, at the very edge of the stage, and when she holds out her free hand, Ariel takes it.

"As most of *Ransom's* fans know," Sally says, as the lighting guys hit the three of us with a single spotlight, and dim all the other lights on the stage, "Josh and Ariel are very much in love."

That one gets a *really loud* round of cheering...

"So tonight, we're going to give them their 'old song' – right here in Wichita. I'm gonna bet that, even as old as the song is, a lot of you will recognize it, so we expect all of you to help us out, and sing along."

"Truth is..." Anna adds from the darkness, her fingers again running down the keyboard, "I fell in love with this song, the very first time I heard it." As a second spotlight drops on her, Anna continues. "Although I don't really know Josh and Ariel, from what these guys tell me, this song totally fits the two of them."

"So Wichita... *are you ready?*" Sally yells.

The entire arena goes totally off the chart again, and I somehow know Emma did this here – *in front of this particular crowd* – on purpose. And yeah, at this point, even though we haven't seen her, Ariel and I are pretty certain this is Emma Campbell's doing...

Anna starts the intro, which she extends out for thirty seconds, giving Sally time to get the crowd going, and even I recognize the silly song – from a TV commercial!

Within seconds, Sally has the crowd – *all 18,000 of them!* – clapping along, in almost perfect unison. And, just as Sally said, it's apparent most of them recognize the song too. Once Sally is ready, she smiles, and disappears behind us.

The very second the guys with the horns join Anna, so do the rest of them.

All Ariel and I can do, is hold on to each other.

Set Up (twice)

Misty Masterson

One day, as the Lord is my witness, I *am* going to sing a duet with Sally Wright. If, as everyone kept telling me when I was younger, my voice is a 'gift', then Sally's is an amazing treasure.

She has a range than shouldn't be possible, I don't think I've ever heard her miss a note, and then there is her *passion*. A deep, intense, passion, that comes from a place that doesn't exist in most vocalists.

And the most important thing about Sally? For her it's *never* about being perfect, but instead, every time the girl opens her mouth, it's about *having fun!*

I'm standing next to Martin, who has his arm around my shoulders, listening to the music, and three bars in, Sally starts singing...

> *Give it just a little more time*
> *And your love will surely grow*
> *Give it just a little more time*
> *And your love will surely grow*

She wanders up, slips in between the Josh and Ariel and sits down, making sure they keep holding hands, and goes right on singing.

Life's too short to make a mistake
So think of each other and hesitate
Young and impatient you may be
There's no need to act foolishly

Sally's amazing voice transfixes *everyone* in the building – there's no way to explain what we are experiencing… well, with words anyhow. Martin and I are stunned to silence. All we can do… is watch.

I do, however, start laughing, when the horn players start dancing in unison. In just a single heartbeat, they have Melinda and Randi in step with them.

You're young and you're in a hurry
You're eager for love but don't you worry
You both want the sweetness in life
But these things don't come overnight

When they reach the break, Anna Rodriguez – the cute little sixteen year old high school kid – lets her heart out. There's simply no other way to say it. Watching how effortlessly her fingers dance over the piano's keys is hypnotizing, and when I glance at my husband, the mass of tears on his cheeks makes me smile. After all, when one keyboardist can bring another to tears, *that* says something.

The lighting guys drop a single spot on Anna and the horn players, and for a full thirty seconds, the three of them totally wreck the place with a mind-blowing solo, as the others back them.

When I look for Vanessa and Rhyan, I find them lined up with Melinda and Randi – the six of them are clapping and doing that silly dance, in unison! I grab Martin and in the blink of an eye, we're dancing right along with them.

Sally gets Joshua and Ariel on their feet, and within seconds the three of them, are dancing away too.

Looks like I owe Anna a dollar...

Someone brings the house lights all the way up, only to reveal that *every single person in the building is on their feet*, clapping, dancing, and singing along. Who knew a forty-year-old Motown tune could raise this reaction, in a crowd this young? Heck, at least half the crowd is so young, their *parents* were in diapers when the song was recorded!

Music... *is amazing.*

Once Anna and the guys finish the solo, she slips right back into the song. When I glance at the top of the stairs, I finally see Emma standing there, in tears herself.

The horn players move back to center stage, and join our goofy line dance, blowing furiously on their horns, as Sally finishes the song. The entire arena watches as Josh wraps his arms around Ariel, and they start dancing together slowly.

> *Love is that mountain you must climb*
> *Climb it together hand in hand over time*
> *You've known each for oh so long*
> *And the feelings you have are oh so strong*

The moment the last note fades, the cheering is so insanely loud, I actually have to cover my ears. Josh sweeps Ariel off her feet, and plants a massive kiss on her – *in front of 18,000 people.* The members of *Saturday Afternoon*, having put down their instruments, rush over and pretty much tackle Anna, pulling her off the stool, and squishing her in one massive group hug.

I jerk on Martin's sleeve, point in the direction of the stairs, and he looks just in time to see the members of *Between Classes*, clapping louder than anyone else, and Emma, wiping her tears.

Ransom: Start to Finish

I'm standing with my arm around my husband, my heart expanded to three times its normal size, when I turn and see Ariel pull a mic from a stand, turn to face Josh, and then raise her hand. It takes about thirty seconds for the crowd to catch on, and go quiet. Once they do, Ariel gets all of us...

"Yes, Joshua Miller, I will marry you. Right this very second if you're up for it..." she calmly says.

The almost total silence that engulfs the arena is so acute, you'd think the place is empty. Then I hear something behind me, and when I turn to look, I find Pastor Wilson – *from our church in Ransom* – bible in hand, coming up the stairs. Right behind him, is Terri Maxwell. Terri says something to Emma as she passes her, and when she reaches center stage, she grabs a mic, flips it on, and says, "How convenient! I just happen to have a minister..."

The crowd is so dumbfounded and disbelieving, they remain completely silent. Then without warning, the entire arena is filled with the Bridal Chorus – more commonly called 'Here Comes The Bride' – and when we turn to look, there at the piano is our happy little high school sophomore, grinning like a criminal, tears streaming down her cheeks, playing her heart out.

And, although it isn't actually 'legal', on a cool October night, Joshua Miller and Ariel Williams get married, on a stage, inside the InTrust Bank Arena, in Wichita, Kansas, in front of 18,000 of the their *friends*, by a minister they've known their entire lives.

In truth, the whole scene is pretty extraordinary.

The next morning, as Martin and I try to sneak out really early to go to breakfast, the Night Manager and the night desk clerk call us over to the front desk. Without a word, the manager unfolds a newspaper, and lays it out in front of us.

Covering the *entire front page* of the Wichita Eagle, is a photograph of Josh and Ariel, locked in the most passionate kiss they have probably ever shared, and Pastor Wilson is standing behind them, smiling.

There's a caption, in bold letters, under the photo that says, *"We Do!"*

Plotting

Georgia Crossman

When the five of them show up at our house, the first words out of my mouth are "are you moving in again?" which of course, makes them laugh.

"Nope… just for tonight. We have a concert to go to, tomorrow night," Vanessa says, hugging me.

"OMG!" I blurt out, "Do they know?"

"Now where would be the fun in that?" Josh asks, also giving me a hug.

I make dinner, and we spend the night talking about the tour, and all the amazing stuff that happened. I find out that Josh and Ariel are 'legally' married now, that they are going to be moving to LA again, and will be working for Terri.

Vanessa has been offered a teaching position – at CSU. She still has to get her certificate to teach, but as smart, and as passionate as she is, I know that isn't going to be a problem. Although I can't prove it, I'll bet the farm, my brother and father had something to do with that whole situation.

Then the big news. Misty is pregnant.

She and Martin intend to continue living in Ransom, and will probably spend their days, volunteering at all the schools in the area. Of all the band members, they are the most ready to slow down.

So... as I expect, the next morning my sister in law calls, and asks if I will consider babysitting, while they play their final show at Moby Arena. Although Carla is with them, they don't want to burden her with the kids, the night of the tour's final show – which I totally understand.

When I say I'll do it, Emma says she'll bring them over, and I have to be quick on my feet. I tell her I'm going to be visiting Dad for a bit, and that I can pick them up on the way, so they can hang out with Grandpa too. She buys into it.

Ransom's presence is still a secret...

One Last Show

Martin Masterson

We do manage to pull it off. With Terri's help we get into the VIP section, and right up against the stage. Their final show – to a *sold-out* Moby Arena – is classic *Audio Distortion*. One of the *many* things we've learned from them – *always* play your last show *at home*.

The highlight of the night comes when, to the audience's total surprise, *Saturday Afternoon* takes the stage to close the show – with the same song they played at our final show, three weeks earlier. Because they're in Fort Collins, getting Anna, Timothy, and James back onstage with them, is simple, and makes them big stars, at Fort Collins High.

And, of course, they once again have everyone in the building dancing and singing along – even a matching set of five year olds, and the most adorable two year old, you have ever seen. Yeah... 'Aunt Georgia' snuck them in, dressed them up, and sent them out onstage, to the complete surprise of their parents. Silly girl.

But for the six of us, the most amazing part of the night is finally getting to see Bailey and Melissa join the girls, to perform *The Time It Takes.* They are *perfect*, and when the five of them take their bow, you can tell by the kids' faces, they know their amazing ride is over...

After the show, *Audio Distortion* obliges the reporters, and does a number of interviews in the Green Room, and we sit quietly and watch. Each reporter has the same question – *'how long before we get more?'* – and each time the question is asked, the band offers only smiles in response. Gotta love these guys.

We end up at the Campbell's house, talking until the wee hours of the morning. About the time the sun comes up, everyone heads for bed.

Just from their demeanor, I'm overcome by a pretty ominous feeling. The first clue that something may be up, is the fact that for the first time, they did three shows at Moby, instead of one big one at Pepsi Center, like they've usually done at the end of their tours.

My heart is telling me that *Audio Distortion* may actually be done this time...

108

Normal Speed?

Joshua Miller

The tours, the interviews, and the personal appearances now finished, everyone goes home for a while and tries to slow down to 'normal' speed again.

For a while, at least.

The Grammy nominations come out in nine days… and although our mentors don't seem all that interested, the six of us are on egg shells. Here's why…

The Time It Takes has owned the #1 spot on the singles charts for the last nine consecutive weeks. Terri says it's because 'tweens' and teens around the world know Melissa and Bailey are a big part of the song.

Being Saved fell to #3, behind *Moving Too Fast,* and when they released their title track – *One More Time* – it entered at #26, went to #14 in a week, and has been steadily climbing since. It's currently #9.

Three tracks in the top ten, for three weeks. Life is good for *Audio Distortion.*

And… we are pretty much deflated.

As if all of that isn't enough, *One More Time* has also occupied the #1 spot on the album chart, *for nine consecutive weeks,* and is certified multi-platinum – breaking the million mark four times!

Taking Chances is currently #5, and has been, for six weeks.

Sometimes, just *wanting* it, isn't enough.

Emily, being the annoying nuisance she is, actually makes a call every Saturday, right after Billboard posts, to our lead guitarist, and all she says, is *"nener-nener-nener"* and then hangs up.

Now, if that isn't childish enough, being the knucklehead I am, and knowing exactly who is at the other end of the call, I actually answer… *every single time.*

No matter how bad it looks, the six of us still hold out hope, that we will at least get nominated…

And It Begins

Misty Masterson

Ransom's interview schedule…

Absurd comes to mind first.

The fact *Being Saved* dominated the VMAs, seems to have the press believing we are online to do the same thing at the Grammys.

Yeah… right.

Being Saved, and the ongoing silliness associated with it, has changed Carla – *a lot*. At first, I was very concerned about it, but in the end, a sixteen year old telling me she has a handle on it, allows me to relax, and let her travel her path.

She agrees – with Cadi and Nick's approval – to hang out with us for a bunch of the interviews. Because everyone we encounter seems in awe of her, she's pretty uncomfortable at first. Then, much to our surprise, it's Joshua who steps up, and gives her a direction.

"If they're making you uncomfortable, for crying out loud, tell them that. Remember that *they want to interview you*, which pretty much makes you the boss…"

At the very next interview, Carla takes charge – just like she did in the cafeteria at her high school, when the 'fame' thing seemed about to get away from her. She asks to speak to the hosts privately, and they agree.

"I'm just a sixteen year old girl... honest. Yes, I can apparently write. Lots of people can. Not a big deal. I'm not a star, or a celebrity. If you guys can keep that in mind, this whole interview thing will be a lot easier..."

Apparently she made her point – because word spread. After that, every interview we did, was smooth, efficient, and most importantly, *fun*. Carla was even cutting up with one of the hosts.

The whole situation has also created the most amazing bond between her and Nick. If the entire world didn't know she lost her parents, they would all assume Nick *is* her father, just by watching them interact. Even Cadi concedes there is an extraordinary bond between them, that like many other things in life, simply isn't meant to be explained... only accepted.

So... the Grammys.

Ransom gets a few nominations – our dominance at the VMAs pretty much demands it. We're up for Album of the Year, Song of the Year, Record of the Year, Best Pop Vocal Album, and Best Short Form Music Video.

Here's a shocker. *Audio Distortion* only gets three nominations.

They're up against us and two other bands for Album of the Year and Best Pop Vocal Album. The nomination they get, that we don't, is Best Pop Group Performance – based we are pretty sure, on Melissa and Bailey performing with them, both on the record, and on tour.

As a group, we've asked Carla to go up and accept the award, if we should win Song of the Year. It takes some effort, but once I – with some help from Cadi, and Emma – explain that the award is about the writers/composers of the song, and not the performers, she seems to understand. The six of us together, explain that we are immensely grateful for the path the song has taken us down, but we all understand that without her – without her willingness to let the world into her life – it wouldn't have happened. Poor Carla is totally freaked. Later, without the rest of the band, I take a few minutes to explain the deep significance of the person who *lived the song*, going up and receiving it, and it seems she is almost ready to concede.

She hasn't said what she intends to do yet, so I guess we'll all be surprised together.

Eight more weeks...

Although for our mentors, it's business as usual, I think the six of us may simply self-destruct between now and then.

Isn't music amazing...

"**This**, is totally about how six amazing musicians gave a girl, and her brother, the means to remember their parents — forever!"

~ Carla Mitchell 

...*Miss Carla Mitchell!*

Georgia Crossman

Because I'm sort of a non-participant in this whole Grammy thing, I've been left to tell you about it. You see, the band is totally lost in the night's insanity – which is really cool to watch.

My husband let me get the most amazing dress, and the shop was happy to alter it enough to make sure it fits my pregnant self, without giving away my secret.

They talked Carla into sitting with the band, in case she decides to go up, should they win Song of the Year. The eight of us are in a line, with me at one end, and Carla on the isle at the other.

Finally, after the TV breaks are over, the lights go down, and we hear...

LADIES AND GENTLEMEN
WELCOME
TO THE 59TH ANNUAL
GRAMMY AWARDS!

...and we watch as the stage spins around to reveal *Audio Distortion* – with a slight change. Melissa is sitting at the

Bösendorfer – which Stanley had shipped here, just for this performance – and Bailey is sitting at her father's drums.

Seems the two of them get their wish – to be *onstage* at the Grammys – even if it isn't exactly as they planned.

Audio Distortion is invited to be the first act of the show, and of course they want them to play *The Time It Takes*, with their stand-in drummer and keyboardist. At this point, the girls have played the song so many times, that even with the pressure of playing at the Grammys, the five of them nail it – and get yet another standing ovation. The girls are in full-out 'giddy' overload, while Emily, Cadi, and Emma can't seem to stop laughing.

They gave *Ransom* the Grammy for Best Short Form Music Video, before the televised part of the show actually started, and for an hour, one at a time, they give away those cute little gramophones... until they reach Best Pop Group Performance. The very instant the words '...and the Grammy goes to, *Audio Distortion*', fill the arena, Melissa and Bailey leap from their seats, to the cheers of all of the artists around them. I have to fight off a laugh, when I watch the two of them actually get high-fived by Cee Lo Green and Bruno Mars, as they jump into the aisle. Dr. Dre – who is sitting behind their parents – put's a hand on Willie's shoulder and while pointing at the girls, says something to him. Willie smiles, and shakes his hand.

Then, as the crowd waits for *Audio Distortion* to go get their award, Emma Campbell does what has to be *the most amazing* thing I have *ever* seen anyone do... in my entire life. She calls Melissa back to her, hands her a sheet of paper and says something to her. Melissa looks at the paper, leans over and hugs Emma, then takes Bailey's hand and the two of them head for the stage. After only a few steps, Bailey stops and goes back to where Emma is sitting, says something to her, and in a single heartbeat, to the applause of the entire crowd, the twins are in the aisle. Hand in hand the four of them make their way down to the stage. Halfway there, the announcer's voice fills the arena…

"Accepting the award for Audio Distortion –
Bailey Morgan, Melissa Faintree, and the
youngest Campbell's!"

Carrie Underwood is waiting on them, grinning and holding two Grammys. She kisses each of them on the cheek, and hands them each an award. They in turn – to the amazement of the crowd – immediately hand them to Paige and Peyton. Carrie takes the twins' hands, and points Melissa and Bailey at the mic, which she has lowered for them.

"We are like so totally petrified…" Melissa offers.

"Seriously!" Bailey quickly adds.

"You guys rock!" comes from somewhere out in the audience, which makes Melissa momentarily cover her face with her hands. She quickly recovers, and with tears on her cheeks, steps up to the mic.

"Aunt Emma gave me this," she holds up the piece of paper, "so I'm going to try to read it for you…"

As Melissa wipes her tears, and starts to read, Bailey squats down, says something to the twins, and whatever it is, makes Carrie start laughing. She too, leans over and whispers to them.

"Thanks to the Academy, and all our fellow artists, for this amazing recognition," Melissa reads, "But mostly thanks to all of *Audio Distortion's* dedicated fans. Those," she points at the Grammys the twins are holding, "are for all of you! As long as their fans keep listening, our parents will keep making music!"

Even as I watch, something I read jumps to the front of my thoughts… a photograph of Melissa and Bailey with the caption *'pop music's future'* under it, and I find myself wondering if they're right.

As the crowd begins to applaud, Carrie pulls the mic from the stand, hands it to Bailey, who smiles, and promptly gives it to Paige.

A six year old, onstage at an awards show, with a live mic...

This should be insanely entertaining...

"AUDIO 'STORTION TOTALLY ROCKS!" Paige yells.

As it reverberates through the Staples Center, *everyone* is on their feet cheering. The kids come down the stairs and back up the aisle, and after they give the Grammys to their parents, everyone again takes their seats.

Forty-five minutes later, the show reaches the 'Big Four'. When they reach Song of the Year, I glance down the row at my husband and the others, and I have to make myself not laugh. My heart knows how much this means to all of them.

John Mayer and Katy Perry read the nominees, and a video clip plays during each one. When the clip for *Being Saved* is played, the place goes pretty much nuts. Then, the presentation...

"Man!" John offers, "That's some stiff competition! But... only one can win... and this year's Grammy for Song of the Year goes to..." he pauses, as Katy, with a huge smile, carefully opens the envelope.

"Ransom – Being Saved!" Katy yells. *"Carla Mitchell and Misty Maitland, song writers!"*

The instant applause is almost deafening, as the video begins playing on the giant monitor above the stage. When it reaches the part where Carla is sitting on the corner in Salt Lake City, a small tear on her cheek, and the newspaper headline superimposed over her, the image freezes, as the audio keeps playing.

                                           Riley Morgan

I again lean forward and look down the row, to see what Carla is going to do. They decided that if Carla's nerves got the better of her, Misty would go up alone. I watch as Misty and Martin – who are sitting next to Carla – stand up, yet she doesn't move.

Then, somehow, Carla finds a way to turn her heart loose. She takes Martin's hand, and he pulls her to her feet. She faces Misty and Martin, says something to them, and then, she steps into the aisle – alone.

Most of the people sitting near her, already know who she is, and they *all* come to their feet, and begin applauding. Seconds after she starts down the aisle, Logan Henderson – one-time member of *Big Time Rush* – steps into the aisle, and holds out his arm. A stunned, and full on crying Carla, takes it, and lets him lead her down to the stage.

"Accepting the award for Ransom,
Miss Carla Mitchell!"

The instant the announcer says it, I glance at Cadi – just in time to see her, hands covering her mouth, burst into tears. Even Nick has tears trickling down his cheeks, as he stands with his arm around his wife. Emma too, has an arm around her.

It takes her close to a minute to actually reach the stage, as person after person hugs her, or kisses her cheek. When she finally makes it, she's gone from crying, to sobbing. Standing at the top of the stairs, waiting on her, is John, and he takes her hand and leads her center stage. Katy hands her the award, as John hugs her, and kisses her cheek. Then they step back and give her the mic. After a moment, she takes a deep breath, and says, "Thank you… all of you."

The entire arena goes totally silent.

"Misty and the band said this," she puts the award down on the podium, and stands quietly staring at it for a few seconds, "is for, *and* about, me. It's not really. Lots of people have lost family, maybe even some of you. My brother and I are just two more…" She pauses again, picks up the Grammy and after gently rubbing the inscription on the front of it with her finger, lifts her head and looks at the audience. *"This…"* she holds the award up, "This is actually about them… *about Ransom*…" She again begins to cry, and with a big smile says, "Stand up guys…"

The six of them stand, to another massive round of applause, and at least three spotlights hit them at the same time. I am suddenly over come with a feeling of intense pride, even though I'm not a member of the band…

"This," Carla says, as Katy and John step up on each side of her, "is totally about how six amazing musicians gave a girl, and her brother, the means to remember their parents – forever. If it has to be 'for' someone, well…" she looks straight up, "it's for you, Mom and Dad. *We're gonna be fine!"*

Instant standing ovation, which turns into a long, and deeply emotional, round of applause – minus the screaming, yelling, and whistling – from *everyone* in the building, as *Being Saved* continues to play. I'm pretty sure this is the most emotional I have *ever* seen my husband. When he sits back down, I reach over and wipe the tears off his cheeks, and gently kiss him.

Instead of following the presenters backstage, Carla immediately goes back the way she came, and no one tries to stop her. Logan, still standing at the bottom of the stairs, leads her back to her seat, where Cadi and Nick are standing in the aisle, both in tears.

After she gets hugs from her parents, she turns, and goes back to her seat. She holds out the award to Misty who, with tears streaming down her cheeks and a huge smile on her face, refuses to take it. After an emotional hug, they sit down, and the show continues.

Adele and Nicki Manaj are the next presenters. As they walk slowly center stage, the crowd gets quiet, and a smiling Adele steps up to the mic.

"So music lovers, Nicki and I are here to present the Grammy for Record of the Year…"

"As soon as my damn heart slows down…" Nicki blurts out, starting yet another round of clapping.

"For all you songwriters out there," Adele continues, "I'm pretty sure there's a song in that last presentation… somewhere…"

"Yeah…" comes from a smiling Nicki, who also appears to be crying, "And whoever finds it, will have a freakin' hit on their hands. How amazing is that girl?"

The entire building again erupts, and when I glance at Carla, she's bright red, and quickly buries her head in her hands.

"So…" Adele offers, causing the crowd to go quiet again. "Record of the Year…"

As they read the nominees for Record of the Year, again the video clips play. This time, when I look at my husband and his bandmates, there is a feeling of total calm – from all of them. They won the one that was important to them – the rest is apparently just fluff.

"And the Grammy goes to…" Adele says, carefully opening the card she is holding, as various opinions are yelled from the crowd. Then, with a huge smile, Adele holds the card out where Nicki can see it, and in unison they yell, ***"Ransom – Being Saved!"***

This time, *Ransom's* response does make me laugh – especially my husband, who along with Vanessa, starts cutting up and acting silly. In seconds, the six of them are in the aisle and headed for the stage, getting high fives the entire way. Carla, still in tears, chooses to stay seated. Misty makes a short speech, and then the band disappears backstage.

I'm about to tell Carla to come down next to me, when Willie appears, and takes her across the aisle to sit with Cadi and Nick – which is where she needs to be.

And then there was one.

One more award.

The Big One.

Album of the Year.

Everyone watches as Paul McCartney and Diana Ross take the stage, and after a brief discussion about the importance of the award, Ms. Ross reads the nominees, as an image of each record's cover art is displayed behind them. Once all the nominees are named, she continues.

"This year's Grammy for Album of the Year goes to..."

As Mr. McCartney carefully and slowly opens the envelope, it seems as if everyone in the building is holding their breath. Then, with a huge grin, he holds it out for Ms. Ross to read...

"Well music fans," Ms. Ross offers, turning and giving Mr. McCartney a 'look' and a laugh, "Just like their song says, they've managed to do it, *One More Time – Audio Distortion!*"

I burst into tears – I can't help it. I stand up, and walk to the aisle, and the moment my brother steps into it, I give him a hug that is emotional to the tenth power. Then I hug Emma.

Emily and Cadi have burst into tears, and poor Willie – heck, he looks like he's actually going to faint.

However, the absolute coolest part of the whole scene, is listening as Paige and Peyton, giggling their little heads off, tell everyone within earshot, *"Mommy and Daddy won!"* in unison – over and over.

It takes them a few moments, but eventually, everyone – with the exception of Carla – ends up on stage. Mr. McCartney and Ms. Ross give each of the kids, one of the Grammys, realizing that it was they who inspired the record. Being totally unprepared, Stanley thanks a few people, and does manage to mention Terri, the label, and most importantly, *Audio Distortion's fans*, before they eventually head backstage.

As they disappear, I take a seat next to Carla, who is sitting next to Vicki. She smiles at me, and then without warning, leans over and hugs me.

"Can it possibly get any more insane that this?" she asks, reaching out and taking my hand.

We sit and stare at each other for a few seconds, then, as the crowds again goes quiet, I smile and shake my head up and down in response to her question. Seconds later, as she starts giggling, she turns and looks at Vicki who, without a single word, also shakes her head up and down.

Even as the stage begins to move, bringing *Ransom* into view, for the final performance of the night, the three of us break into laughter.

Music... no matter which side of it you are on, is always, totally amazing.

Aftermath

Misty Masterson

The six months following the Grammys, is totally insane – to a level one simply can't explain. And of course, the press asks all the inevitable questions…

'Was the outcome fair?'

'Are the bands still friends?'

'Are you working on anything new?'

…and to our complete surprise, *Audio Distortion* quietly disappears, and leaves us to deal with it all!

Gotta love those characters.

However, the best part of the aftermath, was the day Emma – and a guy with a camera – busted into the offices of an obscure tabloid that thought they'd use us as a means to make a name for themselves.

It was the very first time any of us, had seen Emma Campbell, truly angry. Terri and Max even tried to intercept her on her way there, but she managed to avoid them.

She immediately confronted them about comments they printed concerning the relationship between the bands, by tossing a copy of the story, into the face of the 'reporter' (if you can realistically call him that) that put his name on the article. He lasted about a minute with Emma in his face. He repeatedly refused to say who his source was, which served only to make Emma angrier. When the head editor got into it, and asked her to leave, she smiled, told him that of course she would, and that starting the moment she was outside the door, her mission for the remainder of her life would be to bring down their publication, and that she intended to use the video they just shot, to begin the process. The moment one of the employees acted as if they intended to do something to the camera (or maybe the cameraman), through the door came Rhyan Crossman – absurdly huge drummer, and ex-football jock. In a perfectly calm voice he explained that if anyone touched the camera, or the person holding it, there would be a lawsuit. When a guy across the room said something about the tabloid winning it, Rhyan crossed the room, stopped in front of him, and in a voice so freakin' calm, it was terrifying, said, "Oh... it won't be your boss doing the suing, it will be you suing me – for the cost of the emergency room visit, and extended hospital stay you are about to have, smartass..."

Game over.

The very next day, less than an hour after the video made it onto a number of news channels, Terri got a call from the vice president of the parent company of the tabloid. Seems the reporter and the editor tried the same silly 'secret source' crap on her, and they are now both unemployed. She assured Terri that a retraction would be printed immediately, and that they intended to put *in print*, that because the reporter can't produce a valid source, the paper must take the position, he lied. She asked that Terri convey her apologies to both bands, and asked if it would be possible to speak directly to Emma.

Although we know Emma called the woman, to this day, she's never told anyone what was said.

The very next day, *Audio Distortion* and *Ransom*, went on sabbatical...

All eleven of us, simply disappeared.

It will be over a year, before anyone hears from us again.

As Emma Campbell likes to say...

We let life and music take us where they want to...

End Of A Road

Georgia Crossman

Once my husband finds out he's going to be a father, he immediately becomes uncontainable. Just watching him is entertaining, to a power of ten.

Because William James Crossman Jr. already exists (Rhyan's older sister beat us to it) we can't name the baby after his dad. The funny thing is, it's Rhyan who immediately suggests we use my dad. We don't tell anyone, we just hand Dad the birth certificate, the very first time he holds him.

The moment he sees 'Thomas Victor Crossman', he starts crying. Sure, he's not a Jr., but Dad couldn't care less. He is still, and will always be, my father's namesake.

So... speaking of my father...

This chapter is about him.

From the day I was born, I've been a 'daddy's girl'. Although I was pretty young when our parents split, there was never any doubt that I wanted to be with my father. As far back as I can search my memories, there has always been a bond between us, that none of the others would understand.

You should remember my moment of panic when Vanessa called us in the middle of the night, from England. My first thought was that it was about my father. There's a reason for that.

For years, my father has been very private about anything related to his medical condition. After years of listening to the three of us chastise him about it, he finally put his foot down, and told Stanley and I that it was his business, and we needed to leave it alone. Eventually, even Logan gave in, and she too, let it go.

For about the last five years, I've had a seriously ominous feeling that God intends to take my dad... sooner than we realize. His visits to the doctor increased, and there were days when he simply looked really bad.

But... none of us questioned him. Not even Logan.

Bad move – although even if we had, it wouldn't have changed anything. As it turns out, my ominous feeling was justified.

God took our father – fortunately, quickly – the day after my son's first birthday. He had what the doctors said was a full on, massive heart attack, and he died instantly.

I was at school, standing in the office, and I knew the moment it happened. I walked the six blocks to the high school, and walked in on Stanley as he was talking to Logan, who was at the hospital. I sat down at his desk, and then I cried. Even as my brother sat down next to me, and wrapped his arm around me, I was overcome by a feeling of finally understanding Carla and Randall Mitchell...

Logan took it hard, but better than we expected. I'm pretty sure she was, in some way, expecting it. She did, after all, live with him. Once we talked to the doctor, he apologized profusely, and explained that because of rules, he couldn't tell us beforehand. He said he all but begged Dad – more than once – to tell us what was going on. He also said

Dad never even *considered* the possibility of a heart transplant. He told the doctor straight out, that if God intends to call him home, neither he, or doctors – or anyone else for that matter – was going to do anything to interfere with it.

Sounds just like my Dad...

Anyhow, we had Dad's service today, exactly like he told Logan he wanted it done. Once it's over, I borrow Rhyan's Expedition (it's four wheel drive), and the three of us – Stanley, Logan, and me – drive to Horsetooth Mountain Park, in the mountains just to the west of town. It was Dad's favorite area to hike. After we hike the two and a half miles to the top of Horsetooth Mountain, we scatter Dad's ashes to the wind. Now... as long as we stay in Fort Collins, he will always be around.

The thing that really hurts my heart is that his youngest grandchild will never get to meet him...

Yep... I'm pregnant again.

Weird thing is, I'm not sure why. All I can tell you is that shortly after Thomas was born, a persistent voice began telling me I need to have another child...

Weird... I suppose.

Life And Music

Misty Masterson

What happened to *Ransom?*

Although an interesting, and valid question I suppose, I hear it an awful lot.

So... here's what's happened to *Ransom*...

Vanessa is teaching – music history of all things – at CSU. She has her own place, and has even fallen in love! His name is Cullen and he's... well... British! Go figure?

Seeing the two of them together, I'm pretty sure this one is 'forever'.

Rhyan is building bridges. Yeah, that's right, building bridges. He graduated with his engineering degree, and one of the consulting firms Georgia's dad did business with, saw some of his work, and called him in for an interview. Now he designs small and intermediate sized bridges for them. The thing that drives the guy totally nuts (and fascinates the crap out of the rest of us) is, no matter where he may be – jobsite, at the office, or even in Starbucks – he constantly seems to hear, *"Hey! Aren't you...?"*

Who knew he'd be the one everyone recognizes?

Sometimes, one of us will call his cell for no reason, other than to say *"Hey! Aren't you...?"*

Yeah, I know... we suck.

Joshua and Ariel. Married and living happily ever after – thanks to Emma Campbell. They work for Lucky Guess now. A year after we bailed from the limelight, Terri and Max retired – within days of each other. Terri does some mild consulting work on occasion, but for the most part, she has 'retired' down to a science.

Miss Penelope Jane Campbell (no relation to those *other* Campbell's) is now the queen bee at LGR. A wiry guy named Preston Cox is her right hand. Josh and Ariel answer to them.

And yeah, everyone still calls her PJ...

So... me and my husband. Let's see...

Our daughter – Jessica Lynn Masterson – was born a week before Georgia and Rhyan's son, in the peace and quiet of our house in Ransom. I did it naturally, in a tank full of water. Pretty amazing experience. Not sure if I'm gonna do this one that way, or not.

Yeah, I'm pregnant.

The cool thing is, I'm having fun with it. *And...* it has inspired me.

For the last three months, I've actually been writing again. It hasn't been anything real serious so far, just a line here, and a verse there. But I feel like I have a purpose again, and for a non-working musician, that's a good thing.

　　　　　　　　　　　　　　　　Riley Morgan

Babies!

Rhyan Crossman

I'm a father!

AGAIN!

And... the very best part is, he's named after *me*. Georgia told the nurses no one filled out the paperwork except her, and without asking anyone for an opinion, she named our second son, Rhyan Thomas Crossman Jr.

How insanely cool is that?

Anyhow, she is recovering again, and I've taken time off from work to be a dad. Tommy thinks his little brother is about the coolest thing in the entire world.

Once Georgia is up and around again, she and Tommy take the baby, go to the cemetery, and sit at her father's marker. They introduce the two of them to each other, together. Georgia told me later, that Tommy spent half an hour telling his grandfather just how cool his little brother is.

Once she's ready to go back to work, she takes the baby to the daycare center at the university. Tommy spends his day in the pre-kindergarten class there as well.

This is when she discovers an old friend – one that the six of us have pretty much forgotten about...

Babies!

Martin Masterson

My crazy, and massively old-fashioned wife, has named our second daughter, after our oldest living relative – my grandmother on my mother's side – Matilda Elaine Charlton.

Today, Pastor Wilson christened Miss Matilda Elaine Masterson, as her *great-grandmother* sat watching.

She's as beautiful as her sister, and now I have three amazing women competing for my heart.

Thing is… *they all win*. Every time.

I've been snooping in my wife's new notebook, and some of the stuff the kids have inspired, is downright amazing. Even as I read what could easily be lyrics, my mind is putting music to them.

Yeah… I feel it again. Poking at me… telling me it's time. I think Misty does too, based on what I've read.

Question is… are the others feeling it too?

"Oh my gosh! I just figured out who
you are..."

~ Lindsey Kelly 

Resurrection

Vanessa Preston

I've always seen music differently than the others. I tend to lose myself in it – entirely. Over the years, I've learned to play a number of instruments fairly, and a couple really well. A guitar – regardless of type – will always be my passion.

And, after thirty-two years of life, I think I've finally found a guy who *understands* my passion. The other guys I've dated, always tried to accept it, but Cullen relates to it. You see, he has his own passion – English literature. I do honestly believe the man knows everything there is to know about it. The amazing thing is that he never stops learning and never stops sharing.

Anyhow, I'm sitting in my classroom, and just as it has at least three other times today, an odd feeling that something is about to happen – just like the one that consumed me years ago, and made me leave school and go to visit Emily – again sweeps over me.

This time, however, in a matter of seconds, something *does* happen.

When I hear the knock on the door, I lift my head and find a face I haven't seen in at least four years – even though we live in the same city. I'm so totally stunned, all I can seem to do, is stare at her – and the girl with her. After a few seconds, she starts laughing.

"At least you recognize me!" She turns, looks at the girl and says, "Come on, Lindsey – let's go talk to Ms. Preston..."

"Okay, Aunt Sally!" she replies and follows her down the aisle to the platform.

The moment the girl stops in front of me, I'm so stunned, all I can do is mutter *"o...m...g..."* and stare.

"I'm Lindsey Kelly! Aunt Sally says you know my mom."

"Well, Lindsey," I reply, holding out my hand, which she takes, "I'm Vanessa – and, your aunt is right, I do know your mom..."

"Kinda weird, huh?" Sally asks, as she takes a seat at one of the desks in the front row.

"My life has been one ongoing weird event after another – this just adds to it," I reply, as Lindsey stands staring at a large dry-erase board on the platform, next to my desk.

"Mine's been pretty odd too, actually. I have a son, you know..."

"Seriously? Where is he?"

"Over in the daycare center – which is where she was," she points at Lindsey, who has moved up next to the dry-erase board, and is closely examining it, "when I stopped to talk to her mom."

"Excuse me," Lindsey says, still staring at the stuff on the white board, "but are you a teacher?"

"I am. I teach music history," I reply.

She turns and faces me, with a strangely quizzical look on her face. I smile and turn my attention back to Sally.

                                    Riley Morgan

"Yeah… I heard Mindy is running the place now. Rumor has it, *Saturday Afternoon* also owns a club…"

"It's called the Rubber Stamp," Lindsey says, still staring at the notes on the board, "and my dad is the manager."

"Is he now…" I mumble.

Sally laughs, as Lindsey turns and walks over to my desk.

"Yes ma'am. Sometimes, on Saturdays, I get to go and watch the bands practice."

"Pretty cool. Are you a musician?"

"No ma'am. I like music, but I don't play an instrument." She stands quietly for a moment, then as an afterthought, points at the board behind her without looking at it, and asks, "Did you draw that clef?"

"I did."

"I've never seen it before," she replies, her face still a huge question mark, as she turns, and walks back to the board. "What is it?"

"It's the C clef. It has a few uses," I say, standing up and joining her at the board.

"Does it work like the other clefs?"

"What do you mean?"

"Does it change when you move it from line to line?" she asks, pointing at an F clef on the second line of a stave.

Needless to say, at this point, I'm a bit stunned.

"You *understand* sheet music?"

"Oh, yes ma'am – well… sorta. My mom and Uncle Pete have been teaching me."

I reach out and put a finger on a random note, she looks up at me, grins, and says "C on the major scale." I glance at Sally, then turn back and put my finger on a different note.

"That's F and this," she puts her finger on a symbol next to the note, "makes it flat."

Lindsey smiles at me, turns to Sally and asks, "How come Uncle Pete and Aunt Randi never told me about this clef?" as she puts a finger on it.

Sally laughs, as I put a hand on Lindsey's shoulder.

"Young lady, I will be happy to tell you all about the C clef, and to talk music with you, whenever you want. I live for music, and when I find someone else..."

Lindsey goes flush, and she gets the most stunned look on her face.

"*Oh my gosh!* I just figured out who you are..." she says.

"Really?" I reply, and hear Sally behind us, trying her best not to laugh. "Although I do know your mom, I've never met you before."

"Aunt Randi only says that about one single person..."

"Says what?" I ask, a bit perplex.

The kid blushes the brightest red I have seen in a very long time, and glances at Sally.

"Oh... go ahead and tell her, silly," Sally says.

The kid looks at me, takes a breath, and says, "I bet you play bass... like Aunt Randi."

I crack up – I can't help it.

"I do."

Again, the child goes flush – so flush in fact, I'm inclined to question her.

"Are you okay, Lindsey?"

"Yes ma'am... I think. 'She's totally crazy, but the girl lives for music...' That's what Aunt Randi always says..."

Sally cracks up, and I'm right behind her. I put an arm around Lindsey's shoulders, and turn to look at Sally.

"Your bass player is in it now…"

"*You're in Ransom*… aren't you?" Lindsey asks.

"Yes ma'am," I reply with a smile, "I am!"

"No one is going to believe me…"she mumbles.

"Believe what?" I ask.

"That I actually talked to you…"

"Oh please! Your mom's band is pretty famous…"

"Nuh-uh. Not like *Ransom*."

"How old are you?"

I'm eight. I just finished second grade…"

"Where?"

"Huh?"

"Where do you go to school?"

"Oh… at Laurel Elementary…"

"I see. School isn't out yet, is it?"

"No ma'am. We still have next week."

"Cool. See you next Friday." I turn and look at Sally and ask, "And what about you?"

"Well… it isn't actually me. It's Randi."

"And?"

"She was at the store about a week ago…"

"The store?"

"Aunt Sally and Uncle Pete have a music store. It's up in Cheyenne," Lindsey offers, walking over and taking a seat next to Sally. "They let me hang out with them there a lot…"

"I think I'm beginning to get it…" I say, as Sally leans over and hugs Lindsay. "If you have a son, I'm going to assume he has a father?"

"Uncle Pete is Zach's dad. That was a weird question…" Lindsey blurts out.

"We got married as soon as we found out Zachary was coming..." Sally says, adjusting the ribbons in Lindsey's hair, and not looking at me.

"I see..." The muffled snicker that follows my comment makes her blush.

"We were already planning to... we just did it sooner."

This time I laugh – and roll my eyes.

"So," I shift my gaze to Lindsey, "Do *you* remember going on tour?"

Her face lights up the whole room.

"Dad shows me the video all the time. I think I kinda remember it, but I was only three."

After a few moments of contemplation, she glances at Sally, and then returns her attention to me.

"I do remember Ms. Meredith... mostly cuz she always seemed to be around...and well..."

"I know," I quickly offer, in an attempt to save her, "she's crazy hard to understand."

Sally cracks up, and Lindsey blushes.

"And I totally remember Paige and Peyton."

I'm getting teary eyed, and I know it. It's rushing back into me, all at once. When I stand up, Sally does the same, and even before I can take a step, she puts her arms around me and squeezes. And yeah, I lose a few tears. The moment we break the embrace, she gets me again...

"We need your help – again..."

"Huh?" I blurt out, while at the exact same instant, my cell phone, which is lying on my desk, starts to vibrate.

Sally smiles, as I wipe my eyes and check the Caller ID to see who it is. The moment I see the name, I answer it.

"Hey, little sister. What's new in Kansas?"

Sally goes so pale, I'm concerned she may actually faint.

"I just heard something on the radio – you won't believe what it was."

Okay so… remember what I said about my life – maybe thirty minutes ago – being 'one ongoing weird event after the other'? The moment the stars align, I crack up. I simply can't help it.

Lindsey, who has been quietly listening, asks, "What's so funny?"

"My life mostly, Lindsey," I reply.

"Lindsey?" immediately comes from the phone, her tone telling me she already gets it.

"Uh-huh… Lindsey. And, I'm thinking – and this is just a guess mind you – that you heard *All About The Music* on the radio."

Silence. Total, and complete silence.

"Misty?"

"Yeah… I'm here. As usual, I'm just weirding out."

"Guess who's standing in my classroom, as we speak?"

"Jezzz…" she mutters. "That's almost creepy…"

I laugh.

"Is it her mother?"

"Nope… The lead singer."

Again, total and complete silence.

"Go get a glass of water and sit down. I'll call you back, as soon as I find out what's going on, okay?"

"Uh-huh," Misty mumbles. "Bye."

I hear the click even before I can say anything. I laugh and turn to Sally.

"PJ did it – got the airplay. I heard it earlier today, too."

"Because?"

Sally smiles at me, and actually blushes.

"You know why Ness... Terri did it with *Ransom*, and *Audio Distortion*, a bunch of times."

"OMG! Tour prep? Are you guys headlining?"

"Not sure yet. All we are certain of, at this point, is that we *really* want to do it. It's like since we've gotten older, and have maybe grown up some too, we all sorta get it now. Pete caught Randi staring at a poster of *Ransom* and *AD* – when you guys played Red Rocks, and when he asked what she was thinking, she laughed and said, 'I was just wondering how far we might have made it...' The next thing I know, Patty and Pete are talking to PJ."

"Oh how insanely cool!"

"Headlining or otherwise," Sally continues, her face now awash in excitement, "we just want to go and *play for people* – and PJ said the label is willing to give us the chance."

"What do you need from me – or us?"

"Help with the writing. We have some stuff, but it needs work – lots of work. PJ said she could get us with some writers, but if you guys have some time, we'd rather try this with people we know. You guys got us through it last time..."

When all I do is stare at her, she opens the satchel that is over her shoulder and starts to pull something out.

"I have some stuff..."

"Cool!" I blurt out, and jump up from the desk. I reach over and pull Lindsey to her feet, and she starts laughing. "Let's go to the house where we can spread it out all over the place, and have a good look at it! Come on... I'll drive."

Fifteen minutes later, we're in my truck headed for my house.

"Melinda said that if you went for it, to call her, and she'll bail from work to help. She has her guitar with her..."

"Do it!" I say, and then glance in the mirror at Lindsey. "You okay back there?"

"*Yes ma'am!* I mean heck, *I'm going to your house!* How cool is that?"

Sally again falls into full-on laughter.

It takes twenty minutes to get to the house, and once I shut the truck off, as I turn to look at Sally, I hear a door opening.

"What did Mindy say?" I ask, and at the same time notice someone in front of the truck.

"She'll be here in thirty minutes. She's bringing Zach with her."

"Awesome!" I reply, turning and looking for the person who was just in front of the truck, and finding no one. "What the..." I mumble, and then with a twist of my head, find Lindsey, already standing on my porch, waving for us to hurry up.

"She got it from Randi – her preoccupation with you, I mean," Sally says. "For about the last year, she's been driving Keith and Mindy nuts with 'I want to meet *Ransom'*..."

When I turn to look at her, the coolest grin covers her face. I raise my eyebrows, and she again laughs.

"Just go with it, Ness... that's what Pete and I do with all her friends, once they find out who we are. And FYI... she has the biggest crush on Josh..."

She gets me big time, and I simply can't stop laughing. We get out of the truck, and head into the house, collecting an insanely giddy eight year old at the door.

And yes, the following Friday, *all six* members of *Ransom* walk into a room full of unsuspecting second graders, on their last day of school, and asked if any of them can tell us where to find Lindsey Kelly.

Yep... totally freak out the whole bunch of them – even their teacher.

The second Lindsey sees Josh... well... you get the idea.

Back To Basics

Misty Masterson

"Hey babe!" I hear my husband say, as he comes in the door.

"Daddy!" comes out of his daughter's mouth even before the door clicks shut.

Martin kneels down, opens his arm, and Jess is in them in an instant. When I don't respond to his greeting, he picks her up, crosses the room, and stops behind me.

"Whacha doin'?" he asks, as he leans over and looks. Then I hear, *"no way…"* almost in a whisper.

"I've got six so far."

"Seriously?"

"Uh-huh… and I want all of them to be up-tempo…"

"Like the *hostage* CD was…"

"Exactly!"

"Well… let's have a look then…"

I spin around, definitely surprised he isn't questioning what I am suggesting, and pull out the chair next to me so he can sit down. With his daughter in his lap, Martin goes over each set of lyrics I've written, and when he reaches number five, his facial expression changes, and I know what's about to happen.

"Hey, Jess… you want to hear Daddy make some music?"

He stands her up, stands up himself, grabs the six pages of lyrics he was just reading, and heads for the family room, with Jess right behind him.

Fully aware that I just flipped my husband's switch, I smile and go about making some dinner. Thirty minutes later, Jessica comes in, looking depressed.

"Mattie woke up, and Daddy's busy…"

"Awww… come on. Let's go get her." I reply, taking her hand.

Once we have the baby, we take her back into the kitchen with us, and put her into a small playpen in the dining room. As I go about setting the table, I ask Jessica, "Do you want to help me?" She grins, holds out her hands, and I give her the silverware to put out. It takes us another half hour to get dinner on the table, and once we do, I send Jess to get her father. When he comes into the kitchen, he's grinning, and as he takes a seat at the table, he hands me the same pages he took with him.

Thing is… they now have music on them.

I put Jess in her booster chair, and take a seat next to Martin. We wait as he says Grace, and once he's done, we dig in.

The silence lasts less than five minutes.

"You sure about this?" I ask.

"Wouldn't have started composing, if I wasn't," he replies, stuffing food into his mouth. After he chews and swallows, he smiles at me, and says, "It's what we do, Misty – *what we are good at.*"

After five or six bites, he pauses, and again looks at me.

Riley Morgan

"Figured out how you're going to get the others to play?"

"Somehow, I don't think that's going to be a problem…"

Once we start laughing, so does Jessica. For the first time in a long time, I am completely relaxed, and know that I have a direction.

My husband and I have just created the beginnings of *Ransom's* fifth album.

And… if I have my way, just like our first record, this one is going to be created by *six kids, from the middle of nowhere Kansas…*

"Are you my aunts too?"

~ Jessica Masterson 

Powering Up (again)

Ariel Miller

A week ago Vanessa called me, so wound up, that it took me ten minutes to calm her down. Once I found out what was going on, it was my turn to freak.

Now, having abandoned my husband in LA, I'm sitting in Vanessa's living room, staring at Sally, Melinda, and Patty.

"This is going to be epic!" Vanessa says.

"Are you sure you can put your lives on total hold?" I ask. "PJ is going to want a full tour you know…"

"Pete's older sister, and his mom, are going to handle the store," Sally says, "They've done it before, but only for ten days while we were on vacation. If they have any disasters, they can always call us."

"Kenneth's exact words were, *'don't ask, just do it!'*" comes from Mindy. "I think he's more psyched than we are…"

The three of them laugh.

"And Randi? Hard to tour without your bass player," I offer.

"She told her boss she had to go make some music," Patty says, grinning. "When he questioned her, she told him she wanted to come back, but if that wasn't an option, oh well."

The three of them break out laughing, I glance at Vanessa, and when she sees our confusion, Sally explains.

"It's her brother-in-law. She works for her older sister's husband."

"Well," I offer, "six months to get the CD out, and six months to get a tour online."

"We're ready!" Mindy says.

"We're gonna need a studio..." Vanessa says with a wink.

I pull out my phone, and dial.

"Discovery Studios," Riley's bubbly voice says.

"Hey kid – we need a studio. How's your dad's schedule looking?"

"Aunt Ariel!"

"Yep. So... can you check the schedule, or do I need to talk to your dad?"

"Let me look. When are you gonna need it?"

"Most of next month. Hours are negotiable..."

I can hear her fingers on the keyboard in the background.

"Well... he has a lot of time blocked – mostly Monday thru Wednesday, during the day. You should probably talk to him, or Mom, if you want to try to squeeze in. Are you guys gonna make a new CD?"

"Nope... but another band you use to hang out with is..."

"Which one?" she quickly asks.

"I'm not telling," I reply, getting laughs from the girls. "You'll just have to be surprised."

"Okay… I'll have Mom call ya back as soon as she gets here. Talk to you soon!"

"Bye, Riley."

"So," I start to say, and am interrupted by Vanessa's doorbell ringing.

Even before we can stand up, we hear the door open, and instantly a happy little female voice, that I know all too well, screams, *"Aunt Nessa! I'm here!"*

Within seconds, Jessica – complete with Mom's pigtails – races across the living room, and jumps into Vanessa's lap. Of course, everyone starts laughing, and seconds later, around the corner comes our lead singer, and our keyboard player.

"What about your other aunt?" Martin says, to Jessica.

The child stands up, looks around the room at each of us, and seems for a moment, to be lost in thought. Thinking I am rescuing her, I squat down, and say, "Forgot me, did you?"

"No ma'am, Aunt Ariel," she replies, turning and hugging me. "But I don't 'member them…" she points at Sally, Patty and Mindy, all of whom are sitting on the couch, trying not to laugh. Jessica lets go of me, walks across the room, and after scrutinizing the three of them for a moment, smiles and asks, "Are you my aunts too?"

Everyone breaks out in almost hysterical laughter.

Aren't children amazing?

Jumping In

Martin Masterson

Once they get over the shock of us being here, and all the laughter subsides, without a word, my wife walks over and hands Vanessa (she's *sooo* much more excitable than Ariel) what we have been working on. The moment she reads the first page of the first song, she quickly finds the first page of the second one. Seconds later, she's on to the third.

Although we try, Misty and I can't control it – the laughs just come. The interesting part is when I glance at Ariel, and her face tells me that, just by watching Vanessa, she's figured out what we are up to.

"What do they need?" Ariel asks.

"You and Josh, mostly," I reply, smiling at her.

When Vanessa lifts her head, we all see the tears trickling down her cheeks, as she smiles at us. She pulls one set of pages from the stack, and hands them to Ariel. We, of course, know it's the song Misty wrote about her grandmother – and once Ariel reads it, she too, loses a few tears.

"What's going on guys?"

Having forgotten about the other musicians in the room, the four of us turn and look at the couch, only to find Jessica being tickled relentlessly by all three of them. Misty laughs, takes the pages from Vanessa, walks over, and hands them to Melinda. It takes her a single heartbeat to figure it out.

"oh... my... gosh!" she mutters.

She reads a bit more, and then hands the first few pages to Sally. A page into the second song, she looks at Vanessa.

"We didn't realize..." she says, with an odd look on her face.

"Neither did I, Mindy... neither did I."

My turn to be confused.

"What's going on guys?" I ask, mimicking Sally.

"They need some help..." comes from a now grinning Ariel, as she hands Misty a stack of pages that have been on the table the entire time.

"Oh how totally cool!" my wife blurts out, dropping to the floor next to the couch, and going through the stack.

"And?" I ask, as Jessica comes over and grabs my leg.

"We're trying to come up with some original stuff, and need some help putting it all together," Sally says.

"Seems we're all going to be recording together," Vanessa says, laughing.

"Seriously?" I ask, picking up the kid, and taking a seat.

"We're hoping to come up with eleven – so we can actually pull off a full CD of *our music*," Melinda adds.

"Nope... you'll only need ten," Misty offers, as a devious little grin starts to show on her face.

"Huh?" the three of them blurt out at the same time.

"This record *has to have* your cover of *Vacation* on it... understood?"

"OMG!" Vanessa yells, making everyone jump. "You are *sooo* totally right, Misty!"

The room erupts in laughter, as the high-fives follow.

"I had Josh talk to PJ," Ariel says, "and she wants to put them, with two other bands, and get them on the road."

"This stuff is totally workable," Misty says. "Did you write it, Sally?"

"Some of it. We've all hand our hands in it at some point. Pete and Randi are responsible for most of the music…"

"Have you guys looked at it?" Misty asks, looking at Ariel and Vanessa.

"Yep," Ariel quickly replies. "I already have some ideas for music too."

"This is going to be so phenomenal! All of us writing and recording together?" Misty blurts out, truly excited about the idea.

"And… you guys are totally freakin' nuts…" I mumble, following it with a laugh. "Rhyan and Josh are gonna flip…"

"You're still going to help us?" Patty asks, sounding totally confused. "What about…"

"Heck yeah!" Vanessa pretty much yells.

As the bunch of them starts talking among themselves, I take Jessica and head for the front porch. There's one person I fully intend to involve in this journey of insanity – and this is right up her alley.

Outside, I put Jess on the top step, then take a seat next to her, and pull out my phone.

"What do you say we call Carla, kid?"

As I am searching for the number, my daughter is quick to ask, "Who's Carla, Daddy?"

"You remember Momma's nice little statue – the one you like so much?"

"Uh huh…"

"Carla helped her get it," I say, hitting autodial.

"Does she like music too?"

"That she does, Jess… that's she does."

"Martin?" comes from the phone.

"Maybe…" I reply, fighting off a laugh.

"You still have my number?"

"Why wouldn't I?"

"Uh… well… I dunno."

"At school I take it?"

"Uh huh. I'm studying for a test I have tomorrow."

"And after the test?"

"Huh?"

"Once the test is over, what's on the schedule?"

"Okay… what's going on," she asks, actually laughing.

"I'm going to need your help with something…"

"Seriously? My help?"

"Uh huh. You *and* that notebook. You still have it, right?"

"Yes sir, of course. I'm still writing in it, too."

"That's what I needed to hear. Can you come up here?"

"Up where? And for how long?"

"Fort Collins. And, for a few days this time…"

"This time?" she repeats, laughing again.

You'll understand once you're here. Can you come?"

"Sure. I can get by, skipping a couple of days. But I have to be back on Monday. And remember, it will take me *an entire day* to make the drive."

"Nope – not happening. Can you get a ride to the airport?"

"I guess... but..."

"I'm buying, you goof. Up here tomorrow night – I'll pick you up – and home Sunday. Will that work?"

"Sure!" she replies, and after a few seconds, adds, "So just tell me – is Misty writing again? Are you guys actually going make another record?"

"Yes. And yes. But that isn't what I need *you* for..."

"You are being a pain, Martin!" she blurts out.

"My wife says that all the time. See you tomorrow, kid!"

"See you then. Bye!"

"Is Carla going to help Mommy get a new 'tatue?" Jess asks, as I hand her my phone.

"Nope... not exactly dear. But you can do Daddy a favor if you want..."

"*OKAY!*" she yells and jumps up.

"Run inside and tell Momma that Carla is coming to help, okay?"

I stand up, and the instant the door is open, the child disappears in a flash. A few seconds later I hear, *"Is so! Daddy said!"* – which is immediately followed by *"Martin! Get your butt in here!"*

Just as *One More Time* was *Audio Distortion's* swansong, I know this is going to be ours. And just as my wife said, *'it's going to be phenomenal'*...

Falling Into Place

Ariel Miller

When Carla actually turns up, it's as if everyone shifts into high gear. Words hit paper, music follows the words. At one point, armed with a stack of possible songs, we invade the Campbell's basement. Sometimes, the only way to figure things out, is to record them.

Emma and Stanley are great, and spend a lot of time, laughing and shaking their heads.

When they discover the little ones, the Campbell kids are totally amazing. We're all kind of baffled when the twins, for whatever strange and bizarre 'kid' reasons, recognize Lindsey the very second they see her! Even Carson knows who she is – after almost five years.

When Emma sees Lindsey for the first time, I swear the woman almost cries.

For eighty-five days, we become one huge musical family.

When it's time for Pete and the girls to put down some real, finished tracks, Misty calls Willie. He says he's kind of available for the next thirty days, and when Misty asks if he'll squeeze us in, he says yes, but that there's a catch. She asks what it is, and he says Josh and I have to be there.

Yeah, we're all curious now.

Josh gets PJ to let him cut out for a long weekend, and heads for Tahoe. I load a rented van with *Saturday Afternoon* and their equipment, and we head out to meet Josh at Discovery Studios, to cut the band's very first CD, of all original music – *Timing Is Everything*.

I think the six of us are more psyched than the band recording...

"Congratulations, Mr. and Mrs. Miller.
You **own** Discovery Studios!"

~ Willie and Emily's Lawyer 

Taking A Chance

Joshua Miller

When I walk in the door at Discovery Studios, I find a depressed looking Riley, sitting alone in the lobby.

"Hey kid! What's with the face?"

"We're moving..."

"What?"

"We're going back to Fort Collins..." a different voice says from behind me. When I turn around, there stands Vicki.

"What about..." I start to ask.

"It's for sale."

I'm so utterly dumbfounded, all I can do is stare at her.

"That's why Willie wanted you here. You and Ariel get first shot at it."

I suck in a huge breath, and drop onto the couch next to Riley. After a second, I look at Vicki again, and find a big grin on her face.

"Vicki... there's no way..."

"Oh bullshit!" I hear Willie say, as he comes in, spins around, and drops over the end of the couch, coming to rest in Riley and my laps, and making his daughter crack up.

"Dad!" she yells, trying to wiggle out from under him.

"We can work something out, and you know it, Josh..." Willie says, grinning.

"If of course," Vicki adds, "you guys want to work for yourselves."

Willie sits up, lets Riley escape to an adjacent chair, and turns to face me.

"PJ and Preston say you're good, Josh – maybe even better than the two of them. You been at it a long time, and I believe you can handle this place with little or no effort. Having your wife with you, will make it that much easier."

"And..." Vicki adds, a cute little smirk on her face, "When *Saturday Afternoon* gets here, you are going to get the chance to prove him right, or wrong."

"Huh?"

"Josh Miller is their engineer – start to finish."

"Seriously?"

"Yep!" Willie says. "Lucky Guess has signed off on it. PJ says they'll go with releasing the final master you cut."

Again, I'm at a total loss. Sure, I've cut masters – lots of them. But always under the scrutiny of one of the senior engineers at LG. Now, I'm on my own. But... this is what I was after, when I first told Richard I wanted a job. The day I heard the master of *The Time It Takes*, I told Ariel that one day, I would create something just as amazing.

Apparently, I'm going to get my chance.

"You guys honestly think we can do this?"

"I *know* you can," Willie replies, with total conviction.

"Well... I suppose we can ask Ariel when she gets here..."

"Cool!" Willie replies, standing up. "Come on down stairs and look at the stuff your wife faxed before they left. It may give you some ideas..."

It takes forty-two, fourteen hour days, to get a complete master. Willie does actually turn me loose, and *Timing Is Everything* becomes my very first *solo* project. Even when I am struggling with something at one point, he never intervenes. He lets me – *and Ariel* – figure it out.

I opt to use two songs they recorded in the Campbell's basement, instead of recording them again. One of those – titled *Precision* – tells the story of how the band discovers the process of 'creating'. It's filled with all the background chatter that occurs when a band records, and is actually more about hearing the *process*, than about the song itself – although it *is* a pretty cool song. The members of *Saturday Afternoon* think it's an amazing way to draw the listeners in.

Once we have the final clean master of all eleven songs, *Saturday Afternoon*, Willie, Vicki, Riley, Ariel, and I, sit and listen to the entire disc. No matter how many times I hear it, I will always be totally captivated by Sally Wright's voice...

We send the band and the master to LA – PJ is all kinds antsy to hear it. When I hear Willie tell her that he couldn't have done it any better, my heart almost comes out of my chest. Once they are on their way, it's down to business.

We're sitting on the floor of the upper studio – a strange place for a business deal for sure. Ariel has a firm grip on my hand, and I can't tell which of us is shaking the worst.

"Look guys," Vicki says, "every single one of our clients knows what we are doing. When we told them you two were buying the place..."

Ariel interrupts her midsentence.

"You 'told them'? How did you know we'd say yes?" she blurts out, making Vicki and Willie crack up.

"Really?" Willie asks, shaking his head.

"Yeah..." Vicki quickly adds, "...what my husband said."

This time, Amy – who we discovered is Willie and Emily's lawyer, and has so far been silent – even lets out a laugh.

"Anyhow..." Vicki continues, "...they've all agreed to give you guys a chance – even the artists who aren't with LG. You aren't going to be lacking for work."

"The last six weeks have proven you *can* do this, guys. Now... you just have to decide you *want to*," Willie adds.

"Sign next to the yellow flags on each page," Amy says, grinning and handing me a clipboard full of paper.

Willie and Vicki again laugh, when they see how badly the clipboard is shaking as I take it.

"Eighteen years ago, at a high school in Kansas, I asked six kids if they wanted to make some music. They stepped up, and took the chance..."

I feel the huge grin as it spreads across my face. I look at Ariel, whose eyes have glassed over, and when she kisses my cheek, I pull the pen loose, and start signing. Once I'm done, my wife does the same, and then hands the clipboard back. Amy then hands it to Vicki, and after she signs, it's Willie's turn – and of course, he's grinning the entire time.

The rest of the blocks are signed by the attorney – as proxy for Emily and Leonard. As soon as she signs the last block, she leans over, smiles at me, and holds out her hand, which I take.

"Congratulations, Mr. and Mrs. Miller. *You own Discovery Studios!*"

Just hearing her say it, is a total heart-stopper.

Our Tragedy

Stanley Campbell

Hey! Remember me? I'm in another band, which also had their story told by the same amazing author.

Thing is, this part of the story, never made into the books Riley wrote about our band, because it happened after the fact. Even though our story ended, *Ransom's* is... well... a *Continuing Evolution* – right?

The reason I'm involved in telling their story, is because I forbade Riley from asking Rhyan to do it. We all believe it would be asking too much of him.

She's my baby sister, but she's the love of Rhyan's life... and the mother of his kids.

Thing is, this is an important part of *Ransom's* story, and it had a profound effect on all of them. It truly needs to be shared, in telling their story, so I'm going to do it.

Now... about Georgia...

Shortly after Rhyan Jr.'s birthday my sister started feeling ill, and as most people do, she figured it was just the flu. She went to the doctor, got checked, and followed his instructions. Ten days later, when she realized she was getting worse – not better – she went back. This time, the doctor ordered a bunch of tests, and sent her home to rest, and wait.

Three days later, after he called Emma to come get Thomas and Rhyan Jr., Rhyan put his wife in his truck, and took her to the hospital where, after only a cursory exam, she was quickly admitted. We knew then, it wasn't good…

They diagnosed Georgia with an acute form of leukemia. They started treatment within hours, and the doctors did their very best – we *all* honestly believe that – but her condition got worse so rapidly, they lost control of the disease.

In my heart, I had to accept that God apparently has something else he wants my sister to do. A different path she has to travel.

The strange thing was, just like my father, my sister knew how it was going to end. Realizing that her death would affect a lot of people, she got me alone so we could talk. As sick and weak as she was, as I sat at her bedside, holding her hand, she made me promise her a few things.

"Tell Emma that she is the *only one* I trust to make certain the boys understand. No child psychologists or shrinks – *no one. Just Emma.* Promise me…"

I made the promise, hoping with everything in me, that my wife would be up to the task.

"They can't cancel the tour – do you understand me, Stanley?" she continued, pushing herself into a sitting position. "It won't stop me from going, and they've all said this is the last time. I haven't watched the six of them go through what they have, only to become the thing that destroys them. They deserve to go out in an amazing way – like you guys did. Not like this. *Please* promise me you will make *them* – not just Rhyan – understand that."

I again made the promise, even though, in my heart, I wasn't sure I would be able to keep it.

"Finally, I go the same way Dad did. You, Logan, and Rhyan will have to do it. You can put a marker at the cemetery, with Dad's, so the boys will have a place..."

I made the last promise, knowing that at least it was one I *could* keep.

The radiation treatments, and the chemotherapy, took a massive toll on my sister, and unfortunately, Georgia's body simply couldn't tolerate it. Eventually, I believe she willingly gave up the fight, and conceded to God's plan.

On August 19th, ninety-nine days after she was admitted to the hospital, at the age of thirty-two, God took my sister, to be with my father. Alone with Rhyan, she smiled at her husband, squeezed his hand, said "I love you", and then simply closed her eyes. Rhyan sat there, holding her hand, and sobbing, for close to an hour. Logan eventually went and brought him out, so the doctors could tend to things.

Rhyan's grief was so overwhelming that, for a short time, we all thought we might lose him, to his own heartache. My wife spent two months, doing the impossible – giving a four year old boy, an understanding of why God choose to take his mother. And, in the end, it's that same four year old boy, who rescues his father.

Georgia gets promise #1, when, on a sunny Sunday afternoon, Thomas Crossman walks up, sits down next to his father on the front steps of their house, takes his hand, and says, "Aunt Emma says that Mom is still here – and that she'll always be, if we believe it." Then, after a couple of seconds of silence, the child turns, tugs on his father's sleeve, and when Rhyan looks at him, asks, "Do you believe it, Daddy?"

That's the moment we recovered Rhyan Crossman – the soft-spoken, amazingly talented drummer that completely stole my sister's heart, the moment she met him.

Rhyan stopped grieving that day, and with the help of his son, chose instead, to talk about, and celebrate his wife's life. He went back to work, *and* to being a parent. Emma watched the boys until, after two full months of research, he found a nanny he was comfortable with. The boys – especially Thomas – were at first, kind of leery of her, but eventually accepted her.

When he tried to explain to Emma that he did it because he didn't feel right being dependent on her, she told him to hush, kissed him, and told him that when needed, we will always be here for the three of them.

The others spent time dealing with the loss of Georgia in their own personal ways. Over time, she touched each of their lives in different ways.

The five of them continued helping the members of *Saturday Afternoon*, prep for their first headlining tour. They committed to it, and none of them knows how to quit. Eventually, having done as much for Pete and the girls, as they could, they each went back to their own lives. They all accepted that *Ransom* was done. Life pretty much dictated that, and not a single one of them had a problem with it.

The outpouring of emotions from *Ransom's* fans was astounding. Lucky Guess got so much mail addressed to Rhyan, they had to ship it to him in boxes. At least a dozen websites appeared, dedicated to Rhyan, Georgia, and the kids. The best one I came across had a copy of an image someone took at the *No Purchase Required* show in Denver. It's of my sister, up on her husband's shoulders, fist-pumping away. The caption under it said *'Georgia – Forever on our minds'*.

Even with all the stress and craziness during that time, *Ransom* managed to finish *Circular Motion*, which ends up being their final album. It tells the story of how life – and everything it affects – tends to circle back to the beginning, and repeat itself.

The CD turned out to be totally upbeat – just the way Misty wanted it. With Rhyan's consent, they told PJ to release it, but in the days following Georgia's death, Misty called PJ and told her to wait. The next day she and Jessica vanished, and we didn't see them for three full days. When the two of them finally returned, Jessica walked up to her father, held out a stack of sheet music, and with a big smile said, "It's for Aunt Georgia..."

A week after my sister's service, the five of them locked themselves in our basement, and six days later, *In The End* came to life. They called Willie for an assist with the percussion part of the song, because they weren't ready for Rhyan to know about it yet. The next afternoon he knocked on our door, with Bailey standing beside him. It may be the most amazing idea Willie Morgan has ever come up with.

They sat Bailey down at the drums, played the track for her a couple of times, and told her to close her eyes, and to let her heart make the music. Knowing exactly what – *and who* – the song is about, the kid put her entire being into it, and the results were beyond amazing. Neither Rhyan nor Willie could have done it better. As far as *Ransom* is concerned, Bailey's percussion work made the track *perfect*.

Once they were done, they took the *basement version* to Lucky Guess, and told PJ they wanted it added – *as is* – to the other masters, and that the song was the new title track. PJ played the song, and the moment she realized what – more specifically, *who* – it was about, she immediately asked if Rhyan knew about it. Misty instantly said "No" and followed it with "Do *you* want to ask him about it?" PJ shook her head, laughed, and said "Okay then…"

The graphics guys quickly changed the CD's insert to read…

in the end

…in lower case, across the bottom, this time in Bailey's handwriting – and left the rest of the image alone. The label also issued a statement saying that, due to circumstances, *Ransom* wouldn't tour in support of it.

The music world's response was off every conceivable chart there is. *Circular Motion* and *In The End* entered the charts at number 1 – *five weeks apart* – and occupied the #1 and #2 positions for *five weeks*. The CD managed to cross the platinum barrier the *fifth* time, *eighty-eight days* from its release date, and the airplay was insane – not one or two songs, but *eight of the eleven* on the CD make it to air. It quickly became, and will probably always be, *Ransom's* most successful record.

PJ would have given anything to have produced a video – of *any* of the songs on it.

And yes… as the world quickly discovered, Misty wrote the amazing title song about her very good friend, Georgia Crossman – about the silent strength my sister showed, right up until the end.

Here's the thing though… Those *'circumstances'* that the press release mentioned? They've never had to deal with Rhyan Thomas Crossman… *Senior*.

"Are we going too, Mom? Are we?"

~ Jessica Masterson   

Promise #2

Misty Masterson

I'm on my way home, from my parent's house, and as I pass through the intersection of Wilson and Cross streets, I see the big truck in front of the Crossman's house, half-backed into the driveway. Without thinking, I pull on the wheel, and make an instant left, making Jessica squeal and laugh.

"Do it again, Momma!" she blurts out, as I pull up to the curb, facing the wrong way, at the end of the driveway.

The moment I see Rhyan standing outside the open garage, my heart simply stops. When he sees me, he smiles and waves.

"Can Mom go talk to Uncle Rhyan for a minute?"

"I wanna come too!"

'Thank God' I think to myself, as I go about getting her out of the car seat, 'I left Matilda with my mother!' The moment the child's feet hit the ground, she races over to Rhyan.

"UNCLE RHYAN!" she screams, and jumps into his arms.

Seconds later, Tommy comes racing out of the garage.

"Jessie!" he yells, as Rhyan puts her down.

We watch them disappear into the front yard, chasing each other around, and cutting up.

I'm about to say something to Rhyan, when I realize what it is, the crew is so diligently packing up.

"What's going on?" I ask, pointing at a guy who is putting a well-worn, and very familiar, glittery purple floor tom-tom into a box of puffed cornstarch packing peanuts. "That's your…"

"…'going on tour' kit," he says, looking more devious than I have ever seen him look. "You know I never play any other drums on the road…"

When all I do is stare at him, he leans over, and gently kisses me.

"I heard *Ransom* is going on tour, and I figured I'd better be prepared. Besides, I have a new percussion piece I need to learn too – although the drummer that created it, totally kicked butt…"

I burst into tears, I can't help it. I reach out and gently touch his cheek.

"We all understand Rhyan… you don't have to…"

"Yeah, little sister, *I do…*" he replies, taking my hand and gently squeezing it.

I'm lost… totally and completely lost. All I can seem to do is stare at him… which makes him laugh.

"My brother-in-law and I got drunk about a week ago. First time since a hotel room in Sydney…"

This time, I laugh – I can't help it.

"And… we talked. Stanley told me, that he told all of you, about the promises he made her…"

I involuntarily suck in a huge breath, now beginning to understand. When I look around for the kids, I see them sitting on the porch, and Mrs. Crossman giving them small glasses of something. She must have sensed me, because she turns, looks at me, smiles, and puts her hand over her heart.

"I hope you guys still want to do this – to tour I mean…"

"But…" I start to say, and he quickly interrupts me.

"After I talked to Stanley, he sent me to see PJ. I walked in last Tuesday, told her I was ready, and I swear, I thought the woman was gonna faint…"

As he is talking, I feel the tears as they continue to slowly trickle down my cheeks, and I'm pretty sure I know where this is going.

"Here's the thing…" he continues, reaching out and wiping the tears from my cheeks, "PJ and Preston never cancelled any of the set-ups. Casey sent out the press release about us *not* touring, but never followed up on things. PJ immediately called Stephen, and he told her that Mystical Productions *has everything in place* for *Ransom* to open the *In The End* tour, at Staples Center, in thirty-seven days. Tickets go on sale day after tomorrow, assuming *the six of us* are up for it…"

I am – *honest to God* – completely speechless.

"*And…*" Rhyan adds, as a *huge* grin spreads across his face, and he points at the kids, still sitting together on the steps, giggling and poking each other in the ribs, "a certain four year old gave me *very specific* instructions – '*you guys gotta do it for Mom*'."

I'm full on crying again, and when I look Rhyan in the eyes, the magic I find there, tells me that this absolutely has to be done… *for Georgia.*

And… for the most amazing little boy I know.

I'm hugging Rhyan when, as if on cue somehow, my daughter comes running across the yard, yelling at the top of her little lungs, ***Are we going too, Mom? Are we?*** When she reaches us, it's as if she forgets to stop, so when she grabs my pant leg, she almost knocks me over!

"Going *where*, Jessica," I ask, as I regain my balance, and try to peel her off my leg.

"Tommy says Uncle Rhyan is going on a tour and he's going with. *I wanna go too! Pleaaasssseeee!*"

More tears. No way can I stop them.

Tommy, who followed Jess across the yard, stops next to his father, takes his hand, and gives me the most amazing smile. Then, as the smile turns to a devious little grin, he looks at my daughter and says, *"Don't worry Jessie – your mom is the singer – you guys have to come!"*

I take a step over, and standing on my tiptoes, I gently kiss the strongest man I know, right on the lips. Jess and Tommy both say *'ohhhhh'* at the same time, and then start laughing. I kneel down in front of my daughter, gently touch her cheek, and then ask, "You want to tell your dad we're going on tour, or should Mom do it?"

Without warning, the child launches herself into the air, and screams so loudly, it makes my ears hurt, and makes Rhyan fall out in hysterical laughter. Even before I can grab her, she tears off down the street in the direction of home – which is only three blocks away. I smile at Rhyan, say, "I'll be back for the car in a bit..." then turn and take off at a run, in pursuit of my daughter.

Watching her explain it all to her father, turns out to be insanely entertaining...

Who?

Allison Chambers

Who, you ask, is Allison Chambers?

Bass guitar – *Inverse Polarity* – at your service.

No, you've never heard of us.

No, we've never recorded anything.

No, we never got famous.

No, we don't even play together any longer.

Life took us in different directions.

But, the five of us did share an amazing, twenty-two week adventure, that will be with us until we die.

You see... *we opened for Ransom on their final tour...*

When Mrs. Mitchell turned up at my front door, and told me what she wanted, I broke up laughing. Then, she handed me one of her books – the ones about *Audio Distortion*. Needless to say, it wasn't all that funny anymore.

Anyhow, I spent two days talking to Mrs. Mitchell, and what you are about to read is, to the best of my recollection, the story of how five unknown kids, walked into the experience of a lifetime – compliments of one of the biggest pop bands of our generation…

"You want us to do what?"

~ Dawson Cox   

No Freakin' Way!

Allison Chambers

We are diligently packing the van for a trip to Twenty-Nine Palms, when Ms. Silva walks into Dawson's garage, and totally freaks us out...

"You want us to do *what?*" Dawson blurts out.

"Open for *Ransom*. Their tour starts in less than a month," Ms. Silva says, grinning at the five of us.

"We're a garage band, for crying out loud!" I reply.

"That's why they want you. Martin and Josh are coming by to hear you live, if that's cool?"

When we all stand staring at her, she cracks up laughing.

"When PJ told me to find a new band, Preston said he might know of one. At the time, we didn't know he was your," she points at Dawson, "dad. The moment Josh saw all the YouTube stuff on you guys, he sent me to find you..."

Still, we do nothing but stare.

"Someone gave them a chance – twenty years ago. They thought it would be cool to do the same for you – if you're interested."

"What you are talking about is way different than playing parties or fairs. Two or three hundred is way different than ten thousand," Angie says.

"Actually, it isn't. One is just way louder than the other is all. The truth of the matter is, *fans... are fans,* no matter how many there are."

"Talking to Josh is one thing – he works at LGR, like my dad. He's totally cool and all, but *opening for his band* is... well..."

"*Ransom* is massive, Ms. Silva..."

"Yep... they damn sure are. And you guys have just gotten the chance of a lifetime. If it's too much, say the word and I'm outta here. I'll let the guys know, so they don't fly out here."

Although Blake and Carter never say a word, I think we all pretty much know, right then, that even as completely insane as the idea is, we *are* going to do it...

Newbies!

Joshua Miller

"I don't know, Josh... they seem awfully iffy," Dani says.

"Yeah, well... so were we. We even tried to keep Emily and Willie from finding out we played together."

I hear her laugh.

"Where are they playing next, or do you know?"

"Of course I know. It's what I do. Seems they've been paid to play a wedding reception out in Twenty-Nine Palms, near the Marine base. They were loading a van when I caught up to them."

"So... they didn't say 'no', right?"

Again I hear her laugh.

"You want the address of the reception?"

"Well *duh*... that is what you do, right?"

As she reads the info, I copy it down – including the name of the bride and groom. Helps to know who got married, if one intends to crash a wedding reception.

Our Opening Act

Martin Masterson

We're standing in the lobby, waiting for the Groom's father to come meet us. That's when we hear them live, for the first time. They are tearing up a cover of *Stuck In Reverse* by *No Purchase Required*, and Josh is just as stunned as I am. We know they're a cover band – we've seen the videos – but what we are hearing is so precise, that unless you knew better, you'd think *NPR* was playing!

Once Dad shows up, he's so shocked he just stands staring at us. He actually thought someone was messing with him, when they told him two members of the pop band *Ransom* were in the lobby asking for him. He invites us in, and we find a nice, quiet, obscure place to watch, *and listen* from, and we manage to remain unnoticed for most of the reception.

The kids play *Moving Too Fast, Time Out* – by a group called *Big Trouble* – and eventually, much to our surprise, *The Way Home*. Their vocalist definitely has a set of pipes. The bride and groom ask them to play *Destined To Be* for their first dance as husband and wife, and the moment the girl hits the first high note, it seals the deal.

Ransom: Start to Finish

We have our opening act...
I don't care how freaking 'unsure' they are...

Riley Morgan

Testing

Ariel Miller

"We need a big favor, Sally."

"Sure! Name it!"

"Preston says you guys are in Denver this weekend, and we need a stage to put a new act on."

"You mean live? During the show?"

"Uh huh – if you and *Back Alley* are up for it."

"Of course we'll support you…"

"Yeah, but you need to ask Chris and the guys. It's as much their show, as yours. We're hoping to slip them in between the two of you, for one song."

"Hang on a sec…" she says, and then starts talking to someone. A moment later she comes back on. "I'm gonna do a conference call – don't hang up."

I hear some clicking, then Sally talking, then a male voice.

"Hey, Mrs. Miller! Sally said you need to talk to me?"

I laugh, and say, "Can I mess with your show?"

"Huh?"

"I want to slip an act in between the bands – just to see how they handle it. Will *Back Alley* have an issue with that?"

This time he laughs.

"Not at all. Who are they?"

"Our opening act."

"Seriously?" comes from Chris and Sally at the same time.

"Yeah... no major stage time yet. We need to test them before we turn them loose."

"How totally and insanely cool!" Sally says, which gets another laugh from Chris. "You're still as crazy as ever."

"So... if Dani turns up with them on Friday morning..."

"No!" Sally says. "Send them sooner – like on Thursday, or even Wednesday, and let us hang out with them."

"Wicked idea, Sally!" Chris adds.

"You got it. We'll need you to send us some video, and tell us how they handle it, okay?"

"You betcha! What's their band name?"

"They don't have one. Maybe you can help with that too!"

I hear almost hysterical laughter from both of them.

"We're on it! Talk to you later."

"Bye guys."

I spin around, and find a grinning Dani standing there.

"Get them, and take them to Denver – tomorrow. Preston can tell you what hotel the bands are at. Don't babysit them – let Sally and the others do that, okay?"

"Uh-huh. I'm going to meet my husband, and do some shopping."

"Rhyan and I will turn up before show time Friday. Abbie knows we're coming, and will get us inside. I swear, one day, I will actually be able to understand that girl's Irish accent..."

"And the bands are in the dark, right?"

"Uh huh. All of them. Good luck lady."

"No luck necessary. These kids are good, and they will be in good hands. When you guys open in twenty-one days, it's going to be phenomenal. Your fans are already off the chart about the tour."

"As *Audio Distortion* once said… *'One More Time'*…"

I hug her, and watch as she disappears out the door.

In my heart, I hope with all that I am, that she's right…

Showtime!

Misty Masterson

Yet another opening night.

For *Ransom*, it will be the last.

But we're all good with that.

We're standing together at the bottom of the stairs, each of us holding up a hand. As the kids pass us, the high-fives are exchanged, and they disappear into the darkness of the stage. I know every one of us is flashing back to a night at the O2 – so many years ago.

Then, we hear the announcer...

Welcome music fans!

Tonight, on the Staples Center stage, we have an interesting pairing.

One band the world knows... the other they don't.

One band is making a return... the other a beginning.

Ladies and Gentleman – Lucky Guess Records, Mystical Productions and the Staples Center, are proud and honored to present, playing on their first major stage – be sure to remember their name – five amazing musicians that call the City of Angels home...

Inverse Polarity!

The moment the lights come up, the kids totally cut loose. Even though all their songs are covers, the crowd is still all over it. The cool part is that they recognize each song, and before you know it, are singing along with the band. They play through their set – they manage six songs which are so close to perfect, even the audience is amazed – and when they reach the final song, they pull a fast one on us. The stage goes dark, a single spot comes on, and standing alone at the front of the stage, is Angie – their singer.

"Wow! You guys have been totally amazing! Who would have known you could be this supportive of a cover band? The five of us thank you, from the very bottom of our hearts!"

As she sits down on the edge of the stage, Carla appears behind us with Tommy and Jess in tow, and stops at the bottom of the stairs. We watch as she stuffs foam plugs into their little ears, makes them promise not to take them out, and then, to our complete astonishment, sends them up on stage.

"Hey!" Rhyan starts to say...

"You hush, Rhyan Crossman!" Daniela replies, so fast it freaks all of us out.

"Now, for this last song, I've enlisted the help of a couple of new friends..." Angie says, as the kids rush over, laughing, and jumping around, and take seats on each side of her. It's apparent from the kids behavior, and how careful they are near the edge of the stage, that they have practiced this at least a few times – thanks no doubt to Carla. "Their parents are the ones who made it possible for the five of us to be up here tonight, entertaining you."

The crowd, now strangely quiet, watches intently.

"The last song we're going to play has touched thousands of lives since the day it was recorded. I even called the woman who wrote, and originally performed it, and asked for her permission to sing it tonight."

She pauses, waits for a lighting adjustment, and when a spotlight lands on each of the kids, on cue, they wave at the audience, and then Angela continues.

"Tell them who you are," she says, holding the mic in front of Tommy.

"Tommy Crossman."

There's a collective deep breath that could very well be the entire audience, telling us they know who he is.

"And you?" she continues, holding the mic in front of Jessica.

"Jessie Masterson."

"So… you guys know what song I'm gonna sing, right?"

"Yes ma'am!" they yell at the same time, getting a rise out of the people right in front of the stage.

About this time, I feel my husband's arms slip around me, and his chin come to rest on my shoulder. When I glance to my left, I see Vanessa holding tightly to a teary-eyed Rhyan's hand.

"Do you know who the first person to sing this song is?" Angie asks.

"Aunt Emma!" the kids again yell at the same time.

The moment the music starts, I burst into tears, and the crowd, immediately recognizing the intro, goes totally nuts.

"This song is about these guys!" Angie yells over the applause and whistling, putting a hand on each of their heads, "and all the little ones each of you have at home!"

Then the girl proceeds to pump every ounce of her being into what turns out to be a *perfect* cover of *The Time It Takes*, and by the first chorus, Staples Center is filled with *thousands* of multicolored light sticks, glowing brightly, and swaying slowly, from side to side.

"God!" Ariel blurts out through her tears, *"I sooo wish Emma could see this!"*

Martin turns to her, and with a big smile, says, "I'm thinking she will... even before it's over..."

He's right. Just as *Saturday Afternoon* owned YouTube after their first show, years ago, even before we take the stage, there are hundreds of video versions of *Inverse Polarity's* monumental performance of *Audio Distortion's* song, everywhere on the internet.

For the entire week following the performance Miss Angela Sutton pretty much owns YouTube. One fan goes so far as to take six or seven different versions of the video, and combine them into one. Then, in an almost professional manner, he lays the audio back over the finished product. A week after it's posted, it has over *three million* hits. Then, with no warning, clips of the video turn up on both MTV and VH1, as well as on a number of local stations.

Stunned beyond all explanation, each member of *Inverse Polarity* posts a public 'thank you' response to the video, so that everyone can read them.

Yep... *Inverse Polarity* is famous...

Whether they want to be or not.

Always Remember...

Rhyan Crossman

Time for me to get back into this. My wife would expect nothing less.

I've learned to live with the fact that our new title song is about Georgia, and how she lived her life. At first, it was weird knowing I'll have to play it every night for audiences, and listen to Misty sing the lyrics.

Then *He* steps in – in the form of an ambush by two four year olds, while I'm sitting on the stage, only hours before the opening show…

"Hey, Uncle Rhyan!" Jessica yells, as she and Tommy come tearing across the empty stage.

They slide to a stop right in front of me, laughing, shoving each other around, and generally being four year olds.

"What's up guys?"

"Did you know that Mom has her *very own song?*"

My heart stops, and I sit staring at my son, who has the most amazing smile covering his face.

"Mom showed us! She's gonna sing it tonight!" Jess adds.

"And what do you think of that?" I ask Tommy, pulling him into my lap, and hugging him.

"It's really cool. Carla," he pauses and points across the stage to where she is sitting on the stairs, "read it to us, and 'splained what it means."

When I glance at her, she smiles and waves, and I know I'm gonna cry. It's in this exact moment that I know – Georgia will truly, never be gone…

Our show opening night comes off perfectly. We're all completely psyched, and on our A-Game. I think that maybe, over time, we've forgotten how much fun performing *live* actually is. And, of course, *IP's* amazing opening doesn't hurt our mindset either. But, I'm not even remotely prepared for how the show will end.

Penelope Campbell, Preston Cox, and Daniela Silva are… well… amazing comes to mind, but doesn't even come close to being enough. Anyhow, their little plan involves our new title song…

Misty made the decision that *In The End* was going to be the last song on the playlist. None of the others questioned her. I'm about to find out why…

The crowd is singing along, as a couple thousand light sticks sway back and forth in rhythm. When we reach the last stanza, the arena goes dark, the crowd goes quiet, the light sticks stop moving, and a single spotlight lands on Misty. With only Martin's keyboards backing her, she sings the last four lines, and as the spot on her gets smaller and smaller, darkness slowly engulfs the stage.

I'm sitting at my drums, sticks in hand, smiling, and thinking that there could never be a better ending to this particular song, when, without warning, the entire stage suddenly lights up, as the giant twenty-five foot tall monitor behind me comes to life.

Having no idea what's going on, I spin around on my stool, and the moment I see it, I drop to my knees, and start sobbing. Vanessa and Ariel are next to me instantly, both putting arms around me.

Covering the entire monitor is my wife, sitting on my shoulders, pumping her fist, and singing...

Across the bottom is her name, the dates she was here with us, and a single line of hand-written words...

Mother, Wife, Sister, Daughter, Amazing!

One Last Surprise

Misty Masterson

Emma Campbell is the most devious surprise planner I know. When she managed to sneak an entire band – *undetected* – into one of our shows, I conceded she very well may be the best too!

The moment she calls my cell and tells me, "I have a plan", I'm all over it. Having seen numerous videos of a recent performance of *The Time It Takes*, this time her victim is a cute little brunette named Angie.

Just as they have done for the entire tour, *Inverse Polarity* is setting up to play their last song. And now having become accustomed to the process, Jess and Tommy are anxiously waiting at the top of the stairs, for their chance to go out and sit with Angie while she sings. Everything works just as it has the last nineteen times, in ten different arenas, and once the lights go down, the band starts playing. But... before Angie can sing a single word of the intro, *someone else does...*

I can't remember life
Before you

> *Was there ever life*
> *Without you?*

...and the voice is unmistakable. I'm fairly certain every person in the building recognizes it the moment she sings the first line. Although Angie and the kids are under a single spot at the front of the stage, a second one lights Mrs. Emma Campbell, as she casually crosses the distance between the soundboard platform, and the stage. The amazing thing is, *without any urging from Security,* all the fans step out of the way and give her a clear path. When Angie sits stunned, staring at her, Emma laughs and waves at the sound guys, who tell the band, via their earpieces, to loop the song back to the beginning, which they are quick do – even as stunned as *they* are. Of course, the kids immediately recognize Emma.

"AUNT EMMA!" they yell almost simultaneously, which cracks up everyone who hears it.

She stops within inches of them, whispers to the kids to be still, and then as the band reaches the intro the second time, Emma looks at Angie and says, "I'll start, you follow. Sound like fun?" and then reaches out and puts a hand on her leg, while at the same time, she sings...

> *I can't remember life*
> *Before you*
> *Was there ever life*
> *Without you?*

This time, a still completely confused Angie, is on the first stanza instantly...

> *In the time that it takes*
> *For a leaf to fall*
> *You will grow up strong and tall*

...which is followed by Emma's...

Riley Morgan

In the time that it takes
To tie your shoes
You will surely be making news

Between stanzas, two really big Security guys pick Emma up – to the applause of the crowd – and set her on the edge of the stage, right next to Tommy, who immediately wraps both arms around her. The woman never misses a beat...

Back and forth, and back and forth, as the now astonished crowd claps and listens, the two of them give what is probably the most incredible performance of the song, there will ever be.

As the lights go out, Angie sings the last line, and instantly, the big monitor jumps to life. The song's video begins to play, and seventeen seconds into it, at the point where Emma says, '*Standing right there actually*', and points at the kids, the image freezes on the four of them, standing in the doorway, smiling. Three seconds – and a couple of heartbeats – later, the monitor goes blank, throwing the entire arena into almost total darkness.

I'm sorry... there are simply no adequate words to describe what happens next.

Only the 20,000 people in the American Airlines Center in Dallas that night will ever understand.

You simply had to be there...

Closure

Martin Masterson

The rest of the *In The End* tour comes off flawlessly. We even develop a rapport with the members of *Inverse Polarity*, who end up thanking us repeatedly for...well... we aren't sure for what. Having talked to each of them over the course of the tour, it's pretty apparent they don't intend to take the whole 'band' thing any further. They are each going back to the paths they have always been destined to travel – and will have a pretty cool memory to take with them.

The morning after the final show in Wichita, PJ has a huge breakfast party for the bands and the production team. And of course, she invites the press. She knows we are done, and is giving us an opportunity to tell them in a calm, controlled environment. And yes, Misty uses the word 'finished' – which the press seems to accept.

When we are finally ready to 'go home', it's kind of a weird situation. There are no tears, or heavy sighs, but instead, we're all jovial, and in excellent moods – even PJ and Preston. We exchange hugs, and then one at a time, head back to our lives – the ones will be living from now on.

Ransom: Start to Finish

It's been amazing, incredible, astonishing – and a million other adjectives I can't come up with at the moment, and we will all treasure the last twenty years forever. What we have all finally come to accept is, no matter what happens from this point forward, the six of us are – *and will always be...*

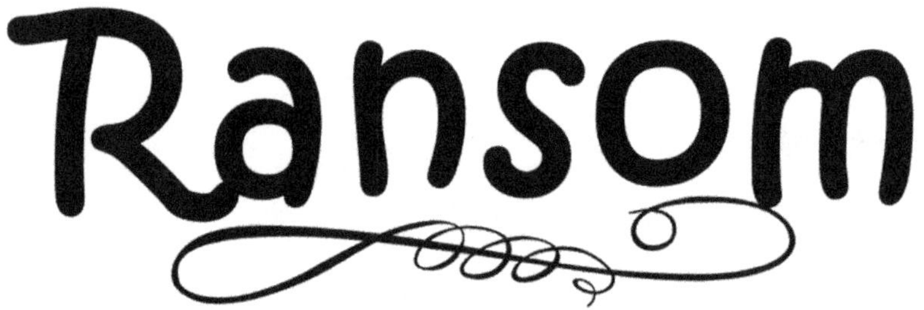

Riley Morgan

Epilogue

Riley Mitchell

It's been four years since *Ransom* survived their last tour, and I spent the last year of that, talking to all of them, and writing this story.

Even before the final show in Wichita, they all agreed, it was their last tour. Martin told me *'it's time to let those younger than us – the up and coming bands, who so desperately want their shot – to take over'*. So far, none of the other members has said anything to the contrary.

Are they still part of the music world?

Joshua and Ariel are – without a doubt. Discovery Studios is still supporting Lucky Guess, and a pretty long list of other artists. The two of them have become pretty incredible engineers, and have built on the studio's already impressive reputation. Their attitudes, however, about what makes good music, have changed, and it shows in the types of artists they choose to work with now. No matter what anyone says, I'm convinced it all has a lot to do with how – *and where* – they were raised.

The rest of the band? Life, as usual, stepped in.

Vanessa married Cullen, and they moved to Wales – of all places. Apparently Cullen inherited a rather nice estate in the seaside community of Tywyn, which is on the southern end of the Snowdonia National Park. I bet Nessa that she'd be speaking Welsh within two years, but still don't know which of us won. They are teaching – free of charge – at the village's primary and secondary schools, simply because they can.

Sounds like an amazing retirement, if you ask me.

Misty and Martin are back in Ransom, and will be forever. As the tour was winding down, Carla asked Misty what was next for the band. Misty told her she couldn't speak for the others, but that she, Martin, and their kids, *belong* in Ransom – and that's where she could find them. They went home right after the tour ended, and have been there ever since. The really cool thing about the Masterson family is, to this day, *anyone* can walk up, knock on their door, and get invited in. It's just how things are done in Kansas...

And of course, *The Three Musketeers* – Rhyan Jr., Thomas, and Rhyan. That's what we all call them. They are inseparable.

Rhyan has remained single. He's said that maybe one day, he will again open his heart to someone, but not until the boys are old enough to understand. He refuses to give anyone reason to believe Georgia has been – or for that matter, *could be* – replaced. They have a mother, and there will – as far as Rhyan is concerned – never be a step-mother.

Just recently, Meghan – their nanny of four years – had to go. She graduated, and her life – and an amazing job offer – awaits her elsewhere. Because Emma is still a homebody, and the twins are still at home, she has stepped back in, and looks after the guys when Dad is tied up with work. The funny thing is, the twins think having two younger brothers, totally rocks! Being the youngest myself, I completely understand their enthusiasm.

But, make no mistake – Rhyan Crossman is 100%, full on *Dad*. When he isn't off building another bridge somewhere – with the two of them supervising – he's at a football, a baseball, or soccer game, and is of course, the loudest parent in the stands. And, if it's important to the boys, no matter what it is, Dad makes certain he's there.

And, for the record, yes… the poor guy *still* hears, *"Hey! Aren't you…"*

So… there you have it.

Ransom: Start To Finish

One More Thing... 😉

Randall Mitchell

Yeah, right...

Riley is an amazingly talented writer, but she's full of it.

And yeah, the eight of us made my wife add this...

You see, we did a survey – the Campbell kids, my sister, my wife's sister, and the Faintree sisters – and we agree on one thing. *Not one of us* believes for a single heartbeat that *Ransom* is finished. Not even Riley.

Neither do any of you – *their fans.*

Neither does anyone who was ever fortunate enough to have been exposed to, or to have worked with them over the years.

Emma Campbell said it best when, twelve years ago, in a grassy field, on the Isle of Man, she told Ariel and Misty...

"...at some point in the future, the urge will strike you – maybe one or two of you, or maybe all of you at the same time – and before you know it, you'll be making music again. It's part of who you guys are!"

And, as Donna Dollar said about *a different band*, at the end of Meghan Milton's MTV Special, *twenty-two years ago*...
"*All we have to do is **believe** they'll be back...*"

Riley Morgan

If you haven't already done it, now is a great time to start reading your way through the story of the band that started it all... over twenty years ago.

The band that the critics keep saying may never go away...

The phenomenon the world has always called...

Available in print and digital formats online at

audio-distortion.com
and
amazon.com